D0350620

8/14

9/16
9/17

9X. 3/18. 9/20

EYE FOR AN EYE

ALSO BY BEN COES

Power Down
Coup d'État
The Last Refuge

EYE FOR AN EYE

BEN COES

3 1336 09257 3865

ST. MARTIN'S PRESS ⚏ NEW YORK

This is a work of fiction. All of the characters, organizations, and events portrayed in this novel are either products of the author's imagination or are used fictitiously.

EYE FOR AN EYE. Copyright © 2013 by Ben Coes. All rights reserved. Printed in the United States of America. For information, address St. Martin's Press, 175 Fifth Avenue, New York, NY 10010.

www.stmartins.com

Design by Phil Mazzone

Library of Congress Cataloging-in-Publication Data

Coes, Ben.
    Eye for an eye : a Dewey Andreas novel / Ben Coes.
        p. cm.
    ISBN 978-1-250-00716-2 (hardcover)
    ISBN 978-1-250-02609-5 (e-book)
    1. Special forces (Military science)—Fiction.   2. Terrorism—Fiction.
I. Title.
    PS3603.O2996E93 2013
    813'.6—dc23

                                                          2013009103

St. Martin's Press books may be purchased for educational, business, or promotional use. For information on bulk purchases, please contact Macmillan Corporate and Premium Sales Department at 1-800-221-7945, extension 5442, or write specialmarkets@macmillan.com.

First Edition: July 2013

10 9 8 7 6 5 4 3 2 1

To Oscar,

the Navy SEAL of nine-year-old boys

I will make my arrows drunk with blood, and my sword shall devour flesh.

—DEUTERONOMY 32:42

EYE FOR AN EYE

Prologue

I don't know."

The three words Amit Bhutta, Iran's ambassador to the United Nations, had repeated for the past day and a half, three words that Dewey listened to with a blank look on his face. It was, by his rough count, approximately the thousandth time Bhutta had said them.

He and Tacoma had been taking turns interrogating Bhutta. Two hours on, two off. They had a distinctly different style. Tacoma, the former SEAL, was less patient. Bhutta's bloody face showed the practical implications of that impatience. Dewey assumed it was Tacoma's youth that made him slap the Iranian around. Not that he cared. But his style was different. With Bhutta, Dewey felt that screwing with his head had a better shot at getting them the information they needed. That and not feeding or giving Bhutta anything to drink.

The interrogation room was located in the basement of Rolf Borchardt's mansion in Kensington. The room was soundproof and windowless. At the center of the room, a steel table was bolted to the wooden floor. Behind it was a steel chair, also bolted down. The table had wet blood on it, not for the first time.

A lamp in the corner provided the only light.

Bhutta was stooped over, leaning forward, his cheek pressed against the steel table. His left eye was shut, black and blue.

The heat inside the room was cranked up. Both men were sweating, but Bhutta, with his wrists shackled behind his back—and the muzzle of Dewey's Colt M1911 aimed at his head—was sweating a little more.

It had been a week since Dewey infiltrated Iran and stole the country's first nuclear device. Dewey's disguise, his overgrown beard and moustache, were gone now. His face was clean-shaven, his hair was cut to a medium length.

When Dewey asked to borrow a pair of scissors to cut it himself, Borchardt insisted on taking him to a Belgrave Road stylist. Now Dewey looked like a model, ripped from the advertising pages of *Vanity Fair*, though the savageness which the professional photographers endeavored to manufacture in their models was, on Dewey, real. His unruly brown hair was combed back; his eyes were bright, cold, and blue; his large nose was sharp and aquiline, despite the fact that it had been busted on two separate occasions. Dewey didn't think about his looks. Truth be told, he didn't like the way he looked. He didn't like attention. Dewey preferred blending in, remaining anonymous. Today, with no stubble on his face, a tan, and a $450 haircut, it was not hard to see why the thirty-nine-year-old American could still turn heads.

Yet, as Bhutta had learned over thirty-six hours of interrogation, there lurked something beneath the attractive veneer of the kid from Castine, Maine. It was a toughness, a coldness, an anger deep inside. Most who knew Dewey Andreas thought that anger had been forged by the long, bitter winters of his youth along the Maine coast, or on the unforgiving football fields of Boston College, or still later, during Ranger school, or in the otherworldly trials that separated warriors from mere men called 1st Special Forces Operational Detachment—Delta—along with the Navy SEALs, America's most fearsome Special Forces soldiers.

Only Dewey knew it was none of the above, that what had hardened him was the morning he'd watched his six-year-old son die of leukemia so long ago. That was what made him, when necessary, ruthless. It was also what kept Dewey, in the innermost part of his being, just, fair, flawed, and vulnerable—human.

Even Bhutta could see the toughness now, as he stared at the American. It was the same meanness and detachment that had probably coursed in the blood of the men who so long ago had kicked the crap out of the British, a determination that, to the Iranian's mind at least, was as defeating as anything he'd ever experienced.

"What's his name?" asked Dewey.

"I told you, I don't know. He's China's asset."

Dewey was seated in a beat-up, torn leather club chair. He had his right leg draped over the right arm.

"What's his name?"

"Fuck you."

"What's his name?"

"I don't know."

"Ambassador Bhutta, we can do this all night."

"I don't know, asshole."

Dewey smiled.

"Language," said Dewey.

"Fuck you."

"If your mother could hear you swearing, she'd be really fucking pissed."

Bhutta's mouth flared slightly, nearly a smile.

"You laughed."

"Fuck you," Bhutta whispered. "You're not funny."

"Then why'd you laugh?"

"I wasn't laughing."

"Okay, I have one for you," said Dewey. "What do you do if an Iranian throws a pin at you?"

Bhutta paused, then finally relented.

"What?" he asked.

"Run like hell."

"Why?"

"Because he's got a grenade between his teeth."

Bhutta laughed.

"You're worse than the other guy," whispered Bhutta, shaking his head. "That's stupid. Just beat the shit out of me, will you?"

Dewey laughed, then pumped the trigger on his .45. The bullet struck Bhutta's right kneecap, blowing it to shreds. Blood sprayed onto the wall. Bhutta screamed, lurching against the chair, pulling at the shackles.

"Jesus, I didn't think it would hurt that much," said Dewey.

Bhutta turned and looked at Dewey, a horrible grimace on his face. His knee was bleeding profusely.

"*I don't know his name! How would I know China has a mole inside Mossad?*"

Dewey ran his fingers back through his hair.

"Here's the deal," said Dewey, wiping the muzzle of the gun on his jeans. "You can either tell me the name of the mole, or you can tell Menachem Dayan and those nice fellas at the madhouse. I have a feeling their jokes aren't going to be as funny as mine. Also, they'll kill you. After they dunk your head in water a few hundred times."

Bhutta screamed again.

"You tell me the name, and the only one who gets hurt is the mole," Dewey said. "You go free. We can arrange some sort of relocation program inside the United States. Some sunny state."

Bhutta's face was pale and drenched in sweat.

"What about my daughter?" asked Bhutta, tears streaming down his face.

"Her too."

"What about my knee?" asked Bhutta, in agony.

"It can go too."

"Fuck you!" Bhutta howled. "You know what I mean."

Dewey sat up and aimed the gun.

"No, not again. I want something in writing. An affidavit from the CIA or the Justice Department."

"Not going to happen. If you want me to choose between shooting your kneecap off or calling some lawyer at Langley and explaining why I haven't already dumped you off to the Israelis like I was supposed to, all I can say is, that ain't gonna fuckin' happen."

4

"You're a bastard."

"Yeah, I am," said Dewey. "But if I say I'm going to do something, I'm going to do it. Tell me the name of China's spy inside Mossad."

"Fuck you."

Dewey stood up, then chambered another round. He aimed the gun at Bhutta's left knee.

"*No!*" Bhutta screamed. He looked at Dewey. "Dillman. His name is Dillman. That's all I know. Tell me you won't fuck me over."

Dewey stuck the Colt M1911 in his shoulder holster and walked to the door.

"I never break a promise."

Dewey walked down the hallway and pulled out his cell.

"Get me Menachem Dayan," he said into the phone as he walked upstairs.

A moment later, Dewey heard the raspy cough of Israel's top military commander, General Menachem Dayan.

"Hello, Dewey."

"I finished interrogating Bhutta," Dewey said. "I know the name of China's mole inside Mossad."

"Who is it?" asked Dayan.

"I want your word, General," said Dewey. "Kohl Meir gets to put the bullet in him. Then he's buried."

"You have my word."

"His name's Dillman."

I

MOSSAD SPECIAL UNIT, AKA "THE MADHOUSE"
TEL AVIV, ISRAEL

Dayan stepped into Fritz Lavine's sixth-floor corner office, which overlooked the Mediterranean Sea, the U.S. embassy, and downtown Tel Aviv. Lavine was the director general of Mossad, Israel's intelligence service. He was a tall, rotund man with receding brown hair and big ruddy cheeks pockmarked with acne scars. Dressed in a white button-down shirt, sleeves rolled up, he stood behind his desk, inspecting a sheet of paper. Two men were seated in chairs in front of Lavine's desk: Cooperman, Mossad chief of staff; and Rolber, head of clandestine operations.

All three turned as Dayan entered, slamming the door behind him.

"What the *fuck* happened?" asked Dayan as he crossed the office, his voice deep, charred by decades' worth of cigarettes. "How many years did you three work with this son of a bitch traitor and you never suspected a goddamn thing?"

"There'll be plenty of time for blame, Menachem," said Lavine, icily. "Right now, we need to find this motherfucker and put a bullet in his head before he does any more damage and before he escapes."

"What *is* the damage?"

"It's extensive," said Cooperman. "So far, we can trace the exposure of at least sixteen MI6 and CIA operatives back to Dillman. As for Mossad, the number appears to be seven dead agents."

"Jesus Christ," Dayan whispered, looking in disbelief at Cooperman.

"TGI succeeded in rebuilding Dillman's digital biograph, correspondence, you name it," said Lavine angrily, throwing the paper down on his desk. "He gave the Chinese everything. Every Far East operation we conducted over the past decade was known ahead of time by Fao Bhang and the ministry. Their knowledge was so extensive that it appears they even tolerated certain activities inside China so as not to raise suspicion. Dillman passed on detailed aspects of anything Langley supplied to us. This includes nuclear infrastructure."

Dayan walked to the glass and looked for a few brief seconds toward the U.S. embassy.

"Have we notified Calibrisi?" asked Dayan, referring to the CIA director, Hector Calibrisi.

Lavine nodded. "Chalmers too," he added, referring to Derek Chalmers, head of MI6.

"And what was the reaction?" asked Dayan.

Lavine stared back at Dayan but remained silent. He didn't need to say anything. They all knew Dillman had set all three agencies back years, decades even, and that both London and Langley would be extremely angry.

Dayan shook his head. He sat down in one of the chairs in front of Lavine's desk.

"Where is he?" asked Dayan, calmer now, his hand rubbing the bridge of his nose, eyes closed.

"We don't know," said Rolber. "We're looking, carefully. If he suspects anything, he'll run."

"If he goes to China, we'll never see him again," said Dayan.

The phone on Lavine's desk chimed, then a voice came on the speaker.

"Director, they're waiting for you."

"Patch us in."

The phone clicked.

"Hector?" asked Lavine.

"Hey, Fritz," said Calibrisi on speaker. "You have me and Bill Polk here at Langley along with Piper Redgrave and Jim Bruckheimer at NSA."

"MI6 is on also," said Derek Chalmers, in a British accent. "Where are we on this?"

"We have nothing," said Lavine. "We're looking everywhere. Last contact with the agency was two days ago. General Redgrave, has NSA developed anything?"

"No," came the female voice of the head of the National Security Agency. "And to be honest, I'm not going to start using NSA assets on Dillman, or on anything else, until we make damn sure our systems and protocols haven't been contaminated by this mole. If the Chinese are inside NSA, we have bigger problems than Dillman."

"What's the plan if and when we do find him?" asked Calibrisi.

"We have three options," said Rolber. "One—we watch him, use him, plot an architecture of disinformation back into Beijing. Two—we bring him in, interrogate him, then let him rot. Three—termination."

"Why not two and three?" asked Calibrisi. "Grill him then kill him."

"If we bring him in, China will find out, Hector," said Cooperman. "There has to be some form of check-in and tip-off. If he misses that check-in, Fao Bhang will immediately try to exfiltrate him, or, more likely, just kill him."

"Then Bhang will move on Western assets before we have time to clean up inside the theater," said Chalmers. "Every MI6, CIA, Mossad agent in China will die, not to mention anyone else Dillman has exposed. It will be a bloody mess."

"It already is a bloody mess," said Dayan.

"So what about option one?" asked Calibrisi. "What would the design look like?"

"We locate him then hang back," answered Rolber, "carefully monitor his movements, and tightly control information flow to him. In the meantime, we put our assets in the Chinese theater on high alert and prepare for exfiltration. When Dillman is no longer useful to us, or he suspects something, we bring out our teams, then bring him in. We can shoot him later."

"Fuck that," yelled Dayan, hitting the desk with his hand. "We're not waiting. Dillman dies right now. Period, end of statement. If I have to do it myself in downtown Shanghai with a dull butter knife, this motherfucker dies."

"Dillman is just a symptom, General," said Calibrisi. "It's Fao Bhang who's behind it all."

"Then let's kill that son of a bitch too."

"Nothing would please me more, but we've never had a shot at him," said Calibrisi. "Bhang doesn't travel outside the People's Republic of China. He hasn't been seen in the West since 1998. Inside PRC, forget it. He's as well guarded as the premier."

"Let's cut our losses and kill Dillman," said Dayan. "I'm not a fan of fancy intelligence operations—double agents, disinformation, whatnot. They never work. We're seeing firsthand how they get all fucked up. It's time to clean up this mess and tie it off. As for Bhang, we're wasting our time. The man's a ghost. Let's focus on what we can do, namely kill what has to be the most important intelligence asset Bhang possesses in the West. That's at least something."

"I have an idea," said Chalmers.

"Go ahead, Derek," said Lavine, picking up an unlit cigar stub from his desk and sticking it in his mouth, then looking at Dayan.

"Even before this Dillman episode, Fao Bhang has done damage to all of us. Bhang and the ministry are a country unto themselves. He's the third-highest ranking member of the Chinese State Council, but he's the most powerful by far. Premier Li fears him, as does the country's military. His tentacles extend into China's economic affairs. He's been an instrumental part of the currency manipulation that has plagued Britain and, on a much more dramatic scale, the United States, for years. For all I know, his hackers are listening in right now."

"They're not," said Cooperman. "I assure you of this."

"Forgive me, but your assurances mean nothing."

"What's your point?" asked Lavine.

"Bhang is rising," said Chalmers. "His malevolence grows. This is simply another chapter in a very dark book."

There was silence in the room and over the intercom as Chalmers paused.

"My question is, when are we going to do something about it?" he asked.

"So what's your idea?" asked Calibrisi.

"We have to find Dillman," said Chalmers. "Obviously. Then, my

9

suggestion is, we use him. But not in the way you're thinking, Hector. No, instead of using him for disinformation then killing him, we're going to switch the order around. Kill him, then use him. We're going to lure Fao Bhang out of his hole, and Dillman is going to be our bait."

"I'm not sure what you mean," said Rolber.

"Bhang won't care about the loss of one human being, even his most treasured asset in the West, but he will care if the loss of Dillman exposes him as weak, as not in control," said Chalmers. "If we can undermine him in the terribly cutthroat drama that is Chinese leadership, it will endanger him. It will, potentially, signal those who fear Bhang or who covet his power. It's time to destabilize Fao Bhang and let his enemies move against him. Otherwise, there will be no end to his reach and the damage he inflicts upon the West."

Cooperman suddenly reached for his chest pocket and pulled out a vibrating cell phone.

"What?" he whispered into the cell.

Cooperman listened, then signaled at the phone, indicating to Lavine to mute the conference call.

"We found him," whispered Cooperman, looking at Lavine, then Dayan and Rolber. "He's in Haifa."

Lavine pressed the mute button on the speakerphone.

"Haifa?" asked Lavine. "What do we have there?"

"I have a kill team in the city," said Rolber. "Boroshevsky, Malayim. They're good to go."

"No," said Dayan. "This is not Mossad's kill."

"You don't trust us now, General?" demanded Rolber.

"It has nothing to do with whether or not I trust you," said Dayan, his gravelly voice rising. "I gave my word to Andreas; it's Kohl Meir's kill. Get Meir up to Haifa, brief him en route, get him whatever weapons he wants. That's an order."

"Yes, sir."

"In the meantime, Fritz and I will coordinate with MI6 and Langley. I'm not sure I understand what the hell Derek Chalmers is talking about, but I like it. These British always have brilliant ideas, even if their food does suck."

2

Dillman walked through the lobby of the hotel, stopping outside the sliding glass doors. He stared at the rising sun, then glanced around. Like all Mossad agents, he'd been looking over his shoulder for so long it was second nature.

He was dressed in blue tennis shorts, a white shirt, and black-and-white Adidas tennis sneakers. In his hand, he held a yellow Babolat racket.

Dillman began his morning jog in the hotel driveway. He ran down the steep, winding road toward the neighborhood called Carmeliya. He ran past large stucco homes until he came to a school, then ran across the parking lot to the public tennis court. There he would hit the ball against the backboard for an hour or so, then jog back to the hotel.

As he came around the corner of the school, he was surprised to find somebody already at the backboard, hitting tennis balls. Dillman thought about turning around and heading back. He didn't feel like waiting God knows how long for the court.

Instead, Dillman approached the man. He was young, bearded, and scraggly-looking. He was dressed in red sweatpants, a long-sleeve gray T-shirt, topped with a yellow baseball cap and mirrored sunglasses.

The man tossed the ball up and swatted it toward the backboard. Dillman could tell by the rhythm and pace that the player was decent.

"How long will you be, my friend?" asked Dillman in Hebrew.

The player turned, raising his hands.

"I only just arrived," the man said, slightly annoyed.

"No worries," said Dillman. "I'll go for a run instead."

As Dillman started to walk away, he heard a whistle. He turned around. The tennis player waved him over.

"Would you like to hit some?" the man called from the court.

Dillman shrugged.

"Sure," he said.

They played for the better part of an hour. The stranger was good. His strokes were a little unnatural, but he was fast and was able to get to everything, despite a slight limp. He beat Dillman 6–3 in the first set. Dillman took the second 7–5. Then, in the third, the bearded stranger jumped to a 4–0 lead.

In the middle of the fifth game, they both heard the string break, after the young man ripped a particularly nice backhand up the line, out of Dillman's reach. Dillman welcomed the interruption. Not only was the younger man beating the crap out of him, but Dillman was sweating like a pig and hungry for breakfast.

"That's too bad," said Dillman, breathing heavily. "I guess that means I win, yes?"

Dillman had been kidding, an attempt at a joke, but the stranger either didn't hear the joke or, if he had, didn't think it was funny.

"I have another racket," the man said, walking to the bench at the side of the court. Other than the score, it was the first thing the young man had said the entire match.

He unzipped his racket bag.

Dillman walked toward him as he reached into his bag.

"Are you from the area?" asked Dillman as he came up behind the stranger.

The man kept his back to Dillman as he searched inside his bag.

"No," he answered. "Tel Aviv."

"Are you a student? Do you play at the university? You're very good."

The stranger turned around and removed his sunglasses.

"No, I'm not a student," he said. "I'm in the military."

Dillman stared into the stranger's eyes. Something in his dark, brown eyes triggered Dillman's memory. Then, slowly, Dillman looked to the man's right hand. Instead of a graphite shaft there was a thick piece of wood; instead of a racket head and strings, there was the dull steel of a large ax, the kind of ax you could chop down a tree with.

"Your second serve needs some work," said the man, who Dillman now recognized: Kohl Meir. "Other than that, you're actually not bad."

Dillman lurched to run away, but Meir swung the ax, catching him in the torso. Dillman fell to the ground, gasping for air, the ax stuck in his side. The pain was so intense he couldn't even scream. His mouth went agape, his eyes bulged, and blood gushed down his chest and side.

Dillman reached desperately at the ax handle.

Calmly, Meir knelt next to him.

"You like my ax?" asked Meir, smiling. "It's for chopping the heads off traitors."

Meir stood and placed a foot on Dillman's chest then jerked up on the handle, pulling the steel ax head from the traitor's body. Dillman whimpered in agony. He was bleeding out, drifting into shock, moments away from death.

Meir lifted the ax over his head. He swung down, burying the blade into Dillman's skull.

A white van moved slowly around the corner of the school, crawling toward Meir. The van stopped a few feet from the corpse. Meir watched as the back of the van opened and two men in blue unibody suits climbed out.

The Mossad cleanup crew jogged forward, placing a stretcher next to Dillman's blood-soaked corpse.

"One thing," Meir said.

"Yes, commander."

"Don't touch the ax," he ordered.

3

A small brown pony with a fluffy tan mane stood patiently in the large backyard of a simple red building with an ornately decorated roof. At least twenty school girls gathered in front of the pony, waiting their turn.

It was a balmy Saturday afternoon at the official residence of the premier of China, Qishan Li, who was elevated three years ago. Li's face sported a large smile as he watched his granddaughter, Meixiu, climb atop the animal. Her friends all clapped loudly and screamed as Meixiu moved the pony away from the house.

The crowd in the backyard included Meixiu's classmates from the private all-girls school she attended, their parents, and an assortment of other well-wishers, staff members, and sycophants. Li adored his granddaughter, and his annual birthday party for her was a well-known event. It was a chance not only for Meixiu and her friends and family to celebrate, but an opportunity for Chinese politicians and ministers to curry favor with the premier by giving the young girl elaborate gifts.

Meixiu had opened all of them, and the back terrace was cluttered with gifts: bright sweaters, jewelry, toys, shoes, flowers, and a hundred other items large and small, stacked on tables for the guests to admire.

A half mile away, a dark blue delivery van pulled up to Xinhua Gate. The driver lowered the window and handed his ID to one of the armed soldiers guarding the entrance.

The soldier inspected the identification. The driver was from the Ministry of State Security.

"Who is it for?"

"The girl," said the driver. "A present from Minister Bhang."

The soldier passed his ministry ID back to him and nodded to another soldier to let the van through the gates.

The van moved at a placid speed through the massive multibuilding compound that served as central headquarters for the Chinese government, including the Communist Party and the State Council. Pretty trees and manicured lawns separated the ancient, beautifully maintained buildings. Every few hundred yards stood an armed soldier or two. The van stopped outside Li's residence. The driver climbed out of the van as a pair of armed soldiers in paramilitary gear crossed the front lawn of the house.

The driver opened the back of the van. All three men stood and stared inside. Sitting in the back was a lone object, a large brown shiny-new Louis Vuitton trunk with a pink ribbon wrapped garishly around it, then tied in a bow.

"It's heavy," said the driver. "Give me a hand, will you?"

The three men lifted the trunk and carried it across the lawn. Another guard, this one in plain clothes, opened the front door.

They carried the trunk through the house. At the door to the outside terrace, Li's wife caught the sight of the three men, then let out a delighted laugh.

"What have we here?" she yelled in a high-pitched giggle.

"From Minister Bhang, madam," said the driver.

"Oh, delightful," she said, waving them toward the door. "Just delightful."

They carried the trunk to the back lawn amid excited *oohs* and *aahs*. Meixiu, still atop the pony, let out a squeal as she suddenly saw the present being set down on the lawn. She practically jumped from the pony and ran across the grass to the trunk.

A bright yellow envelope was taped to the top of the trunk.

"To Meixiu," said Meixiu, reading the note aloud as Li and his wife stood at the young girl's side, surrounded by the rest of the children and adults. "On this, the happiest of days, happy birthday to you, from Minister Fao Bhang."

Li glanced at his wife, a slightly confounded smile on his face.

"Who is that, Grandfather?" asked Meixiu.

"Just someone I work with," said Li.

"What a kind gesture," said Li's wife.

"May I open it?" asked Meixiu, a huge smile of excitement on her face.

"Of course," bellowed Li, gleefully.

The girl pulled one end of the ribbon and let it fall to the ground. She unclasped the two buckles on the front of the trunk, then lifted it up.

At first there were smiles and shouts of delight, as many people didn't understand what it was they were seeing. Then came the silence, as smiles disappeared. Finally, there was the scream, the first one, from Meixiu herself, a piercing yelp of a scream that ripped the air. Her scream was soon joined by others from her grandmother, schoolmates, and everyone else within sight of the trunk.

Inside the trunk was the body of a dead man, stuffed unnaturally into the trunk, dressed in tennis shorts, a tennis shirt, covered in a flood of dried blood and mucus. In the middle of the man's head was an ax, which had been hacked deep into the skull.

As Meixiu suddenly vomited and everyone else scrambled to leave amid a chorus of quiet hysteria, Li turned calmly to one of the plain-clothed security men.

"Return this to the ministry," said Li as he reached for his chest and tried to control his anger. "Then tell Fao Bhang I want to see him immediately."

4

D o you recognize him, sir?"

Fao Bhang, China's minister of State Security, the top intelligence official in China, stared at the mangled corpse. It was stuffed like a side of beef into the Louis Vuitton trunk. The smell was overwhelming, but the pungent aroma didn't stop Bhang from looking. The dead man had on tennis sneakers, shorts, and what had been a white tennis shirt. A long gash had been cleaved into the torso, at least a foot long and four inches wide. His ribs were visible. The skin around the gash was swelled up, septic and rotting. From the man's skull, a large ax jutted out, the ax head embedded deep into the dead man's forehead. At the nape of the neck, a silver Star of David lay still, attached to a thin necklace.

Bhang had met Dillman more than a decade before. Bhang had been sent to Israel to kill a Chinese dissident hiding out in a Jerusalem tenement. The operation had gone flawlessly; it would be a one-day hit; in and out, bragging rights back at the ministry. But it had gone awry at the airport. They'd stopped him; his cover had been blown somehow.

Within hours Bhang was tied up and sweating in a Mossad interrogation house, located in a quiet Tel Aviv suburb called Savyon.

Dillman was his interrogator. He was Mossad's deputy chief operating officer, and Bhang recognized him immediately.

"Welcome to Israel, Fao," Dillman had said. "Did you finish the job on the old man? A seventy-four-year-old with arthritis. That must have been pretty hard, yes?"

Then, the words that changed it all, that changed everything. And they came from Bhang's mouth, as if from a ventriloquist.

"We'll pay you fifty million dollars to spy for China," Bhang had said to Dillman. "Agree, promise to set me free, and it will be wired within the hour."

He'd guessed, correctly as it turned out, that it needed to be an awe-inspiring number. Anything less, and the Israeli wouldn't have done it. The ministry had paid Dillman the $50 million and at least another $50 million over the years. In return, Dillman had been a virtual treasure trove of information, not only about Israel, but America too.

The turning of the high-ranking Israeli had propelled Bhang upward within the ministry. He bathed in the reflected glory of the mole's revelations.

"Dillman," said Bhang, looking at the corpse, at rest in the trunk.

"Are you sure, sir?"

Bhang did not answer or show any emotion, as he stared at the dead Israeli.

Fao Bhang did not like idle talk. In fact, on the day when Bhang was elevated to his leadership post of the Ministry of State Security, leapfrogging over more than a dozen more senior officers who were, on paper, more experienced than him, Premier Zicheng had remarked, "Fao, you seem more like a librarian than a spy."

Bhang, in typical fashion, had not responded, except to nod a humble thank-you. Premier Zicheng then presented him the Order of the Lotus—the ministry's highest honor. Bhang was appointed, at the age of forty-three, to arguably the third most powerful position in China.

Only Bhang knew that Zicheng's remark really could not have

been further from the truth. It demonstrated a critical lack of under-standing about him, another underestimation of his abilities, his strengths, and his cunning. In order to claim the ministry's top office, Bhang had engineered a bold, highly ruthless plot. Over the course of a year, he had systematically destroyed the one man standing in his way, Xiangou, his boss, mentor, and caretaker. Machiavelli himself would have cringed in fear.

It had all begun with a phone call from Bhang's half brother. Bo Minh was an electrical engineer by training, who'd started at the min-istry at the same time as Bhang. But whereas Bhang had political am-bitions, Minh was more interested in the obtuse recesses of abstract technology. Minh became a mid-level functionary within the minis-try's electronic espionage and surveillance directorate, designing de-vices used to listen in on enemies and allies alike, helping to arm agents with increasingly tinier, more-potent tools, which could be deployed in different environments across the globe and used to eavesdrop on any sort of conversation.

Minh had called Bhang past midnight, awakening him in a hotel room in Cairo, where he'd been sent to kill someone.

"I have discovered something," Minh had whispered conspiratori-ally.

"Why are you whispering?"

"I can't talk," whispered Minh urgently. "Listen to me. There is to be a change at the top echelon of the ministry."

Bhang had rubbed his eyes, then looked at his notebook, lying next to the bed. The word **CAIRO** was written out in bold letters. It was a habit he'd formed early on, so that in the jumbled chaos of hotels and cities he traveled to, he could wake up and know immediately where he was.

"What time is it?"

"What time is it? Did you not hear me?"

"How do you know?"

"I was testing a listening device. I had placed it in a bathroom on the seventh floor. The minister himself spoke. He must have gone into the bathroom near the cabinet room. He was alone, on a phone call. He has cancer. He is to resign within the year."

"Did he say who he would pick as his successor?"

"Xiangou."

A wave of electricity went down Bhang's spine. Xiangou was Bhang's boss, the head of the ministry's clandestine paramilitary services bureau. He ran the kill teams. In its own way, this was good news. It meant the minister would be selecting a killer over a functionary as the next head of the ministry.

Unfortunately, Xiangou was only forty-eight years old. He would have a long career as minister, which meant Bhang's chances of running the ministry would effectively be over.

A stark realization occurred to him then. This whole thing was, in fact, his death knell. For while Bhang was Xiangou's protégé and the most effective assassin within the clandestine bureau's ranks, Xiangou feared him. There wasn't a more vicious man alive than Xiangou. As soon as he found out he was to become China's next minister of State Security, Bhang would be dead within the hour.

"When will it happen?"

"I don't know."

"Don't tell *anyone*. Do you hear me?"

"Yes, Fao."

And so it had begun.

Bhang knew he would have to design the operation outside of the architecture of the ministry. The ministry was everywhere, and any action he might contemplate involving Xiangou would be detected.

Bhang realized as he sat in that Cairo hotel room that next morning, he would need to do this one off the grid.

He picked up the phone.

"Dillman."

"Mikal, it is me, Fao."

"Good morning, Fao. Who will the ministry be putting a bullet in today?"

"I need to see you. It's urgent."

"I'll be in Brussels tomorrow. Meet me at noon at the Metropole. The room will be under Seidenberg."

In an opulent suite at the Metropole, Bhang laid out his dilemma to Dillman. Not only did Bhang need Dillman's ideas on how to remove Xiangou, he needed Dillman to actually do it. He needed Mossad to terminate Xiangou. Bhang couldn't be involved. He'd asked many people to do many things over the years, but always with the threat of violence or the promise of money behind the request. It was the first time Bhang had ever asked anyone for a favor.

"I'll do it for you," Dillman had said, placing his hand on Bhang's knee and patting it. "Anything for you, my good friend."

Dillman fabricated a cover story to explain why Israel needed to assassinate Xiangou. He doctored a photograph of Xiangou dining with a high-level Hamas operative in Budapest. For his madhouse compatriots, that was more than enough paper to approve the kill.

Mossad began by infiltrating Xiangou's personal life and looking for vulnerabilities. He was married but kept a mistress in Macau. He liked to gamble. It was decided that they would strike Xiangou during one of his monthly visits to the sprawling city, China's version of Las Vegas.

Macau, Dillman knew, would be a challenge. Chinese intelligence was everywhere, particularly inside the big casinos, layered throughout the staffs and monitoring cameras, looking for suspicious or even just interesting Westerners to spy on. The casino where Xiangou would be gambling was the most logical place to hit him. But there were thirty-two casinos in Macau, and trying to guess which one Xiangou would throw away his money at was like trying to find a needle in a haystack.

Then there was the building where his mistress lived, a modern glass skyscraper in the central business district. Her apartment was on the penthouse floor, fifty-six stories up. The building was highly secure, with armed guards at the entrance. More important, Xiangou always brought a two- or three-man detail with him. If the casinos were going to be difficult, the apartment building would be next to impossible.

Dillman's overarching concern was the possibility Xiangou's death might be traced back to Mossad. It had to look like an accident.

From public construction records, they studied the apartment building at its various stages. A British structural engineering firm had been hired as a subcontractor, and part of their purview had been the scope and plan for the elevators. A phone call to London was made.

Three weeks later, on a sun-splashed Thursday afternoon, Xiangou landed at Macau International Airport. He went directly to the StarWorld Casino, where he spent several hours playing craps and drinking vodka, with three ministry agents hovering over his shoulders. At dinnertime, he went to his mistress's apartment. At just before 9:00 P.M., Xiangou and his mistress stepped into the elevator. As the doors shut, Xiangou winked at the young girl, reaching for her hand. Then, as a pair of cables attached to the roof of the cabin failed, the elevator dropped fifty-six stories. Screams from Xiangou's mistress could be heard at various points by people waiting for an elevator, as the couple rocketed down the air shaft to their violent deaths.

The following June, after the current minister of State Security surprised almost everyone with his resignation, for personal reasons, Fao Bhang was named China's next minister of State Security.

He owed Dillman his job. He owed Dillman his life.

Bhang reached into the trunk, grabbed the Star of David from Dillman's neck, ripped it off, then turned and walked out of the morgue.

Back in his office, Bhang assembled his three deputies; Ming-húa, head of clandestine operations; Quan, who ran the ministry's intelligence-gathering unit; and Wuzhou, Bhang's chief of staff.

"Where did the trunk come from?" asked Bhang.

"Hong Kong. It arrived yesterday."

"And the girl saw it?"

"Yes. She opened the trunk herself. Premier Li was present as well, as was the first lady."

Bhang's nostrils flared.

"Do we know who it was actually sent from?" he demanded.

The two aides looked at each other, neither wanting to be the one to answer Bhang's question. Finally, one spoke.

"The origin on the manifest was Hong Kong. That's all we have."

Bhang sat down. He leaned back in silence, then lit a cigarette.

"Minister Bhang," said one of the men, "Premier Li insisted you see him immediately."

"Please," said Bhang, holding his index finger up for silence.

Bhang took several deep drags without speaking. His mind raced. He processed what had happened. There was a strategy here. Whoever found Mikal Dillman—presumably Mossad—was up to something.

He took several hard puffs, looking for inspiration in the rush of nicotine.

If terminating Dillman was the objective, they could have simply done so, then deposited the corpse in a landfill. When Dillman missed his weekly check-in, the ministry would have assumed he'd been found out. But Mossad had done no such thing. Dillman checked in three days ago and then they put the ax into his skull. The Israelis could have—should have—brought him in and interrogated him. But they didn't. They killed him, stuffed him into a box, shipped him to Hong Kong. They could have kept Dillman alive and used him, as Bhang would have, to penetrate back into Beijing and the ministry, to try to learn who Dillman's handlers were, perhaps even tried to blackmail Dillman. They didn't. Instead, Dillman's killers not only sent him back, they did so in a particularly interesting and provocative way.

Their target was Bhang himself.

It was unmistakable. This thrust was aimed at him. There could be no other explanation.

Not bad, thought Bhang.

They were smart enough to know they would never be able to get at Bhang themselves. He was too well guarded, his movements too unpredictable, his activities too secret. His enemies would attempt to get at those surrounding Bhang. Premier Li, the most powerful man in China, would be furious over what had happened to his granddaughter. Much worse was the subtle effect Dillman's corpse—and its flamboyant delivery—would have on everyone surrounding Bhang. It was a dagger, sent to pierce the shroud of invincibility that Bhang had built and enforced over a decade atop the ministry, through terror, force, and fear. If Dillman's corpse could be delivered in such an ostentatious, unexpected, and undetected manner, well, then, someone out there, perhaps one of the three men seated in his office, might develop the confidence to strike at Bhang as well.

"And so the game begins," said Bhang quietly, to himself, as he stared at the burning ember atop his cigarette.

"Minister?"

Bhang stood up. He reached for Dillman's Star of David, which was on his desk. He picked it up and held it, examining it.

"Who outside of the ministry was aware of Dillman?" asked Bhang.

One of the men handed a single sheet of paper to Bhang. The list was short, only four names. Bhang studied it, then nodded his head slowly up and down.

"Aziz," said Bhang.

"The Iran station chief? He's not on the list, sir."

"Please see that he's here, in my office, as soon as possible."

"Yes, Minister."

"Then see that the first three gentlemen on this list are killed, in a manner that is quiet, and, if possible, dignified."

"Yes, sir."

Bhang stubbed out his cigarette. He removed his blazer from the back of his chair.

"Tell the premier I'll be there in ten minutes. Also, have gifts sent to his granddaughter; wonderful gifts—a large teddy bear, flowers, sweets. I want you to personally oversee the wrapping of the presents as well as their delivery. Is that understood?"

"Yes, Minister Bhang."

5

WHEATON ICE ARENA
WHEATON, MARYLAND

Dewey Andreas climbed out of his Ford F-150 and glanced up at the sky, still dark at 4:55 A.M. It was cold out, not Maine cold, but cold enough to see his breath. He reached into the back of the pickup and grabbed his equipment bag and a pair of hockey sticks.

"You must be the ringer Jessica was bragging about," said a brown-haired man walking by, carrying his equipment.

Dewey nodded and smiled but said nothing. He recognized the speaker; Mark Hastings, chief justice of the United States Supreme Court. Hastings, Dewey knew, had played goalie at Harvard. His equipment bag was twice as big as Dewey's.

"You need a hand?" Dewey asked.

"Do I really look that old?" Hastings laughed.

"Let me get your stick."

Dewey took Hastings's goalie stick and walked with him toward the rink doors.

It was the most exclusive pickup hockey game in Washington. It was probably the most exclusive pickup hockey game in the world. After all, where else on a cold Saturday morning at five o'clock could you find three members of the cabinet, a Supreme Court justice, four U.S. senators, half a dozen congressmen, a few assorted Pentagon officials, and a variety of other denizens of the Washington elite gathering to lace up their old pairs of CCM Super Tacks, pull on equipment last used in high school or college, and play an hour of hockey?

Of course, the main attraction was the occupant of the black limousine now pulling into the rink's parking lot, with small American flags waving from the front and rear corners of the vehicle, flanked by a convoy of Chevy Suburbans: The president of the United States, J. P. Dellenbaugh.

Dellenbaugh and Senator Anthony DiNovi were the only participants in the weekly pickup game to have actually played professional hockey, Dellenbaugh for the Detroit Red Wings, DiNovi for the Boston Bruins. Most of the other players played hockey in college. A few only made it to high school. The only requirement was that a player played through high school and that Dellenbaugh like them. There was also a no-business rule—no talking politics, legislation, poll numbers, upcoming elections, nothing political whatsoever. Also, no lobbyists.

Originally, the game was Dellenbaugh's idea, begun when he was a freshman senator. It became a slightly more exclusive ticket when Dellenbaugh was selected as Rob Allaire's running mate. When Allaire was elected president, and Dellenbaugh became vice president of the United States, it became still harder to get an invite to the game. After Rob Allaire's untimely death, and J. P. Dellenbaugh's swearing in as president of the United States, everyone assumed Dellenbaugh wouldn't be able to continue the game. But they were wrong. Except for the occasional vacation, foreign trip, or crisis, Dellenbaugh had kept it up.

Now it was next to impossible to get an invite to the game, played every Saturday morning at the blue-roofed Wheaton Ice Arena. Dellenbaugh himself needed to approve everyone invited. The Secret Service screened the names of all participants. Every week, FBI bomb dogs came out to the rink at 3:00 A.M. to sweep the facility.

If you were an ex–hockey player, you probably knew about the game. That was the way the hockey world worked. Even if they were despised opponents in college, after the rivalry was over and the skates were off, hockey players reunited, like a tribe. Ex–hockey players didn't like to brag or call attention to themselves. They were secretive too. Until recently, few people outside of the tight-knit D.C. community of former hockey players knew about the game. That is, until one of

26

the players—still unidentified—leaked word of the weekly pickup game to a female reporter for *The Washington Post*. The reporter, a long-legged, beautiful sports reporter named Summer Swenson, wrote a piece entitled "The Pickup Artists," with an old photograph of Dellenbaugh, showing him beating the daylights out of some unfortunate member of the New York Rangers. The article detailed the ins and outs of the president's weekly game. It caused the Secret Service to move the time and location of the game.

Checking wasn't allowed, though that didn't stop the game from occasionally getting chippy. Usually, it was Dellenbaugh himself who was the instigator. One thing about hockey players was that once they laced the skates on, each player invariably reverted to his habits and ways of old. The former puck hogs still hogged the puck, the former playmakers still set up plays, and the former fighters, such as Dellenbaugh, well, they caused trouble.

Dewey hadn't asked to be invited to the game. In fact, as he followed Hastings inside the rink, bag slung over his shoulder, he cursed Jessica under his breath. He hadn't skated since his senior year at Castine High School. At Boston College, given the choice of football or hockey, he'd decided to play football. Dewey had been captain of his high school team. Back then, more than two decades ago, Dewey could handle himself on the rink pretty well. He played defense, scored the occasional goal, led the team in assists. But what he'd really been known for, the quality that caused his coach, a gruff old Mainer named Mark Blood, to nickname him "Mad Dog," was his ability to hit.

A slight tinge of adrenaline spiked in his blood as he walked through the door and caught the sight of a rusted blue-and-white Zamboni chugging around the ice.

Dewey followed Hastings into the locker room. Inside, the benches on both sides of the room were filled with men getting dressed. Dewey didn't recognize many of them; he couldn't have told most U.S. senators apart from the guy driving the Zamboni. But he did recognize a few. In addition to Hastings, there was Attorney General Rickards, and DiNovi, the senior senator from New Jersey.

Dewey glanced quickly around the room at the senators, congressmen, and other officials in various stages of undress.

"I heard we had a new guy in town," said a tall, black-haired man, who walked over to Dewey. "I'm Tony DiNovi." He extended his hand.

"Hi," said Dewey, shaking his hand. "Nice to meet you, Senator."

"Call me Tony. So I hear you're the lucky guy who's marrying Jessica Tanzer. Congratulations."

"Thank you."

"When's the wedding?"

"We haven't set a date yet."

"I've known Jessica since she worked on Capitol Hill," said DiNovi. "She worked on the Intelligence Committee before she went over to the FBI."

"I didn't know that."

"She has one of the best strategic minds I've ever known. Most effective national security advisor we've had in a long, long time, certainly since I've been around. You're a very lucky man, Dewey."

"Thanks, Senator."

Dewey pulled his shirt over his head, then leaned down and unzipped his hockey bag.

"That's one hell of a scar," said DiNovi, looking at Dewey's left shoulder. The scar had that effect; it was two inches wide and ran from the apex of his shoulder down to the midpoint of his biceps, like an ugly ribbon. "If you don't mind my asking, what happened?"

Dewey looked at DiNovi without answering.

Just then, the door swung open and the president of the United States, J. P. Dellenbaugh, walked in. His brown hair was slightly messed up, and he had a big grin on his face. His hockey bag was slung over his shoulder. He was wearing red sweatpants and a faded blue-and-yellow University of Michigan sweatshirt. He threw his bag down next to Dewey's.

"Hi, Dewey," said the president. Dellenbaugh reached out and shook his hand. Everyone was watching. Dellenbaugh glanced around the room. "Hi, boys. What's the matter, haven't any of you ever seen an American hero?"

Dellenbaugh kept his eyes on Dewey as he shook his hand.

"Tony," continued Dellenbaugh, "he got the scar fighting terrorists. Now let's stop giving the guy the third degree and play a little hockey. Sorry I'm late, everyone."

Dellenbaugh took the seat next to Dewey and got undressed. It was refreshing to see the U.S. president in this unrehearsed, raw light; seeing him as just one of the guys.

"You and I are probably the only guys in this room who went to public high school," whispered Dellenbaugh, smiling at Dewey. The implication was clear: the rest of them, at least for the next hour, were all a bunch of prep-school pussies.

"Where did you go?" asked Dewey.

"You mean you don't know my life story, up and down, left and right?"

"I apologize."

"Don't," laughed Dellenbaugh. "I live for moments like that, finding someone who doesn't know every damn thing about me. That's why this hour is the best hour of the week. People don't treat me like I'm president. The best is when Desmond over there tries to lay me out with one of his pathetic Dartmouth checks."

A large brown-haired man, tightening his right skate, looked up at Dellenbaugh from across the locker room.

"You're goin' down, Dellenbaugh," he said, smiling.

Dellenbaugh paused, staring at Desmond with mock fury.

"Bring it, bitch," said Dellenbaugh, taunting him back.

The room erupted in laughter.

Dellenbaugh turned to Dewey.

"To answer your question, I went to Trenton High School, outside of Detroit. Then Michigan on a scholarship. My dad and mom both worked for General Motors."

Dewey didn't say anything as he pulled out a pair of ancient CCM Super Tacks, the blades partially covered in rust.

"My God, those are old," said Dellenbaugh. "I'm going to buy you a new pair as a wedding present. Speaking of which, congratulations."

"Thank you."

"I asked Jessica where you popped the question. She wouldn't tell me."

Dewey smiled but said nothing. He pulled his laces tight, tied them, then reached into the bag for his helmet.

"So you're not going to tell me?" asked Dellenbaugh.

"No."

Dewey pulled out an old, bright yellow Jofa helmet. Before he put it on his head, he looked inside. He reached down and removed a layer of cobwebs.

"Jesus, Mary, and Joseph," said Dellenbaugh. "That is one nasty-looking helmet. I'm starting to worry about you, Dewey. When was the last time you played?"

Dewey laughed at Dellenbaugh's ribbing.

"Twenty years ago," said Dewey.

"It's pretty mellow out there," said Dellenbaugh. "I don't want you getting hurt. I promised your fiancée I'd return you without any major injuries."

Dewey stood up and pulled his helmet on.

"I'll see you out there, Mr. President."

"I'm right behind you," said Dellenbaugh. "Hey DiNovi, did you bring me a Dunkin' Donuts coffee, like you said you would?"

"Yes, Mr. President," said DiNovi, who was pulling his right skate on. "Decaf, right?"

"Wise ass. If it's decaf, I'm going to veto any piece of legislation with your name on it for the next year."

Outside the locker room, Dewey walked on the rubber mat to the rink door. The stands were empty except for a dozen or so Secret Service agents, spread out around the bleachers. Agents stood at both entrances; each man held what looked like a laptop bag across their torsos, one hand concealed. Inside were submachine guns.

Several players were already on the ice, skating in circles to warm up. Dewey stepped onto the ice and proceeded to go flying onto his butt. He slowly got to his knees, then stood. He began a slow circle around the rink. His skates, though rusty, were sharp. Still, it had been almost two decades since he'd skated and he was rusty. He watched as an older player, perhaps in his fifties, went flying by him. Then he caught Dellenbaugh, climbing onto the ice. The president quickly leapt into a full sprint around the outer edge of the ice, his skates making sharp cutting noises as he moved gracefully around the rink. Dellenbaugh was a sight to behold, his strides smooth, with tremendous speed. He circled twice, then came over to Dewey, slowing down alongside him.

"How you feeling?" he asked.

"Not bad," said Dewey.

"You're on D, next to me. Stay away from Tom DeGray."

"Which one is he?"

"He's the guy with the red helmet," said Dellenbaugh, nodding at a player stretching next to the boards. "Congressman from Chicago. He can't skate for shit, but he can hit and he plays dirty. More to the point, he used to have a thing for Jessica."

"A thing?"

"They went out to dinner. That's all I know. Just keep an eye out. He's the vengeful type."

Dewey skated along next to Dellenbaugh for a few minutes, working hard just to keep up. Even relaxing, Dellenbaugh moved with a speed that, at least to Dewey, was stunning, barely pushing his legs, yet flying along.

Dellenbaugh gathered everyone at center ice. He and DiNovi picked teams. Even though Dewey was clearly one of the worst players on the ice, Dellenbaugh picked him first. Each team had ten players, enough for two lines and a goalie. Hastings, chief justice of the Supreme Court, was one of the goalies; the other was a staffer from the White House Communications Office named Gus Edwards, who had played at Williams. When a young White House intern named Pitchess finally showed up, he was handed a striped jacket and told to referee.

The game started with Pitchess dropping the puck at mid ice. Dewey started at defense, next to Dellenbaugh, who was passed the puck by the center. Dellenbaugh flipped it to Dewey, who skated up the right side of the rink, then passed it back to Dellenbaugh, who proceeded to weave in and out of three players on his way to the opposing net, where he deposited the puck between Edwards's pads—*five hole*—for the first goal of the game. Technically, Dewey got an assist on it. Dellenbaugh skated back to defense as Pitchess retrieved the puck from the net. The other team booed rather loudly as Dellenbaugh skated by their bench.

31

"Puck hog!" hooted one player on the opposing team.

"Republicans never pass the puck!" barked another, to the howls of his teammates.

Dellenbaugh took his place on the blue line, next to Dewey.

"Nice shot," said Dewey.

"Thanks, kid. Good assist."

"Yeah, right," said Dewey.

The next face-off was won by the other team. DiNovi, who was playing center, took the puck and dumped it into the zone behind Dewey and Dellenbaugh. Dellenbaugh gave chase as the other team's right wing came after him. In the corner, Dellenbaugh grabbed the puck and banged it along the back boards to Dewey. Just as Dewey was about to get the puck, he felt a sharp pain at his ankles—a stick from behind, slashing at his skate. He went flying over and tumbled to the ice, sticking his left arm out as he collided with the boards so that his head wouldn't hit. Turning and looking up, he saw the back of a red helmet, the only red helmet on the ice: DeGray, the player Dellenbaugh had warned him about. He took the puck and centered it to DiNovi, who stuck it past Hastings to even the score.

Dellenbaugh skated over and helped Dewey up.

"You okay, kid?"

"Fine," said Dewey.

The teams changed lines, tied at one apiece. On the bench, Dewey glanced over to the other bench, catching the eye of DeGray, who was smiling and talking with someone.

"You want me to clean his clock for you?" asked Dellenbaugh, smiling.

Dewey laughed.

"No, not a big deal."

Dewey had liked Rob Allaire, Dellenbaugh's predecessor, a lot. Initially, Dewey wasn't sure how he felt about Dellenbaugh. Now, as he saw the president in his element, as a human being, as a teammate, even as a friend, Dewey was starting to like him. Dewey wasn't very good at relating to people or forming friendships. Dellenbaugh was a genius at it. He made him forget the fact that he was president; if anything, he made Dewey feel like they were two kids playing pond hockey back in Castine;

Dellenbaugh had a big shit-eating grin on his face as he not-so-subtly encouraged Dewey to take revenge on DeGray.

It was different from how he'd felt about Allaire. With Allaire, Dewey felt nothing but respect and admiration, even awe. When Allaire had awarded Dewey the Presidential Medal of Freedom, it was one of the proudest moments of his life. But with Dellenbaugh, it was something different that made Dewey like him. He was closer in age to Dewey, and his working-class roots were ones they had in common.

The ref blew the whistle, and Dewey climbed over the boards for another shift, this time starting in the opposing team's zone. Dewey was on the blue line, at the point, and the center won the face-off and shoveled it back to him. Dewey stepped forward with the puck, went left, then took a slap shot—which sailed with decent speed into the jumble of players in front of the net. Despite the no-checking rule, as he fired the shot, Dewey got leveled from behind. From the ground, he watched as his shot somehow found its way into the back of the net, the goalie having been screened. Looking up, he saw Dellenbaugh pushing DeGray back against the boards and saying something to him. Dewey hadn't seen who'd hit him, but obviously Dellenbaugh had.

As he skated back to mid ice, the red-helmeted DeGray skated up to Dewey.

"Hey, sorry about that."

Dewey ignored him.

The game went back and forth, becoming progressively sloppier as the hour went on, with the exception of the play of Dellenbaugh and DiNovi. Though they were clearly taking it easy, they stood out; both had awesome speed and stick-handling ability. Once Dellenbaugh had racked up a hat trick—three goals—he stopped taking shots, instead passing it whenever he had a clean shot.

Dewey played respectably, racking up two more assists.

With only a few minutes left, Dewey found himself with the puck at mid ice. He passed it to a wing, who brought it into the opponent's zone and took a shot, which went wide. Behind the net, Dewey saw the red helmet of DeGray as he made his break out from behind the net, skating up the ice.

Dewey began his run at the congressman from his own blue line.

He tracked DeGray as his red helmet weaved through several players. Had DeGray passed the puck, Dewey would have aborted his run, but DeGray held on, gathering speed and momentum. By center ice, DeGray was at full speed. So was Dewey.

A good hockey player, like Dellenbaugh, can skate with the puck without looking down, stick-handling blind and thereby avoiding hard checks that seemingly come out of nowhere. But most players needed to occasionally glance down at the puck to make sure it is still on their stick. DeGray was mediocre at best.

Unfortunately for the Democratic congressman from Chicago, Dewey chose to make a temporary exception to the no-checking rule. As DeGray crossed mid ice, lurching left past his own centerman, Dewey was skating at full speed. Dewey was as locked into DeGray as a torpedo is locked into the hull of a battleship. DeGray looked up at the last second as Dewey crossed mid ice, lowered his shoulder, and struck him squarely in the numbers. DeGray was pummeled. He went flying off his skates, backward, dropping his stick and landing with a loud groan on the ice. His red helmet went flying off his head, spinning toward the boards.

Play stopped as DiNovi grabbed Dewey to keep him away from DeGray, who lay facedown on the ice. When DiNovi attempted to push against Dewey, Dewey stood his ground. Dellenbaugh broke them up.

"I got him, Tony," said Dellenbaugh.

Dellenbaugh skated with Dewey toward the door. Dewey glanced over his shoulder as a few players helped DeGray to his skates.

"I wouldn't want to get on your bad side," said the president, laughing. "I was going to politely level him into the boards. That was brutal."

Dewey said nothing as he stepped off the ice.

Hastings filed in behind Dewey and the president as they stepped off the ice.

In the locker room, Dewey, Dellenbaugh, and Hastings were the first to sit down.

Hastings pulled his goalie mask off. His face was bright red and his brown hair was matted in sweat.

"It's about time someone took out that little bastard," said the chief justice, giving a thumbs-up to Dewey.

34

The door opened and DeGray stormed in, a trickle of blood on his chin, coming from his mouth.

"You son of a bitch!" he screamed at Dewey, stepping toward him. His helmet was off. Dewey didn't flinch, calmly continuing to untie his skates, ignoring him. "That was the dirtiest hit I've ever seen."

DeGray stood in front of Dewey, who pulled his helmet off and put it down. Dewey looked up at him.

"Fuck off," said Dewey dismissively.

DeGray looked around, his face beet red with anger. Suddenly he swung at Dewey. Dewey caught the fist with his left hand, then stood and, in one fluid motion, grabbed DeGray by the neck. Holding De-Gray's forearm in his left hand and neck in his right, Dewey thrust up at him, throwing DeGray backward, off his skates, to the ground in front of Hastings.

"It was a clean hit," said Hastings, as he untied his right skate and stared at DeGray on the floor. "And don't forget, I'm the chief justice of the United States."

"I thought there wasn't any hitting, Mr. President," said DeGray from the ground.

"Dewey just gave you a little dose of your own medicine," said Dellenbaugh, laughing. "Now stand up like a man, take your skates off, and get the hell out of here."

DeGray slowly sat up. He looked around for sympathy but found none.

"Does this mean . . . can I come back?"

"Absolutely," said Dellenbaugh. "Just not between the hours of five and six on Saturday mornings. If you do, I'll have one of the agents put a load of buckshot in your ass."

6

RESIDENCE OF THE PREMIER
ZHONGNANHAI
BEIJING

The black sedan carrying Fao Bhang passed through Xinhua Gate. A four-man watch of armed soldiers needed only for Bhang's driver to lower his black-tinted window a few inches to see whose limo it was; Bhang's drivers, a rotating group of three, were all known to the guards at Zhongnanhai.

At the front entrance to the premier's residence, Bhang was escorted by a soldier down a long hallway, its walls decorated with murals. At the end of the hallway was a set of closed double doors, where another soldier stood. Upon seeing Bhang, he turned and knocked.

"Send him in," came a voice from inside the room.

The soldier nodded at Bhang, then opened the door and showed Bhang in. As he went to shut the door, Premier Li called out.

"Stay inside the room," he ordered to the soldier.

The soldier followed Bhang in, shut the door, then stood at attention just inside the door.

The room was a library, its crimson red walls lined with books. Premier Li was seated on a maroon sofa, beneath a chandelier. Across from the sofa were two leather chairs.

Li was dressed casually; a button-down beneath a green cashmere V-neck sweater. He stared at Bhang as he entered.

"Premier Li," said Bhang, bowing before him. "My humblest appreciation for seeing me on such short notice."

Li said nothing. Instead he glared with a blank, seething anger at Bhang. He did not ask Bhang to sit down. Understanding the signal, Bhang stood between the two chairs, across from Li.

"What happened?" asked Li curtly, in a manner that contained what could only be described as controlled fury. "You destroyed a little girl's birthday today, Bhang?"

"I am here to apologize," said Bhang, in a soft voice. "I am most sorry. I have all ministry resources trying to determine what vile creature played such a mean-spirited joke."

"Joke?" Li yelled. "He had an *ax in his skull!* An *ax!* Covered in blood! Who would do such a thing?"

"I did not send it, so I don't know," said Bhang. "This was a cruel strategy employed by China's enemies for God knows what reason. Perhaps to do what is occurring right now, to foment anger among the leaders of our government. But I will find out who did this, sir, and justice will be brought to them."

"My granddaughter had to be sedated," said Li. "My wife is distraught."

"And for this, I am deeply sorry. Sometimes, it would seem, the world in which I live and work, a world of secrets, spills over. It's not something I chose."

"Who was this dead man?"

Bhang remained silent.

"Who was this man?" bellowed Li.

"I'm here to apologize," said Bhang. "There is nothing more I can say, with all due respect, sir."

"I am ordering you to tell me who this dead man was," seethed Li.

Bhang returned Li's angry glare with a calm, kindly expression.

"Mr. Premier," said Bhang, "there are aspects to every job that do not necessarily bring clarity or edification to the world. This question would fall into a category of what I would call unnecessary detail."

Li sat back, considering his next words.

"You're not going to tell me?" he asked, taken aback, his voice rising. "What have you exposed China to, you insolent bastard? Your arrogance knows no boundaries, Bhang."

Li pointed at the soldier. The soldier, standing at the door, looked nervously at Li. Then he reached to his holster and removed his gun. He targeted it at Bhang.

Bhang registered the sight of the muzzle, now aimed at his head. He nodded calmly, pondering what to say, remaining silent for several seconds. Then he cleared his throat.

"Mr. Premier," said Bhang, "his name was Dillman. He was an Israeli. He provided China with much information over many years."

"And why was his corpse sent to my granddaughter?"

Bhang swallowed, saying nothing. He stared meekly at Li for several seconds, letting the premier vent his anger. Finally, Li waved a finger at the soldier, ordering him to put the pistol away.

Bhang bowed.

"I must reiterate my humblest apologies to you and your family. This afternoon, a bounty of gifts is being delivered to your granddaughter, sir, and I can assure you, because my own deputy was responsible for their purchase, their packing, and their delivery, that there will be no similar mishap. Good day to you, sir."

Li said nothing, looking toward the window. He waved his hand dismissively, telling Bhang to get out, then made eye contact with the soldier, letting him know he was to escort Bhang out of the residence.

Bhang turned and walked toward the door. He walked quickly down the corridor, with the soldier trailing him. Outside, he crossed the brick walkway in front of the residence. He climbed into the back of the idling sedan.

The soldier followed Bhang to the sedan and stood watching as Bhang shut the door quietly. After a moment, the black tinted window lowered a few inches.

"Well done, Lieutenant," said Bhang, quietly looking at the soldier who minutes before had aimed his sidearm at Bhang's head. "Your performance was most convincing."

"Thank you, Minister Bhang."

Bhang raised the window and looked in the rearview mirror.

"Drive," he said.

The sedan moved slowly away from the house as Bhang removed a cigarette from his suit-coat pocket and lit it. He took a long drag on the cigarette, staring at the burning ember, feeling new emotions: embarrassment, shame, and humiliation. Even the harsh burn of the nicotine could not quell the taste of bitterness in his mouth.

"You'll pay," he whispered to himself.

But he wasn't thinking of Li. Li was a sideshow. Rather, Bhang pictured nothing but a figure, a dark, featureless face, the anonymous one who'd found Dillman. "Yes, you'll pay, my friend, whoever you are."

7

As national security advisor, Jessica Tanzer had carte blanche to enter the president's office whenever she wanted to, but on this particular morning she'd made an appointment. Jessica checked her watch, then walked to the door that led to the Oval Office.

She knocked lightly on the door.

"Yeah," came the voice of J. P. Dellenbaugh from inside.

Jessica opened the door and popped her head in.

"Hi, Mr. President."

"Come in, Jess."

Jessica closed the door behind her. Dellenbaugh looked up from a document he was reading, returned to the document, then looked up again, scanning Jessica from head to toe.

Her auburn hair was braided back in a thick, neat ponytail. She wore a diamond necklace, a blue sleeveless Prada dress that clung tightly to her body and came barely halfway down her thighs, and shiny brown riding boots that climbed to her knees.

"Don't take this the wrong way," said Dellenbaugh, "but you could get arrested for wearing that in some places."

"Are you harassing me, Mr. President?" Jessica laughed. She walked across the office and took a seat on one of the chesterfield sofas at the center of the room.

"Trust me," said Dellenbaugh, laughing, "after I saw what your future husband is capable of doing, I'm the last person who'd harass you."

"What does that mean?"

"Dewey didn't tell you what happened at the rink?"

"No."

"Nothing," said Dellenbaugh, who grinned, stood up, and walked to the sofa across from Jessica. "He got a goal and three assists. He's good. He's got a very graceful, almost gentle way about him out there."

"Gentle?" she asked. "Are we talking about the same guy?"

"You look like you just stepped off a Hollywood set, Jessica."

Jessica blushed light red.

"Thank you," she said. "Dewey and I are leaving for Argentina at lunchtime. I thought I'd wear my travel outfit to work."

The morning sun shone brightly through the French doors, creating a checkered, geometric pattern on the tan leather. Dellenbaugh reached forward and poured two cups of coffee from the silver service atop the table, handing one to Jessica.

Dellenbaugh raised the cup to his lips to take a sip.

"So what's up?"

"I'm resigning," said Jessica.

Dellenbaugh paused as he was about to take a sip. For a moment, he didn't move.

"I know the timing isn't great, sir. But I want you to know it has nothing to do with you or the team here. I love my job."

The president put the coffee cup back down on the table. He leaned back, put his hand to his tie, loosened it, then unbuttoned the top of his shirt.

"Wow. I definitely was not expecting that. You and Hector are the linchpins of our national security team. You more than anyone. I need you here."

"I'm sorry, Mr. President."

"Does Hector know?"

"Not even Dewey knows," said Jessica. "I felt it was my duty to inform you first."

"Is there something wrong?"

"Not at all. I love it here. And, President Dellenbaugh, I truly enjoy working with you. To be perfectly frank, I didn't think I would. I thought after President Allaire died, I'd hate my job and resent you. But the opposite is true. You're doing a fantastic job. Every day has been a blast. I understand now why Rob Allaire asked you to be his vice president. And, you've given me the freedom to do my work, and you've given me your trust. That's all a national security advisor can ask for."

Dellenbaugh ran his hand back through his hair.

"You didn't answer me, Jess."

"I'm thirty-seven years old," said Jessica. "I've got a wedding to plan, and that's just for starters. I also want to make some money, sir. I've never held a job outside of government."

"There's plenty of time for that," said Dellenbaugh. "You are at the center of this administration. You are a critical component to our national security. This might sound corny, but we need you. America needs you."

Jessica smiled.

"I can't tell you how much it means to me to hear you say that. But I've made up my mind."

Jessica's eyes were red with emotion.

Dellenbaugh paused, then smiled. He stared at Jessica in silence for several moments. He sighed.

"I understand," he whispered. "I understand, and, as sad as I am right now, I'm very proud of you. How much time do I have?"

"A while," said Jessica. "I'd like to work with you to find the best possible individual to serve as your next national security advisor. Then, from the private sector somewhere, I'd like to remain your friend, as well as be a part of the team that gets you reelected in two years."

Dellenbaugh laughed.

"Jessica, I can't stop you. But I'm going to try and talk you out of it."

"I'll always listen to anything you have to say, President Dellenbaugh."

Jessica stood up. She walked around the coffee table and put her hand out, but Dellenbaugh ignored her outstretched hand and wrapped his arms around her and gave her a hug.

"You have fun down there, will you?" he said.

"I will. Thank you, Mr. President. I'll check in from the ranch."

"Don't do that," said Dellenbaugh. "You're on vacation. I've got things covered here. You go have fun with Dewey. Let him know I already ordered him a new helmet and a decent pair of skates."

8

Headquarters for the Ministry of State Security comprised six large buildings in a sprawling rectangular campus on the southern outskirts of Beijing, the buildings connected underground by tunnels and, on the ground floor, by concrete courtyards. Each of the six buildings was indistinguishable from the next: ten stories high, square, built of drab gray concrete and small windows, not so much ugly as boring and bureaucratic. The courtyards were largely empty except for a few people milling about. The occasional low rumble of the underground subway system, which ran in an internal circular loop connecting the six buildings, could be heard above the din of traffic beyond the unexpectedly ornate steel fence that enclosed the campus. The complex was guarded by armed soldiers stationed every few hundred feet.

The black limousine carrying Hasim Aziz, Iran's highest-ranking intelligence official in China, turned through the main entrance at the northeast corner of the campus, then entered the subterranean parking garage. The vehicle stopped in front of a glass-enclosed lobby with yet more soldiers standing about, submachine guns held aimed at the ground. This was building 6.

Aziz had been to the ministry many times before. To say that Iran relied on the Chinese ministry of intelligence was an understatement.

Annually, the ministry provided Iran with more than one billion dollars in covert aid in the form of cash payments. In addition, and more important, the ministry doled out intelligence about Iran's enemies and allies alike, gleaned from ministry agents spread like flies across the Middle East. In return, China did not ask for anything specifically. Anything, that is, except to be obeyed at those times when they called.

They took the elevator to the tenth floor. Aziz followed one of Bhang's staffers down a long corridor. At the corner of the building, two men in suits stood in front of a set of imposing steel double doors. As Aziz approached, the man on the right reached for the doorknob and opened the door.

Inside the office, to the left, the wall was covered in an ancient Chinese tapestry, which hung from the ceiling. Two green sofas faced each other across a simple glass coffee table. The other side of the office faced the outer part of the building; both walls had windows looking out on Beijing. Fao Bhang was seated behind a desk in the corner, his fingers interlocked, still. He stared at Aziz as he entered. Two other ministry officials stood to the left, next to the desk. A single chair sat unoccupied in front of Bhang's desk.

"Minister Bhang," said Aziz, bowing slightly, out of respect, then stepping toward Bhang, his right hand extended.

"Good evening," said Bhang, ignoring the Iranian's hand. He pointed to the chair. "How was your trip, Mr. Aziz?"

"Fine," said Aziz, sitting down.

"Are you curious as to why you're here?"

"My assumption is that you'll tell me at some point, Minister Bhang."

Bhang nodded his head up and down, then his lips spread in a forced smile.

"Does China ask much of you, Mr. Aziz?"

"What do you mean, sir?'

"Do we ask much of you? The question is self-explanatory."

"Do you mean Iran?"

"I mean you, Hasim Aziz," said Bhang.

Aziz shifted in the chair.

"China is very generous. It's no secret that the ministry helped us acquire weapons-grade uranium. In addition, your financial aid has been very important. As for me, in my five years as station chief, I have always enjoyed my relationship with the ministry."

Bhang was silent for several moments. Without taking his eyes away from Aziz, he reached with his left hand to the desk drawer, opened it, and pulled an object from the desk. It was a necklace. He tossed it onto the wood top of his desk so Aziz could see it.

Aziz looked at it. Then his eyes moved back to Bhang. He remained silent.

"For more than a decade, Iran has enjoyed the fruits that come from China's friend inside Israeli intelligence. I pulled this from around his neck this morning. He was the unfortunate recipient of an ax to the skull."

"This is most disturbing," said Aziz, looking perplexed. "As you said, Iran benefited greatly from your man."

"Do you know what his name was, Mr. Aziz?"

"No, sir. I knew of the existence of a man, of course, but his name was always a secret to me. Nor did I ever ask my contact for further information. As you said, his insights were a benefit to our republic."

"His name was Dillman."

Aziz was silent. Sweat broke out on his forehead.

"Two months ago, in a Shanghai restaurant, we provided photographs to you," continued Bhang.

One of the men placed a pair of photos on the desk in front of Aziz. The first showed a tall Iranian, dressed in a suit, walking with a woman. The other photo showed an American, white shirt, blue blazer, stubble, big, tough-looking.

Aziz looked at the photos, sat back, then looked at Bhang.

"Lon Qassou," said Aziz. "And the American."

"Dewey Andreas," said Bhang. He reached for his pack of cigarettes and lit one.

"Yes."

"It was Andreas who stole the Iranian nuclear bomb, correct?"

"Yes, he did, Minister."

"And how did he do that?"

Aziz stared dumbfounded at Bhang. His eyes darted left and right. "He infiltrated the Turkish border."

"And replaced the bomb with a replica, correct?"

"Yes."

"How did he know what it looked like? Its dimensions? Even I did not know, despite the fact that I provided the yellowcake, the trigger, and the money to build it."

Aziz nodded, then was silent as he considered the question.

"I'm thinking of what I know, sir," said Aziz.

"I suggest you think faster," said Bhang, impatience in his voice. "How did he know what it looked like?"

"He had knowledge from someone who had seen it," said Aziz. "Perhaps Qassou?"

"Qassou was a functionary," said Bhang.

Aziz looked up.

"I realize you would perhaps like to move on to another subject, Mr. Aziz," said Bhang. "But you will answer. I know you know the answer to my question, as do I."

"Then why are you asking me?"

"I suppose I would like confirmation."

"In New York City," said Aziz, "Andreas kidnapped Iran's ambassador to the United Nations."

"Bhutta," Bhang said, his nostrils flaring.

"Yes," said Aziz. "Bhutta was involved in the creation—"

"I know who Amit Bhutta is," said Bhang, his voice rising, staring daggers at Aziz.

"I'm sorry, Minister Bhang," pleaded Aziz. "I had nothing to do with it."

Bhang's eyes darted right, to one of his aides. The man stood and motioned for Aziz to stand.

"Minister," said the Iranian, his brow furrowing in worry as the aide grabbed his arm. "I'm sorry. I had no control over Amit Bhutta! Please, sir!"

The other aide joined the first, grabbing the Iranian's other arm and yanking him toward the door.

Bhang's eyes were black with rage, his pale face flushed red, yet he found a way to control himself. He reached for another cigarette and lit it. As Aziz was dragged to the door, his protestations grew louder, more desperate. Bhang inhaled, then glared at the back of the Iranian's head.

"Have a safe trip, Mr. Aziz," said Bhang.

9

Dewey felt a hand on his shoulder, gently rubbing it.

"Wake up."

He registered the soft, dry whisper of Jessica's voice, then the smell of her perfume, before he opened his eyes or so much as moved. She rubbed his shoulder. He slowly opened his eyes and looked at her.

"Mile High Club?" he asked her in a whisper.

"Pig," she said, smiling.

"We could squeeze into one of the restrooms."

"Don't you think people would notice?"

"I'll shut the door."

"Oh, my God. You're demented."

"Probably, but you look so good in that dress."

"Wait 'til we get to the ranch. We have an entire week."

"I can't wait 'til the ranch."

She glanced around, making sure nobody was looking, then leaned forward and kissed him on the lips. Her hand went down to his crotch and pushed against his jeans.

"Buenos días, señor," she whispered.

"Come on, we can do it right here. Everyone's either asleep or reading."

"You know what I really want right now?" she purred.

"What?"

Jessica reached beside her and picked up a catalog.

"For you to help me pick out our wedding china."

"You're evil," he said.

She giggled.

"I've got it narrowed down to sixteen patterns."

"Oh, God," Dewey said. "I thought this was going to be low-key. Why don't we elope? Why do we need china? What's wrong with good old-fashioned paper plates?"

"This is the only time I'm ever getting married, farm boy. Fine, don't help me."

"I'll help you," he said. "Just promise you won't tell anyone."

Jessica giggled, leaned toward him, and kissed his cheek.

"President Dellenbaugh told me you're a good hockey player. He said you scored three assists."

"You don't score assists, Jess. You make assists."

"Oh, whatever. What is there, some sort of hockey grammar book you guys carry around? Last time I checked, most hockey players can barely form a complete sentence without drooling."

"Did he say anything else?" Dewey asked.

"Oh, you mean did he mention how you almost decapitated Tom DeGray?"

Dewey grinned.

"He didn't tell me," said Jessica. "Tom did. He called me and said he acted like a jerk. He said he wants to apologize to you."

"Honestly, I can't believe you dated that guy."

"Well, you put him in his place, from what I hear."

Dewey smiled.

Jessica placed her head on Dewey's shoulder. She held up her left hand, admiring her ring finger. On it was a beautiful diamond ring: an antique setting, three diamonds of equal size set in a row atop a platinum band. She ran her right index finger over the top of the stones.

"I think it's sort of cute that you were jealous," Jessica whispered.

Dewey cleared his throat.

"I wasn't jealous."

"Oh, really?"

"The guy's a douche. He tried to chop my foot off. I exacted a little justice, that's all."

"I think you were jealous, and I think it's cute what you did. I guess I don't blame you. He's not that bad, though. Do you get jealous? We should probably talk about that. I mean, I definitely get jealous. If you so much as look at one of these South American bombshells walking around Córdoba, I will . . ."

Her voice trailed off as she looked at Dewey.

"I'd rather talk about china settings, Jess."

She sat up and laughed.

"Okay, okay, I'll drop it. By the way, wait until you see Argentina. It's beautiful."

"I've been," Dewey said.

"Oh, really?" Jessica asked. "When did you go to Argentina?"

Dewey smiled but said nothing. He put his hand on her left thigh.

"That's classified, sweetie," he said.

"You know I can find out, Dewey. Was it Delta or later?"

"It was an operation. A week in Buenos Aires. Interdiction. We were chasing a narco. Colombian, some sort of money guy. Bad dude."

"Did you get him?"

Dewey nodded.

Jessica took his hand, leaned forward, and kissed his ear, clutching his neck.

"I think I'm starting to like you," she whispered, laying her head on his shoulder, shutting her eyes, pushing away all thoughts except for the simple thought of them.

10

By 5:00 A.M., Fao Bhang was seated in the conference room next to his corner office at the ministry, reading Dewey Andreas's file. He held a cup of coffee in one hand and a cigarette in the other. With him was Ming-húa and Hu'ang Li, head of the ministry's intelligence-gathering unit, the intelligence bureau.

Several other senior ministry staffers were also present. Cigarette smoke was cantilevered across the air. Through the conference-room windows, Beijing was beginning to turn gray as dawn approached.

On the wall, two large plasma screens were lit up. The first showed three photos, all of Andreas, taken at Odessa International Airport a little over three months ago. The first was taken at a distance, from a side angle. Andreas towered over Ukrainian customs agents as he handed them his passport. The second photo was head-on, from a distance and blurry, as Andreas unwittingly approached a security camera in the main terminal of the airport. A third photograph was clearest. It showed Andreas up close, looking at the same camera. A blank, calm expression was on the American's face. He wore a blue suit, no tie, and had a few days' worth of stubble. The camera seemed to capture not only Andreas's cold suspicion, it also showed a flicker of intelligence and, in some sense, enjoyment.

The second plasma had a file sheet on Andreas: one slide, upon which was highlighted everything that was known about him:

ANDREAS, DEWEY   Citizenship: USA
DOB: unknown   Home: Castine, ME
Boston College: May 93   English B.A., 3.1 GPA
Varsity Football 90–93(captain 92–93)
U.S. Army: enlistment Jun 93
U.S. Army Rangers, Fort Benning, GA
Winter School: Jan–Mar 94
Rank: 1 in class of 188
1st Special Forces Operational Detachment, aka Delta Force: Recruitment Mar 1994, Graduate Dec 96, Fort Bragg, NC, Rank: unavailable

CAREER (known):

- Lisbon, POR: Jan–Mar 96: (mission unknown)

- San Isidro de El General, COS: Oct 96–Jan 97: Anti-narcotic: NIC, COL, VEN

- London, ENG: Apr 97: Assassination (attempted) Subhi al-Tufayli / Hezbollah (mission failure)

- Munich, GER: April 97: Exfiltration Constantine Vargarin (wanted by GUR-RUS) (mission success)

- Buenos Aires, ARG: Sep–Dec 97: Anti-narcotic: ARG, COL, CHI, and BOL

- Montreal, CAN: Jan 98: Assassination Constantine Vargarin (mission success)

- Lisbon, POR: Mar 98: Assassination Frances Vibohr (Siemens VIP suspect in sale of TS info to SAU) (mission success)

- Bali, IND: Aug 98: Assassination of Rumallah Khomeini (mission success)

- Jun 00–Dec 11: (nonmilitary) roles offshore oil & gas industry

     Aberdeen, SCO
     Edinburgh, SCO
     Belfast, IRE
     Cardiff, WAL
     Valparaiso, CHI
     Buenaventura, COL

- East Hampton, NY: Dec 11: Andreas kills Alexander Fortuna (sanction: believed to be unofficial)

- Washington, DC: Jan 12: U.S. Presidential Medal of Freedom and U.S. Congressional Medal of Honor

- Islamabad, PAK: Jun 12: Overthrow of Omar El-Khayab (sanction: assumed to be official JSOC/CIA)

- Broumana, LEB: Jul 12: Assassination of Aswan Fortuna (sanction: believed to be unofficial)

- Mahdishahr, IRA: Oct 12: Infiltration/theft nuclear device (sanction: unknown)

ACTIVE FILE(s):
- VEVAK Tehran, IRA
  98-05: (inactive: kill or capture)
  12-pres: (active: kill or capture)

- IRG Tehran, IRA: 12-pres: (active: capture)

- AL-MUQAWAMA/Hezbollah
  Tehran, IRA: 98-01: (inactive: kill or capture)
  Tehran, IRA: 11-pres: (active: kill or capture)
  Damascus, SYR: 12-pres: (active: kill or capture)

- HAMAS
  Gaza, ISR: 12-pres: (active: objective unknown)

- GRU
  Moscow, RUS: 97-04: (inactive: capture)

MISC:
- Fort Bragg, NC: May 99: Wife (Holly) dies: Andreas charged with murder

- Arlington, VA: Jul 99: Discharged from 1st Special Forces Operational Detachment, U.S. Army, and stripped of all honors

- Fort Bragg, NC: Jan 00: Acquittal on all charges

- Nov 12: Engagement to U.S. National Security Advisor Jessica Tanzer
  Date of marriage: (unknown)

Several photographs were imposed on the right side of the file sheet, including a photo of Dewey taken as former U.S. president Rob Allaire awarded him the Presidential Medal of Freedom, as well as a photo showing Dewey many years ago, when he was a soldier. The photo showed Dewey in a military uniform, a Ranger tab visible on the right arm. Despite its age, this image was the clearest of the lot. He held an

M60 carbine targeted at the sky, his hair was short, he was tan, and beneath his eyes were two black paint stripes.

Bhang walked to the plasma screen and stood in front of the photo, staring, then pointed at the tab.

"That's a Ranger tab," said Bhang. "Do you know why it has white thread?"

"I believe they were out of black thread," replied Ming-húa, laughing. He was joined by the others.

Bhang abruptly slammed his right hand down on the table.

"Does anyone know why the American's patch has white thread?" Bhang repeated, an edge to his voice.

The men at the conference table grew silent.

"It's an honor," continued Bhang. "Soldiers who make it through Ranger school during winter are allowed to sew on their patches with white thread. It's the hardest time of year to do it. We're dealing with an unusually talented individual here."

"I have no doubt he's a threat, Minister," said Ming-húa, chastened. "But not to us."

Bhang glared at his deputy.

"We're not here to discuss your opinion as to who does or does not constitute a threat to China," said Bhang, icily. "The loss of Dillman is the single greatest intelligence loss the ministry has incurred in the past decade. This meeting is to determine how we are going to terminate Dewey Andreas. Whether or not he's a threat is no longer relevant. The decision has been made."

Ming-húa nodded.

"My apologies, sir."

"Where is Andreas now?" asked Bhang.

"On a plane, minister," said Hu'ang Li. "Flying to South America. We are fortunate in that he purchased his tickets using an American Express card."

"Tickets, plural?" asked Bhang.

"Yes, two tickets to Córdoba, near the Sierras Chicas."

Bhang's mind raced.

"What do we have in the theater?" he asked.

"We have a woman in Santiago, Chile," Ming-húa said, looking at

55

his laptop. "She's junior. I don't think she's the best option. I have a contractor—a sniper—in Lima. Very talented. He could be in Córdoba in a matter of hours."

"What else?"

Ming-húa typed on his keyboard, and a map suddenly lit up one of the plasmas on the wall. On the map, in different colors, was a manifest of all active MSS agents. Ming-húa pointed a red laser at the map.

"We have a team inside the United States," said Ming-húa, "a cell we could, theoretically, pull out, but it's a couple; the woman is inside NSA, a subcontractor. They've been in the U.S. for a decade. We'd be foolish to risk the loss of this project."

"What else?"

Ming-húa scanned the map, then pointed.

"We have a kill team in Caracas. They're excellent."

Bhang picked up a photo of Andreas. He stared at it for a few moments.

"I want the sniper on a plane immediately," he ordered. "Use a charter out of Lima, and make sure he knows he's responsible for bringing in any weaponry necessary for the operation. Also, get the Caracas team in the air."

"Yes, sir."

Bhang quickly rescanned the dossier on Dewey. "Castine, Maine. Find out if he still has any family."

"And do what?"

"Send them flowers, you imbecile," said Bhang, seething. "Find out if he has family! *Period!*"

II

Two men moved through the central terminal at Maiquetía. It was early morning and Maiquetía was packed.

"I'm going to duty-free," said Chang, the younger of the two. He had an easy way about him, unlike Hu-Shao, who, while only two years older, looked and acted like he was from another generation.

"Why?" asked Hu-Shao.

"Cigarettes."

"You should stop smoking."

"And you should start," said Chang.

Chang walked toward a line of retail shops in the central terminal. At duty-free, he spent a few minutes ogling the exotic European vodkas, vodkas he could have purchased any day of the week in Caracas but that somehow looked more tempting here at the airport. Finally, he went and bought a carton of Marlboro reds. On the way back to the gate, he stepped inside a sunglasses boutique and bought the first pair he tried on, a pair of white Guccis that made him look, at least he thought, like a movie star.

At the gate, Hu-Shao did a double take as Chang walked up with his sunglasses on.

"You look like a fool," said Hu-Shao. "Please. Pretend you don't know me."

Chang ignored him. He was sick of his colleague. Any man would be sick of someone they spent day and night together with, months on end, living and working together. In truth, Hu-Shao had taught him much. He'd taught him to be an operative: surveillance, infiltration, weaponry, how to kill. But sometimes his partner's cold demeanor grew old.

On the LAN Airbus A320, they sat in first class. Bhang believed agents should be comfortable during operations. Once airborne, they took turns studying the fifteen-page briefing sheet on the American, Dewey Andreas. The file contained everything the ministry had pieced together about the former Special Forces soldier they were now going to find and kill.

Had anyone somehow gotten hold of the papers, even if they could read Chinese, what they would have found was illegible. The briefing papers had been sent in one of the three encrypted alphabets every agent was trained to memorize, alphabets that were reconfigured every six months. It was one of the hardest parts of being an agent.

The two men spent several hours reading about Andreas's background. The summaries of his operations were staccato, devoid of wordy descriptions, in many cases incomplete. Yet even without the sort of descriptive detail that would have made the reading more pleasurable, the document was formidable and sent a wave of anxiety through each man.

Chang read the mission summary four times in a row, each time feeling increasingly sick to his stomach:

PROJECT: 816G
TARGET: ANDREAS, DEWEY
PRIORITY: 2

1. Recent activities by Target resulted in the loss of key ministry assets. Target is an enemy of the State.

2. Target is classified as a level 1 combatant. He should be considered extremely dangerous.

3. Previous attempts by others to kill Target have failed, and the result has been, in virtually every known instance, the death of those attempting to harm him.

4. Target has extensive combat experience. He is a gifted face-to-face combatant and received advanced training in various CQB systems, including KAPAP/LOTAR and Eskrima while in Delta.

5. Target will be proficient with cold weapons, including knives and implements, and will be prepared to improvise with nonlethal objects.

6. Target is expert in all aspects of firearms and explosives. If Target acquires arms, proximity to Target should be considered an active kill zone.

7. Team should expect the mission to be highly treacherous and should take precautions, both in terms of settling up affairs at home as well as in-theater tactical design.

8. Target is traveling with a woman who is a VIP in the United States government. Assume Target will be guarded and/or under surveillance.

9. Team will rendezvous with Lima-based contractor in Córdoba. Contractor is a level 12 marksman and will have responsibility for the kill. Contractor will have all necessary weapons and materials for mission. The strike should take place at night.

10. Target is classified as a Priority 2 termination so directed by the minister. He should be terminated with prejudice.

11. Mission success will earn team members two level pay and one level rank promotion and two additional weeks of paid annual vacation.

After Chang and Hu-Shao finished reading, Hu-Shao removed a small object from his carry-on. It looked like a set of binoculars but in fact was a secure photo viewer. They took turns studying photos of Andreas as well as photos of some of his victims.

After they finished, Chang looked at Hu-Shao.

"What will the design be?" Chang whispered.

"Read the sheet," said Hu-Shao. "A distance kill at night. The merc is a mark twelve."

"Two level pay increase?" said Chang. "We must succeed."

"Typical. You should be honored that, of all the agents in South America, you and I were selected for this mission."

"I could live without the honor," said Chang. "I could, however, live with two more weeks of vacation."

12

VISTA TOWERS
1198 MALECÓN CISNEROS
MIRAFLORES DISTRICT
LIMA, PERU

Raul awoke to the sound of his cell phone. He reached to the bed-side table and picked it up.

"What."

"One hour. Be at the private terminal."

"Where am I going?"

"Córdoba."

Raul reached up with his left hand and rubbed his eyes. He reached behind him, to the wall above the bed, and flipped a switch on the wall. The curtains moved slowly away from the windows, which took up the entire wall. Sunlight exploded into the room, and he shut his eyes.

"Who?"

"China."

"How long will I be gone?"

"Well, that depends now, doesn't it?"

"What time is it?

"Five-thirty."

Raul's eyes opened again, as he became more alert.

"Who's the target?"

"I don't know. You'll find out when you get there. You're part of a team out of Caracas."

"Who is it?"

"I told you, I don't know."

"You forget I know you, Pascal."

"He's American. That's all he told me."

Raul felt the naked backside of his girlfriend, Marisol, pressing under the sheets against his groin. He was thirty-one years old, still young, but compared to her, he was an old man. They'd had sex twice the night before. *How can she still want more*, he thought to himself as she continued to grind against him.

"Pascal, I'm back three days," said Raul into the phone.

"I already wired a hundred thousand. You get another hundred on completion."

"How much are they paying?"

Marisol turned her head and smiled at Raul.

"Two million."

"I want half, or else get somebody else. Call me when you wire the other nine hundred."

"Three hundred. I'll give you all of it before you go."

"One million. You heard me."

Raul hung up. He pulled away from Marisol.

"I need coffee," he said, throwing the sheets off.

He climbed out of bed. Marisol looked up at him.

"Come back to bed."

"My God," he said, shaking his head and laughing. "Did you not get enough attention when you were a child?"

"I still am a child," she said. "Technically, seventeen is still a child."

From the floor, he picked up a pair of black silk boxers and pulled them on.

"What's the matter?" she said. "Can't you get it up? My old boy-friend could do it like six times a day."

Raul stared at her for a moment, then lurched forward and slapped her hard across the face, sending her flying to the side of the bed. She let out a scream. Blood trickled from her lip.

"Animal!" she yelled. She started to cry.

"Get out," he said, calmly. "You're going to be late for school."

"It's Saturday."

"Whatever. Get out."

Raul walked to the window. He looked out at the ocean, a bold shelf of glimmering black that spread to the horizon. He walked out of the bedroom, down the hallway, into the kitchen. He flipped on the coffee maker. From the black marble countertop, he took a cigarette and lit it.

A minute later, Marisol came running down the hallway, dressed in a black miniskirt, high heels, and a blouse. She was disheveled. Her long brown hair was tousled, her makeup smudged from tears. She held a small washcloth to the side of her mouth.

"You fucking asshole," she said as she walked by him. "When I tell my father—"

"When you tell your father?" asked Raul.

He reached for a drawer, then pulled out a Glock 18, with a stainless-steel suppressor screwed into the muzzle. He took three quick steps toward her. She put her hand up, between the tip of the weapon and her face. She cowered, crying, as he stepped closer, a maniacal look on his tan, stubble-coated face.

"If you tell your father, if you tell anyone for that matter—your father, your mother, your brother, your sister, your priest, the police," he whispered as he moved the suppressor to the side of her head, "if you so much as tell your parakeet, you'll die. So will they. Got it?"

Marisol nodded her head, eyes closed, cheeks wet with tears, as she cowered against the door.

"Now leave," he said quietly.

At the private terminal near Lima's Jorge Chávez International Airport, Raul parked his red Kawasaki Ninja ZX-10R. He wore a light green T-shirt that showed off his muscled arms. He wore jeans and red running shoes. He had a backpack. His hair was long, down over his shoulders, and unbrushed. He had on silver sunglasses that reflected the sun. He walked across the tarmac to a white-and-blue jet, a Gulfstream G280. He climbed up the airstairs.

Inside, he popped his head into the cockpit, saying hello to the two pilots.

Seated on one of the four white leather captain's chairs inside the cabin was a tall, distinguished-looking gray-haired man. He wore a charcoal suit, no tie, and smoked a cigar. He studied Raul as he climbed aboard, tossed his backpack in one of the empty seats, then sat across from him.

"Are you coming?" asked Raul.

"No," said Pascal.

"Why are you here? Is it the money?"

"No," the man said, "Ming-húa called back. He's worried about blowback."

"I've killed Americans."

"Not ones connected to the government. Not ones who know the president."

Raul smiled.

"I'll be careful."

"After he's killed, the United States is going to investigate."

"Are the weapons clean?"

"Yes, of course. The point is, don't get caught."

"Thanks for the advice."

"Bhang has informants scattered all over Argentine Federal Police. You need to understand what I'm saying. If you get caught, you'll die. I know Fao Bhang. If you're caught, you'll be dead before America has time to interrogate you and find out who sent you."

Raul nodded at a large steel box lying across two seats.

"RPGs, M4s, UZIs," said Pascal. "German, Russian. It won't raise any eyebrows when they run the ballistics."

"Is my rifle in there?"

"Yes, the Dragunov. You meet the agents in Córdoba. A guy named Hu-Shao has tactical authority, but you're the shooter. Get it done as soon as possible, then get out. I wired the entire million."

"Who's the American?"

"His name is Andreas. He's ex–Special Forces."

"Why are we doing this?"

"It's what we do. That penthouse apartment you live in?"

"I want more money."

"You're a greedy kid, you know that? I'll get someone else."

"Fine," said Raul, standing up. "This sounds like a shit show anyway."

"Sit down."

Pascal was silent for several moments.

"I'll pay you two million."

"Okay," said Raul.

"Call me when you're done."

13

CÓRDOBA, ARGENTINA

It was morning when Dewey and Jessica landed in Córdoba. The Córdoba airport was small, quiet, and nearly empty, despite the fact that it served the second-biggest city in Argentina.

Inside the terminal, after going through customs, a teenager stood, holding a small sign that said ANDREAS. The boy was tall with long brown hair, a cowboy hat, in khaki shorts, an orange polo shirt, and knee-high riding boots. Standing next to him was a beautiful girl, perhaps a year or two older than him, with long blond hair, wearing tan riding pants stained with dirt, knee-high black boots, and a white T-shirt. She had a big smile on her face. Dewey guessed she was seventeen or eighteen years old and that the boy was perhaps fifteen or sixteen.

"Ms. Tanzer?" the boy asked as they entered the small lounge. He stepped forward, his hand outstretched. "I'm Alvaro Sabella, from El Colibri. This is my sister, Sabina. Welcome to Córdoba. How was your flight?"

"Hi, Alvaro," said Jessica, shaking Alvaro's hand, then Sabina's. "It was great."

"Mr. Andreas, nice to meet you."

"Hi," said Dewey, shaking their hands.

"Our truck is out front," said Alvaro.

"Your mother said to tell you not to drive too fast," said Jessica, looking at the boy.

"She did?" he laughed. "That's embarrassing. I don't drive too fast. Always she says this, but it's not true."

"What are you talking about?" asked Sabina. "Are you crazy? You're insane. I'm driving." She rolled her eyes and looked at Jessica. "He's terrible. He drives like he rides. Crazy."

"I'll be careful," said Alvaro. "And please don't forget, Sabby, I have the keys." He taunted Sabina by dangling them over her head.

Dewey glanced at Jessica, then smiled.

Alvaro drove the white Range Rover reasonably well, not too fast, except for a few times, at which point Sabina would scream at him to slow down.

The Córdoba region was located halfway between Buenos Aires and Chile, at the geographic center of the country. The region was an important agricultural center, home to wineries, as well as cattle and sheep farms. It was also home to some amazing ranches, including Colibri, nestled in a lush valley that spread for hundreds of miles in the vale of the Sierras Chicas mountain range.

The ranch was an hour's drive from Córdoba, between the towns of Jesús Maria and Santa Catalina. It was ranch country, and everywhere to the west were the undulating peaks of the Sierras Chicas. The ranch began as a dirt road off the main road north of Jesús Maria. There were no signs or visible outcroppings to distinguish it from any of the other dirt roads.

"How many acres?" asked Dewey.

"Five thousand," said Sabina. "Our grandfather bought the land when he was twenty-two. Most is prairie, some woods."

"Did he build the ranch?" asked Dewey.

"Father did. Grandfather bought it when he was on a hunting trip, then he never returned, not once. Our father was given the land. He came to visit when he was twenty and fell in love with a woman from Santa Catalina, our mother."

The gravel road seemed to go on forever. After more than a mile, a small, modern building appeared in the distance, illuminated by lights.

Next to the glass-and-stucco building was a neatly manicured polo field.

"The polo house," said Alvaro. "Have you played before?"

"Not me," said Jessica.

Just past the polo house, a dark green picket fence marked a new road off to the right. In the distance, a massive, rambling building could be seen, sprinkled with yellow light from windows. They drove down the driveway to the front of the building. A small fountain at the center of the circle driveway shot water up. The main house was white stucco with brown trim and looked Spanish. It spread out from left to right, a picturesque, stunning expanse of windows, rounded dormers, columns, porches, and beautiful flowers; in fact, in every direction, the grounds were covered in flower gardens.

Already parked in front of the entrance was a black sedan and a black Suburban.

Jessica glanced at Dewey.

"Our welcome party," she whispered.

Dewey and Jessica climbed out, then went inside. A group of people were standing just inside the entrance. Two people who were tanned and dressed in casual clothing, a tall man with deep tan lines, and his wife, a dark-skinned beauty: the owners, the Sabellas. Next to them were two men with pasty white skin, golf shirts, and khakis. Perhaps at a public golf course in some American suburb somewhere they would have blended in, but here they stuck out like sore thumbs.

"You must be the Sabellas," Dewey said to the Secret Service agents as he walked inside. Everyone started laughing.

"I'm Nico," said the tall tan man, stepping forward. "Welcome to Colibri."

"Nice to meet you," said Jessica.

"I'm Maria," said the woman. "How was the ride? Did Alvaro manage to scare you to death with his driving?"

"He was fine," said Dewey.

Jessica turned to the agents.

"So who's in charge?" she asked. "You, Morty?"

"Hi, Jess. We promise you won't see hide nor hair of us. We're going to run four-hour shifts. We'll take up position at the driveway entrance."

"I hope you brought a good book," said Jessica.

"Jessica told us you're a pretty good rider," said Nico, looking at Dewey.

"I'm okay," said Dewey.

"Would you like to take a ride after lunch?"

"We'd love to," said Jessica.

Nico nodded to Alvaro, telling him to go get the horses ready.

The Sabellas gave Dewey and Jessica a tour of the mansion. They were the only guests. Their suite had a wall of French doors that overlooked a large garden filled with roses, and just behind it, a gunite swimming pool.

They went to the suite to change for the ride.

Jessica unpacked both of their bags while Dewey stared out at the peaks of Sierras Chicas through a set of binoculars. Halfway through unpacking her belongings, she came across a black, see-through teddy. Behind Dewey's back, she surreptitiously removed her jeans and blouse, then put on the lingerie, while Dewey's eyes remained transfixed on the mountains.

"This place is unbelievable," said Dewey, still staring through the binoculars. "You're the fucking best, Tanzer."

Jessica walked up behind him and wrapped her arms around him.

"No, you're the best, Andreas."

"Can you believe we're getting married?"

"Yes," she said. "I can."

14

CÓRDOBA

As the Gulfstream G280 taxied across the tarmac at the Córdoba airport, Raul sat back, unstrapped his seat belt, and put his feet up on the seat opposite him. He looked out the window at the terminal in the distance.

Raul wasn't nervous, but it didn't take a genius to realize this wasn't a typical job. Something was bothering him.

He opened the weapons box and did a quick inventory:

Dragunov sniper rifle, PSO-1 scope, suppressor
SR-3 Vikhr assault rifle
AKMS-74 assault rifle, folding stocks
ASh-12.7 CQB assault rifle
Two Arsenal Strike One 9mm handguns, suppressors
Three Makarov PMM 9mm handguns

He shut the box and walked to the front of the jet.

"Any sign of them?"

The pilots both shrugged.

"Where's the car?" he asked.

"In the lot," said one of the pilots, "top floor. A black Land Cruiser."

Raul went back to the seat. He looked at his watch. It was noon.

In the sky above Córdoba, at that very moment, the landing gear on the LAN regional from Caracas moved into place.

After passing through security, the Chinese agents moved to the private terminal. Inside the lounge, Hu-Shao felt his cell vibrating. He stopped.

"Where are you?" asked Ming-húa.

"We just arrived."

"The sniper's name is Raul. He has the weapons and the vehicle."

"Do we have schematics for the ranch?" asked Hu-Shao.

"They're on your phone."

"Anything else?"

"Yes. After Raul kills the American, kill him. Leave him on the ground."

Raul watched through the round porthole window next to his seat as two men exited the private terminal and walked quickly toward the plane. One of the copilots opened the stairs to the jet. A few moments later, they entered the cabin.

The first agent nodded.

"You must be Raul."

Raul nodded, saying nothing.

"Hu-Shao," said the agent. "This is Chang. Where are the weapons?"

Raul pointed with his thumb toward the back of the cabin.

Raul watched as Chang walked down the aisle. Hu-Shao sat down and eyed him with a blank expression on his face.

After a minute, Chang returned to the seat.

"It's decent," he said. "A little run-down. Russian. Some nice new Strike Ones. But the sniper rifle's a Dragunov. I didn't know they still made Dragunovs."

"I'm the one who has to use the Dragunov, so it's my problem," said Raul contemptuously. "If you don't like the guns, go buy your own."

"If the weapons aren't right, that's all our problem," said Hu-Shao. "You're earning a lot of money in the next twenty-four hours."

"They're fine," said Chang, looking at Hu-Shao, trying to calm the tension. "They'll do."

"Who's the target?" asked Raul.

"He's American, a former soldier, Special Forces, traveling with a do-not-touch."

"Which unit was he with?"

"Delta," said Hu-Shao.

Raul nodded. Pascal had already told him the target was ex–Special Forces, but the fact that he was Delta gave Raul a small kick in the stomach. Like many ex-cartel men, Raul knew of the Deltas.

"That's all I know," continued Hu-Shao. "As for the design, we need to study the security at the ranch. Once we know how many men are there, what type of coverage there is, and the rotations, we'll set up the nest."

Raul glanced at Chang, who wore a blank expression on his face, as did Hu-Shao. Had either of these two ever run into Deltas, he wondered?

Raul had been exposed to Deltas on more than one occasion when he worked as a fast-boat runner for the El Chapo cartel. Everyone referred to the American group of soldiers as the "locos." The Deltas were known for working alone. Their specialty was counternarcotics interdiction at the source of production, as well as assassination: selective targeting of cartel higher-ups, usually a clean, surgical kill involving a slug to the head. Raul was lucky in that sense: as a fast-boat runner, he rarely had to deal with them. Instead, they had the Coast Guard to deal with, which, compared to the Deltas, was like outrunning tortoises.

As he stared out the window, Raul tried to remember some of the stories about Deltas. What he did recall is that the Deltas liked to blend in. They never wore uniforms, and it was practically impossible to tell the difference between a Delta and anyone else walking down the road—a local farmer, a tourist—and that was only if you could see them. Most of the time they operated at night. The Deltas were a mystery.

Raul stood up, moving to the weapons box at the back of the cabin.

"You—" said Raul, nodding at Chang, "a hand, will you?"

15

By one in the afternoon, the black Land Cruiser arrived at Estancia el Colibri.

Raul drove as Hu-Shao navigated with coordinates provided by Beijing.

"Cut in farther up the road," said Hu-Shao as they passed the dirt road entrance.

In the backseat, Chang looked out the side window with a high-powered monocular scope. Fifty feet down the drive, he spied the shiny grill of a parked Suburban.

"There's someone there," said Chang.

They drove a few minutes longer, then Hu-Shao pointed to the right of the road.

Raul slowed, then took a right off the paved road and cut into a field. He drove for nearly a mile, until Hu-Shao held up his hand, telling him to stop.

Chang opened the door, climbed to the roof, and scanned in the direction of the ranch. A minute later, he jumped from the roof, then climbed back into the SUV.

"We're out of visual range," he said.

"Let's get moving," said Hu-Shao.

The three men climbed out of the SUV. They rubbed black and

green paint on their faces and changed into camouflage. The two Chinese agents each packed a rifle and a handgun. Raul carried the Dragunov, strapped over his back.

They skulked in a low traverse toward where they knew the Suburban was parked. They walked for ten minutes. When they came to a rise on a low hill, Chang raised his hand, stopping the others. He pulled out the scope and scanned the distance.

"I have a visual on the security vehicle," he said.

The three men took up position on the hill, lying down on their stomachs. The sun was beating down.

"What's next?" asked Raul.

"We wait," said Hu-Shao. "We need to understand the security protocol. I want to know how often they're rotating shifts."

Raul took the scope from Chang and looked for the vehicle. He found the small specter of the Suburban in the distance. There were no signs of life from the black SUV.

"How do you know someone's even in there?" asked Raul.

"There's someone there," said Hu-Shao. "Be patient."

16

ESTANCIA EL COLIBRI
CÓRDOBA

Dewey and Jessica arrived at the polo house, which looked deserted. Out back of the building they came upon Alvaro, sitting on a chair, shirt off, soaking in some morning sun. His eyes were closed. Earbuds were in. In his right hand was a joint, which he was puffing away on, as his head moved rhythmically up and down to the music.

"Awkward," said Jessica, as the boy eyed her, then Dewey, then abruptly turned and fell from the chair, onto the grass. He leapt to his feet. He dropped the joint and stomped on it with his boot as he exhaled.

Dewey started laughing.

"If you tell my parents—"

"Oh, man, that's insulting," said Dewey.

"Aren't you government people?" he asked, getting to his feet, embarrassed.

"Tell you what," said Dewey. "Get us a couple of horses and we won't fly you to Guantánamo."

Alvaro got a big grin on his face.

"Deal," said Alvaro. "I have the perfect horses for you."

Alvaro showed them around the stables. The barn itself was a long, light green rectangular building with a red tin roof. Inside, more than forty horses were stabled. Near the middle of the long line of horses, Alvaro stopped at a large, black stallion.

"This is my father's," he said. "A beautiful horse. A champion. Very smart. You can handle him."

"What's his name?"

"Da Gama."

In the stable next to Da Gama, a smaller, black-and-tan filly leaned over the railing and put her snout next to Jessica's head, then licked her before she even knew the horse was there.

"Thea," said Alvaro. "My mother's."

Alvaro outfitted Thea while Dewey got Da Gama ready. They climbed onto the horses and moved out through the stable door.

The stallion beneath Dewey gave him a familiar feeling. He'd grown up riding and loved the feeling, the bond, between a rider and a horse. As he rode Da Gama out onto the green grass next to the stables, looking at the mountains in the distance, he reached down and ran his right hand along Da Gama's neck.

Jessica trailed behind him.

Alvaro came out onto the lawn.

"What's the lay of the land?" asked Dewey. "Anything we need to watch out for?"

"Don't go beyond the northern fork of the river," said Alvaro, pointing toward the mountains. "Da Gama will know how to get back, but I would keep in sight."

Dewey grinned at Jessica.

"You ready?"

"I'm ready."

They rode south for two hours. The views were stunning, the kind no picture book could ever do true justice to. Mountains streaked blue-green and, on top, white with snow; valleys of fields that ran for miles, balkanized by wildflowers, heaving in the breeze, like a Chinese fan;

red-tailed hawks soaring above, then streaking through the air toward earth, diving at the ground and grabbing a rodent before lifting back off into the blue, cloudless sky.

When they hit a slow-running stream, they stopped beneath an ancient elm tree to let the horses drink.

For as long as she could remember, Jessica had wanted to fall in love, to get married, to have a family. She'd dreamed of wedding dresses, bridesmaids, china settings, a honeymoon. Yet Jessica had never found someone. She'd lived through the marriage whirlwind of late twenties to mid-thirties, attending at least two dozen weddings of her friends.

The truth is, she could've married any number of men who'd courted her over the years, accomplished men, one of the top attorneys in Washington, a widowed U.S. senator, the British ambassador to the United States, wealthy businessmen.

Jessica looked toward Dewey. He turned and smiled.

"Nice out here, isn't it?" he asked.

"Yeah," she whispered. "Not bad."

They leaned in, toward each other, beneath the shade branch of the big elm, and kissed.

"I love you," she whispered.

"I love you too."

A tear came to Jessica's eye and ran down her cheek, even as she smiled.

"Why are you crying?" he asked.

"Because I'm so stinkin' happy," she said.

Four miles to the north as the crow flies, Raul, lying still on his stomach, saw movement through the scope. A sedan pulled in and parked in front of the Suburban.

"I have movement," said Raul.

Hu-Shao and Chang both put binoculars against their eyes and watched as two men stood next to the cars, talking. After a few minutes, the Americans climbed back into the cars. The man who'd been in the Suburban climbed into the sedan and pulled a U-turn, then drove quickly out of the driveway.

76

"What now?" asked Raul, impatiently.

Hu-Shao watched the sedan pull out, then put his binoculars down. "We wait. In the meantime, make sure the Dragunov is calibrated."

"We could've killed him by now," said Raul.

"And he could've killed us, Raul. Now please, if you will be so kind, shut the fuck up. Go make sure that twenty-pound bag of shit Russian rifle is working."

17

The apartment building was made of gray concrete. It was nine stories high, neat, and well maintained, though plain-looking, with small windows. It was in an area of Beijing that was considered remote, naturalistic, with close proximity to gardens, trees, lakes, and nature.

The dark sedan pulled up to the front of the building, and Bhang emerged. He carried a large plastic grocery bag filled with fruit, milk, juice, chocolate, and vegetables.

He climbed the stairs to the ninth floor and was winded, as always, by the time he arrived at the door to unit 9B. He wheezed as he looked down at the straw welcome mat, the same worn mat that had been there for as long as he could remember.

Bhang knocked. A few moments later, a series of dead bolts could be heard, turning. The door finally opened.

"Hello, Fao," said Bhang's half brother, Bo Minh, a large smile on his face. "I didn't know you would be coming. It's Sunday. To what do I owe this honor?"

"Since when can a man not stop to pay a visit to his brother?"

With a calm smile, Bhang registered the disheveled visage of Minh. He was shirtless. His chest was so thin he could see his brother's rib cage. His skin was approximately one shade brighter than a corpse's. His hair was down to his shoulders, unbrushed, streaked with gray, shining with several days' worth of grease. Minh's thick glasses were smudged and made his eyeballs look three times their actual size.

Bhang stepped forward and wrapped his arms around his brother.

"I brought you some food," said Bhang, hugging him.

The apartment was one large room, lit brightly, with little furniture except, along the walls, long tables atop which sat more than two dozen computer screens, all lit up with various photographs, charts, and data. The tables were chest high so that Minh could move easily between computers, remaining on his feet as he worked. At the ministry, where Minh was the chief technology officer, he worked up to twenty hours a day for months on end. At home, he didn't stop either, as the flashing computer screens attested. Bhang still didn't know when his brother slept.

The apartment had only two windows, at the far wall, and Bhang walked to the one on the right. He looked through the window. He could see the lovely flowers of the Beijing Botanical Garden in the distance, and Kunming Lake to the far right. As Bhang was the minister of State Security and Minh was the top technologist at the ministry, Minh could have lived anywhere he wanted. But this was where the lonely, brilliant man wanted to live. Near the flowers.

"Will you stay for tea?" asked Minh, an infectious smile on his face. "With honey and ginger, how Father made it?"

"Yes," said Bhang.

At the mention of their father, at the sight of his frail, malnourished, wonderfully kind brother, a memory stirred.

He had never known his real father. That man had died while working at the tire factory when Bhang was only two. Bhang's mother had remarried, to a man named Ni Minh, a kind man, who raised him like a son.

It was a warm, summer day in the alley behind the small house on the outskirts of Chengdu, where he grew up with his mother, stepfather, and little Bo.

The neighborhood boys were playing soccer, shouting and screaming, long after sunset.

Ni had asked Bhang to include Bo. Little Bo. Even at that age, he

79

wore thick glasses and was thin and small. The other boys made fun of him. Even Bhang sometimes participated.

Bo was put in one of the nets as goaltender. It was a close game and Bo let in the winning goal. His own teammates yelled at him, pointing at him, taunting him. One of the boys picked up the ball and hurled it at Bo. It hit his head, and his glasses fell to the ground, shattering. Bhang had watched as Bo searched the ground for the glasses, feeling with his hands, tears streaming down his face. It was the moment Bhang remembered. It was the moment Bhang realized what love was and what loyalty was. It all coalesced at that moment, seeing Bo on the ground, so helpless, looking for glasses that no longer existed.

Bhang beat up the boy who hurled the ball at Bo, breaking his nose with a vicious punch. He knocked a tooth from the mouth of another boy and delivered a black eye to a third before they descended on him and thoroughly beat him, then left him on the gravel, his nose bloody, his lip too, his entire body like a large bruise. But Bhang had never felt better than at that moment.

It wasn't long after that fight before Bo started to show his genius. He could take apart and put back together anything—radios, the air conditioner at the school, Ni Minh's electric razor. Then he started to create machines on his own. Over the course of a winter, he'd built a small combustion engine for the house that could generate electricity. Bo had carved his own path in this world, with or without Bhang, and Bhang was proud.

Bhang found himself staring out at the gardens, lost in the childhood memory, when Minh returned to the room, two hot cups of tea in hand.

"Where shall we sit, Bo?" asked Bhang, smiling and taking one of the cups from his brother.

"Wherever you like," said Minh, waving his gaunt arm through the air, as if the room were a suite at the Ritz-Carlton Hotel instead of a furnitureless hovel that looked more like a computer closet than anything else.

Bhang laughed enthusiastically along with Minh as he sat down on the wooden floor, crossed his legs, and took the first sip from the cup.

18

Behind the hill, out of view of the others, Raul went to work.

He found several pieces of wood bark, then set them up like targets in a line. He walked off five hundred feet, then set up the Dragunov.

He sited the first piece of bark in the rifle scope. He centered it, focused in, then fired. Nothing happened. He fired again, and still nothing. He made an adjustment to the placement of the scope on the side-rail mount. He fired again. This time, the top of the bark went flying away in a cloud of dust. It wasn't the spot he was aiming for, but it was a start.

Hu-Shao had been right; the rifle was out of sync. Raul wouldn't admit that to him, however. Raul loved the old Dragunov.

Raul made several more small adjustments, finding the small knob that enabled him to compensate and adjust for bullet drop over long distances.

He test-fired several more times, adjusting the knob in between shots, until he hit a piece of bark precisely where he was aiming.

Over the next hour, he went down the line of bark, at increasing distances, testing the rifle until he felt confident that the aiming mechanism was perfect.

Finally, he took his shirt off and draped it over a shrub. He walked off approximately one mile. He got down on his stomach, aimed, then fired. Leaving the rifle on its bipod, he jogged to his T-shirt. A few inches off dead center, a large tear was visible.

Raul put the shirt back on and walked back. He was ready.

Dewey and Jessica rode under the warm sun until midafternoon. They came to a bend in the river. A small promontory of meadow formed in the notch of the running water. A tree jutted out over the water. The water was dark blue and bulged at the bend, forming a deep pool. It was hot out but dry.

Dewey removed his shirt, boots, and jeans, then walked naked into the water. Jessica removed her clothing too, following him to the stream. The water was bitter cold.

"Ouch," she said as she stepped in behind him. "That's freezing!"

He took her hand in his. He was used to swimming in Maine. The stream was almost as cold as a Castine plunge in October, but not quite.

"Comes down from the mountains," said Dewey. "Melting ice. It's nothing compared to Maine, sweetie."

"Well, I'm not swimming in this," she said. "It's too cold."

"Trust me, it's refreshing. My dad used to swim up until Thanksgiving. Now, that was cold. He called them polar bears."

"Polar bears?"

"Yeah. Like, let's go for a polar bear."

"Oh," said Jessica. "Well, I'm not some crazy Mainer, and this is too cold for me."

"No worries," said Dewey. He bent down, near Jessica's legs.

"What are you doing?" she asked.

Dewey wrapped his right arm around the back of Jessica's thighs, then lifted her into the air.

She screamed.

"No!" she howled. "Put me down! Put me down right now!"

Dewey walked into the deeper water, as Jessica, dangling over his shoulder, slugged him in the back, hitting him as hard as she could.

"Help!"

"You'll thank me after," he said, barely noticing the pummeling Jessica was delivering. "Besides, you called my dad a crazy Mainer. You hurt my feelings."

"Stop!" she yelled. "Help! Someone help me!"

When the water reached his waist, Dewey dived forward into the frigid water, still holding Jessica. Her screaming was muffled as they crashed into the water. A moment later, when she surfaced, Jessica began howling all over again.

"You bastard! I'll get you!"

She splashed water at him, but all he could do was laugh.

They swam in the pool for a while, eventually getting used to the temperature. On the far shore, Jessica swam to him and wrapped her arms around his shoulders.

"It actually is kind of refreshing," she said.

"Does that mean you're not mad?"

"No, I'm still mad. I like being mad at you. It's fun."

"How can I make it up to you?" he asked, wrapping his hands around Jessica's back. She wrapped her legs around his torso and moved closer.

"Well," she said, kissing his lips, "I can think of something that might make me forgive you."

Dewey carried her to the shore. They made love in the warm grass just above the stream, without a soul for miles.

Afterward, they swam back across the stream. Jessica spread out a red chamois blanket in the shade of the tree. They ate—ham-and-cheese sandwiches made by the chef back at the ranch—then lay on the blanket. Jessica put her head on Dewey's shoulder. They fell asleep to the sound of the stream running by.

By the time they awoke to head back to the ranch, the sun was gone and the sky was turning into a beautiful dark purple.

Chang sat with his legs crossed, staring through the scope at the Suburban. The sky was growing dark.

He saw the sedan pull into the driveway at a few minutes before eight o'clock.

"He's back," said Chang.

Hu-Shao sat up abruptly, his eyes growing alert. He glanced at his watch.

"They're running four-hour rotations," he said. He turned to Raul, who was lying on his back, eyes closed. Hu-Shao snapped his fingers. "Let's go."

Raul stood and walked to the Dragunov, which was set up on its bipod and trained at the Suburban. He got down on his stomach and studied the vehicle through the high-powered thermal night scope. The two Americans were chatting again. Finally, one of the men climbed into the sedan. He pulled a U-turn and sped away. The other man climbed into the front seat of the SUV.

The Suburban was blocking some of the heat of the man's body, and Raul wasn't getting a very good heat print in the scope, but he was getting enough. He was, he guessed, just under a mile from the target. Raul rubbed his finger along the steel trigger. Then he fired.

A low boom exploded from the Dragunov as the high-powered rifle kicked back and a 7.62mm Kevlar-tipped cartridge ripped from the muzzle of the rifle. He heard nothing; yet through the scope, he watched as the front side window shattered.

"What happened?" barked Hu-Shao.

Raul said nothing as he retargeted the scope and prepared to fire. He concentrated, searching for the heat spot of the target. Then he found it, in the same place it had been before; he'd killed the American.

"Bull's-eye," he said. "Let's go. We have four hours until he's discovered."

At the polo house, Alvaro took the horses from Dewey and Jessica. They walked beneath the darkening sky back along the gravel road to the ranch. Inside their suite of rooms, they took showers, then dressed for dinner in the main house.

Raul drove the Land Cruiser in a slow, circuitous arc toward the back of the ranch. The headlights illuminated knee-high grass, night bugs, and darkness. His destination was a field of low hills at the back of the ranch house. Had they moved in a direct line, the route would have been just over a mile. Instead, they drove in a two-mile arc.

Raul stopped when Hu-Shao gave the signal. They climbed out of the SUV.

On foot, Raul, Hu-Shao, and Chang traveled light. Hu-Shao and Chang carried assault rifles and handguns. Raul carried the Dragunov, strapped across his back. He also packed his sidearm, a well-worn Colt .38 Super "El Capitan," with a custom snub-nose suppressor in the muzzle, his most prized possession, a present his father had given him on his ninth birthday. He tucked it between his belt and back.

From the Land Cruiser, they moved in the darkness, Hu-Shao navigating with his phone. Eventually, they came within sight of the ranch house, far in the distance, its yellow lights twinkling.

Hu-Shao took out his night scope and scanned the house.

"Here," he said, pointing at a small grassy knoll.

"What's the distance?" asked Raul.

"Half a mile."

Raul sighted the sniper nest atop the knoll, setting the Dragunov on its bipod. He spent several minutes calibrating the scope as well as adjusting for bullet drop. Once he had the rifle good to go, he moved it slowly back and forth along the back of the rambling stucco mansion.

Chang pulled an MRE from his pack and ripped the tinfoil lid from it, then stuffed the food into his face.

"We have three hours before the dead guard is discovered," said Hu-Shao.

Raul listened, studying the house, looking for signs of life.

"What if I don't get a shot?" asked Raul.

"Then we hit the house. If you haven't killed Andreas in two hours, we move in."

Raul pulled his eye from the end of the rifle scope. He stood up.

"Where the hell are you going?" said Hu-Shao angrily.

"To take a piss," said Raul, pointing to his crotch. "I might work for you, Chinaman, but he doesn't."

As Raul walked off into the darkness to pee, Hu-Shao put the scope to his eye, pretending to study the house; but his eye glanced sideways, watching Raul as he walked away.

Hu-Shao removed a 9mm Strike One from his shoulder holster. He reached into his front pocket for a suppressor, screwing it into the muzzle of the handgun.

Chang, on his back, looked up from his MRE.

"What are you doing?"

"Following orders," answered Hu-Shao, checking the magazine. "Eat your dog food and shut the fuck up."

He gripped the weapon and stuck it into the pocket of his Windbreaker, clutching the grip, prepared to fire.

"What did he do?" whispered Chang.

Hu-Shao sat down on the ground, against a rock, behind the sniper rifle. He was directly behind where Raul would be after he shot the American.

"That's the wrong question," said Hu-Shao.

"What's the right question?"

"The right question is, am I going to kill you too?" Hu-Shao whispered, smiling viciously.

Chang laughed nervously.

"When will you do it?" whispered Chang.

"After he shoots the American."

Raul walked behind the hill for several hundred feet, whistling. The sky was black and blue and dotted with stars. He unzipped his pants and peed on the ground, then began a slow walk back toward Hu-Shao and Chang. He walked nonchalantly over the hill, to the right of where he'd left. The dark outline of the ranch house was visible in the far distance, the lights from windows casting dull yellow into the evening.

He saw Chang first, lying on the ground, next to the Dragunov. He was staring through his night optics at the ranch house.

Hu-Shao was behind Chang and the rifle, reclined against a rock. His hand was stuffed inside the pocket of his Windbreaker. He was looking in the opposite direction, waiting for Raul to return.

Raul removed the Colt from his jeans. He moved the safety off. He walked in silence down the slope of the hill. He aimed the gun at the back of Hu-Shao's head. He paused for a moment, then two. Finally, as if by instinct, Hu-Shao turned.

Hu-Shao's eyes met Raul's. Hu-Shao's mouth went agape. He tried to say something but couldn't. Then he ripped his hand—clutching the weapon—from the Windbreaker and swung it up at Raul.

Raul pumped the trigger. There was a low mechanical *thud* as a slug tore a hole just above Hu-Shao's lip, at the center of his mustache. The back of his skull exploded across the rock. Raul fired again, this time ripping a hole into Hu-Shao's right eye, destroying the front of his face.

Chang turned at the sound. He stared in silence and horror at the destroyed skull of Hu-Shao.

Raul knelt and picked up the spent cartridges from his gun. He moved to Hu-Shao, picked up his weapon, then began to search for the slugs that had ripped through him.

"It goes without saying," said Raul, patting the grass in the twilight, not even looking up from the ground, "don't do anything stupid or you'll end up the same way."

Raul stood up and stuck the gun between his belt and back.

"What do we do with him?"

"Carry him out," said Raul. "Tell them Andreas shot back."

Chang nodded in stunned agreement.

"How did you know?" Chang asked.

"I knew it the moment he stepped on the plane. In fact, I knew it before you stepped on the plane. Now let's kill the gringo and get the fuck out of Argentina."

19

ESTANCIA EL COLIBRI
CÓRDOBA

On the terrace outside the main house, Dewey and Jessica ate a dinner of trout, fresh tomatoes, and rice with toasted pine nuts. They shared a bottle of wine. Candles, and the stars above the Argentine sky, provided the only light.

After dinner was done, Nico and Maria sat down and had a glass of wine with them. At some point, Maria brought out homemade strawberry shortcake.

The couples sat talking for a long time, laughing, finishing off the bottle of wine. Finally, Nico and Maria stood to clear off plates.

Dewey felt his eyelids getting heavy.

"You tired?" Jessica asked.

"I'm getting too old for this," he said.

Jessica shook her head, giggling.

"Too old for what?" she asked. "Luxury ranches half a world away from anyone or anything? Sex on demand with a smoking-hot Irish girl? Gourmet dinners by candlelight?"

"All of the above," he said. "Especially the sex part. I think we need to slow things down a little."

Jessica rolled her eyes.

"You really are *not* funny."

Raul lay on his stomach, his right eye against the rifle scope, studying the terrace. The dim light made it hard to discern between the figures sitting at the table. Despite the relatively short firing distance, all he could see was silhouettes. There were at least four people, and while he knew he could take out several of them, he didn't like the odds of shooting all four. So he waited, as patiently as possible. But time was running out. The guard would soon return. When he did, any chance of killing the American would be gone.

"How long do we have?" asked Raul, keeping his eye glued to the scope.

"It's nearly eleven," said Chang, trying not to sound worried. "We have an hour."

Raul felt his heart pick up a beat, and he shut his eyes for a brief moment, trying to calm down.

At eleven, Dewey and Jessica said goodnight to the Sabellas and walked to their suite.

Jessica went to the French doors, opening them to the nighttime air. The moon and stars created a golden hue of ambient light.

Dewey went to the armoire and took off his shirt. From the top drawer, he removed two small shiny gold objects, which he'd been hiding from Jessica. He examined them in the palm of his hand.

He'd bought them in Manhattan. Each had cost ten thousand dollars at Tiffany's. He could've bought them for half the price from a less well known jeweler, but it's what Jessica wanted, and that was all he cared about. Dewey smiled as he looked down at the two rings.

"Can I show you something?" he asked.

Jessica turned from the doors, tilted her head, and smiled.

"Sure."

"It's eleven fifteen," said Chang, whispering urgently. "We can't wait any longer."

Raul, on his stomach, breathed very slowly now, as he'd been trained to do. He looked in utter stillness through the high-powered PSO-1 scope at the woman standing in the middle of the French doors. She was facing him. Her mouth was centered in the crosshairs of the scope.

Behind her was a man. He was tall. He stood with his back turned at the far side of the room. Andreas. Raul pressed his finger against the trigger, almost hard enough to fire the rifle but not quite.

"She's too close."

"You hit the guard from a mile out," said Chang, encouraging him. "You can do it, Raul."

A tremor of fear made Raul shiver for a brief moment.

"Be quiet, please," said Raul.

He slowed his breathing to the point of holding his breath. He studied Andreas in the scope, just to the right of the woman.

Raul became aware of movement—to the left, back on the terrace off the kitchen. He moved the rifle ever so slightly, finding the terrace. Someone had flipped lights on. He registered a tall man with dark skin along with a woman. He moved the weapon back to the bedroom, reacquiring the sight of the woman, standing in the middle of the doorway.

Suddenly, the woman turned, moving away from the French doors. Raul had a clean shot.

He yanked back the trigger. The low boom of the Dragunov echoed across the dark plain, then kicked back as the rifle sent a slug through the night.

Dewey went to open his hand and show Jessica the two rings, just as the bedroom was interrupted by a sharp noise—abrupt, violent, an unnatural sound—the fracturing of wood, the sound combining, in a terrible second, with the smell of sawdust.

Dewey's head jerked right. The armoire lay mauled, a large hole cleaved, just inches from where he stood, splintering in a web of slivers and wood dust.

His eyes turned to Jessica. She looked panicked and lost.

Dewey, instincts suddenly taking over, lurched toward her.

"*Get down!*" he screamed.

Raul retargeted the rifle, finding the bedroom, then Andreas. He was still standing. Raul fired again.

The second slug tore into Jessica's back. The bullet kicked her sideways and down. Dewey caught her as she fell, his eyes meeting hers. He laid her on the ground, out of the way of the open doors. He looked down at her white dress. A pool of blood grew quickly, forming a neat crimson circle above her heart.

Dewey leaned down to her. Her lips moved as she tried to say something, but no sounds came out, only a small trickle of red at the corner of her mouth.

Dewey held her gaze as tears came to his eyes and a terrible look crossed his face. He began to cry as he held her. He kissed her forehead, unable to say or do anything. He held his lips against her forehead for several moments as his body slowly heaved. When, finally, he lifted his lips away from her, she was gone, her eyes blank pools of green that stared straight up past him.

Dewey opened his hand. He slid one of the two rings onto her finger. He reached up and closed her eyelids.

Dewey shut his eyes as tears came down. He was gripped by pain and grief, paralyzed; but then he heard words, a voice, speaking to him:

Leave her now. Walk away. Leave her behind. Now isn't the time. No you have to do the thing you were trained to do. What you were meant to do. The only thing you can do.

Fight.

20

CÓRDOBA

Through binoculars, Raul watched in horror as the woman was pummeled to the ground.

He'd hit her—the do-not-touch—and missed Andreas. The slug had ripped her dead center in the back. She was dead.

It didn't take Raul too long to do the math. If Bhang was willing to kill him before, for no reason other than to frame him, he couldn't imagine what lay in store for him now.

"You killed the woman," said Chang.

Not only had Raul fucked up by killing the woman, he hadn't completed the primary—the only—objective. If there was to be any mercy from Bhang, it would come by finishing off Andreas.

Raul moved the rifle, ever so slightly, staring through the scope, scanning the bedroom for signs of life. He paused on the area above where she'd fallen. He waited a few moments, then pulled the trigger, firing another cartridge, blindly, into the room.

He saw a shadow move toward the back of the room. This time he didn't hesitate. He pulled the trigger.

As Dewey clutched Jessica, glass abruptly shattered just a foot above his head. The gunman was still out there.

He crawled to the armoire as another slug ripped the wall, just inches in front of him.

He yanked out the bottom drawer, dumping its contents on the ground. He searched frantically for Jessica's tan diplomatic pouch. He found it beneath clothing. Lying on his side, shielded by the bed, he unzipped the pouch. Inside was his handgun: Colt M1911. He slammed in a mag, then aimed at the ceiling light. He pumped a bullet into the bulb. The room went black.

The sound of gunfire made Maria look up from the kitchen sink, where she was washing a copper pan. She dropped the pan into the soapy water, then dried her hands on her apron. A look of fear came to her face.

"*Nico!*" she yelled to her husband, who was on the terrace.

"What?"

"*Come quickly!*"

Raul swept the weapon slowly left, finding the light of the main house.

"We have less than an hour!" said Chang, desperately. "The guard—"

"The guard isn't our problem," said Raul, calmly scanning the house.

Raul saw movement on the terrace. It was a tall man. Was it Andreas?

Raul pumped the trigger. The slug hit the man in the chest, throwing him backward and down to the ground.

Reaching into the pouch, Dewey found two more magazines, along with his combat knife. He fastened the knife sheath to his calf, crawled to the door, and sprinted down the hallway toward the kitchen.

As he got to the main house, he heard breaking glass coming from the kitchen.

Dewey charged into the kitchen, searching for Nico and Maria.

Maria was kneeling in the corner, pointing in silence out at the terrace. Dewey crossed in a low crouch to the doors that led outside. Nico lay in a contorted heap, surrounded by a mess of food, broken plates, and blood. His chest showed a pancake of blood where the bullet had struck.

Anger fueled with sorrow, hatred, and every other dark force that had ever compelled any man to kill and it took over Dewey. It washed over him like a storm tide, and he knew in those moments it would never leave him, never again; it would always be there, forever, and every step for the rest of his life, whether they killed him tonight or he lived to be a hundred, would be scarred by the pain that now coursed through him.

He shot out the terrace light, then crawled to the wall near the French doors. He shut out the lights inside the kitchen.

Dewey moved to Maria, kneeling against the wall. He'd never seen someone as scared. Pure terror was spread across the woman's face. Her mouth was ajar, her lips moving in a silent scream, as tears flowed down her cheeks. Her right hand was still pointing toward her dead husband.

Dewey felt his instincts taking over then. Whatever pain, whatever sorrow, whatever trauma was to come, it would have to wait.

He felt himself going back to a familiar place. He was in Panama City, in the basement of the tenement, four dead SEALs by his side, trying to fight his way out of an ambush by one of Noriega's kill squads. He was in the cold water six hundred feet below Capitana, on the ocean floor, oxygen running out, fighting for his life against two of Alexander Fortuna's mercenaries. He was on the tarmac at Beirut Airport, side by side with Kohl Meir, hemmed in by Hezbollah to the south and Lebanese Special Forces to the north.

It was that time he'd come to recognize, the crucible that alone was Dewey's, a gift and a curse: the moment of the warrior.

Dewey reached his hand out and took Maria's hand in his own. Calmly, he placed his gun on the ground, and held her hands, comforting her. He looked into her eyes, just visible in the dim light from the night sky.

"I need you to do something, Maria," said Dewey.

She stared, eyes transfixed on nothing, into the distance.

Dewey gently squeezed her hands.

"Can you do something for me?" asked Dewey, trying to get her back.

Slowly, Maria's head moved up and down, nodding yes.

"I need you to be strong," said Dewey, calmly. "He needs you to be strong. Can you do that?"

She shut her eyes. She started sobbing. Her body heaved as tears came down.

"Where are Sabina and Alvaro?" asked Dewey.

At the sound of her children's names, Maria's eyes suddenly became more alert. She tried to stand up. Dewey put one of his hands on her shoulder and held her down.

"Where are they, Maria?"

"Her boyfriend's, in El Brillante."

"That's good," said Dewey. "What about Alvaro?"

Maria paused, thinking, then again tried to lurch up, as she suddenly let out a low scream.

"At the polo house," said Maria, desperation in her voice. "We need to find him."

Dewey kept his hand on Maria's shoulder, holding her there, against the wall.

"I'll take care of Alvaro. You need to hide. Is there a basement?"

Maria pointed to a door at the far side of the kitchen.

"Good," said Dewey reassuringly. "Are there guns?"

"They're in Nico's gun safe. I don't know the combination."

Dewey reached for his Colt and handed it to her.

"Have you ever fired a sidearm?"

She nodded.

"This one will kick," said Dewey. "Hold it with both hands. I want you to take the gun and go to the basement. Find a place to hide. The next people you'll see will probably be police; don't shoot them. But if they're not police, you need to kill them."

"How will I know?"

"You'll know. If it's the bad guys, they'll be quiet, and they probably

95

won't be Argentine. The police won't be quiet; they'll be looking for you, calling your name."

Maria thought for a moment, then nodded at Dewey.

"Now go," said Dewey. "You need to move."

Maria crawled across the kitchen floor, opened the basement door, and disappeared into the cellar.

Seconds were passing, precious moments. Dewey needed to think quickly. They could be getting away.

It had been a black-on-black design, sniper, informants, technological know-how, and, above all, audacity.

The safe thing would be to get the authorities in here. Secure the scene. Then call Hector. Get a Langley forensics team down here to analyze the slugs. But Dewey didn't feel like doing the safe thing. He needed to find the man who triggered the rifle that killed his fiancée, and then find the men who sent him there.

He felt adrenaline surging inside him. His heart raced. He stood, took one last look at Nico's corpse, then sprinted out of the kitchen.

Back at the bedroom, he paused outside the door, steeling himself for what lay inside. He stepped inside, trying not to look at Jessica.

Don't look. You said your goodbye. Walk away. Leave her behind.

There's only one thing you can do now, Dewey. It's what you were made to do, what you were meant to do, the only thing you can do.

He went to the bureau and searched until he found Jessica's sidearm, a government-issued Glock G30S. He slammed in a magazine, grabbed the other mag, then ran to the terrace, into the darkness.

"It was supposed to be surgical," said Chang, to Raul's right, watching through the binoculars.

"And I was supposed to be a doctor," said Raul. "Things don't always turn out as planned."

Both men watched as, in the distance, the lights of the ranch went out one-by-one.

"Start packing up," said Raul. "We need to get the hell out of here."

"He's still alive."

"So are we. Now pack up the shit."

"What about him?" asked Chang, nodding toward Hu-Shao.

"We'll carry him. Let's get moving."

Dewey sprinted away from the ranch, through uncut fields, beneath the night sky. He ran at a grueling pace, ignoring the burning in his lungs.

The front of Dewey's foot hit a root sticking up, and he went tumbling forward, landing on his chest. He paused for a moment on the ground. He scanned back toward the house. He could make out the dark silhouette of the ranch.

Dewey searched for something to hold on to, a feeling, a moment, to stave off the terrible thoughts. The darkness, the burning in his lungs—it all brought him back to Fort Bragg, to training, to Delta:

You'll get used to the dark. It will become your ally. When it does, no man will be safe from you.

Dewey got up and began to run, harder this time, charging across the fields.

His mind flashed to a picture of Jessica in the river, swimming toward him. He took the memory, folded it up, then tucked it there, in a box, somewhere deep inside. Next to Robbie. He closed the box and shut it away.

Before him, on the ground, he saw a trail of beaten-down grass.

The tracks came from the south, toward the river. He scanned the horizon, seeing nothing but darkness and stars. Dewey fell into the path of beaten-down grass, sprinting, the Glock clutched in his right hand. His nostrils flared, sweat trickled down, and he felt it now, the warmth of the hunter.

He saw a flicker of light in the distance, then heard an engine.

Dewey ran faster, his lungs burning, aiming toward the light.

He came to a small hill and took it in five quick steps. There, less than a hundred feet away, was an SUV, headlights on. In front of it were two silhouettes, leaned over, carrying a body.

Dewey raised the Glock in stride, then fired.

The men saw him and dropped what they were carrying, both men lurching toward the SUV.

Dewey pulled the trigger as fast as his finger would let him. Bullets hit the vehicle, breaking glass. He hit one of the men, who fell to the ground. Dewey ran closer, firing again as the fallen man got up and limped toward the back of the SUV. The engine revved as Dewey came closer, suddenly peeling out and driving away from Dewey as he emptied the mag.

Dewey stopped, watching as the taillights receded in the distance. He could barely breathe. For nearly a minute, he leaned over, catching his breath.

He walked to the body. The man was lying facedown. The back of his head was missing. His shirt and the back of his pants were drenched in blood.

Dewey put his foot beneath the man's torso and kicked him over. His face was partially destroyed. He had a mustache that was interrupted in the middle by a hole, the entry point to a bullet someone had fired at close range, a dollar's worth of metal and gunpowder that had blown out the back of his skull. Another slug had been fired into his right eye. The left one was still in place, a bulging eye that looked blankly up at the sky. He looked Asian.

The lights from the SUV disappeared. It was eerily quiet.

Dewey ran back to the ranch. In the bedroom, he found his shoulder holster. He put it on, inserted the handgun, then looked one last time at Jessica. Her face was calm and still, like a sculpture.

In the driveway, he slid open the garage door. A Range Rover was parked inside, and he climbed in, found the keys on the dash, and started the car. When he flipped the lights on, they illuminated a bright red motorcycle which was parked in the back of the garage. It had letters in black cursive along the side:

DUCATI CORSE
1199 PANIGALE S

Dewey turned off the car, climbed out, and hopped on the bike.

He turned it on. It rumbled to life, the engine purring smoothly, low and loud. He revved it several times and let it scream in neutral. He put the bike in gear and moved slowly out of the garage.

At the gravel, he opened it up. The Ducati burst down the driveway. Within seconds, the bike was going sixty. As he approached the polo house, Dewey slowed to a stop. He put the kickstand down and ran inside.

He found Alvaro in one of the bunk rooms, asleep. Dewey placed his left hand on the boy's mouth, waiting for him to wake up, which he did, struggling beneath Dewey's hand, startled. He was a strong kid, but Dewey held him down with his right hand, with his left he put a finger to his mouth, telling him to be quiet.

"Come with me," said Dewey.

Back on the Ducati, Alvaro sat behind Dewey, clutching him around the waist.

He pushed the throttle now as far as it would go. The front tire popped up from the ground. Dewey leaned in, pushing to settle it back down. He was at eighty miles an hour as he reached the end of the driveway, where, in the distance, he saw the Suburban. The front side window was shattered. He slowed as he came upon it. He saw the back of Morty's head, slumped over the steering wheel.

Dewey revved the bike and sped toward the main road.

"Hold on," he yelled over the engine.

He reached the end of the driveway and banked a hard left, then let the bike rip. The engine roared. In seconds, he'd cycled the gearbox and was moving at more than 120, chasing the killers of the only thing that mattered to him.

A few seconds later, he glanced at the digital pictograph on the console: 154.

The country road became more crowded as he approached Córdoba. He saw a gas station and cut in, then stopped.

"Get off," said Dewey.

Alvaro climbed off the back of the bike. He was barefoot. He looked thoroughly confused, and scared.

"What's going on?"

"Call your sister in El Brillante. Tell her to stay where she is."

"What happened?"

Dewey looked into the boy's eyes.

"Then call AFP. Tell them the ranch was attacked. Your mother is alive."

"My mother is alive—"

"They killed your father."

Alvaro looked as if he was about to faint.

"Tell AFP your mother is in the basement, hiding," said Dewey, a hard, emotionless expression on his face. "Alvaro, you need to be tough. Your mom, your sister—they need you to be tough. That starts right now. Do you understand?"

Alvaro appeared daunted by the sudden realization of what was happening. Finally, he nodded at Dewey.

"Yeah, I understand."

Dewey ripped out of the gas station on the Ducati, leaving a scorched line of smoking rubber. He cycled quickly through the gearbox, taking the bike back up to 100, 110, 130, and still, he didn't slow.

He swerved past cars and trucks, swinging into the oncoming lane, then back again, as horns blared. At the outskirts of the city, he saw a sign with a picture of a plane on it. He banked right, feeling his knee scuff against the road, then opened the bike up again. He was quickly back up to 150.

Move quickly. Always have a weapon. If you're in danger, you must be prepared to risk your own life.

Just past another sign for the airport, Dewey hit the crest of a hill he didn't see coming. As the road dropped, the momentum of the bike thrust him forward, into the air. The bike caught air and didn't come down for several seconds, as the engine churned furiously. Dewey fought to keep his balance, to stay straight, until, thirty feet down the road, the back tire of the bike touched down, with Dewey gripping the handlebars. The front tire hit tar a second later.

Dewey banked right into the airport entrance, again nicking his right knee on the tar as he bent the bike low.

The airport was lit up but quiet. He sped through the arrival area, looking for signs of life, then hooked around the side of the terminal, racing for the runway.

He saw two blue lights. He came on a police cruiser at the gate to the runway. The car door opened and an officer held up his hand, ordering him to stop, but Dewey kept going, past the policeman. He pushed the bike harder, pulled back, lifted the front tire, and hit the wooden gate that that led to the tarmac. It smashed into pieces.

At the far side of the tarmac, he saw a black Toyota Land Cruiser, its lights still on, a door open. He heard a low grumble from down the tarmac, then recognized the oncoming lights of a jet. It was moving down the runway, directly at him. The engine roared.

Dewey dumped the bike, climbed off, then pulled the Glock from his shoulder holster.

"Raul!" yelled one of the pilots from the cockpit.

Chang was seated in the cabin of the Gulfstream. He looked across the aisle at Raul, who lay on his side across two of the leather cabin chairs. The mercenary held his hand against his stomach, where the bullet from Andreas had hit him.

"They're trying to stop the plane," yelled the pilot.

Raul's dull eyes met Chang's. He tried to say something. Blood seeped over his lips as his mouth moved.

"Take off," he coughed. "Get off the ground."

At that moment, Chang thought about killing Raul, but he wouldn't need to. The Mexican would be dead within the hour. Blood oozed out over his fingers as he clutched his stomach.

The plane's engines roared. The jet started moving down the tarmac.

"You need to remove the bullet," said Raul, blood dribbling out the sides of his mouth.

Chang said nothing. He stood and walked to the cabin. He stood behind the two pilots as the Gulfstream barreled down the runway.

"*He has a gun!*" yelled one of the pilots, pointing out the window.

The jet came faster now, down the runway, directly at Dewey. He raised his right arm and stepped into the path of the oncoming jet. He trained the muzzle of the Glock at the front of the plane. Then he started firing. The slugs hit the cockpit glass in front of the pilot.

One, two, three, then the rest of the magazine: Dewey emptied all his ammunition into the glass. As the front wheel lifted off just feet from where he stood, he realized the glass was bulletproof.

"*Stop!*" screamed a police officer behind him.

The blue-and-white jet lifted off. As Dewey was tackled from behind, he watched as Jessica's killers escaped into the dark sky.

Chang leaned forward, looking out the cockpit window. At the end of the runway, a shirtless man was walking down the middle of the tarmac. The jet sped closer to him. The engines roared. The man's arm was raised. He had his gun trained up at the plane. Above the din, Chang heard the faint sound of gunfire, then the chink of the slug hitting the plane. Reflexively, he flinched.

They came closer and closer to the figure. Chang knew it was Andreas. Even without looking, he knew it was him. A slug hit the glass of the window, pockmarking it. Andreas kept firing as the jet moved closer, dotting the glass with small indents.

The jet's wheels began to lift off as they came right upon Andreas, who didn't move. Chang craned his neck to see him. He was big, wearing only jeans, his expression angry and unflinching. Then the Gulfstream climbed fully off the tarmac.

Chang's heart raced as he felt the smooth embrace of liftoff. He stood at the edge of the cabin for several moments.

In one day, his life had changed entirely, and not for the better. He couldn't begin to imagine how he could fix it. Andreas was alive. The woman was dead. Hu-Shao was back at the ranch with a pair of holes in his head. He had no friends or allies. Whatever money he had was being monitored by the ministry. He had nothing.

He knew he should report in and tell the truth. After all, he wasn't the one who killed the woman. He wasn't the one who shot Hu-Shao. It was Raul.

But none of that mattered. The ministry didn't tolerate failure. He was a dead man.

Chang returned to the cabin.

Raul lay still, his eyes wide open, staring permanently into oblivion.

Chang ransacked his pockets for cash, finding nearly four thousand dollars in cash.

He sat down and looked out the window, trying to think. From his pocket, he removed his ministry-issued SAT phone. He was at a crossroads. He could call in to Beijing and confess to everything that had happened. Or he could run.

He'd seen firsthand how Bhang treated people who failed him.

He smashed the SAT phone against the floor. He removed the tracking device from the phone and stomped on it until it was pulverized.

He went to the cabin.

"Give me a map," he said.

Both pilots turned. Their eyes drifted down to the handgun that Chang now clutched, moving it back and forth between the two men.

The pilot on the left pulled a navigational chart from a pocket on the side of the cockpit. Chang flipped through it, then studied the area.

"What's the nearest city?" he asked.

"Santiago."

"Head for Valparaiso," said Chang, pointing, "on the coast."

21

UNITED STATES TREASURY DEPARTMENT
WASHINGTON, D.C.

From outside the closed office door of U.S. Treasury Secretary Woodrow Uhlrich, a passerby could, on occasion, hear a mysterious thumping sound.

Those who were close to Wood Uhlrich knew that it only happened toward the end of the day, a stressful day, a day in which Uhlrich, sometime past eight or nine in the evening, would venture to the sideboard in his office and fill a highball glass a quarter full with Pappy Van Winkle's. The dull thuds that echoed in the entrance foyer, through Uhlrich's closed door, were the sounds of darts striking the cork of the dartboard that hung on the back of the door.

To say that Uhlrich's staff loved him would have been an understatement. In fact, each and every one of them would have gone to war for Uhlrich. Joanna Traaten, his beautiful executive assistant; Bobby Grace, his overweight but capable chief of staff, and all of the others who'd come along on Uhlrich's wild ride, from mayor of Lexington, to governor of Kentucky, to United States senator, and, upon the election of his best friend Rob Allaire to the presidency, to his appointment as treasury secretary, they had all been there, through thick and thin.

It was Grace who kept the bourbon in ample supply. It was Traaten who made sure his schedule was wiped clean by 6:00 P.M. And both knew that when the darts started hitting, to leave Uhlrich alone.

None of them had ever seen him angry. Even his wife, Daisy, couldn't remember a time when Uhlrich had raised his voice. He was laid-back to the point of being taciturn. He simply couldn't be fazed, didn't like to talk, and yet somehow lured people in with a quiet sort of charisma.

Hitting the dartboard was Uhlrich at his most emotional. Everyone knew that when he started throwing darts, he had something on his mind. After a half hour or so, it was Grace's job to politely knock on the door and see what was going on.

"Wood?" Grace asked as he pushed the door in, a few minutes after eight. "Hold your fire, Mr. Secretary."

Grace stepped inside, then closed the large door behind him.

"Hi, Bobby."

Uhlrich's tie was off. He was standing halfway between his desk and the door, where the dartboard hung. In his left hand was a glass of bourbon. In his right, a green-and-red-tailed dart. Grace glanced at the dartboard. One of the darts was in the center.

"Nice shot."

"I did that one yesterday. Left it there. It reminds me that every once in a while I do something right."

Grace walked to one of the two large black leather sofas, next to where Uhlrich stood, and sat down.

"What's on your mind?" asked Grace.

Uhlrich was quiet. He tossed the dart toward the board, where it stuck into the cork a few inches from the center.

"You want a drink?" Uhlrich asked.

"Certainly." Grace started to get up.

"You sit," said Uhlrich. "I'll get it."

Uhlrich went to the sideboard and pulled out a glass, then poured it a quarter full with bourbon. He walked to the sofas and sat down across from Grace.

"Baum?" asked Grace, referring to Richard Baum, the chairman of the Federal Reserve.

"Yes."

"How much do we need to borrow?"

"Five hundred billion."

"*Mamma mia*," said Grace. "That would be the largest bond sale ever, if memory serves."

Uhlrich took a sip from his glass, then brushed his hand back through his mop of curly blond hair.

"The strategy of trying to force Congress to cut spending has backfired," said Uhlrich. "Frankly, Richard is right about one thing. As long as Congress refuses to cut spending, we need to borrow more money. He doesn't spend the money. Congress is playing chicken with the Fed and with the president. They know Dellenbaugh won't raise taxes. So what they're going to do is keep spending and force us to borrow more money from China."

"China will buy whatever bonds we put into the market."

"That's what I'm worried about," said Uhlrich. "We owe the People's Bank of China nearly two trillion dollars. Trillion with a *T*. That's a lot of money. Soon we'll be at two five, then three. It's not sustainable. What happens when we have to choose between whether your grandma gets her heart medication or China gets their interest payment? What happens when we have to choose between some Marine unit getting a better kind of flak jacket or paying off Beijing? And what happens when we do choose your grandma? What do the Chinese do? Scares me to even think about it."

"We restructure. What can they do? Invade?"

"You're missing my point," said Uhlrich. "The Chinese already invaded. They're here; instead of weapons, they fired money. If they stop buying our bonds, the U.S. economy will collapse."

"So we start paying it back."

Uhlrich smiled.

"I'm going back to Kentucky," he said. "When Rob Allaire asked me to be treasury secretary, I thought it would be an honor, and it has been. But I'm not big enough for this job. We need someone sitting in this room who can figure this all out."

"You're a great treasury secretary."

"No, I'm not. It's gotten beyond me, Bobby."

Grace stood up. He leaned forward and picked up Uhlrich's glass.

"Let's have another one," said Grace, "and talk about that fishing trip we're going on next summer. You're not leaving, Wood. I have too much dirt on you."

Uhlrich leaned back, laughing heartily.

"I'm going to be remembered as the treasury secretary who sold America to the Chinese."

"No you're not," said Grace, standing at the sideboard and pouring two more bourbons. "You're going to be remembered as the guy who fucked up the door playing darts."

22

MINISTRY OF STATE SECURITY
INTELLIGENCE BUREAU
SHANGHAI

In Shanghai, it was dinnertime. But none of the approximately one thousand employees within the ministry's vast intelligence-gathering unit appeared to be hungry.

The desks were lined up in long rows; fifty rows in all, twenty desks per row, most of the desks occupied. The floor was an almost unfathomable collage of visual media. There were television screens one after another for as far as the eye could see, patient onlookers sitting and watching every media from every outlet imaginable in the entire world; earphones plugged in, listening and watching every news channel, television show, and movie released throughout the world, in every country, in every language, looking for information that had anything of intelligence value to China. This meant all geopolitical or economic issues affecting China as well as its allies and adversaries. They were to transcribe all mentions of China onto electronic tablets, which were then forwarded to human ciphers to examine further.

To the left, the job was to listen: radio shows, podcasts, music; again, any and every audio media introduced into the known world, if possible, in every country, in every language. To the right, the job was to pore over domestic and foreign print media, from every country, in every language: newspapers, magazines, blogs, books.

For a room filled with so many people and so much media, it was amazingly quiet.

Under Fao Bhang, the ministry had spent more than five billion dollars upgrading the technological might of the ministry's electronic eavesdropping. This money went into trying to replicate America's National Security Agency. This sophisticated eavesdropping apparatus—computers, satellites, satellite dishes, and software—produced massive amounts of information, which then needed to be analyzed by human beings. This was the room where that work was done.

Near the front of the room, a middle-aged man in a light yellow sweater and glasses stared at his computer screen.

> 11:50:01 PM
> ARG 6/Córdoba
> Gunfire reported
> Location: Airport Córdoba

The analyst's job was to monitor activity in Argentina, including dispatches originating at Argentine Federal Police—the country's top law-enforcement agency—relevant to China. Normally, a generic crime report wouldn't have drawn his attention. But some piece of software or algorithm within the bowels of the ministry had flagged it. He waited for another update. It came half an hour later.

> 12:18:36 AM
> ARG 6/Córdoba
> Multiple deaths reported
> Location unknown

He went quickly into a bypass of AFP's servers, going behind the AFP firewall through a backdoor Chinese hackers had built.

> Locale: Estancia el Colibri
> Mara Road 5'77"
> AFP at scene
> Multiple deaths confirmed

The analyst opened a separate program and typed "Estancia el Colibri." When he hit "enter," a satellite photograph appeared on the screen. The frame zeroed down in, focusing on the location of the ranch.

12:51:09 AM
Three confirmed homicides
**USSS at scene

He typed "USSS" into the ministry code manual.

United States Secret Service

The analyst sat upright. Suddenly, his computer screen went red and locked.

ACCESS DENIED
999999999999999

The number 9 replicated across his computer screen in flashing red until the screen was nothing but line after line of the numbers. He attempted to type, but it was useless.

He stood up from his cubicle and walked to the front of the room, went through a door, then walked down the hallway to the small, glass-walled office in the corner.

"Something has happened," he said to a gray-haired man smoking a cigarette.

"Argentina? What could possibly happen in Argentina?"

"A triple murder, sir."

"So what," he said waving his cigarette dismissively.

"The U.S. Secret Service is at the scene."

The man sat up.

"When?"

"Only minutes ago."

"Well, what the hell are you doing here? Find out more!"

"The system shut me down."

"What do you mean it shut you down?"

"It said 'access denied,' then flashed a number."

He stood up.

"What was the number?"

"Nine."

He stubbed out his cigarette and reached for his phone on the desk.

"Get me Minister Bhang," he said into the receiver.

Bhang's phone buzzed while he was out at dinner with his daughter and her young child.

"What is it?"

"Argentina, sir."

Bhang listened to the information from the intelligence bureau in Shanghai as his grandson bounced on his lap. Perhaps Bhang should have attempted to reach Hu-Shao or Chang at this point. But his mind was already three steps down the line. If the mission had been a success, he would have already been told this by the agents on scene or by Ming-húa. But that's not what happened. Something was wrong. He hung up, then dialed a different number.

"Si," came the voice, a Spanish accent, of Pascal, whom Bhang had woken up.

"What's the tail number of the plane?" asked Bhang.

"What? Who is this?"

"It's Fao Bhang. What's the tail number?"

"I'm sorry, Minister Bhang. Hold on."

With his left hand, Bhang reached to the table and picked up a dried noodle, then pushed it gently into his grandson's toothless mouth. He smiled at his grandson as he waited, the phone against his ear.

"Do you have a pen, Minister Bhang?"

"I don't need one," said Bhang. "Just tell me the number."

23

PRIVATE RESIDENCE
THE WHITE HOUSE
WASHINGTON, D.C.

J. P. Dellenbaugh was awakened by the phone next to his bed. He reached for the light switch, pulled the chain, then looked around the room. His wife, Amy, opened her eyes but didn't move.

Contrary to popular lore, there is no red phone in the bedroom of the president of the United States. There are three phones, each black, with a small console of buttons. It is White House Control—the White House switchboard—that connects the president to the world. It is through a tightly controlled protocol that any inbound phone call gets through to the president, at any hour, and it's a short list of people whose calls get through. In the middle of the night, that list is even smaller, confined to the president's chief of staff, the director of the CIA, the secretary of state, the secretary of defense, and the national security advisor. Someone else might be able to get through, a foreign leader, for instance, but first they would have to go through one of the chosen few.

Dellenbaugh grabbed for the phone before the second ring.

"Yes," he said, sitting up against a pillow, which he pressed against the big ornate cherrywood headboard.

"White House Control, sir, please hold for CIA Director Calibrisi."

The phone made a staccato beeping noise for a few moments. Dellenbaugh glanced at Amy, who had propped herself up on her left elbow and was watching him. Hector Calibrisi came on the line.

"Mr. President, sorry to awaken you," said Calibrisi.

"It's okay," said Dellenbaugh. "What's going on?"

"I received a call a few minutes ago from our chief of station in Argentina. I'm afraid it's very bad news, sir. Jessica is dead; she was killed a few hours ago."

Dellenbaugh reflexively, unconsciously jerked forward, heaving involuntarily, like a cough without noise. With his free hand, his right hand, he reached out and gripped his wife's hand, squeezing it. He was silent for several moments, blinking, trying to process the news, unable to speak. He looked at his wife with a pained expression of disbelief and sorrow.

Amy Dellenbaugh said nothing, instead took her other hand and wrapped it around his, trying to be supportive.

"Killed?" Dellenbaugh finally whispered.

"She was shot. It's still early. We have a forensics team getting on a plane in a few minutes to get down there. She was gunned down by what appears to have been a sniper. It was a planned attack. One of the ranch owners was gunned down; so was Morty, sir. Dewey survived."

"My God," said Dellenbaugh. "I'm sorry, Hector. I know how close you were."

Calibrisi was silent. Dellenbaugh heard what sounded like a low sniffle.

"Who would want to kill our national security advisor?"

Dellenbaugh let Calibrisi regain himself. After more than a dozen seconds, Calibrisi cleared his throat.

"I don't know. It very well may have been Dewey they were after. In fact, it probably was Dewey."

"Iran?"

"Possibly."

Calibrisi paused, then continued in halted speech.

"I should have known, Mr. President. I should have known and insisted on a much broader security detail."

"It's not your fault," said Dellenbaugh.

"Yes, it is, sir."

"Where's Dewey?" asked Dellenbaugh.

"Córdoba. He chased someone—presumably the attackers—to the airport. They escaped on a private plane. He shot at the plane. Local police didn't know what was going on, so they locked him up. We're dealing with it."

"How did we learn about it?"

"The head of AFP woke me an hour ago. He and our chief of station are on their way from Buenos Aires."

Dellenbaugh glanced at Amy. She'd figured out what had happened, and tears were running down her cheeks, which she did not attempt to hide.

After a long pause, Dellenbaugh cleared his throat. He sat up, then stood up. He held the phone in his right hand. Dellenbaugh still retained much of the brawn that had made him a much-feared pugilist during his time in the NHL. He unconsciously clenched his left fist, as if he were about to slug somebody in the nose. His biceps lumped out like a baseball.

"We need to find out who the hell did this," said Dellenbaugh. He stared out the window at a Washington that was dark, except for a few lights here and there, including the ones that demarcated the pinnacle of the Washington Monument. "Whether it was an accident because they were after Dewey or, God forbid, the assassination of America's national security advisor, someone has to pay. If it was the latter, Hector, this is war."

Calibrisi was silent.

"Do you agree?"

"Yes, I do, Mr. President. Intentionally or unintentionally, this is an act of war. We need to find out who did it. I need to speak to Dewey."

"We need to handle how this is announced," said Dellenbaugh.

"I haven't even thought about that, sir."

"You don't need to. Let me handle that. In the meantime, get Dewey back here. I want to know what happened. Let's reconvene first thing in the morning, in the Situation Room. Make sure Harry Black and Tim Lindsay are briefed and ready to talk about military options."

"Yes, sir."

Dellenbaugh hung up the phone. He looked at his wife.

"I'm sorry," she said, tears streaming down her cheeks.

Dellenbaugh said nothing. He fought to hold back tears. He picked up the phone.

"Yes, Mr. President."

"Get me Jessica's parents. They're in Princeton."

24

In a dilapidated concrete building near Santiago's soccer stadium, Chang stood atop a stainless-steel platform, barefoot, naked, sweating profusely, and breathing heavily, as heavily as if he'd just run five miles.

The building looked like an abandoned warehouse. But its external decrepitude masked its true purpose. From the outside, the doors were boarded up and no light was visible. From the inside, two stories below ground, a windowless expanse looked like a laboratory at a pharmaceutical manufacturer.

The facility was owned and operated by a company called Utrecht Promotions, which was, in point of fact, a shell corporation set up by China's Ministry of State Security. It was one of thirty such secret interrogation labs dotting the globe.

The reason Chang was standing, despite the fact that he was exhausted, was because he couldn't sit down. It was physically impossible. Forty-six stainless-steel probes the thickness of pencils jutted out from walls on both sides of him. These steel probes—long needlelike protuberances—were the approximate sharpness of golf tees, not sharp enough to break skin at first contact, but painful nevertheless, and capable, with some pressure, of puncturing skin and even leather. The probes were connected to a computer that monitored all manner of

Chang's physiological state, all in the name of determining if Chang was telling the truth.

Different countries, even different agencies within the same country, had different methods of getting people to talk. Simple lie detectors, while excellent devices for sniffing out lies from the untrained, were beatable with coaching and practice. Torture—electricity, waterboarding, fingernail removal, and dozens of other methods—was effective but often led to false confessions. Then there were pharmaceuticals, drugs, in many shapes and formats, employed in a variety of methods. But like the proverbial cure for baldness, no drug had yet been invented that could compel someone to tell the truth. Truth serum was a fiction, a product of Hollywood and thriller writers. What had been shown to be effective in a pharmaceutical context was the interplay of opiates, such as heroin, intended to make the victim feel good, and any manner of neurotoxins, which caused pain. The lure of the opiates intermixed with the harsh pain of the neurotoxins had been shown, especially by the CIA and Mossad, to be enormously effective at drawing out confessions.

Bhang took a different approach.

Upon his elevation to minister, Bhang had appointed somebody he could trust and who was technically capable—his brother Bo Minh—to design and build a better mousetrap. What Minh invented was now being experienced firsthand by Chang. The device was called the "dragon."

The dragon was simple enough: forty-six stainless-steel probes that pressed front and back against the subject, from head to toe. The probes were intelligent, that is, they performed a variety of functions depending upon the individual probe. First of all, at their most basic level, the probes monitored in real time all life functions of the subject—heart rate, brain activity, lung and heart pressure, levels of various chemicals in the bloodstream, oxygen levels, breathing rate.

These readings were then run through a sophisticated algorithm that had been written after studying more than one thousand individuals in a controlled setting, telling both lies and the truth, over a period of two years. Through this two-year data repository of minute-by-minute reactions, Minh and his team of statisticians, physicians, scientists, computer engineers, and design engineers knew exactly what lying looked like across a complex spectrum of physiological attributes. What they learned is that liars have a wide variety of strategies and physiological reactions, depending on time of day, levels of hunger, levels of exhaustion, and a number of other factors. There was no single way to know if someone was lying. However, there was a finite physiological library of reactions during the lying process—eighteen in all—across all people. Minh and his team discovered that in physiological terms, there are eighteen different kinds of liars, no more, no less.

Once they understood how to identify a liar with one of the eighteen different patterns, they then charted the transition from a state of lying to the state of telling the truth, in precise physiological terms. They mapped each of the eighteen types and, in this way, mapped the precise physiological transition to the truth. They learned that some liars will move to the truth with pain. Others will not, but those liars could be motivated in other ways, such as with drugs, sleep deprivation, hunger.

Thus armed with more than twenty-two terabytes of data, Minh and his team designed an algorithm that was capable of analyzing an individual's various physiological attributes, determine if he is lying or telling the truth, and, if lying, could place them in one of the categories, then administer the most effective way to compel the subject to tell the truth.

The dragon automated the entire process.

Each probe had a different role. Five of the stainless-steel needles, for example, monitored heart activity. Two injected synthetic opiates, heroin derivatives, while four injected different types of neurotoxins designed to cause pain. Ten probes could send electric jolts, and six produced small flames barely visible to the eye but hot enough to char the skin.

Perhaps most important, all probes moved inward, pressing against the subject, sandwiching him in tiny increments, every time a lie was told. This was what Minh referred to as the "dragon teeth." A subject could feel the immediate effect of his own lies. Eventually, if enough lies were told, the individual being interrogated could be punctured straight on through, in forty-six different places. So far, that had yet to occur, as the algorithm had proven incredibly effective at getting the truth before that occurred.

On this day, in Santiago, Chile, it didn't matter to anyone except the algorithm what specific type of liar Chang was. But he was lying.

Chang was alone in the lab. A camera was attached to the ceiling, hanging ominously down like a spider from the rafters, aimed at him, filming him, then delivering the live feed to Beijing. Speakers in the wall delivered the questions.

Chang was drenched in perspiration and his skin was ashen, a product of more than sixteen micro injections of heroin and three injections of a synthetic neurotoxin made from a derivative of household bleach. In addition, he had three large pink marks—one on his neck, another on his testicles, and still another on his left ankle—where the dragon had sent a series of white-hot flames.

Most conspicuous, however, was the wallpaper of reddish dimples, like the outside of a golf ball, that was arrayed across his front and back, as the device moved ineluctably inward, slowly crushing Chang as he attempted in vain to spin his magic tales.

His capture at Valparaiso Airport had been routine. They were waiting for him when the jet landed. Chang would never know how Bhang had found him out so quickly. During the trip to Santiago, the ministry agents hadn't said a word. As he was driven to the ministry laboratory, bound and gagged in the back of a van, he'd asked himself if there was something he could have done differently. Perhaps he should've remained in Argentina and gone into hiding. But even that would've been futile. They would've found him, sooner than later.

"Why did you run?" came the voice from the wall.

Was it Fao Bhang's voice? He'd never actually heard Bhang speak. He sounded polite, like a schoolteacher.

"Answer, please."

"I don't know," said Chang.

A small needle injected something into his neck. Burning pain erupted at the point of injection and flamed out. Chang screamed.

"What happened to Hu-Shao?"

Chang said nothing.

"Where is Hu-Shao?"

"I don't know."

The probes moved in, just slightly, while at his ankle a small torch flared. Chang screamed.

"Why didn't you make contact?"

"I did. I made contact—"

A flame shot out from a different probe, at the lower part of Chang's back. He screamed.

"You were escaping. You're lying."

"I was going to call from Valparaiso."

The probes moved in, pressing a little harder against his skin.

"Stop lying. Where is Hu-Shao?"

"I told you, I don't know."

He felt and heard one of the probes puncture skin above his stomach. Blood oozed out from the puncture wound.

"Where is Hu-Shao?" asked the voice, calmly.

Chang looked up at the camera, resigned.

"He's dead. Raul killed him."

"How?"

"He shot him in the head."

"Where?"

"In the field. He knew Hu-Shao was going to kill him."

Chang's eyes drifted to the camera.

"It was your fault," he added. "All of you. If you'd just left it alone, it would all have been done, as we were trained to do. Instead you told Hu-Shao to kill the mercenary. Why? Why did you do this? Just kill me."

The probes tightened, sandwiching him, while a shot of something cold entered through a probe at his neck. Suddenly, a burning pain riveted him as the neurotoxin entered his bloodstream.

"Where is Hu-Shao's body?"

"At the ranch. On the ground. His head is destroyed. We were going to carry him out."

"Did I hear you correctly?" asked the interrogator, anger and shock in his voice. "Hu-Shao's body is—"

"On the ground," said Chang. "The American was shooting at us."

"Andreas?"

"Yes."

Chang felt warmth, as a tiny dose of heroin was administered, a reward for telling the truth. He shut his eyes and tried to forget where he was. Somehow, he knew it was to be the last moment of pleasure in his life.

"He shot Raul in the stomach. We had to leave the body on the ground and run."

"Is Andreas still alive?"

Chang remembered the sight of Andreas, firing his weapon at the Gulfstream as they took off. But he could be dead now. That was what he told himself.

"I don't know."

"Was Andreas alive when you last saw him?"

"Yes."

"Did you fire at him?"

"Yes."

"Was he hit?"

"I don't know."

The probes moved in slightly, pinching.

"Was he hit?"

"No."

"Was he with someone?"

"Yes. A woman."

"Did Raul shoot the woman?"

"Yes."

In a small windowless room deep in the bowels of the ministry, which looked like the control room on a nuclear submarine, Bhang stood with his arms crossed, a cigarette dangling in his right hand. With him was Quan, who directed the ministry's intelligence-gathering unit, and Bo Minh, his half brother, the inventor of the lie detector, who was managing the controls of the device.

All three men stared at the small plasma screen on the wall, which displayed a live feed of Chang.

At Chang's last words, Bhang leaned forward and hit the mute button.

"Did he just say what I think he said?" asked Bhang, shock and anger in his voice.

On the screen, Chang's bloodshot, nearly lifeless eyes stared into the camera.

Quan shrugged his shoulders.

Bhang lifted his finger from the mute button.

"Please repeat what you just said."

"Fuck you," moaned Chang, delirious.

Bhang nodded to Minh, who grabbed a dial beneath the screen and turned. Blood burst at different points on Chang's body as the probes, with Minh's assistance, pressed in tighter, crushing him.

"Please, Mr. Chang, repeat what you said," ordered Bhang.

"Raul shot her. He killed her. He hit her in the back."

Bhang looked at Minh.

"End the feed, if you would, Bo," he said. "Cut him down. Get rid of him."

Bhang walked to the door. At the door, he turned.

"Please find Ming-húa," he said to Quan. "Tell him to be in my office in exactly thirty seconds. Then take care of Raul's body, the pilots, the plane, everything. Erase all evidence."

25

Two men walked briskly into the provincial police department head-quarters. One of the men was in his fifties, tall, with dark skin and a thick head of black hair. This was Colonel Arman Marti, director general of Argentina Federal Police, the country's top law-enforcement agency, Argentina's equivalent to the FBI. The other man was much younger, in his early thirties, had curly brown hair, and was shorter. This was Charlie Couture, Argentina chief of station for the CIA.

It was five in the morning.

Marti and Couture walked past the front desk without slowing. They entered a hallway that ran along the cellblock. At the last cell, Marti swiped a small steel card in front of a scanner. There was a loud click as the dead bolt popped open.

The two men stepped inside. The cell was dimly lit, humid, and smelled of body odor.

Seated on the ground was a shirtless man. He had on jeans and boots. His brown hair was disheveled, and he had several days' worth of stubble on his face. Marti's head jerked back as he looked at the man, an involuntary gesture as he realized the man was not only awake, but waiting, with a blank, hateful look.

The man was seated against the wall, staring at the two men as they entered the cell.

Couture spoke first.

"Hi, Dewey," he said. "I'm Charlie Couture from Langley. This is Colonel Marti, who runs AFP. First things first: How are you?"

Couture and Marti waited for Dewey to respond, but he remained silent.

"We have the ranch cordoned off," said Marti. "Is there any information you can provide to us? Did you see anything?"

Dewey stared impassively at Marti.

"I can have someone get your stuff," said Couture. "You don't need to go back there if you don't feel like it."

Dewey stared past the two men. He had a distant look, like he was staring at something a thousand miles away.

"We have a jet over at the airport that'll fly you back to the U.S."

Dewey still didn't move or say anything.

Marti glanced at Couture, who returned the look.

Couture pulled a phone from his pocket and hit a button.

"It's me," Couture said into the phone. A moment later, he handed the phone to Dewey. "It's Hector."

Dewey hesitated, then took the phone.

"Dewey," said Calibrisi.

Dewey took a deep breath but remained quiet.

"I've got a forensics team heading down there," continued Calibrisi. "Six of my best guys. Jim Bruckheimer at NSA has a group charging hard as well. We're going to find out who did this."

There was a long moment of silence as Calibrisi paused, waiting for Dewey to talk.

"You there?"

"Yeah."

"I know it's tough, but right now, we need your help."

"I know."

"Did you see anyone? Do you think it was Iran?"

Dewey looked up at Couture, then at Marti. Both men were staring down at him. Couture nodded at Dewey, understanding that he wanted some privacy. He took Marti gently by the elbow and pushed him toward the cell door.

"It was a kill team," said Dewey.

"How do you know?" asked Calibrisi.

"It was a three-man team. I found the sniper nest, five or six hundred yards out. I found someone in the field beyond the nest. He was already dead. The body was cold. Most of his head was shot off. But he looked Asian."

"Did you tell Marti?"

"No. I don't trust anyone down here. They knew we were here."

"There are a ton of ways to track someone. We need to find that body and look at it."

"Hector, I'm asking you, don't tell AFP yet. Let me go look at the body in the daylight."

"Fine."

"Who runs the autopsy?" asked Dewey.

"AFP has jurisdiction," said Calibrisi. "We'll get access to the findings and we'll sit in on the autopsy. The president of Argentina waived protocol and is letting us take Jess home this morning."

"Why would someone . . . ?"

"It could mean anything," said Calibrisi. "You know that. There are a million possible explanations, with Iran being right there at the top of the list. Let's get the body and look at it."

"I have to go."

"Were you in the room when Jessica was shot?" asked Calibrisi.

The question caused a pained expression to shoot across Dewey's face, as he thought of that last sight of Jessica, standing in the French doors.

"Yeah. I watched it happen. They shot her in the back."

"I think you should come back up here. Let us do our job down there."

Dewey tasted salt as tears ran down his cheek into his mouth.

"Her body's at the airport," added Calibrisi. "We'll bring her back to Andrews. Her parents are devastated."

Dewey held the phone against his ear, staring at Couture and Marti, who stood, patiently, outside the cell, out of earshot.

"How will it be announced?"

Calibrisi exhaled deeply.

"I don't know. I'm headed over to the White House in a few minutes to talk about that. It'll happen today."

Dewey felt a sudden wave of nausea.

"I have to go," said Dewey.

"Hold on," said Calibrisi. "I want to say something. I know you want to hit back. I want revenge too. I loved her like a daughter. Heads are going to fucking roll over this."

"What's your point?"

"My point is, let's find out who the hell did this then design a proper retaliation, together."

"There's no amount of people we could kill to get even," said Dewey. "There's no way to bring Jessica back."

"I know we can't bring her back. But we can make anyone and everyone who was involved pay dearly."

Dewey didn't say anything more. He hung up the phone.

Behind police headquarters, Dewey climbed into the back of a dark green AFP Chevy Suburban. They drove in silence back to Estancia el Colibri. Dewey tried to focus on the road ahead, tried to avoid the dark thoughts that kept recurring.

He reached down and felt for his knife. The sheath was gone. Then he remembered being tackled on the tarmac. Hitting the ground as the two police officers strong-armed him down. Watching the Gulfstream lift off.

"I want my knife back, and my sidearm."

In the front seat, Colonel Marti turned. He looked at Couture.

"The knife was given to me. It was a gift."

"I'll give it to you," said Marti, "but you're going to have to wait on the gun."

Marti reached into a steel briefcase in front of the seat. He removed Dewey's combat blade, still sheathed, and handed it back to him.

Dewey looked out the window. He saw her eyes again.

———

Thanksgiving that year was cold, crisp, and cloudless. They bought a turkey from a farm in Virginia. They drove out to get it that morning, the top of her 911 down, freezing cold but tempered by the sun. It was just the two of them. Jessica cooked it to perfection, the skin a crispy mahogany brown, stuffing with sausage in it, sweet potatoes with browned marshmallows on top, her grandmother's recipe. They ate by candlelight then watched football. Dewey made a fire and they sat on the chair, Jessica on his lap, sharing a glass of wine. Silver Oak. He loved that memory. They drank from the same glass. Something so small, so insignificant and trivial, but the memory of sharing that glass warmed him.

"Will you marry me, Jessica?"

The words he vowed long ago never to say again, but when they arrived on his lips he felt the weight fall from his shoulders. He was giving up his freedom with those few words, and yet he'd never felt more free.

"Yes, I will."

Walk away. She's gone. It's all gone. Leave it behind now, Dewey.

There's only one thing you can do now. The thing you were meant to do.

A few minutes later, they reached Colibri.

A long cordon of patrol cars lined the main road, their red and blue lights flashing, creating a security perimeter at the entrance to the ranch. Dewey heard the distant churning of chopper blades, then glanced out the window and counted two helicopters in the sky.

The Suburban moved through the cordon. Several soldiers and various agents saluted as Marti looked blankly ahead through the front window. A mile on, another small swarm of AFP agents was gathered, along with a medical examiner's van.

Dewey glanced at Couture.

"I'm going to pack up my stuff and take a shower."

"Take your time."

Dewey emerged from the back of the SUV. Every AFP agent, police officer, and med tech stared at him. He cut through the middle of the group. At the front door, an armed AFP agent held up his hand.

"*Alto*," said the agent.

Dewey ignored him, brushing past, and as the agent was about to say something else, Marti whistled from the driveway. He waved his head, indicating to let Dewey by and, by the harsh look of reproach on his face, telling the young Argentinian in no uncertain terms to leave Dewey the hell alone.

The ranch house was empty and quiet. The terrace to the dining room was marked off in yellow police tape. The blood had already been cleaned from the bluestone terrace.

To his left, from down the hallway, he heard voices. He walked to the bedroom. Two forensics techs in white smocks were in the room, snapping photographs. They looked up when Dewey entered. They said nothing.

Dewey went into the bathroom and took a shower. He left his bloody jeans on the floor of the bathroom, put on another pair of jeans and a white Lacoste shirt. He packed his belongings into his duffel bag. Then, he packed Jessica's things into her Louis Vuitton suitcase: shirts, shoes, skirts, a couple of bathing suits. Beneath her clothing, he found a simple wooden frame. In was a photo of the two of them. He tucked it into her bag.

Dewey stepped to the doors that led to the terrace. He scanned the horizon, looking for the sniper nest he knew was out there. They hadn't found it yet.

There were maybe a dozen people who knew where he and Jessica were going. He didn't know how they'd found him, but there was no question, they'd been tracked or followed. There was no way it was one of the Americans. Dellenbaugh, Calibrisi, Jessica's chief of staff Josh Brubaker, Morty and the other Secret Service agent, the head of the Secret Service, a handful of others—that was it. It hadn't come from within.

Perhaps he'd never know. But until he was out of the country, he couldn't trust anyone.

He stepped out onto the terrace. He crossed it, then walked diagonally out, across the expansive lawn, then beyond, into the knee-high grass. He knew the general direction, and soon enough he picked up the trampled-down grass from the night before.

If they were looking at him, they would think he was either a member of the search party or, if it was Marti or Couture, a mourning man, taking one last walk, grieving at the death of his fiancée.

A few minutes later, he came upon the dead man.

Under the hot glare of the morning sun, the man's destroyed skull was even more grotesque. Flies hovered.

Dewey knelt. He pulled his knife from the sheath. He grabbed the man's hand and cut off the right index finger. He slipped it into his pocket, turned, and headed back to the ranch house.

He stared at the ground as he walked, deep in thought. Whoever killed Jessica was out there. He would find him. If it took him the rest of his life, he would find him. And when he did, he would pay.

Fight. It's all you can do. It's all you could ever do.

"I'm coming," he whispered, eyes scanning the horizon.

26

Ming-húa was waiting inside Bhang's office when he returned. A cigarette dangled from Bhang's mouth, unlit. Out the window, the Beijing afternoon was a bland mixture of clouds and gray sky. Not that either man noticed the weather. It was just a sideshow to the main event, which was running the largest intelligence agency in the world.

One could say Bhang lived, ate, and breathed the ministry. In point of fact, he smoked it. From the start of the day until the wee hours, Bhang, along with nearly every other top official at MSS, chain-smoked. The result was that headquarters had a rank, stale permeation of smoke, despite constant cleaning.

"Minister—"

"Be quiet," said Bhang sharply as he grabbed a silver lighter from his desk and lit his cigarette.

"I am deeply apologetic," continued Ming-húa, seated on one of three leather chairs arrayed in an orderly line before Bhang's desk. "May I ask—"

"I want silence," said Bhang. "This has been a failure of epic proportions. I knew it was a mistake to elevate you, Ming-húa. You belong in the field, taking orders, not giving them. It was your responsibility to terminate Andreas. Instead, we now have a situation that could become very uncomfortable, very quickly. A situation you likely do not fully understand. So you will keep your mouth firmly shut and you will listen and you will do exactly as I say."

Ming-húa nodded.

"If the Americans ascertain that China was behind the assassination of Jessica Tanzer, it's not unrealistic to think there could be war," said Bhang, puffing his cigarette, staring at Ming-húa. "At the very least, they will be extremely upset. The United Nations will be brought in. The international community will be outraged."

Bhang lit another cigarette with the ember from the first.

"And the blame for all of this will fall on the ministry," continued Bhang, "and, more specifically, on me. Lest you have any illusions as to your own personal safety, Ming-húa, trust me: you will be dangling from the rafters long before they wrap the noose around my neck."

"Minister Bhang, may I say something?"

"No," said Bhang. "Shut up and listen. Your top priority at this moment is to follow my orders. I want you to retrieve the body of our agent. Whatever assets we have in Argentina must be utilized to retrieve Hu-Shao or destroy any evidence of his identity. If Hu-Shao is identified, we will be finished. Do I make myself perfectly clear?"

"Yes, sir, you do. Most perfectly."

Bhang stared for several silent moments at Ming-húa, scorn on his face. He finished his cigarette, then opened the top drawer of his desk. He removed a yellow folder, put it on the desk, then flipped it open. He removed a small stack of photos, all of Dewey Andreas. He picked one up. It showed Andreas in a crisp white uniform, a military hat on his head, shaking someone's hand as he was formally sworn in as a member of 1st Special Forces Operational Detachment—Delta.

Bhang stared at the photo, then handed it toward Ming-húa. Bhang's hand appeared to be trembling slightly as he attempted to control his anger.

"Second, I want Andreas dead. Issue a worldwide termination order. Immediately. I want our top paramilitary project team on this. Their sole responsibility is finding and killing Andreas. I will oversee the group personally, not you. It will be run out of the conference room next to my office."

Ming-húa remained silent. He didn't react, but he was listening.

"Am I perfectly clear, Ming-húa? I want to hear you state that I've been clear."

"Perfectly clear, Minister."

Bhang walked to the door.

"Where are you going, Minister?"

"Where am I going?" answered Bhang, calmly, turning, a vicious sneer on his face. "Your highly paid marksman just assassinated the American national security advisor. I'm going to clean up your mess."

27

PEOPLE'S BANK OF CHINA
BEIJING

Bhang stepped off the elevator on the fourth floor of a modern, low-slung office building, its curvilinear glass wrapped in a half-moon around a squat round granite centerpiece. This was the People's Bank of China. Bhang was accompanied by two security guards. He was here to see Ji-tao Zhu, governor of the People's Bank.

The bank's modest-sized building belied its vast global reach and influence. It was the People's Bank that controlled all monetary policy for the country, the world's second-largest and fastest growing economy. The People's Bank had the most financial assets of any single public financial institution ever, including the Federal Reserve. This small building and the men and women walking through its hushed corridors were sitting on more than $3.5 trillion of liquid reserves and tens of trillions of dollars in other nonliquid assets, such as foreign debt. The bank's tentacles were everywhere, both inside the country and across the globe.

If China's long-term vision was to be the most powerful nation on earth, it was through the bank that such a vision was being slowly but inevitably implemented. Beginning in 1948, when the bank was formed, the People's Bank of China had woven its way into economies large and small, across the world, democracies and dictatorships alike, creating an interlocking grid of influence and dependence in virtually every country on every continent. The bank was owed money by virtually every government of consequence in the world.

The bank rarely if ever used its financial influence, especially in matters of foreign policy. Those who were naïve thought it was because the Chinese government was, deep down, a moral institution, which would never dare use its power to harm others, to exert pressure, or to exact revenge. Those who were smart knew that it was just the opposite. Like a poisonous snake, the bank chose to lurk in the tall grass and the shadows, as it grew stronger and stronger with each passing day, until it was ready and willing to show its fangs and, if necessary, to attack.

Bhang entered through another set of metal detectors into the suite of offices that were the purview of Zhu and his small executive staff. The walls along the corridor were thick, opaque glass, tinted in gold. In a large conference room, he saw Zhu, seated at the end of the table, a half dozen functionaries seated around the table before him. Zhu saw Bhang approaching. He stood up and walked to the door, then stepped into the hallway.

With his hand, Bhang flicked at the security detail, telling them to move away so that he and Zhu could speak.

"I assume you're not here to open a savings account, Minister Bhang?" asked Zhu, smiling.

"We might need your help, Governor," said Bhang, a serious expression on his face.

"How can I be of assistance?"

"We could be in a situation," said Bhang.

"A 'situation'?" asked Zhu, blinking rapidly.

"A situation that requires some of the bank's legendary powers of persuasion, Governor Zhu."

28

Dewey sat on a plush, black leather captain's chair in the cabin of a CIA-owned Citation X jet, heading north, toward America. Except for the two copilots, he was alone. Out the window, the snow-capped peaks of the Andes passed beneath.

He removed the framed photograph from Jessica's suitcase. He stared at it for more than a minute. It showed him giving Jessica a piggyback ride. It had been taken in Castine, during the early summer, along the path that ran near Wadsworth Cove. The photo was lopsided because they couldn't find a flat place to set the camera before putting the timer on and getting into place. They were both laughing. Jessica's hair was in pigtails. He had a big smile. That was why she'd framed it, he guessed. She always said he looked too serious in photographs. On some level, that, more than anything, affected him profoundly. That this was how she saw them. That was the moment that captured, for her, their love.

Fumbling inside his bag, he unzipped a pocket along the liner. He removed another frame, this one made of silver. It was a black-and-white photo, old and faded. It had been a sunny day in Southern California. He was fresh out of college, his hair short, a military uniform on, the Ranger tab visible on his shoulder, before he'd been asked to try out for Delta. When he was still innocent to it all, to the misery of loss, the finality of it, to the feeling of fighting for a country you loved alongside men who were closer than brothers, then watching them die by your side, in your arms. To the feeling of losing a son.

On his lap, Robbie ate a chocolate ice cream cone, his cheeks and the tip of his nose messed with chocolate. His arm was around a beautiful dark-haired woman, who seemed more and more, with time's passage, an ember, barely a memory: Holly, so beautiful, his high school sweetheart, the first person to make him understand what love was, the second person, after Robbie, to teach Dewey what it meant to lose.

He fought to push the thoughts away. He stacked the frames together. He put them in the pocket of the bag and zipped it up.

Leave it behind. Walk away. It's dust now, memories, broken thoughts, and it will only cause you pain.

There's only one thing you can do. It's all you could ever do.

Fight.

Dewey knew what he had to do. He'd been trained to do it, and he was the best at it. He wanted revenge, and he alone, he uniquely, could exact it. But a more-powerful urge swept over him then, an even darker force than revenge or the desire to kill.

He stood and walked to the front of the cabin. He opened one storage compartment after another until he found what he thought might be there. A line of liquor bottles crowded a low shelf. He scanned it then lifted a half-empty bottle of Jack Daniel's. He unscrewed the cap, then raised the bottle to his lips, taking a tremendous gulp before removing the bottle from his lips.

"Sir," said one of the copilots, poking his head out from the cabin after hearing the opening and closing of cabinet doors. "Mr. Calibrisi wants to talk to you."

Dewey put the bottle back to his lips and took a smaller, more-refined slug this time, perhaps self-conscious about what he looked like in front of the Special Operations Group pilot, though, of course precisely the opposite phenomenon occurred; the image of Dewey was already engraved in the man's mind by the swaying, by the large bottle gripped in his hands, by the look of madness on Dewey's face.

"Tell him I'm busy," said Dewey.

"He wants us to take you up to Andrews."

"No," Dewey said, shaking his head. "Like I told you, first airport after you get into the U.S."

29

IN THE AIR

The U.S. Treasury Department–owned Boeing 757 was Wood Uhlrich's favorite perk that came with being secretary of the treasury.

Inside the private stateroom there were three adjoining rooms; a small but comfortable sitting area with a pair of leather couches and two chairs along with a flat-screen plasma television; a large bedroom with a king-size bed that sat beneath a line of windows; and a bathroom, inside of which was a marble-tiled shower. The suite looked like something out of the St. Regis Hotel.

As the plane cruised high above the Atlantic Ocean, Uhlrich sat on the bed, reading *The Wall Street Journal*. After an hour or so, he got up, put his shoes on, walked through the living room, then opened the door and glanced around.

He walked to a conference table at the front of the cabin. He glanced toward the galley kitchen and made eye contact with a woman in a white uniform.

"Coffee," he said, "and two Advils. Thanks, Margaret."

"Yes, Mr. Secretary."

Uhlrich sat down at the table.

"What do we have, guys?"

"I'm not a guy," said one of the two people seated at the table, a pretty woman who smiled as she said it. Beatrix Packard was deputy secretary of the treasury.

Uhlrich laughed as he took a seat next to Packard, across from the only other treasury official on the trip, Lance Rapala, undersecretary of the treasury for international affairs.

Rapala, a former member of Congress, was a seasoned treasury official. Rapala was in his early seventies but still had a thick mane of black hair, aided no doubt by some product of American chemical innovation.

Packard was even higher on the treasury totem than Rapala. Packard, a former managing director at the legendary Boston private equity firm Mustang, was charged with managing the roughly one-trillion-dollar annual treasury-bond-sale effort, a linchpin in the creation of liquidity not only for the U.S. government but the American economy. It was Packard's job to make sure money kept floating within the multilayered channels and back alleyways of the official U.S. economy, a feat that was accomplished via a tricky, mediated dance involving bond sales to foreign governments and corporations and a near-constant arm-wrestling match with the Federal Reserve.

If Packard had one of the most stressful jobs in government, she didn't show it.

"You're starting to sound like my daughter, Trix."

"You're starting to sound like my dad, Wood."

"I wish I was your dad," said Uhlrich. "Retired . . . living in Florida."

"Eating soft food, bored out of your mind."

"Exactly."

"You don't like twisting arms, Wood?" asked Rapala.

"No," said Uhlrich. "I'm getting tired of it. So who am I meeting in Hong Kong?"

"Zhu," said Rapala. "I set up a one-on-one meeting. He knows the subject matter."

"What do we want?"

"England and Germany have each agreed to pick up fifty billion," said Packard. "That means we need China to take the other four hundred billion."

"That's it?"

"No," said Packard. "By year's end, we'll need to put another trillion out there. You should probably mention that to Mr. Zhu."

Uhlrich watched as the attendant delivered his coffee and Advils. He popped the Advils into his mouth and followed it with a swig of coffee.

"Eight months ago, it was difficult to place a quarter billion dollars worth of bonds," said Uhlrich. "Since that time, debt levels across the EU have shot up. Everyone is asking Germany for help; same with Britain. The entire continent is in a recession. So where is this money going to come from, Trix?"

"That's why we're flying to Hong Kong, Mr. Secretary. China is our only option."

Uhlrich leaned back.

"Have you spoken to Zhu?" asked Rapala.

"No," said Packard, looking at Rapala, then Uhlrich. "I don't need to. China will buy the bonds. I'm not worried."

"You better hope so," said Uhlrich. "What's the backup plan?"

Packard shifted in her chair.

"What do you mean, sir?"

"China's always been the backup plan," said Uhlrich. "Now, they are the plan. Which means we don't have a backup plan, do we?"

"No, sir, we don't," said Packard. "We need China to buy the bonds. America's dirty little secret, sir."

30

BIRCH HILL
McLEAN, VIRGINIA

Calibrisi was eating dinner at his home in McLean when his cell rang. He glanced at his wife, Vivian, who smiled understandingly.

"Yeah," he said, putting the phone to his ear.

"CIA Control, sir. I've got Steve Owen patched in from CIA one-two-alpha."

Calibrisi looked at Vivian.

"Do you want me to leave?" she mouthed.

Calibrisi shook his head no.

"Hi, Steve."

"He's refusing to talk, Hector. He's also drinking."

"Where does he want to be dropped?

"First airport inside U.S. territory. I thought I'd give you a chance to influence that decision. Where do you want us to leave him?"

Calibrisi was silent, thinking quickly about what assets he had in the southeastern United States. Technically, he wasn't supposed to have any. But the last thing he wanted to do was drag in the FBI. This one was personal. He knew Dewey was likely headed for a tailspin, and he wanted to be there to catch him when he fell. He could have simply ordered Owen to fly him back to Andrews, but that would've been even worse. Dewey would resent him for a long, long time if he pulled a stunt like that.

"Miami," said Calibrisi. "Drop him in Miami. Thanks, Steve."

"No problem, sir."

Calibrisi waited for Owen to drop off, then spoke to the CIA switchboard.

"Control," said Calibrisi into the phone. "Get me Katie Foxx."

31

The CIA jet landed at Opa-locka Executive Airport on the outskirts of Miami. He wasn't quite drunk, but he was well on his way. For the last hour of the trip, Dewey swigged from the bottle of whiskey, staring out the window, saying nothing, trying to push all thoughts from his mind.

In truth, Dewey was still lucid enough to understand where he was and why he was there. He'd poured enough whiskey down his throat over the years to understand what his limits were. He knew they all thought he was inconsolable, perhaps even suicidal, but he wasn't. He was angry. The last thing he felt like doing was getting the third degree by a brigade of CIA analysts. Actually, strike that. The last thing, the truly last thing he wanted to do, was to listen to people he barely knew express their condolences. He wanted solitude. He wanted to figure out what would come next. More than anything, he wanted revenge.

At the airport gift shop, where he'd stopped to buy a pack of Marlboros, Dewey caught the sight of Chip Bronkelman, the Boston billionaire who had offered him a job running security for his hedge fund. Bronkelman's round, pudgy, friendly face smiled out from the cover of *Forbes*. Jessica had been the one to set up the job with Bronkelman. It would have paid more than a million dollars a year. Still, Dewey had turned it down. Now, as he looked at the cover of the magazine, his mind played a cruel trick on him. If he'd taken the job, he wouldn't have been able to accompany Jessica to Argentina. Whoever had targeted him for assassination wouldn't have tracked him to Estancia el Colibri. If he'd taken the job with Chip Bronkelman, Jessica would still be alive.

He climbed into a cab outside the airport, asking to be taken to a hotel.

"What hotel?" asked the cabbie.

"I don't care," said Dewey. "Any hotel."

"Nice? Expensive? Economy? You want fleas and bedbugs, or caviar and champagne?"

Dewey made out the man's eyes in the rearview mirror.

"Just take me to a fucking hotel."

The cab lurched forward.

"There are more than two hundred hotels in Miami," said the cabbie.

"Well, then you have a lot of choices, don't you?"

"Bars," said the cabbie. "I have a feeling you want to be near some bars."

Dewey sat back, a slight grin spread across his face at the cabbie, but he said nothing.

"What brings you to Miami?" asked the cabbie.

"None of your fucking business," said Dewey, looking at him with bloodshot eyes in the rearview mirror.

"All right, I'll shut up."

Fifteen minutes later, the cab pulled into the Delano Hotel, stopping as a valet grabbed the back door of the cab and opened it.

"The Delano," said the cabbie, grinning. "Great place for assholes like you."

Dewey did a double take as he reached into his pocket for some cash.

"Did you just call me an asshole?"

"You weren't going to tip me anyway."

The fare was thirty dollars and Dewey threw down an extra twenty.

"What's that for?" asked the cabbie.

"For having a set of balls, unlike most people."

Dewey shut the door and went inside. It was an old hotel but mod-

144

ern, having been redesigned and decorated with a meticulous array of uncomfortable-looking modern furniture, strange art, and odd photographs.

"Bonjour," said a pompadoured greeter in a white button-down shirt. "Welcome to the Delano. Consider this your home away from home."

Dewey did a U-turn. He walked down the block to a plainer-looking hotel, the National. There was no greeter, and he walked to the front desk. He paid in cash for three nights and registered under the name Tom Smith.

The room was on the tenth floor, overlooking South Beach. He looked at the clock by the bed. It was 6:00 P.M. He stripped down to his underwear, opened up the door to the small balcony, then ordered a steak from room service. He took a can of beer from the minibar and went out on the balcony. He sat down in one of the chaises and smoked a cigarette as the sky over South Beach turned purple with the coming sunset. The beach below was less crowded than he would have thought. He sat staring at the water and the beach, purging his mind of any sort of semblance of thoughts, until his dinner arrived.

After dinner, he went to the pocket of his jeans and removed the finger. He went into the bathroom and inspected it under the light. The finger was nearly black now, beginning to rot. He examined the fingerprint lines. Who would want him dead? Hector was right: maybe it was Iran. The dead man? Perhaps a mercenary. But who were the other two men?

He went to the minibar and removed a small bottle of Jack Daniel's. He chugged it down, then went to the full-length mirror. He stared into his own eyes.

When Holly died, part of him died with her. Holly had been the only love Dewey had ever known. His first love. He didn't know anything else, and it was pure. Losing her had been devastating. It had taken Dewey more than a decade to will the thought of her out of his head, ten long years of the hardest labor he'd ever experienced just to get over her. Dewey had found the most punishing work imaginable, as a roughneck on a succession of oil platforms, hundreds of miles offshore, first in the bitter winters of northern Europe, then in the miserable heat off the coast of South America. It had taken the punishing hell of hard labor to restore himself.

Jessica was different. He hadn't been expecting it. She understood him, challenged him, accepted him. He'd grown to know her, then love her. They'd talked about different places to settle down. Jessica liked Portland, Maine, close enough to Castine for visits but also a city, with great restaurants. A place you could raise a kid. It wasn't too late for that, they both knew. But there would probably be time enough for only one. Would it be a boy or a girl? They talked about names. For a girl, they liked the name Summer. For a boy, Hobey, after Dewey's brother.

Now it was gone. It was destroyed. And the memories were like ashes in his mouth. They reminded Dewey that he was different. They fed his innermost fear, that he wasn't meant to be happy, that he'd been chosen somehow to be tested in the cruelest of ways.

He stared at his reflection in the mirror.

"She was innocent," Dewey said aloud, to no one.

Dewey swung his right fist against the mirror. He struck it once, but nothing happened. The next time, he swung harder. The mirror cracked, a spiderweb emanating out from the center of the glass, where he'd hit it. He looked at his fist. The knuckles were bloody where the skin had just been torn off. He punched again, harder this time. He felt glass enter his skin, then watched as a few pieces fell to the floor and shattered. He swung yet again, harder this time. The spiderweb disappeared as the wall of glass flashed silver, then cascaded to the floor at his feet, hundreds of shards of glass shattering around him.

He walked into the center of the bedroom, pulling pieces of glass from between the knuckles of his right fist. He got down on his knees, then put his hands down. He did a push-up, then another, and soon was moving up and down, up and down, up and down, his arms burning, sweat pouring off his chest and head.

Walk away, he thought. *Leave it behind.*

After fifty push-ups, he felt like throwing up. Blood dripped from his right fist onto the floor. He kept going. At a hundred push-ups, he did throw up, whiskey mostly. It poured from his mouth as he kept moving up and down. His arms burned like they were on fire.

He was back there, at the edge of it all, back where it began, in

146

Ranger school, that long winter in Georgia. Nothing would ever be harder than Delta, but that first time, that pain that they drove you to, that first time only occurs once, and for Dewey it was Rangers. He threw up so many times that first week of Ranger school that he lost count. He got so used to it that he came to understand that beyond the throw-up, beyond the wall of pain that paralyzed you, came the other pain, the one that was from God, the one that told you that you alone could get to that point, you alone could bear it, you alone were forged in steel strong enough to endure it.

Blood and vomit covered the floor now, and tears of pain dripped from his eyes as he drove himself further, first 130, then, at some point, 200 push-ups.

Dewey needed to go back to that time and place now. He needed to go back and find that inner steel he knew existed, the steel he would need to survive Jessica's death. The steel he would stab into the heart of those who'd taken her.

He lost count sometime after 220 push-ups, passing out on the floor, lying in a pool of his own sweat, vomit, tears, and blood. He curled up into a fetal position, sobbing, and fell into a deep sleep.

32

The phone started ringing precisely at midnight.

The only woman in the small Recoleta apartment was in bed. Francita Marti, a frail woman of eighty-four, let it ring for more than a minute. After that, she realized whoever it was wasn't going away. It required nearly another minute to get out of bed, with her arthritis.

"Yes," she said in a soft but annoyed voice. "Who is it? If this is one of those calls—"

"Good evening," came the voice. It sounded distorted and loud, as if the man on the other end had a disability. She could not have known he was using a device to cloak his voice.

"Who is this?"

"It's about your son."

The woman became alert. She reached for the lamp next to the phone and turned it on. She found a pad and pen to write with. It didn't happen often, but in matters having to do with her son, she knew to listen and to obey. After all, he was the top law-enforcement officer in all of Argentina.

"What about him? What time is it?"

"You must reach him immediately," said the voice. "Tell him to call his friend Juan, in Mexico City."

33

President Dellenbaugh stared out at a particularly bright red rose blooming at the edge of the Rose Garden, a few drops of dew clinging to petals that looked as if they'd been painted by Georgia O'Keeffe.

It was 6:15 A.M. and Dellenbaugh had been awake since four. He'd gone for a run on the treadmill in the private residence, trying to clear his mind, but he'd quit after only two miles.

Dellenbaugh turned and went back to his desk. For the third time, he attempted to read the front-page story, right-hand column, above the fold in *The New York Times*, announcing Jessica's death.

U.S. NATIONAL SECURITY ADVISOR
TANZER KILLED IN ARGENTINA

(*Córdoba, Argentina*)—Jessica Tanzer, America's top national security official, was killed yesterday while vacationing in Argentina. According to sources, Tanzer, 37, was shot to death at a remote ranch near the Andes . . .

Dellenbaugh had been president for only four months. Other than bringing in his own communications director, he hadn't made any changes to the senior staff at the White House or any of the agencies.

Starting from scratch, he wouldn't have necessarily selected the exact same group, but he'd decided that, midterm, he wasn't going to change a thing.

Some cabinet members, of course, had been more helpful than others. But no one had done more for Dellenbaugh than Jessica.

In her no-nonsense, smiling, confident way, she'd cut through the tangled, subterranean web of interlocking moving parts that was America's national security infrastructure. She'd saved him time, so much time, by arguing, forcefully at times, when he was wrong.

Now she was gone.

He took the paper and held it up in front of him. He stared at the large color photo of Jessica that was spread across three columns, above the fold. The photo showed Jessica in the White House Briefing Room, conducting a press conference. She was wearing an elegant Burberry sleeveless dress, tan plaid, a bright string of pearls around her neck. Her auburn hair was brushed neatly back, parted in the middle, with her trademark bangs.

Dellenbaugh shut his eyes and tried to concentrate on not feeling overwhelmed by the loss, not to mention by the questions of who did it and why. He knew the implications were huge and that the country and the world—friend and foe alike—were now looking at the United States, and at him in particular, to see how Jessica's death would be avenged.

The other question that ate at him: Who the hell would he get to fill Jessica's shoes? The value of a president's national security advisor was directly correlated to his or her willingness to be brutally honest, to be unafraid to hit the boss between the eyes with a proverbial two-by-four. The only other individual Dellenbaugh trusted to do this was Hector Calibrisi, but Dellenbaugh needed him across the river at Langley.

Dellenbaugh pushed his chair away. He got down on his knees, behind the desk. He leaned forward and folded his hands together in front of his face. He shut his eyes. And for the second time that morning, he prayed for Jessica.

When finally he opened his eyes, the door to the Oval Office was open. Hector Calibrisi was standing in the door.

"Mr. President," said Calibrisi, "I apologize. Cecily wasn't here—"

"Come in," said Dellenbaugh, standing up, pointing at one of the tan chesterfield sofas in the center of the Oval Office.

Dellenbaugh and Calibrisi sat down across from one another. They shared a long, pregnant moment of silence.

"Time to get back on the horse?"

"Something like that," said Calibrisi.

"From the *Times* article, it appears someone inside AFP is talking."

"It's unavoidable, Mr. President. The news is out. I don't think it matters, though. This is not a Poirot mystery."

"What do you mean?"

"We found a body."

"When?"

"An hour ago. Lying on a hill, near a sniper nest."

Calibrisi popped the latches of his briefcase. He removed a stack of photos. They showed a corpse, in various positions; prostrate on the ground, from the back, close-ups. The anterior of the man's head was badly decomposed. Black and dark maroon from dried blood surrounded a crater at the back of the skull. The next photo showed what was left of the front of the man's face, mostly gone now.

"He looks Asian," said Dellenbaugh. "What does it mean?"

"We don't know yet. My guess is, they were after Dewey. Perhaps Iran or someone affiliated with the Fortunas. The autopsy is happening as we speak. We need to know who this guy is before we draw any conclusions."

"Where's Dewey?" asked the president.

"He was dropped off in Miami last night."

Dellenbaugh nodded.

"I sent some people down there to find him. From what the pilots say, he's not doing well."

"Can you blame him?"

"No," said Calibrisi. "I know how I feel right now, and I can't even imagine what he's going through."

"Did we bring the body back here for the autopsy?"

Calibrisi shifted uncomfortably in his seat.

"No, sir. AFP has jurisdiction."

"Can they be trusted? Should I call President Salazar?"

"I don't trust anyone," said Calibrisi, "certainly not the Argentinians. That said, we're getting complete access to the investigation. They've allowed us to have our forensics team at all stages of the investigation. We have guys in on the autopsy. I don't trust them, but I also don't see any reason for them to fuck around. And if they try to fuck around, we'll know immediately."

"What if Jessica was the target?" asked Dellenbaugh.

Calibrisi sat back, joining his fingers behind his head.

"First of all, regardless of whether they were after Dewey or Jessica, the fact is, our national security advisor was murdered. There needs to be payback. It needs to be significant. Significant enough to let the world understand that America will not tolerate the assassination of our leaders. In my opinion, once we determine who did this, we have two choices. We can either make all of the evidence public, bring it to the United Nations, the media, et cetera, and let justice take its course. Or, we can take it off balance sheet."

"Well, as far as I'm concerned, you do whatever the hell you want," said Dellenbaugh, his voice inflecting. "America has to punch back hard. Hell, give me a gun and I'll go do it."

"That shouldn't be necessary, Mr. President," said Calibrisi. "But the offer is appreciated."

34

Calibrisi sat alone in his office, reading an intelligence report from his Moscow chief of station. But try as he might, he couldn't concentrate.

He reached for a different file and stared for the umpteenth time at photos of Jessica, dead on the floor of the ranch bedroom. It hurt to look at them, but then he would return to the photos. Calibrisi felt like he was staring at a puzzle.

Usually, when he was stuck on something that didn't feel right, something he couldn't figure out, he called Jessica. But now he was alone. His mind felt disheveled and unorganized. He was exhausted.

There was a knock on his door.

"Derek Chalmers called twice," his assistant, Missy, said, referring to the head of British intelligence. "He said it's very important."

"You mind getting me a coffee?"

"Sure."

Calibrisi hit a speed-dial button on his phone.

"Hi, Hector," came the proper British accent of Chalmers, head of MI6. "What took you so long?"

"Sorry. I just got your messages."

"I heard what happened," said Chalmers. "I'm very sorry. You have my thoughts and prayers."

"Thank you."

"I didn't think it would happen so soon," said Chalmers. "We should have known. I blame myself."

"Should've known what?" asked Calibrisi.

"Fao Bhang," said Chalmers. "Obviously, he was behind this. We've drawn him out, just as we wanted. Unfortunately, his response was much more lethal than we anticipated."

"Forgive me, Derek, it's been a long day. What the hell are you talking about?"

"Take me off speaker," said Chalmers.

Calibrisi picked up the handset.

"Jessica was assassinated by Fao Bhang," said Chalmers, his voice sharp with impatience. "It's clear. Our little package to Li's granddaughter had an impact, just as we intended it to. This was revenge for Dillman. He wanted Dewey Andreas dead."

A feeling of uneasiness came over Calibrisi. Had their operation resulted in Jessica's death? There was no way. He pushed aside the thought. But a pang of guilt washed over him. The thought that he might have inadvertently done something that led to her death was too terrible to even contemplate.

"We don't have anything linking Beijing to this," Calibrisi said. "Dewey Andreas has a lot of enemies. China isn't one of them. What evidence do you have?"

"Our sources inside Beijing say the premier's granddaughter has been under medical care for three days now, and Li is extremely angry at Bhang. In addition, we're seeing heightened activity out of the clandestine service. Ming-húa has canceled all vacation for his agents across the Eurasian theater. He's exercised the retainers on an army of mercenaries they keep at the ready. Beijing is preparing for something."

Calibrisi stared at the photos of Jessica.

"Are you there, Hector?" asked Chalmers. "Look, I know this is a hard time for you, but you need to keep your head. Jessica was, tragically, collateral damage in a larger war. It's terrible. But this is our opening. We can't lose sight of the objective. Bhang has popped his head out of the hole. We need to figure out how to chop it off. And we have to be careful. As Jessica's death demonstrates, Bhang doesn't play nice."

Calibrisi's door opened and Missy entered, placing a coffee down on his desk.

"Katie Foxx is on hold," she whispered. "They found Dewey."

"Derek, I have to call you back," said Calibrisi.

35

Pascal clicked send. His intended recipient, Raul, had yet to return even one of his texts. Not to mention the phone calls. Pascal had left so many voice mails on Raul's cell phone that eventually the automated voice of a female came on and told him the mailbox was full.

With each passing minute, Pascal became more vulnerable. Pascal had information, valuable information. It was China who was behind Jessica Tanzer's death. Properly leveraged, that information was worth a great deal. But that knowledge could also be his death knell.

Pascal walked to the window. In the distance, he could see the lights of downtown Lima. The motel room he stood in was disgusting. It reeked of old cigarettes, sex with prostitutes who wore cheap perfume, johns who sprayed on too much cologne, and room deodorizer. The bed was small. He'd slept most of the night on the filthy carpet because he could feel the springs pressing into his back as he'd tried to sleep. Sure, he could have stayed at the Four Seasons, but that's what Ming-húa would be expecting. Ming-húa knew Pascal had expensive tastes, and that's the first place he'd think to look for him. Pascal knew he needed to lay low.

Pascal had begun the slow, ineluctable realization that he had to run. Through the evening, he tried to convince himself that he could reach out to Beijing, to Ming-húa, and appeal to them to trust him.

But it was a naïve illusion. He had to run. He had more than forty million dollars squirreled away, and he could afford to go wherever he wanted.

He heard the chime from his computer.

It was from Raul. Finally.

Help. Need to talk

Pascal double-clicked the chat icon on his laptop. A small video box popped up.

Where are you

Pascal waited for the photo to sharpen. He didn't get a response from Raul. He typed in again.

WHERE ARE YOU

Finally, letters appeared:

Beijing

Suddenly, the video focused and became lighter. It was a live feed showing a hallway. Someone was holding a camera as they walked. Pascal stared into the screen. A door appeared, the number 6 on it.

"Fuck," he said to himself, staring at the video.

Pascal reached for his pack of cigarettes. Behind him, he suddenly heard the sound of the door being opened.

"Maid," came a female voice from behind him.

"Stay out," he barked.

Pascal's eye moved from the computer screen to a red plastic room key on the desk. A gold 6 was etched into the plastic.

In the same moment that the video feed showed a black boot kicking a door, the motel-room door behind him exploded violently, kicked in from the outside.

Turning, Pascal saw a woman. She was Chinese, with a camera on her forehead, and tight black shirt and pants. She clutched a PP-19 Bizon submachine gun, suppressor jutting from the muzzle.

Pascal charged the assassin, but she triggered the weapon. A spray of bullets sliced horizontally across his torso, stopping his forward progress, then catapulting Pascal backward. The assassin stepped forward, stood above him, then watched as Pascal's eyes rolled back in his head. She sprayed another suppressed hail of slugs down at his head, grabbed his laptop, then turned and walked quickly out of the room, leaving the door open and Pascal's cigarette burning on the carpet next to his destroyed skull.

36

Colonel Arman Marti closed the door to his temporary office on the third and top floor of AFP's regional headquarters. The room was dark. He did not turn on the lights. Instead, he groped through the large bottom drawer of his desk, feeling for a pair of night-vision goggles. He pulled them out, then flipped on the power button.

On the desk in front of him was a small manila envelope.

It was 3:00 A.M.

It had been four hours since he'd left Charlie Couture, the CIA chief of station, at the hotel bar, where the entire team was staked out for the duration of the investigation into Jessica Tanzer's death.

Couture was like a bulldog, and Marti was sick of him. The young American clung to Marti like a spider monkey. Marti knew full well he was just obeying orders from his bosses at Langley, but it was grating nonetheless.

Marti knew the CIA didn't trust him, or anyone at AFP, for that matter. Couture and his team from the CIA, as well as an even larger contingent from the FBI, had demanded access to all aspects of the investigation and all phases of the autopsy, as well as deliberations by the AFP forensics team afterward. It was, Marti thought, overkill. As far as he was concerned, he wished AFP *didn't* have jurisdiction over the death of Jessica Tanzer. It was turning out to be a grade-A pain in the ass, and he would be happy when it was over.

But then, just when he thought it couldn't get worse, it did.

The phone call had come to his eighty-four-year-old mother in Buenos Aires. In his typical Machiavellian way, Ming-húa had called Marti's mother, knowing most other avenues to Marti were likely being monitored by the National Security Agency and the CIA. Ming-húa had asked Marti's mother, politely, to call his friend Juan in Mexico City. In the precise code Ming-húa had forced Marti to memorize many years ago, Juan meant Ming-húa, and Mexico City meant "extremely urgent."

Over the years, China had paid Marti more than a million dollars to do nothing more than keep Beijing apprised of activities in Argentina. For the most part, Marti often wondered if MSS even cared about what happened in Argentina. Marti knew he was just another investment, sprinkled across the country and the world by Fao Bhang—an investment that might never get cashed in.

But when his frail, aging mother Francita muttered the words "Mexico City," Marti knew the time had come to pay the piper.

Of course, Marti could say no. But Marti didn't want to find out what happened to people who said no to Ming-húa or, God forbid, Fao Bhang. Ming-húa had called his mother. The message was clear. It wouldn't just be Marti who paid the price.

After leaving the Sheraton, Marti had driven to Córdoba airport. There, taped to the underside of the wing of an aging Cessna turbo-prop with peeling paint, he'd removed a small tan envelope.

Now at his desk in the darkness he removed its contents. Inside were two sheets of thick paper, almost like cardboard, each showing ten separate squares, each of the squares with dark, inky fingerprints.

The typeface at the top of the page showed the AFP crime-scene investigator's specific logo, dark orange font with slightly raised, embossed lettering, a security precaution.

Marti left his office. He skulked down the hall. Removing a key from his pocket, he unlocked a door, went inside, then closed the door behind him. He went to the desk of AFP's lead investigator, Sandoval. Marti searched through three neat piles of folders. He found the folder that held the dead Chinese agent's prints. He removed a piece of thick paper and replaced it with a duplicate, then put the folder back. He folded the original and stuffed it in his back pocket.

Marti moved to Couture's desk. The American's files were stacked on the desk. He flipped through the thick pile. He found the original sheets of prints, replaced it with the new one, then put it back on Couture's desk.

Half an hour later, Marti sat on the brown sofa in his hotel room. He opened a beer from the refrigerator, then lit a cigarette. After lighting the end of the cigarette, he put the match to the corners of the two sheets of fingerprints. He watched as the true identity of the dead Chinese agent vanished up in smoke.

37

MIAMI

It was the sound of the hotel housekeepers that awoke Dewey.

"Housekeeping," called a voice through the door.

Dewey opened his eyes, looking in front of him, trying to remember where he was. Pain kicked the back of his skull.

"Go away," he said, without moving.

"Sir, what time would you like us to come back?"

"Fuck off," said Dewey.

He fell back asleep.

How many hours later it was, he didn't know, but it was knocking at the door that stirred him again.

"Fuck off," he said, barely above a whisper.

He heard the sound of the lock turning. The door pushed in and stopped on the chain. Then came a kick. The chain ripped from the wall as the door slammed open.

From the ground, all Dewey could make out was a blur. A tall green hazy figure. The alcohol was still teeming in his system. He barely moved. Then he felt his stomach tightening. He fought against another wave of nausea.

His eyes began to focus and he saw the man's feet: he had on flip-flops. His eyes moved up. He wore madras shorts and a green T-shirt that read I'D RATHER BE WATERBOARDING. He had long brown hair, past his shoulders.

Dewey looked behind the man, suddenly noticing a woman stepping slowly into the room. She had short blond hair, wore white jeans, and a blue T-shirt.

"Get up, grampa," said the man in the green T-shirt, and Dewey recognized the voice.

"Rob?" Dewey whispered.

Tacoma helped him up, putting his arm under his shoulder and lifting him.

"Fuck, you're a goddamn load, Andreas," said Tacoma, struggling. "You're getting fat, old man."

"Fuck you," said Dewey. "It's all muscle."

"Yeah, right."

Katie and Rob looked around the bedroom. It was a mess of broken glass and vomit.

"I wasn't expecting company."

"It's okay," Katie said, smiling. She walked over to Dewey and gave him a hug. She stepped back and looked up at him.

"How are you doing?" Katie asked.

"Not too good."

"I'm sorry about Jessica," she said.

"Me too."

Dewey walked to the minibar and removed two small bottles of Jack Daniel's from the refrigerator as Katie and Tacoma watched, then glanced at each other. He unscrewed the caps, then stuck the ends of both bottles in his mouth and chugged them down in one gulp. He felt the warmth immediately, and the pain in the back of his head went away.

Dewey went to the bathroom and splashed cold water on his face. He looked into the mirror. He'd been there before. Staring into the eyes of a dead man.

He inspected his mauled right fist. The knuckles were worse than he remembered, the skin missing. He saw a sparkle near the knuckle of the index finger. He reached down and yanked a thin, inch-long piece of mirror that had slid into the skin between the knuckles, easing it painfully out. Blood trickled from the hole, which he unconsciously put to his mouth to try to stop.

Hector had sent Katie and Rob, Dewey knew. Tacoma, a former SEAL, and Katie, who had been number-two inside CIA Special Operations Group, were about the closest friends Dewey had right now, other than Hector. Part of him appreciated the gesture from Hector. But Dewey knew he didn't want to get them involved in what he was about to do.

He dried his face and looked one last time at himself in the mirror.

You need to risk it all, Dewey. To strike back at the one who wants to kill you, you need to put everything you have at risk. In order to fight, you must be willing to be hit. In order to kill, you must be willing to be killed.

Back in the bedroom, Katie was stuffing his belongings into his leather bag.

"What are you doing?" Dewey asked.

"Packing your stuff. We're going back to D.C."

"There's no 'we,' Katie. There's me. Me and the motherfuckers who did this. Remember Iran? You didn't want to take unnecessary risks? You didn't want to die? Remember all that?"

Dewey's face was flushing red. Several moments of awkward silence passed.

"Hector exercised our retainer," said Katie icily. "Whether you like it or not, we're going to be working on this."

"This is not going to be some sort of Langley shit show," said Dewey.

"What's that supposed to mean?"

"No one is going on trial at The Hague or being flown to Gitmo," said Dewey. "Whoever did this is dead. Whoever helped is dead. This isn't about justice."

Katie glanced at Tacoma, then nodded.

"We're on the same page," she said.

Thirty minutes later, they were airborne. The three sat around a small conference table as the black CIA Citation X flew north.

"Someone tracked you to a remote ranch in Argentina," said Katie. "That fact alone indicates a level of organization that could only be a foreign intelligence agency. They did an assessment of the security rotations, then timed the strike around them. They used a sniper, who took a night shot, which, as you know, is much more difficult. That's what we know."

Katie reached into a light blue leather handbag. She pulled out a manila envelope. Inside it were photographs of the corpse, more than twenty in all, from various angles, displaying the crater in the back of his head, and several close-ups of his destroyed face. The fact that he was Asian was obvious. Yet they all knew it was irrelevant. He could have been from anywhere.

Tacoma was looking at his laptop.

"Langley just finished the print runs," he said. "Looks like he popped up at INTERPOL. I'll print them out."

Tacoma walked to the front of the jet. He took the sheets of paper off the printer and returned to the conference table.

The first sheet showed two photos. On the left was a photo of the destroyed skull of the Asian man who'd been found in the field at Estancia el Colibri. On the right was the same man, taken while he was still alive, with a mustache and short black air.

The second sheet was a short INTERPOL dossier:

NAME:	Chiong-il
AKA:	Kwoong, Namkung, Kwon
CIT:	Seoul, South Korea
RES:	Mogadishu, Somalia
DOB:	22/07/69
SERV:	1991–2001
	National Intelligence Service (SK)
CURR:	Security consultant
MISC:	Freelance mercenary working out of eastern Africa. Ties to SSNK (North Korea), Al-Qaeda. Mark X sniper (NIS)

The last sheet displayed what looked like a checkerboard. Two sets of fingerprint blocks were lined up side-by-side, taken from the dead man before and after his death. There were red lines connecting all ten print blocks on the left, the prints taken by AFP, to the ones on the right, from INTERPOL, indicating a perfect match. The AFP logo was stamped across the top of the page.

"The prints match perfectly," said Katie.

"So the question is, who hired Chiong-il?" said Tacoma.

"And why," said Katie.

Dewey sat in silence for several minutes. Finally, he reached into his pocket and pulled out a small, dark object that looked a little bit like a sausage link. It was shriveled, slightly bent, with a long fingernail at one end, dirt beneath the nail, and tendrils of dried scab and skin at the other, with a white nub of a small bone sticking out.

He tossed it onto the conference table.

"Is that what I think it is?" asked Tacoma.

"That depends, Robert," said Dewey.

"On what?"

"On what the fuck you think it is."

"It looks like a finger."

"Then, yes, it is what you think it is."

Katie picked it up.

"That's disgusting," she said, inspecting it. "Care to illuminate us as to who the lucky individual is whose finger you now possess?"

"I don't know," said Dewey. "But I am highly doubtful that it's a South Korean mercenary who lives in Mogadishu named Long Dong Silver or whatever the fuck his name is."

"How did you get this?"

"I cut it off his hand. There should be nine prints on that sheet."

Katie picked up the print blocks, which showed prints from all ten fingers.

"Someone fucked up," she said, smiling.

"AFP is involved," said Tacoma.

"At least in the cover-up," said Katie. "Whoever did this thought they were covering their tracks. They might even think the case is over. That could be useful."

"I'll call Hector," said Tacoma, reaching for the SAT phone. "He can meet us at the farm with a print kit."

38

A gleaming white Mercedes limousine pulled up to the Peninsula Hotel in the Kowloon section of Hong Kong. Treasury Secretary Wood Uhlrich climbed out.

On the second floor of the luxury hotel, Uhlrich walked down a high-ceilinged corridor to a double doorway which was flanked by two armed security guards. He walked past the men and into a vast library with two-story ceilings and huge windows. In the middle of the room, two long sofas in pale yellow leather faced each other. A short, well-dressed man with square, thick-framed glasses, stood up.

"Good afternoon, Governor Zhu," said Uhlrich, crossing the room and shaking Zhu's hand. "It's a pleasure to see you."

"And you, Mr. Secretary. How was your flight?"

"Uneventful," said Uhlrich, sitting across from Zhu. "I appreciate your making the trip from Beijing."

"Tell me why you wanted to see me. I assume it has something to do with the upcoming bond sale?"

"That's correct," said Uhlrich. "Given the size of the issue, I thought it was important for us to get together. I want to head off any questions China might have."

"How big is the issue, Mr. Secretary?"

"Five hundred billion dollars."

Zhu nodded, looking without emotion at Uhlrich.

"The bonds are plain vanilla," said Uhlrich. "Typical terms."

"If the United States Treasury secretary is willing to fly all the way to Hong Kong, I'm assuming the appetite for the paper has not been as avid as you might have wished."

"The People's Bank is the first and, hopefully, only conversation we're having."

"I'm concerned about America's level of indebtedness," said Zhu. "The recession forced Europe to impose fiscal discipline, but in the U.S., your Congress keeps spending money it doesn't have."

"I was a United States senator," said Uhlrich. "I share your concerns. But we'll grow out of our current fiscal dilemma long before these bonds mature."

"According to my figures, our current balances show that the U.S. owes China almost two trillion dollars," said Zhu. "How much of the five hundred billion do you expect us to take?"

"All of it."

"All five hundred?"

"That's right."

Zhu sat back, crossed his legs, and said nothing for at least a dozen seconds. He reached up and brushed his hand back through his hair.

"Will there be more after this, Mr. Secretary?"

"We're going to need another trillion dollars by the end of next year," said Uhlrich. "Above and beyond the current issue."

Zhu nodded.

"I appreciate your visiting us first, Mr. Secretary," said Zhu. "I would feel very bad if you were to have waited and then learned of our disinterest only after exhausting all other avenues."

"What are you saying, Mr. Zhu?"

"I suggest you spend some time in Riyadh," said Zhu. "The Saudis might very well have some appetite for the U.S. bonds, though I highly doubt it will be to a level that meets your needs."

"Both of us know China is our only option."

"But we're not going to buy them," said Zhu. "Do we have the financial capacity? Yes, of course. But for reasons which I shall not be sharing with you this afternoon, we are fully allocated in terms of our exposure to U.S. risk."

"Governor Zhu, do you understand the ramifications if we're unable to sell these treasuries?"

Zhu stared at Uhlrich but remained silent.

"If America can't borrow money, we'll either stop paying foreign interest, or the Fed will start printing money. When inflation comes, it won't just hurt us. The world will go into recession."

"Let me be very clear," said Zhu calmly, leaning toward Uhlrich. "If the United States halts interest payments or in any way materially alters its obligations to China, I will order my treasury to start selling on the free market from our current inventory of U.S. bonds. I will start at par and then move pricing down as fast as possible. My guess is, once my counterparts are aware of what I'm doing, the price will drop precipitously. By my own estimates, we would end up liquidating the entire portfolio at between forty-five and fifty cents on the dollar."

Uhlrich's smile disappeared. It took him less than a second to calculate the implications of Zhu's threat. America would still owe the full amount of each bond, but by selling them for half price, China would in effect destroy the market for U.S. bonds. No one would ever buy another bond, certainly not for a full dollar when they could get the same thing for fifty cents from China.

Zhu stood up.

"Now, Mr. Secretary, I must get back to Beijing," said Zhu, extending his hand. "Thank you once again for making the trip. And best of luck with the sale."

Uhlrich sat silently on the couch. He stared at Zhu's extended hand until Zhu, after not receiving any response, started walking to the door.

"Your message has been delivered," said Uhlrich, standing, an angry look in his eyes. "What the hell do you want?"

Zhu turned. He paused, then walked back across the room to Uhlrich. He was shorter than the American. He stood just inches away from Uhlrich, uncomfortably close. He craned his neck to look up at him.

"Perhaps there is a way for us to reconsider our decision," said Zhu. "I will be in touch."

39

RUMIANA FARM
MIDDLEBURG, VIRGINIA

A set of headlights moved down a long dark gravel driveway. On each side of the simple drive was low white picket fence, behind which lay fields of freshly cut grass.

Katie and Tacoma owned the farm, tucked away in the rolling horse country of Middleburg. It housed their consulting firm, which provided various services to government and private industries alike. Those services tended to be top-secret, clandestine activities, categorized under the broad rubric of security.

Until two years before, both Katie and Tacoma had worked at Langley. Katie was the deputy director of Special Operations Group, running covert paramilitary operations across the globe. Tacoma, a former Navy SEAL, who was recruited by Katie to the CIA, had been her deputy.

Their firm didn't have a Web site, glossy brochures, or a listed phone number. What they did have was the backing of Hector Calibrisi and a reputation for being able to do almost anything, in any country, using its extensive network of former spies, former Special Forces soldiers, and a willingness to bend the rules. But Katie and Tacoma had one overarching rule: they considered themselves proxies for the United States of America. They didn't do anything that was not in the best interests of the United States. Calibrisi usually had them on retainer, often calling on them when the bureaucracy of Langley threatened to slow him down.

In the circle outside the main house, Dewey, Katie, and Tacoma climbed out of Tacoma's orange BMW M5, after a hair-raising drive from Andrews Air Force Base. It was almost midnight. The sky was awash in stars as they crossed the driveway toward the front door.

"Listen for it," said Tacoma, pointing to the sky.

All Dewey could hear was the sound of crickets. A few seconds later, the faint rhythm of a helicopter hit his ears.

"Good ears."

"You're just getting old, Dewey."

"What's with all the insults?" asked Dewey, grumpily. "I'm really not in the mood for kicking your ass, but I will."

"You could try," said Tacoma.

Katie shook her head.

"You two are like children," said Katie. "I should get babysitting pay."

The sound of the chopper grew louder. Flashing lights moved across the sky. The wind picked up as a jet-black Bell 525 descended from the sky and landed on the grass next to the driveway. The door opened and Calibrisi climbed out. He walked toward them carrying a steel briefcase.

"Well, look who it is," Calibrisi yelled, above the din.

Dewey walked toward Calibrisi, putting his hand out, but Calibrisi wrapped his arms around him and hugged him.

"Hi, kid."

"Hi, Hector."

"How you feeling?" asked Calibrisi.

"Okay," said Dewey.

Calibrisi lifted Dewey's hand and inspected his gashed knuckles.

"That doesn't look too bad," said Calibrisi. "Rob told me you beat the shit out of a mirror."

Dewey laughed, then looked at Tacoma.

Katie and Tacoma walked toward the door and went inside.

"Hold up," said Calibrisi.

Dewey stopped and looked at Calibrisi.

"I've always known it's part of this business we're in," said Calibrisi, putting his arm on Dewey's shoulder. "I've had friends killed standing next to me. But I've never felt like this. I can't imagine what you're going through."

Dewey nodded but said nothing.

"If you need someone to talk to—"

"Let's go inside, Hector."

"Okay."

They followed Katie and Tacoma inside. The entrance foyer looked like a weapons room at a large police station. The walls were crowded with gun racks that held a variety of high-powered rifles, assault weapons, submachine guns, and handguns.

They went to the basement, to a large steel door that looked like the door to a bank vault. Tacoma punched a code into the digital lock. The door opened.

Inside was a large windowless basement-level room that housed Katie and Tacoma's computers, communications equipment, and more weapons. The room was enclosed in walls made of thick steel and was accessible only by the iris scanner outside the steel door. Katie and Tacoma were the only people capable of opening it.

The room itself was sprawling, eighty feet long by forty feet wide. It had been built by KBR, in conjunction with a team of electrical engineers from the CIA, and was linked to the CIA's powerful mainframes. The room looked like mission control at Cape Canaveral, with walls of large plasma screens, all of which were dark. Long steel desks were lined with computers. But there was one big difference; unlike NASA, the back of the room had a red felt pool table, a Ping-Pong table, and several leather sofas.

On a table near the wall, Calibrisi opened the steel briefcase. He took out what looked like an oversized iPad with a pair of cords sticking out one end. Tacoma plugged one of the cords into the wall. The other he unfurled and plugged into a server in the middle of the room. Calibrisi turned on the biometric scanner. Six of the plasma screens suddenly came to life, lighting up the room.

Dewey handed Calibrisi the dead man's finger. He took it and pressed it against the green screen. After a few moments, the plasma screens showed large photographs, all of the dead sniper. Two were grainy, in black-and-white. The other three were in color. The center photo showed the man, his face now familiar to them all, with the same thin mustache. He was very much alive. The photo was taken from a distance. He wore sunglasses. He was walking down a busy city street, the word UTRECHT stamped into the upper corner along with a date: 05/2004.

The other photos were both black-and-white. Each was a military photo. The man appeared much younger and was wearing the starched gray uniform of Chinese defense forces.

On the last screen, which the four of them stared at in silence, were the results of the print analysis from the finger Dewey had cut off. The finger belonged to a high-ranking operative in the clandestine paramilitary bureau at China's Ministry of State Security. His name was Hu-Shao.

```
ID:        LING HU-SHAO
DOB:       AUG 8 74
BIR:       CHENGDU, PRC
ED:        TAIPEI MILITARY INSTITUTE
           CLASS OF 1992
LANG:      MANDARIN
           ENGLISH
           ARABIC
           FRENCH
OCC:       OPERATIVE (LTK BLANKET)
           MINISTRY OF STATE SECURITY, PRC
           LEVEL: V1 (WITH SILVER SCROLL)
POS:       CARACAS (CURRENT)
           MADRID (2009-11)
           CAIRO (2007-09)
           BUENOS AIRES (2007)
           NEW YORK CITY (2006-07)
           CAPETOWN (2005-06)
           RIO DE JANEIRO (2004-05)
           BAGHDAD (2004)
           DAMASCUS (2002-04)
           BAHRAIN (2000-02)
```

Calibrisi stared stone-faced at the plasma screen.

He thought back to his conversation with Derek Chalmers. As

173

much as he trusted his counterpart in London, he'd had a difficult time believing China was behind it. Now the truth was irrefutable. It all added up in a single moment, an instant, as if someone somewhere had flipped a switch.

It was China after all. And it was Dewey they were after.

"Why would China want Jessica dead?" asked Katie. "Or Dewey for that matter?"

Calibrisi's mind raced as it all came together, like pieces of a puzzle suddenly falling into place.

By outing Dillman, Dewey had given Chalmers, Fritz Lavine, Menachem Dayan—and Calibrisi—the means by which to go after their shared nemesis, Fao Bhang. It was they who'd upped the ante, without Dewey's permission or knowledge. It was they who, in the interest of trying to get at Bhang, had designed an operation that exposed Dewey and Jessica to reprisal. The ax in the head, the Louis Vuitton trunk, Premier Li's granddaughter—all of it the brainchild of spies who'd failed to see the very simple human beings they had inadvertently placed in the crosshairs of one of the world's most brutal men.

Calibrisi felt a sudden wave of guilt wash over him. He felt faint. He looked over at Dewey, who stood in front of the plasma screen, studying the dead agent's background.

Dewey had done his job. He'd gotten the identity of the mole out of Amit Bhutta. They had returned the favor by starting a lethal blood feud against one of the most powerful and ruthless men in the world, which ultimately led back to Dewey.

As far as Dewey knew, Dillman was to be killed by Kohl Meir, then dropped in a Tel Aviv landfill. Clean and simple. Instead, the brightest minds in Western intelligence had used Dillman, just as they used Dewey, and now Jessica. It was their fault. By not seeing it ahead of time, it was his fault.

Calibrisi felt sick to his stomach. A sharp pain stabbed his chest. He put his hand out on the table to steady himself.

Dewey turned and looked at him.

"You okay, chief?" he asked.

Calibrisi knew that if he told Dewey the truth, Dewey would have every justification in the world to kill him, right then and there. He

174

was the one who got Jessica murdered. But what was even worse, Calibrisi knew, was the fact that Dewey wouldn't blame Calibrisi or Chalmers or Menachem Dayan. He'd blame himself.

It didn't matter any longer. He had to come clean. Dewey deserved to know.

"It was my fault," Calibrisi whispered. "I'm the one who got her killed."

"What are you talking about?"

"Dillman."

"Who?"

"The Israeli."

"He's dead," said Dewey.

"We used the body. We used it to launch an operation inside China."

Dewey stared at Calibrisi.

"You what?" he asked, incredulous, his anger suddenly flashing.

"We used the corpse to expose Fao Bhang. To bring him out of hiding so we could kill him."

Dewey lurched at Calibrisi, grabbing him by the throat and slamming him hard against the wall.

"*He was supposed to be killed, then buried!*" screamed Dewey, clutching Calibrisi's throat and holding him against the wall. "*You arrogant son of a bitch!*"

Dewey felt nothing but anger and betrayal as he stared into Calibrisi's eyes and listened to him cough. He heard the click of a round being chambered, next to his head.

"Let him go," said Tacoma, holding a SIG SAUER P226, now trained at the side of Dewey's head.

Dewey waited a moment longer, then let Calibrisi drop. He stared for a moment longer at him, then turned and walked to the door.

"Where are you going?" asked Katie.

Dewey didn't answer. At the door, he turned. He had a confused look as he stared across the room at Calibrisi.

"I'm sorry, Hector," he said.

He walked through the steel door. Katie went to follow him, but he shut the door before she could get to it. When she tried to open it, she couldn't.

"Goddamn it," she said.

"What?"

She slammed her fist against the door.

"He locked it. It's on a timer. We won't be able to get out for five minutes."

Five minutes later, the bolts on the vault door made a loud clicking noise and it swung slowly open.

Katie, Tacoma, and Calibrisi ran down the basement hallway, then climbed the stairs. Tacoma sprinted through the kitchen to the entrance foyer, then ran through the open front door. In the distance, two headlights flickered as a car sped down the driveway, out of sight. Tacoma turned around and ran back inside.

"Keys, Hector," shouted Tacoma as he ran toward the front door.

Calibrisi looked frantically around the kitchen table, where he'd left them. They were gone.

Calibrisi walked to the door as Tacoma sprinted in. Tacoma stopped, then looked at Calibrisi and Katie behind him, all of them realizing at approximately the same time that Dewey had left, had taken Tacoma's car along with Calibrisi's keys and God knows what else.

Calibrisi pulled out his cell phone.

"The president?" asked Katie.

"No, that's my second call," said Calibrisi, a flash of anger appearing on his normally placid face. He put the phone against his ear. "Control, get me Couture. He's in Argentina."

As he waited, Calibrisi looked at Katie.

"It's time to start hitting back."

40

Couture stood in his Córdoba hotel room, staring out the window, phone against his ear.

"Yeah, I'll handle it, Hector," he said, anger sharpening his eyes. "I know precisely who the fuck did it."

He hung up the phone.

Charlie Couture wasn't a very complicated individual. Physically, what you saw was what you got—five feet nine inches of raw muscle and bad attitude, weighing in at precisely two hundred pounds. As for Couture's demeanor, it was a cross between a pit bull and a wolverine. Like many CIA paramilitary, he didn't have many friends. He'd risen not because of his political skills but because of his *lack* of political skills. He was reliable, a workhorse, sent to places that were on the cusp of anarchy, where political turbulence was just beginning to boil up and threaten America. Once there, Couture had a relatively straightforward job, and it wasn't diplomacy.

Buenos Aires was a plum assignment. There was occasional unrest and a strong strain of remnant communist anti-Americanism, but for the most part the country was stable. But Buenos Aires wasn't about Argentina. It was about the rest of South America, particularly Bolivia, Peru, and Brazil. These were trouble spots.

Couture speed-dialed Timms, his lead investigator in Córdoba.

"We're leaving," said Couture into his cell phone. "Have everyone pack up their shit and be downstairs in five minutes."

Couture stuffed his green nylon duffel bag with all of his belongings. He walked out of his hotel room, leaving the door wide open. He walked quickly down the hall, carrying his duffel bag, and entered the fire stairs. He climbed from the fourth floor to the ninth floor, two steps at a time. He walked down the hallway until he came to room 955. He knocked loudly on the door.

"Colonel, it's Charlie Couture," he barked. "Open up."

He pounded the wood a few more times. Then, from the inside, he heard Marti's sleepy voice.

"What is it, Charlie? Can it wait?"

"No," said Couture. "I just got off the phone with Hector Calibrisi. It's urgent."

There was a long silence, at least ten seconds. Then Couture pounded the door again.

"Open the fucking door, Colonel," said Couture. "We found something."

Couture leaned in toward the door.

"We found evidence linking Iran," he whispered.

"Really?" said Marti.

The dead bolt turned. The door opened slightly. Marti put his head behind the chain.

Couture kicked viciously, ripping the chain off and slamming the door into Marti's face, where it struck his nose, crushing it.

Couture followed the door in and leapt at Marti, wrapping his thick muscled fingers around the older man's neck and tackling him to the floor. He straddled Marti as he choked him.

"Did I say Iran?" asked Couture, gripping his throat and strangling the life out if him. "I meant you, motherfucker."

Couture felt the weak swings of Marti's fists against his back. He watched as Argentina's top law-enforcement official turned reddish blue and suffocated to death.

41

OFFICE OF THE CHIEF OF STAFF
WEST WING
THE WHITE HOUSE
WASHINGTON, D.C.

The White House chief of staff's office was a stone's throw from the Oval Office, connected by a short private hallway.

The doors to the interconnecting hallway sometimes stayed open, usually during crunch times, such as just before an important speech, like the State of the Union. During these times, the president, chief of staff, and various senior-level White House and administration staffers walked freely between the two rooms.

Then there were times when the doors between the two offices were shut. Usually this happened when the president needed to conduct a private meeting, outside the earshot of anyone or anything. But for the most part, the president's life, and consequently the Oval Office, was a relatively open book.

It wasn't the Oval Office where the shit hit the fan. That took place in the chief of staff's office.

If the Oval Office was large and fancy, with every inch of space, wall, curtain, fabric, photograph, and painting as orchestrated and thought-out as a symphony, the chief of staff's office was more private, intimate, comfortable, luxurious in its own special way, with stunning views of the White House grounds.

It was the place where the grittier business of running the hardball, day-to-day, between-the-lines work of the presidency took place. The Oval Office was where hands were shaken; the chief of staff's office was where arms were broken.

Adrian King Jr. was the White House chief of staff. King, thirty-five, was five feet eight, with brown hair that was as thick as shag carpeting. His trademark feature was a set of bushy eyebrows that looked like some form of rare caterpillar.

King was the most feared man in Washington. He didn't play politics. He was loyal to a fault and the most hardworking person at the White House. But if you fucked with the president, with anyone under his general purview, or with him, watch out.

King stood behind his desk. In front of him was the complete dossier on Hu-Shao, including photos, a complete biography, and indisputable evidence that placed the Chinese agent in the sniper's nest in Córdoba.

He pored through the dossier with the speed, thoroughness, and efficiency of a trained prosecutor. When he was done, he put the papers back into the folder.

"Hector, I'm going to ask this once," said King, looking at Calibrisi, who was seated on the houndstooth sofa against the wall, beneath bookshelves lined with leather volumes and silver-framed photos. "Are you absolutely, positively fucking sure Dewey cut the finger off himself?"

"Yes," said Calibrisi.

"Would Premier Li have to sanction this?" asked King.

"Not if Dewey was the intended target."

King breathed heavily. He looked at the other man in the office, Secretary of State Lindsay.

"And was he?"

"Yes," said Calibrisi. "Dewey exposed the identity of a high-placed MSS asset inside Israeli intelligence. This was payback."

"Some fucking payback," asked King. "If this was sanctioned by Li, this is war. If it wasn't, well, what the hell is it then? They still assassinated America's top national security official. It's still war."

Lindsay put his coffee cup down on the table in front of him.

"We all know that's not practicable," said Lindsay.

"Tell that to Jessica, Tim," snapped King.

Lindsay sat back, chastened.

"What I mean, Adrian, is we can't just go to war with China. We don't have the troops. We would have to reinstitute the draft. I mean, it's an absurd conversation to even have."

"Oh, yeah," said King, seething. "We might not have the troops, but we have enough fucking nukes to turn that miserable fucking no-good goddamn rice bog into a glow-in-the-dark cockroach park."

Lindsay, a former admiral and chief of naval operations, who was almost thirty years King's senior, nodded calmly.

"I'm angry too, but we're not going to war over it," said Lindsay. "You know it. I know it. Hector knows it."

"The Chinese tried to alter the identity of the dead operative," said Calibrisi. "They planted prints from a known terrorist with no ties to China. They think we don't know. They had help from someone inside Argentina."

"Who?" asked King.

"The head of AFP," said Calibrisi.

King looked as if he was about to flip his desk over.

"Do you know how much we give those ungrateful bastards!" yelled King, reaching for the speaker button on his phone console.

"Yes, Mr. King," came the voice of King's assistant.

"Get me President Salazar down in Argentina," he yelled at the phone.

He looked at Calibrisi.

"Who is the head of AFP?" asked King.

Calibrisi leaned forward and pressed the speaker button, cutting off the phone.

"You mean, who *was* the head of AFP?" answered Calibrisi calmly.

King smiled.

Lindsay glanced at Calibrisi, incredulous.

"Your guys killed—"

"Spare me," snapped King, interrupting Lindsay. "He got what he deserved. As far as I'm concerned, Hector here can do whatever he feels like. But that's *that* world. Right now, we're in *this* world. And the question is, what do we do?"

"I think it's appropriate to expel their ambassador from the country," said Lindsay, "along with the entire embassy staff and the entire staff of the mission to the UN, and any satellite missions—L.A., San Francisco, Chicago, et cetera."

"That's symbolic horseshit," said King. "What about the fuckers who actually did it?"

"It's Fao Bhang," said Calibrisi. "It's his operation."

King straightened his tie.

"Do you have a recommendation?"

"We need to confront the Chinese," said Calibrisi. "They might deny it, but they also might administer their own form of justice and remove Bhang. That would be significant."

"I'm going upstairs to brief the president," said King. "When I get back, I want the Chinese ambassador in my office."

King walked to the door.

"One more thing," he said, looking at Lindsay. "You call Li. You call him or I'll call him."

"I'll call him."

"Tell Li the president expects him at Jessica's funeral," said King. "And tell him to bring Fao Bhang's head in one of his suitcases."

42

The taxicab pulled up to Borchardt's limestone mansion as the sun was setting over London.

The usually quiet street in front of Borchardt's palatial estate was busy. A long line of limousines was queued up, along with taxis, assorted sports cars, and luxury sedans, and a Range Rover or two thrown in for good measure. A line of valets was opening the doors of the cars and taking those cars that needed to be parked to a parking lot around the corner. Well-dressed men, many in tuxedos, along with women in elegant, formal gowns, drifted up the dimly lit front steps toward the entrance to Borchardt's house.

Dewey paid the cabbie, grabbed his leather bag, and climbed out. He was dressed in what he'd been wearing when he drove out of Middleburg eight hours before; jeans, T-shirt, boots. His face was covered in stubble.

Borchardt and Dewey had an unusual relationship, to say the least. Borchardt was a German international weapons dealer with ties to not only most Western countries, including the United States, but also to virtually every known terrorist organization in the world. Borchardt had few morals, but he didn't sell terrorists anything more powerful than guns and ammunition. His reasoning was simple: he didn't like jihadists, and he thought guns would mostly be used to kill each other. Anything more powerful, and he wouldn't have been able to sleep at night, constantly worried that it might be his plane or boat or car that got heated up by an angry freedom fighter.

Borchardt was worth more than ten billion dollars and was considered the most powerful weapons dealer in the world. Interestingly, he made almost as much money selling information as he did selling weapons. He'd learned long ago that every time he sold centrifuges to the North Koreans, for example, the South Koreans were more than willing to pay handsomely for that information, nearly as much as the North Koreans had paid for the centrifuges themselves.

Borchardt had almost gotten Dewey killed two years before. It was Borchardt who plumbed contacts within the Pentagon to identify who killed Aswan Fortuna's son, Alexander. Aswan paid Borchardt four million dollars for a photo of Dewey. A year after selling it to Fortuna, that photo had come within a hairsbreadth of getting Dewey killed by Hezbollah.

But the five-foot-four, waifish-looking Borchardt had made amends by helping Dewey infiltrate Iran the year before. Afterward, Borchardt told Dewey he would be more than happy to help him when he needed it. There was something Borchardt saw in the rough-hewn American. Perhaps it was the way Dewey had stood up to him, without fear, and had given him the opportunity to make amends. Maybe it was the way they each approached the world, reliant on no one. Borchardt had even allowed Dewey and Tacoma the use of one of his basement rooms for the interrogation of Bhutta, an interrogation that had yielded the name of China's asset inside Mossad.

Of course, Dewey trusted Borchardt about as far as he could throw him. Borchardt was unscrupulous, amoral, and self-interested. Yet the moment the true identity of the Chinese sniper had appeared on the plasma screen back in Middleburg, Dewey knew he needed Borchardt's knowledge and connections to Beijing. He needed information on the man behind Jessica's death, Fao Bhang. And, he needed to start planning his infiltration of China and, ultimately, Fao Bhang's world.

Dewey knew full well that Borchardt might betray him to the Chinese. As a matter of fact, he was counting on it.

Dewey climbed the wide marble steps up to the mansion's entrance. A few people stared at him but said nothing. Violins could be heard from somewhere inside the mansion, along with the sounds of laughter and conversation. He saw Borchardt, dressed in coat and tails, greeting guests as they came in. They made eye contact. Borchardt finished speaking with a young blond woman in a black dress, excused himself, and made a beeline for Dewey.

"I see you got the invitation," said Borchardt, smiling as he shook Dewey's hand.

"Wouldn't have missed it for the world, Rolf," said Dewey.

"Did you rent that tux," asked Borchardt, pointing at Dewey's orange T-shirt, "or do you own it?"

"Rented it," said Dewey. "I need to have it back by midnight."

Borchardt grinned.

"Let's get a drink," he said.

Dewey followed Borchardt into a room off the entrance foyer. Borchardt shut the door. It was a large library with vaulted ceilings of dark wood, a huge crystal chandelier, fireplace, walls lined with books, several big couches, a bar in the corner. Borchardt poured two drinks.

"Whiskey, as I recall?"

"Yes, thanks. What's the party for?"

"Some board I'm on."

"Do you need to get back to it?"

"They don't come to see me," said Borchardt. "They come to eat my food, drink my wine, and see my house. Frankly, I know very few of them, and those I do know don't like me."

"Then why are you on the board?"

"I get to look legitimate because I'm on the board of some museum, and they get my money. It's like an arms deal."

Borchardt finished pouring and turned back to Dewey.

"What happened to your hand?"

Dewey didn't answer. Borchardt handed him a glass and clinked his against it. Dewey downed it in one gulp.

"You can tell me later, I guess," said Borchardt. "What do you need?"

"It's complicated," said Dewey.

"Let's start with a country."

"China."

Borchardt tipped his glass back and took a large sip.

"Is this about Jessica Tanzer?"

Dewey stared at him. He was silent for a few moments.

"Yes."

"Why?"

"She was my fiancée. They sent a kill team to Argentina. They were after me, but they shot her."

Borchardt nodded.

"I'm sorry, Dewey."

Dewey was silent.

Borchardt drained the rest of his glass.

"So you want vengeance?" asked Borchardt.

"Yes."

"Against who?"

"Two days ago, I would have wiped out the entire country if I could've. But I don't want that. I want to kill the ones who were responsible for her death. Fao Bhang. Anyone close to him. If I could make it hurt, that would be an added bonus."

"A well-planned infiltration into the PRC could take months. There's getting in. There's the design of the operation itself. There's getting back safely. In addition, there's the simple challenge of accessing Bhang. He's going to be extremely well guarded. Look, they were after you. They sent a wet crew to Argentina? That means if you set foot in PRC and they capture you, you're toast. They'll simply kill you."

"Yeah," said Dewey. "I've thought about it. I'm not looking for a nice, clean round-trip ticket here."

"I need to tell you something," said Borchardt. "I have very deep ties to the PRC. I helped them modernize their military infrastructure, probably more than anyone. I've dined with Premier Li on at least half a dozen occasions. The Chinese ambassador to Britain is here tonight with his wife."

"I'm putting you in a difficult position," said Dewey. "I don't know where else to turn."

Dewey walked to the bar and poured himself another glass of Jack

Daniel's and another scotch for Borchardt. He walked to one of the sofas and sat down.

"That's not what I meant," said Borchardt. "I'm used to being in difficult positions. I'll help you. But I don't want to be exposed. That means you can't tell anyone, not Calibrisi, no one. I cannot afford to get in the crosshairs of Fao Bhang."

"Not a problem," said Dewey. "I don't want anything elaborate. But it needs to happen soon. It needs to be loud and obnoxious. A big fuck you."

"I have to tell you, Bhang is a dangerous man," said Borchardt. "So is Ming-húa, his deputy, who runs the kill squads. A couple of evil bastards. China is one large booby trap. You never know who you can trust. The old man working at the shoe factory is just as likely to be an informant as the cashier at the hotel or the anchorman on the evening news. Your little foray into Iran was a cakewalk compared to this. They could very well already know you're here. The ministry's use of technology would blow your mind. They are far more aggressive than Langley or NSA."

"I take it you don't want to come with me?"

"The problem is," said Borchardt, ignoring Dewey, "even if you had a very clean set of documents, with an INTERPOL back pull—a so-called 'clean insertion'—the problem is, PRC has altered the entire architecture of its entrance protocols."

"I'm only fluent in English and Spanish, Rolf," said Dewey, taking a sip of whiskey.

"Your photograph, in other words, now exists in a highly sophisticated database inside China that is fed, in real time, by border security. Photos are ported from all border crossings, whether it's the airport or the one-room train depot in Erenhot."

"Erenhot?"

"The only border crossing between Mongolia and China. It's a facial-recognition appliance that cost PRC more than two billion dollars and six years to design and implement. It's causing plenty of headaches for people trying to get into PRC with false papers. Bhang's brother, Bo Minh, designed it."

"He has a brother?"

"Yes. Bo Minh. A genius. He's the one who designed the new border security system. It's extremely sophisticated. Every visitor to PRC, whether it's by plane, boat, train, or vehicle, by foot, or by bicycle, is going to have their photo snapped and scanned against a massive database. If you attempt to enter China with a fake ID, it might work, but if it doesn't—you tell me—what do you think Fao Bhang will do? I can tell you what he won't do: he won't let you ever see the light of day again."

"How do you know they have my photograph? Don't tell me you sold it to them too?"

Borchardt grinned. "Were you in the U.S. military?"

"Yes, you know that."

"Then they have your photograph."

"You're kidding."

"No, I'm not kidding. The Chinese are serious. They're not fucking around. America has spent hundreds of billions, trillions even, to try and wipe out radical jihad, while the Chinese pose a capability, and thus a threat, that is several quanta more dangerous than terrorism and radical Islam."

"What do they want?"

"I have no idea. No one does. I'm not sure even they do."

"So why do you deal with them?"

"They have lots of money. They like weapons. They love information. And most important, they wire their money seven days after I send the bill."

Dewey sat back on the deep leather sofa.

"I'll have Karina put you in one of the suites," said Borchardt. "In the meantime, don't venture out into the party. If Bhang is after you, I can guarantee that every embassy official in the world has already memorized your photo. Also, no phone calls; I know what Bhang and his minions are capable of. The lines were swept before the party, but for all I know, one of the caterers works for him and already stuck a bug on the switch."

Dewey nodded.

"Pour a whiskey. Pick out a book. Karina will set you up. You look like you could use a good night's sleep. We'll talk in the morning."

43

PRIVATE RESIDENCE
THE WHITE HOUSE
WASHINGTON, D.C.

King stepped off the elevator into the private residence of the president.

Amy Dellenbaugh greeted him.

"Hello, Mrs. Dellenbaugh."

"For the hundredth time, call me Amy. Come in; he's in the kitchen."

She led King through the luxurious, intimate living quarters of the first family, to the kitchen, where J.P. Dellenbaugh was standing at the counter, sleeves rolled up, making a sandwich.

"You hungry?" asked Dellenbaugh. "I made you a sandwich. I hope you like roast beef."

"Thank you. I do like roast beef."

King walked to the counter, where a sandwich was piled on a plate.

"You really made that?" asked King. "There are people who are paid to do that for you, Mr. President."

"I like doing it myself. If the Secret Service would let me, I'd mow the lawn too."

Dellenbaugh picked up the two plates and carried them to a long table in the center of the kitchen, where they sat down. King picked up the sandwich and took a bite.

"Not bad, sir."

"Not bad?" asked Dellenbaugh, grinning. "How about, 'Great sandwich, Mr. President'?"

"It's a little heavy on the mustard, sir."

"You can't have too much mustard," said Dellenbaugh, taking a large bite of his sandwich. "What do we got?"

"It was China."

"You're sure?"

"The evidence is indisputable. We found the body of one of the men sent to Argentina. He was a high-ranking agent in the Ministry of State Security. Hector believes they were after Dewey."

Dellenbaugh took another bite, then chewed in silence as he thought. His face went from calm to disgusted, followed by irate.

"Motherfuckers," the president said, finally. He put the sandwich down.

"I believe, Hector and Tim believe, we need to confront them. Fao Bhang and whoever else was involved in this need to be held accountable."

"I'll call Li," said Dellenbaugh, standing up.

"Not yet, sir. Tim is going to call him. Let's see what their response is. Let's keep some dry powder, in case we need it later."

44

Borchardt walked with his eyes on the ground, through the party, ignoring those guests who called to him. In the central ballroom, beneath a Rembrandt painting of a young girl in a meadow, he saw Sūn Mǎ, the Chinese ambassador to England, speaking with a woman. Borchardt walked close enough to Mǎ to make eye contact. When the smiling Mǎ looked up from his conversation, Borchardt nodded to him.

Mǎ followed Borchardt into a hallway off the kitchen, then down the stairs into the basement. Mǎ trailed in silence. Both men walked quickly. At the end of the hallway, a large guard in an ill-fitting suit stood. In his hands, aimed at the ground, was a close-quarters combat machine gun.

Borchardt and Mǎ passed the guard in silence and entered a windowless, brightly lit room. Inside, two men were seated, monitoring a wall of plasma screens, all displaying different views of the mansion, both inside and out.

"Go to the Equinox Suite," said Borchardt.

One of the men punched a few keys. The screen cut to a large, empty bedroom suite.

"Would you mind telling me why we're in your basement, Rolf?" asked the ambassador.

Borchardt turned to Mă.

"You'll see," said Borchardt. "Make it fast and don't make a mess. I don't want to know what you're going to do, or how you're going to do it. I want no part of it."

"Of what?" asked Mă.

There was movement on the video screen. A woman walked through the door, followed by a large man in an orange T-shirt, carrying a duffel bag.

Mă moved closer to the screen to get a better look. His smile slowly dissipated and shock overtook his face. He pulled a cell phone from his pocket.

"Get me Minister Bhang," barked Mă, in Mandarin. "Now!"

45

Calibrisi was asleep in his chair when loud knocking on his glass door woke him up. It was two in the afternoon. After staying up all night and working through the morning, Calibrisi had finally succumbed to exhaustion a few hours before.

"We found Dewey."

It was Bill Polk, deputy head of the CIA's National Clandestine Service and director of Special Operations Group, the CIA's paramilitary outfit. It hadn't taken long for Polk's team to figure out where Dewey went.

They started with a fast scan of the three airports within reach of Middleburg by car: Dulles International, Reagan National, and Baltimore/Washington International. They also dispatched three on-the-ground teams to look for Tacoma's BMW M5, which happened to be, in typical Tacoma flamboyance, orange.

At first, the team thought they'd gotten lucky early. There weren't a ton of flights to look at in the immediate hours after Dewey left the farm, but a 2:00 A.M. Dulles-to-Frankfurt flight popped up Dewey's name on the Lufthansa manifest. The CIA team, however, couldn't find Tacoma's M5 at Dulles, though that could have been easily explained away. Perhaps he'd parked it at a local motel, then taken a taxicab. A back-scan of the manifest against customs data, however, showed that Dewey had bought the ticket, gotten his boarding pass, but hadn't been aboard the plane when it took off. Then, sometime in the wee hours of the night, Tacoma's M5 was found at Reagan National, parked in the employee lot. Dewey had flown the Delta shuttle to JFK. At 7:00 A.M., he'd been in seat 4A of a British Airways flight to Heathrow.

"What time did he land?" asked Calibrisi, sitting up.

"An hour ago."

Calibrisi looked at his watch.

"Get a plane ready for takeoff," said Calibrisi. "I want to be airborne in exactly thirty minutes."

"You got it."

Calibrisi leaned forward. He hit the button on the phone console atop the brass-and-glass coffee table, then quickly dialed a number he knew by heart.

"Foxx."

"Katie?"

"Hi, Hector."

"What are you doing?"

"Well, let's see. I just finished adjusting the locks on the vault, so Dewey can't lock us in again."

"Speaking of Dewey," said Calibrisi, "we found him."

"Congratulations," said Katie. "Say hi to him for me, will you?"

"He's in London."

"That's really exciting. Maybe he'll send me a postcard? I'll be waiting by the mailbox. If you talk to him, would you mind relaying a message for me?"

Calibrisi breathed in deeply, grinned, then shook his head.

"And what is that?"

"Tell him to fuck off."

"I will. Anything else?"

"Don't ever ask for Rob and me to help that ungrateful son of a bitch ever again. What a jerk. What if that room didn't have an oxygen circuit?"

Calibrisi let Katie finish blowing off steam.

"You done?"

"Yes."

"Where's Rob?"

"Shooting things in the backyard."

"Well . . . so . . . the reason I called."

"Yeah?"

"I got you two into this whole thing, and I feel sort of bad. I'd like to make it up to you."

Katie was silent.

"Something special," added Calibrisi.

"That's nice. What did you have in mind?"

"I was thinking it might be fun to go on a trip."

"Oh, no, Hector," said Katie, warily. "You're not serious."

"London is so pretty this time of year," said Calibrisi. "The rain. The clouds. The rain. The drizzle. Then there's the fog. Harrods. Buckingham Palace. Changing of the Guard. What do you say? Throw a few shrimps on the barbie?"

"That's Australia, jackass."

"We can go there afterward," added Calibrisi, enthusiastically.

Katie was silent.

"I take off from Andrews in twenty minutes," said Calibrisi. "I'll swing by Dulles private."

"Do we have a choice in the matter?"

"No," said Calibrisi, standing up. "And tell Rob to bring something nice to wear, in case we get to meet the queen."

The black Sikorsky S-76C chopper picked up Calibrisi on the roof helipad at Langley, then delivered him, ten minutes later, to the tarmac at Andrews. He climbed down the airstairs then walked 150 feet to the waiting CIA-owned black-and-silver Gulfstream G150, whose turbines were already buzzing as the pilots prepared for takeoff.

Twelve minutes later, after landing at the private terminal at Dulles, Katie and Tacoma climbed up the jet's stairs, each carrying a small duffel bag.

Tacoma had a wide smile on his face. His hair was a mess. He had on cutoff khaki shorts with paint stains and a faded yellow T-shirt with a trident shield stamped on the chest—symbol of the Navy SEALs. He had on a pair of heavily beat-up cowboy boots.

Katie, as usual, looked slightly more elegant than Tacoma. She had on knee-high brown leather boots with a silver Gucci insignia on the sides. She wore short green-and-white flower-print shorts, which showed off her legs, and a thin white cotton sweater with a black stripe across it. Her hair was braided into a ponytail. Unlike Tacoma, there was no smile on her face.

"Hi, guys," said Calibrisi. "Thanks for coming."

"Wouldn't have missed it, chief," said Tacoma, sitting down in one of the white leather captain's chairs, diagonally across from Calibrisi. "I hear Polky found my Beemer."

Katie sat down across from Calibrisi but remained silent.

The plane taxied down the long tarmac, turned, then roared down the runway, lifting smoothly into the sunny Virginia sky.

Calibrisi briefed Katie and Tacoma on his meeting at the White House with Adrian King and Secretary of State Lindsay.

"So basically, we're going to ask China to turn over their top intelligence official so that he can be prosecuted at The Hague?" asked Katie, incredulous.

"That's the plan."

"Did you speak with the president?"

"Not yet. King is meeting with the Chinese ambassador as we speak. We're going to get on the phone after that."

"Why don't they let you deal with it?"

"That's not off the table yet," said Calibrisi. "Look, if China will hand over Fao Bhang, that would be adequate for me. He should pay. If going the official route is what gets that done, then so be it, I'm happy."

"Happy?" asked Tacoma.

"Well, not happy. I'm still pissed. But the staging of something like a hit on Fao Bhang is not straightforward, guys. We need to let things run their course. Dellenbaugh isn't going to go to DEFCON five right from the get-go. I don't disagree with him either."

"Understood."

"Coffee anyone?" asked Tacoma.

"Sure," said Calibrisi.

Katie held up two fingers, indicating she wanted one also.

Tacoma stood and walked to the galley kitchen at the aft of the jet. He made three cups of coffee, then returned to the seats.

"Why London?" asked Calibrisi, as Tacoma sat down.

"If I had to guess, he's going to see Borchardt," said Tacoma.

"Deep connections to Beijing," agreed Calibrisi, nodding. "Whatever weapons Dewey wants. There's a certain logic to it."

"Dewey is asking him to help get back at Bhang," said Katie.

"The problem is," said Calibrisi, "Borchardt would flip Dewey in a heartbeat. China is his biggest client by far."

"Do we have someone tracking him from Heathrow?" asked Katie.

"No."

"Why not?"

"I didn't want to exacerbate the situation," said Calibrisi. "He's extremely pissed off. If I sent a spotter, he would've seen him. At that point, he'd feel even more betrayed than he does already. Then he'd shut us out permanently. I don't think we want to be shut out."

"We need to get a team over there," said Katie. "Who do we have in London, Hector? Should I call Danny?"

Calibrisi unfolded the SAT phone. He pressed one of the speed-dial numbers, then put the phone to his ear.

"Who you calling?" asked Katie.

"Derek Chalmers," said Calibrisi. "We need to find Dewey and bring him home before he gets in any deeper."

46

When King walked back into his office, Zhai Jintao, China's ambassador to the United States, was seated in front of his desk.

Jintao was fifty years old. He had a neatly coiffed head of black hair that was a tad long, and wore a stylish pair of round, tortoiseshell eyeglasses. Unlike many of his fellow Chinese government officials, he wore beautiful clothing, brightly striped button-down shirts, Hermès ties, Prada shoes, and suits that were made on Savile Row in London. Most unusual, however, was his smile. It was, in a word, infectious. That and his good looks had done much for him over the years, and there weren't many people, inside or outside of diplomatic circles, who didn't like Jintao.

Jintao was alone. As King entered, he stood up immediately. King took off his sports coat and hung it on the back of his door, then shut it.

"Adrian," said Jintao, stepping toward him, "good to see you, my friend."

King ignored his outstretched hand. He went behind his desk.

"Let's dispense with the pleasantries, Mr. Ambassador."

"It's your meeting."

"Do you know why you're here?"

"Not exactly, though I can probably guess."

King pushed the manila dossier on Hu-Shao across the desk to Jintao. Jintao picked it up and leafed through it as King watched in silence. It took Jintao only a minute or two to pore through it. When he was done, he placed it back on the desk in front of King.

King stared at Jintao, who stared back.

"The question, Mr. Ambassador," said King, with anger in his voice, "is not whether China was behind the assassination of our national security advisor. The question is, what the fuck is China going to do about it?"

Jintao remained calm.

"What do you mean, 'What is China going to do about it?'" asked Jintao.

"I mean, what are you going to do about it? Simple fucking question. Hu-Shao was a high-level MSS operative. He killed Jessica Tanzer. This is an act of war."

Jintao nodded, not in agreement but out of respect, acknowledging he had heard King's words and was not ignoring them. But he said nothing.

"Do you deny it, Mr. Ambassador? Is that what you're going to try and do? Deny this guy worked for you? Or maybe he was rogue, off on his own? Is that it?"

Jintao's smile transformed into a kind, if icy stare.

"No, I don't deny it," said Jintao.

King stared, incredulous, at Jintao.

"As you said," continued Jintao, "let's dispense with the pleasantries, cut the bullshit, as you say."

King leaned forward.

"Okay. Go."

"You know as well as I do why he was there," said Jintao. "Hu-Shao was part of a three-man team sent in for Andreas. Unfortunately, Jessica was shot by accident. She was not the intended target. Andreas was. I am being honest with you, Adrian. Do you think we would intentionally harm America's national security advisor?"

"You did harm her," yelled King. "You killed her."

"Yes, we killed her. But it was an accident. And, yes, Premier Li will be coming to the funeral, but not because you threatened him, something which I did not pass on to him when we spoke. That would have only inflamed the situation."

King sat back in his large red leather chair. Jintao's honesty had caught him off guard. King had expected him to deny it, then to bow out, tail between his legs, and, ultimately, to help broker the deal that would appease an angry president and an even angrier chief of staff, not to mention CIA director.

"You are to leave the United States by tomorrow night," said King. "All embassy staff are to leave America. The PRC mission to the United Nations, all staff, as well as any PRC regional missions located in U.S. territory: out. Then we'll discuss what happens with China. At the very minimum, Fao Bhang is to be turned over to authorities for prosecution at The Hague, along with any ministry staff involved in Jessica Tanzer's death. Do I make myself clear, Ambassador Jintao?"

"Perfectly clear," said Jintao. "But there is one problem."

"What is that?" asked King, leaning forward.

"China has no intention of withdrawing from the United States, nor of turning over Minister Bhang."

King was starting to feel a little nervous.

"Mr. Ambassador, your diplomatic missions that are within U.S. sovereign territory are the purview of this country and, specifically, the president of the United States. I was with him approximately half an hour ago. Not only does he want you out of the country, I had to fight to get an extra day for you and your people. President Dellenbaugh wants you gone."

Jintao smiled.

"I certainly understand," said Jintao. "And I would never want to imply that our presence in your country is anything less than a privilege, determined and decided by your president. If you want us gone, we will be gone. Indeed, if President Dellenbaugh wants me gone today, that is something that could be arranged. But . . ."

King stared.

"But what?" he snapped.

"But then, who will buy the five hundred billion dollars' worth of U.S. Treasury bonds which the People's Bank of China is being asked to buy? And, in six months, when Secretary Uhlrich comes to us yet again with his hat in his hand and asks us to buy another trillion dollars' worth of bonds, as he has already informed us he will do, what will happen then?"

King's face flushed red. He sat back, loosened his tie, then ran his right hand back through his hair.

"Premier Li, myself, even, believe it or not, Minister Bhang all regret what happened to Jessica," continued Jintao. "Perhaps nobody more so than me. I had a close relationship with Jessica, closer than anybody else in my government. I sincerely liked her. It is not an exaggeration to say that I'm embarrassed, and that Premier Li is embarrassed. And there will be people who suffer the consequences of this tragedy. But it will not be Fao Bhang. If you would still like China to withdraw, well, of course, we will do so immediately. But before you and your president make such a decision, I encourage you to speak with Secretary Uhlrich. You might also want to consult with the chairman of the Federal Reserve. And, while you're at it, you should probably let your leaders in Congress know."

"Know what?" whispered King, furious now.

"Let them know China will not be in a position to lend the United States another trillion and a half dollars. As they will no doubt tell you, without that money, the government of the United States will have to shut down, or, of course, you could stop paying Social Security benefits, or paying your hardworking U.S. soldiers, or paying hospital bills for the elderly. I could go on."

"Fuck you," said King.

Jintao stood.

"Is that your answer?" asked Jintao.

"That's a question for the president," said King. "The fuck you was from me."

201

47

Karina, one of Borchardt's servants, led Dewey through a small door at the back of the library, which fed into a thin, windowless servants' hallway. At the end of the hallway was a curving iron stairwell.

At the third floor, Karina led Dewey down a long corridor. She opened the door to a spacious bedroom, with a large living room and bathroom.

"If you need anything, please press four on your telephone, Mr. Andreas," said Karina. "That will ring someone in the service wing."

"Thank you."

The bed was massive, with a large white canopy draped overhead. Two large windows looked over the gardens at the back of the house. A crowd of at least two hundred mingled in the gardens. Music drifted up to the window. Dewey opened one of the windows and stood watching the crowd, then yawned, raising his hands over his head. He lowered the curtain, shutting out any outside light.

He drained the last of the whiskey, went into the bathroom, stripped off his clothes, and took a shower. He brushed his teeth, then climbed into bed and turned out the lights.

———

Sūn Mǎ had removed his tuxedo jacket. He paced Borchardt's basement security room. Two of Borchardt's security men were seated, monitoring video screens. Standing behind them was another man. He was short, wiry, crew-cut, young, and Chinese. He was dressed in black tactical military clothing. This was the lead MSS agent in London, one of the ministry's top assassins in all of Europe.

The agent stood, arms crossed, behind the seated security men. His eyes darted about the panoply of screens, keeping an eye on Dewey's bedroom while also monitoring the party, which was beginning to thin out.

"You need to go," said Mǎ, speaking in Mandarin to the agent. "Now. The chances of being seen are practically nonexistent."

"Mr. Ambassador," the agent responded, without moving his eyes from the screen, "if I need your advice, I will ask for it."

The agent stared at a pair of screens that displayed the terrace. A small crowd continued to hover near a fountain.

In the alley behind Borchardt's mansion, a white truck was parked. On its side was written MAYFAIR & LIME CATERING CO. LTD.

Inside sat four MSS agents, awaiting the go from the agent in the basement.

Each man wore the same black tactical military outfit, running shoes, and clutched automatic weapons—close-quarters combat submachine guns, with suppressors screwed into the muzzles.

Night-vision optics were strapped to each man's head, ready to be pulled down at a moment's notice.

The four killers sat in silence, earbuds in, waiting.

Half a world away, Fao Bhang was seated in the conference room next to his office. Ming-huá was with him. They were patched into Borchardt's VPN, monitoring the operation in real time. It was 6:00 A.M. in Beijing.

On the wall, a large video screen was live-linked to Borchardt's security system. The screen displayed a dozen different views, tiled across the screen. In the upper left corner was the live feed of Dewey's bedroom, now dark.

A triangular speaker phone sat on a table in front of Bhang and Ming-huá.

"What floor is he on?" asked Bhang, leaning toward the mic.

"Three," came the voice of the agent in London, "in back."

"I believe we're close," said Ming-huá.

He pointed at the screens. At least three-fourths of the screens were devoid of activity. One screen showed the front steps of the mansion. Couples were filing out.

"Is that a tactical order?" came the voice of the agent in London.

Bhang pointed at a screen showing a man and a woman kissing in a shadowy corner of the back terrace.

"No," said Bhang sharply. "Mr. Borchardt was kind enough to notify us. In return, what he asked for was discretion and cleanliness. We wait until the party is over."

Borchardt stood near the front door, saying goodbye to his guests as they filed out. The party was coming to a close, though many people still continued to mill about. The sound of a Mozart sonata, played with utmost skill by the violinist, lent a soothing, elegant air to the din.

When one of Borchardt's servants walked nearby, Borchardt snapped his fingers.

"Go tell the violin to pack it up," he said. "Last song."

Dewey lay in bed for just over an hour, eyes open, staring at the dark bedroom, with the sounds of the party echoing softly up from the terrace and gardens at the rear of the estate.

In the dark, he climbed from his bed. He pulled on his jeans, T-shirt, and a pair of running shoes from his duffel. He went to the window and stepped behind the curtain.

Quietly, he climbed onto the brass banister and stared down at the gardens below. The party had thinned out. Only a few couples were still on the terrace. The music from the violin abruptly stopped.

Dewey reached up and placed his hands on the eave. He wrapped his fingertips around the front of the eave. He stepped off the banister into the open air, clinging onto the eave with both hands. For several seconds, he hung from the eave, dangling above the gardens three stories below, then threw his right foot up onto the eave. He pulled himself up to the roof.

The roof was pitch-black. Floodlights every six feet cast light up, out, and down from the flat roof, toward the gardens, the sides of the house, and, in front, at Upper Phillimore Gardens.

He stood in the shadows catching his breath.

He moved quietly across the roof to the front of the mansion. He leaned over the edge, clinging to the roof eave, and lowered himself. He was hanging now, staring into a well-lit room, inside of which stood a large red billiards table. A couple, a young blond man with glasses and his tuxedo jacket off, and a woman in a pink dress, was in the room. She was watching him prepare to hit the ball.

Dewey inched along the roof eave, dangling three stories over the sidewalk. He could see people below, couples talking, a man walking a black Labrador retriever. Down the sidewalk, at the entrance to Borchardt's, a pair of armed guards stood watch.

The next window was dark. Dewey swung in and dropped, grabbing the railing. His feet slammed into the limestone beneath the window, barely missing the glass. Slowly, cautiously, he lowered his hands from the banister to the landing where his feet were. He clutched the edge of the landing, then lowered himself again, so that he now hung outside a window on the second floor.

As he dangled in the dark, he scanned the room. It was the biggest bedroom in the house. It was also the only bedroom that wouldn't have security cameras peering in; Borchardt liked his privacy.

Dewey felt for the railing with his shoe. He stepped delicately atop the railing, then climbed down onto the small terrace in front of the window.

From his pocket, Dewey removed a small ice pick, which he'd taken from the bar. He stuck it into the seam between the upper and lower windows.

Dewey knew Borchardt had a state-of-the-art security system, more than capable of detecting penetrations at doors and windows. He guessed that the system would be off for the party. He popped the latch, then lifted the window open.

The agent in the basement security room pulled a pair of thin leather gloves from his pocket and pulled them on. He reached to his ear.

"We're near hard count," said the agent, scanning the screens, which were mostly blank and lifeless. "The right gate is the open access. Move in one-minute intervals along the right side of the gardens to the door closest to the swimming pool. I'll meet you inside the door. Give me a weapons check."

Inside the delivery truck, the four agents, one by one, checked their machine guns, then responded to the lead agent.

"Over one."

"Two."

"Over three."

"Four, out."

Each man pulled the night optics down over his eyes.

"Hold," said the lead agent. He continued to stare at the screens. He saw movement in one of the rooms.

"What's that?" he asked in English, pointing.

"Staff," said one of Borchardt's men with a heavy Russian accent. "Cook."

The agent swung his submachine gun from around his back, to his front. He checked the magazine without looking, then pressed his ear.

"On my go," said the agent in Mandarin. "I want dark COMM. No talk. We move on my lead."

Dewey moved silently to Borchardt's bed. He opened the drawer of a bedside table. Beneath a book, a handgun lay in the drawer: Glock 24 with a suppressor. He checked the magazine, making sure it was good to go.

He went to a closet, pulled a shoelace from one of Borchardt's shoes, then put it through the trigger guard and tied a knot around his neck so that the Glock now hung at his neck. He stuffed an extra mag in his jeans pocket.

Dewey got down on his knees and looked beneath the bed. He reached under the bed and pulled out an MP7A1.

Dewey knew Borchardt was paranoid. He didn't think he was this paranoid.

At the window, he took the ice pick and jabbed it into the curtain. He tore off a long strip of silk from the curtain. He tied it through the MP7's trigger guard, then made a knot. He made a sling, wrapping it around his neck. He strapped the MP7 across his back, then tightened the sling.

Bhang lit a cigarette as he waited in the conference room, watching the operation unfold.

Ming-huá glanced up at him.

"Are we good?" he asked.

"Something doesn't feel right," said Bhang, deep in thought.

"What do you want to do?" asked Ming-huá. "I can abort."

Bhang shook his head without saying anything.

"Proceed," said Bhang.

Ming-huá turned and leaned into the mic.

"Lead one, you have tactical authority," said Ming-huá, into the mic. "You're hot."

Borchardt sat in the library, leg bouncing nervously, sipping a vodka, staring at the Chinese ambassador, Sūn Mǎ, who paced back and forth across the room.

"The guests are gone," said Mǎ, looking at Borchardt. "Honestly, what can be taking so long?"

Borchardt stared at Mǎ.

"Stop talking," said Borchardt. "I told you, I don't want to know about it. I don't want to hear about it."

"I apologize," said Mă.

Borchardt shut his eyes. He took another sip of his drink, trying to quell the guilt he now felt.

"Tell me about the party," said Borchardt. "How was it? Did the guests enjoy themselves?"

"Yes, Rolf," said Mă, smiling, attempting to relax. "It was a wonderful evening. The food was absolutely out of this world."

Dewey climbed back out through Borchardt's bedroom window. He stepped up to the railing. He reached up to the eave and pulled himself to the third floor. From the third floor landing, he grabbed the eave and lifted himself back onto the roof.

He sprinted in the darkness to the rear of the roof.

The terrace and gardens were empty. A staff member carried a tray of glasses toward the house.

Dewey leaned down to the edge of the roof.

The lead agent scanned the video screens one last time. He unlatched his night optics from his belt and pulled them over his head, then down over his eyes. He walked to the door and exited into a darkened basement. He flipped on the optics.

"Go," he said.

The order came to the four agents in the truck. The agent closest to the rear of the truck opened the door.

He pointed at the agent across from him. That man jumped from the truck to the ground. He scanned the alley, then moved to the gate. He opened it and skulked in silence along the right edge of the property, clinging to the shadows. He came to a swimming pool, moved around it, and entered the mansion through a glass door.

In one-minute intervals, the other agents followed.

The four men gathered inside a darkened greenhouse, next to the swimming pool. They waited in silence.

Lead one, the agent from the basement, arrived a few seconds after the last man from the truck. He signaled for the agents to follow him.

They moved two by two, with one man trailing, down a dark hallway to a stairwell, then climbed quietly, one step at a time, up the stairs. At the third floor, the lead agent halted the others with a hand signal. They listened for more than a minute, hearing nothing except the occasional clink of glasses or a faint voice from downstairs.

Dewey stood next to the bed. He was drenched in sweat and breathing hard.

He untied the sling from around his neck, then the shoelace, putting the Glock between his jeans and his back.

He went to the bed and stuffed pillows under the sheets to make it look like he was asleep.

He moved to the corner, feeling the wall for a light switch. Just before the corner of the room, he found it.

To his left, six feet away, was the door. In front of him was the bed. He checked the magazine on the MP7, then moved the safety off. He set the fire selector to full auto. He spread his feet and waited.

He gripped the SMG in his hands, right finger on the ceramic trigger, and thought of Jessica. He could never get her back. But tonight would begin the healing process. He heard his own breathing, counting as he breathed in and out, trying to calm his rapidly beating heart.

He heard a noise from the hallway. The distant creaking of wood, like someone had stepped on a loose board. Dewey suddenly heard the metal of the doorknob as it turned. Dim light came in through the crack as the door opened.

He counted the first man, then another, and still a third. They moved in silence, like ghosts. He saw the outline of suppressors sticking out from machine guns, then the telltale geometrics of the night optics on their heads.

The three agents moved to the end of the bed, raising their weapons, preparing to fire.

A fourth man entered and stood at the door.

It's all you can do, Dewey. It's all you could ever do.

Dewey put his left hand to the light switch. One of the gunman, at the back of the bed, nodded to the others. The metallic thuds of suppressed submachine-gun fire echoed softly in the room as they triggered their weapons at the bed, full auto, sweeping across the mattress, leaving no area unscathed.

Dewey flipped the switch. The room burst yellow as light filled the room.

He pulled the trigger. The MP7 didn't have a suppressor. The staccato peal of submachine-gun fire was shocking. Dewey took down the agent at the door, then swept the MP7 right, head-high, across the three gunman, who, in the confusion and in the sudden light, started pelting the walls with slugs. The three men tumbled to the ground amid the sound of shattering glass and gunfire.

Dewey sprinted to the door and, clutching the butt of the MP7, reached around the doorframe, trigger depressed, firing on full auto. He caught the last killer at the end of the hallway, ripping slugs through his legs, sending him tumbling to the ground.

He stepped into the hallway and walked to the fallen agent, who lay on his back groaning, trying to clutch at his legs. Dewey stood over him. He leaned forward and, with his left foot, kicked the night-vision goggles from the man's head. He was Chinese. Dewey triggered the gun one more time, sending a quick burst into his neck, killing him instantly.

Dewey walked back down the hallway, past his room, to the service stairwell. He descended two flights, then moved down a thin back hallway to the library. The door was slightly ajar. He could see Borchardt seated inside the room. There were two other men with him. One Dewey recognized from his last trip, a member of Borchardt's security detail. The other man was Chinese, dressed in a tuxedo.

Dewey pushed the door in with his left hand, MP7 trained in front of him.

Borchardt was seated at the far side of the large room. The guard stood in the middle of the room. The Chinese man was at the bar, to the right, mixing a drink.

For a moment or two, none of the men noticed Dewey.

Dewey stepped forward. He caught the eye of the security man, who turned, made eye contact with him, then reached for his shoulder holster. Dewey waited a split second, long enough for the guard to get the handgun out of the holster, long enough for him to begin the sweep of the weapon across the room, toward Dewey. Dewey watched it all. Then, as the muzzle moved closer, he fired. A hail of slugs from the MP7 ripped the man across the chest and pummeled him back against the wall.

The Chinese man jerked around from the bar, dropping a glass on the ground. Borchardt merely looked up, a calm, slightly bemused look on his pale face.

"Hi, Rolf," said Dewey.

Borchardt stared in disbelief. His eyes drifted down to the muzzle of the MP7.

"I take it this is the Chinese ambassador?" asked Dewey.

"Yes," said the Chinese man, indignant. "I am Sūn Mǎ."

"Nice to meet you."

Dewey fired. Bullets ripped into Mǎ's chest, knocking him off his feet, kicking him backward.

He stepped toward Borchardt, weapon trained on his skull.

"Ready to stop fucking around?"

Borchardt's lips moved, but no words came out.

"Let me give you the correct answer," said Dewey: "Yes, Dewey, I'm ready to stop fucking around."

"I'm ready to stop fucking around, Dewey."

"Attaboy. Now go get your Depends and your toupée glue. And wake up your pilots. Tell them to fuel up the plane. We're leaving town tonight."

"Where are we going?"

"You know damn well where we're going."

48

Bhang and Ming-huá stared at the screen in anticipation, trying to control their excitement as they awaited the arrival of the kill team.

Ming-huá had punched the picture up for better viewing, and the view of the dark bedroom in Borchardt's mansion occupied the entire screen, like a movie.

For several tense minutes, they watched in silence, both men standing, both smoking. The audio had been shut down by the lead agent, only adding to a sense of unease.

Then it started.

A furious spray of red, orange, yellow, and silver abruptly appeared, like firecrackers at night, as the muzzles of the machine guns erupted in a fusillade of sparks.

The screen suddenly exploded in bright yellow light, as if a light switch had been turned on.

The view was grainy, a fish-eye lens that provided a wide picture of the entire suite.

Four men, clad in black, stood front and center; three at the foot of the bed, weapons trained at the bed, night optics on, and a fourth commando just behind them, near the door.

As the light went on, the agents appeared frantic, swinging their weapons around.

Bhang lurched for the screen, pointing at the corner of the live video feed.

"Watch out!" he screamed, to no one, pointing at a large figure in the corner of the room, who Bhang realized was Andreas.

Bhang and Ming-huá watched in silence and horror as Dewey stepped forward, toward the unsuspecting commando at the door, and the muzzle of his machine gun sparked black and silver. The agent at the door was kicked by bullets. The American swung the weapon right, slashing a hail of lead across the three agents at the foot of the bed, all of them collapsing to the ground.

Bhang and Ming-huá watched, transfixed, as Dewey ran to the door, then disappeared around the corner.

Bhang's face turned beet red, but he remained calm. For a long time, he stared at the picture. He even lit another cigarette. The scene was grisly. The light-colored carpet was quickly overtaken in dark as the four dead agents bled out.

When Bhang completed the cigarette, he dropped it to the ground and stepped on it with his shoe, then stepped to the plasma screen. He placed his hands on the top edge of the screen and yanked. The screen came tumbling to the ground and smashed.

Bhang looked at Ming-huá.

"Could Borchardt have betrayed us?" Ming-huá asked quietly.

"No," snapped Bhang.

"There is no other explanation, Minister."

"Yes, there is," said Bhang, storming toward the door. "Andreas is smarter than we anticipated. I want leadership in my office immediately."

In his office, Bhang removed his coat and tossed it on his desk. He went to the credenza and opened the doors. Inside was a whiteboard. He picked up a marker and removed the cap.

Ming-huá trailed Bhang, taking a seat at the table. Several other members of the ministry's senior leadership team arrived soon thereafter.

Bhang wrote three things on the whiteboard:

1. SANITIZE LONDON: XIAO
2. FIND BORCHARDT: MING-HUÁ
3. WARN: DHENG

"Is this clear?" asked Bhang, looking at the table. "Top priority is cleaning up London. Xiao, coordinate with the Ministry of Foreign Affairs. We want to get those bodies out of there or, failing that, cut off any connection these men had to the ministry."

"Yes, Minister."

"Second, find Borchardt," said Bhang, pointing at Ming-huá. "Find out if he's dead. If not, track him down. Planes, cars, homes, credit cards—everything."

"Yes, sir."

"Third, Dheng, get a warning out to all personnel in the UK, Europe, and Russia. Include a photo. He could be going for more of our people. They need to be warned."

"Yes, sir."

Bhang scanned the table.

"Go," he barked, "except you." Bhang pointed at Ming-huá.

After the others left, he looked at Ming-huá.

"I want a security detail on Bo," said Bhang. "Two men. Good men."

"Yes, Minister. It will be done immediately."

49

Dewey and Borchardt arrived at Heathrow just after midnight. They climbed aboard the plane and were greeted by Borchardt's two copilots. Dewey still held the MP7, which he kept trained on Borchardt as they passed the men, who were seated in the cockpit with the door open.

Both pilots were ex–Israeli Air Force, and they knew their boss and the rough world he ran in. They were paid many times more than any typical pilot, in exchange for their silence and discretion and, of course, their loyalty. Still, a look of stunned shock hit their faces when they saw Borchardt at gunpoint, walking up the airstairs.

"It's okay," said Borchardt as they climbed aboard, smiling at the two men. "This is Dewey. Do what he says."

Borchardt's Boeing 757 was a flying fortress of luxury. There was no other way to describe the customized jet. It had cost Borchardt next to nothing, except for the three million dollars he'd spent on the cosmetic aspects of the jet, including removing more than a dozen different murals of Saddam Hussein, painted on the ceiling and on various walls throughout the plane.

It was no secret to anyone that Borchardt had sold many things to Hussein over the years, including centrifuges and more than a half ton of low-grade enriched uranium; both of which had gone relatively unused and had ultimately been sold by Hussein—through

Borchardt—to Iran. Hussein's appetite, Borchardt always said, was bigger than his bite. While he liked many people in Iraq, including one of Hussein's sons, Borchardt privately believed the Iraqis were too undisciplined and unfocused to develop nuclear weapons. He was more than willing to profit from their ambitions, however.

When the United States invaded Iraq the second time, the government of Iraq owed Borchardt fifty-five million dollars. Borchardt knew that when Hussein went on the lam, as the Americans got close to capturing him, he'd lost any chance of collecting on his debt. So instead, Borchardt had simply appropriated one of Hussein's many planes.

The plane had two staterooms, which looked like suites at a Four Seasons Hotel, including marble-tiled bathrooms with showers and bathtubs. There was a state-of-the-art media room with several large plasma screens built into the walls. The plane had a small but luxurious general seating area, similar to the first-class section of a normal airliner, with spacious black leather captain's chairs and a large wet bar. The galley kitchen was small but adequate.

The cargo area below was used for weapons. Hussein stocked it with enough firepower for a small war—with dozens of machine guns, carbines, shoulder-fired missiles, grenade launchers, handguns, stores of ammunition, explosives, first-aid equipment, in-theater communications gear, parachutes, even a small portable field surgical unit, with basic life-monitoring systems, oxygen, and a retinue of surgical equipment for basic battle-theater fixes and repairs.

Borchardt had left it all alone. As with many of Hussein's weapons, the cache aboard the jet was shiny and unused, like a spoiled child's toys.

Dewey pushed Borchardt into the passenger section, then tethered him to one of the leather seats, flex-cuffing his skinny wrists and ankles to the seat. He started to wrap tape around his mouth to gag him, but Borchardt protested.

"That's not necessary," said Borchardt. "Please. I can understand the cuffs, but do you really need to gag me? I won't talk if you don't want me to."

Dewey wrapped the tape around his mouth anyway.

"I'm not doing it to shut you up, Rolf," said Dewey. "I'm doing it to make you uncomfortable."

When he finished a couple of turns of the tape, Dewey walked back to the cockpit.

"Hi, guys," he said, leaning into the cockpit.

The pilots shared a glance, then looked at Dewey.

"I'm not here to hurt you," said Dewey. "Borchardt either. Just get this thing in the air and aim for China."

"Why China?" asked one of the men.

Dewey didn't respond.

"I know you guys are ex-IDF. I was part of the team that got Kohl Meir out of Iran."

The pilots nodded, saying nothing.

"I'm not telling you this because I expect you to betray your boss," continued Dewey. "I don't. I expect Borchardt to do what I say and you guys to just do your jobs. Got it?"

"Yes," said the pilot on the left.

"I know you guys are smart, ex-military, all that. I know you could make things difficult for me. You need to understand that if you do that, I will kill Borchardt and then I will kill you. *Capiche*?"

"Yeah," said the pilot on the right.

"Got it," said the other.

"We'll need to file a flight plan," said the pilot on the right.

"No you don't," said Dewey.

"Yes, we do. You want to pop this thing on an INTERPOL screen, the best way to do that is for us to leave Heathrow without filing a flight plan."

"Fine, file a flight plan."

"Where to?"

Dewey thought for a moment.

"Moscow," said Dewey.

"What's the final destination?"

"You'll be the first to know," said Dewey. "One more thing. Don't close the door. Don't lock the door. Trust me, you don't want to be on that side of the door if I have to break it down."

The two pilots nodded; the one on the right grinned.

"Now let's get the fuck out of here."

50

It was three in the morning London time when Calibrisi, Katie, and Tacoma landed at Heathrow.

A black Range Rover waited on the tarmac, its parking lights on and engine running.

The back door of the SUV opened as they crossed the blacktop. A tall man in a blue suit, no tie, with longish, slightly unruly blond hair moved toward the three Americans. This was Derek Chalmers, director of Britain's MI6, England's foreign intelligence service.

"Hector," he said, reaching his hand out toward Calibrisi as they met under the wan yellow lights of the Gulfstream. "Good to see you."

"Hi, Derek," said Calibrisi, shaking Chalmers's hand. "You remember Katie and Rob."

"Sure, of course."

Chalmers shook their hands. They followed him to the Range Rover and climbed in.

Chalmers tapped the back of the driver's seat, telling his driver to move. They shot down the tarmac toward the airport exit.

"Well?" asked Calibrisi. "We got anything?"

Chalmers nodded.

"It's a bloody mess."

"Why didn't you call?" asked Calibrisi.

Chalmers stared at Calibrisi, a slightly annoyed look on his face.

"Because there are five dead Chinese commandos at Borchardt's house and one dead Chinese ambassador," said Chalmers. "I have no idea if they're listening in, and I don't want to find out."

"When did it go down?" asked Tacoma.

"Sometime late last night. The team we sent in last night found the bodies. They were still warm. We haven't pulled them out."

"Have you run any of the prints?"

"Yes. They were all MSS. This was a kill team."

"They're all dead?" asked Calibrisi.

Chalmers nodded.

"As doornails. Your man Andreas redecorated the bedroom with them."

"Does China know about their dead ambassador?" asked Calibrisi.

"I assume," said Chalmers. "Borchardt's security team was coordinating with Beijing. The entire operation was run out of Beijing. They had live video of the OP."

"So it's escalating."

"Yes," agreed Chalmers. "Bhang is now fully engaged. It's going to get violent, but we can work with it. I know you don't want to hear this, Hector, but Dewey is proving to be a rather tempting morsel for our friend in Beijing."

Fifteen minutes later, the Range Rover pulled into the alleyway behind Upper Phillimore Gardens and extinguished its lights. A plainclothes agent, hand against his ear, was standing near an iron gate at the back of Borchardt's darkened gardens. He flicked a quick thumbs-up at the driver. Chalmers, Calibrisi, Katie, and Tacoma climbed out, then moved through the gate, meeting another agent who was waiting for them beneath the shadow of a Japanese maple tree.

Inside, they followed Chalmers into the library, whose curtains were drawn. A woman in a black bodysuit, a MI6 coroner, with blue rubber gloves on, was waiting.

On the floor were two bodies, both riddled with bullet holes and drenched in blood that had begun to blacken as it dried. One was a large man with dirty-blond hair in a gray plaid suit, who looked Russian. The other was a Chinese man in a tuxedo. His torso looked like a knife had been taken to it, though the blood-splattered wall behind him told a different story, of slugs having passed straight on through.

"The ambassador?" asked Calibrisi.

"The Honorable Sūn Mǎ," said Chalmers. "The other's ex-KGB. I assume one of Borchardt's men."

They followed Chalmers up the ornate central stairwell. At the third-floor landing, a large pool of blood shimmered under the light from the hallway. A few feet from the top step, a dead Chinese commando lay on his back, his head half blown off.

Down the corridor stood another coroner. He nodded at Chalmers but said nothing.

Chalmers led them into the bedroom. Inside were four more dead agents, littered on the oriental rug—three near the foot of the bed, one just inside the door. Blood was scattered in pools on the ground and splattered on the wall.

"China wasn't fucking around," said Calibrisi.

"Nor was Dewey," added Chalmers.

Calibrisi moved to the bed, stepping around the corpses. The bed was torn apart by slugs. Feathers were scattered all over the bedspread.

"Any calls from the neighbors?" asked Calibrisi.

"Yes," said Chalmers. "But nothing to worry about."

"No sign of Dewey or Borchardt?" asked Katie.

"Nothing. But we do know this: Borchardt's plane is gone. It left Heathrow around midnight."

As they walked back through the gardens, Calibrisi stopped to talk to Chalmers one-on-one.

"What are you thinking?" Calibrisi asked.

"We leave it exactly the way we found it," said Chalmers. "Let Scotland Yard take jurisdiction."

"Why?"

"We have an advantage as long as Bhang believes Dewey is acting alone," said Chalmers. "We can't risk Bhang thinking this is a sanctioned operation by CIA or MI6. The fact that they targeted Dewey while he was with your national security advisor means they're really bloody serious. We need to keep our heads down, and we need to find Dewey. If we play our cards right, he'll lead us straight to Bhang."

"I want to make something very clear, Derek," said Calibrisi, sharply. "I need help finding Dewey. But I have absolutely no intention of doing anything more than taking him back to the United States. He is not part of any operation to kill Fao Bhang."

"It's too late for that," said Chalmers. "Andreas is in the middle of this thing, Hector, whether you like it or not. A dead ambassador? A dead squad of commandos? This is going to anger the hell out of them. You need to put your guilt about Jessica aside and focus on the objective."

"I don't care about the objective," said Calibrisi, stabbing his finger at Chalmers. "We find Dewey, then he's out. I'm not going to have his blood on my hands too."

"This is what we wanted," Chalmers shot back. "Dewey's going to lead us to Bhang. You want to do your friend a favor? Help him get revenge. That's what he wants. It's what he deserves."

51

Dewey slept for the first two hours of the flight, seated a few rows behind Borchardt. When he awoke, he went to the galley kitchen at the front of the cabin and made a cup of coffee. He returned and sat down across from Borchardt, whose mouth remained taped shut.

"You want some?" Dewey asked.

Borchardt looked miserable. His eyes were bloodshot and angry. A sheen of sweat covered his head. His comb-over dangled down by his ear. He nodded up and down, indicating yes, he wanted a cup of coffee.

"What do I look like, a waitress?" asked Dewey.

Borchardt glared at Dewey. He screamed, though it was muted by the tape around his mouth.

"What?" asked Dewey, innocently. "I can't hear you."

Dewey took a sip.

"Mmmm, that's good coffee," Dewey said. "You know, Rolf, you need to stop reading too much into things. I never said I was going to get you coffee. That's called taking someone for granted. I read somewhere it's one of the main reasons relationships fall apart."

Borchardt again screamed from behind the tape, then yanked against the flex cuffs, as Dewey took small sips from his coffee cup and made satisfied purring noises.

"I wonder if those Chinese guys liked coffee?" pondered Dewey. "What do you think?"

He looked at Borchardt.

"Oh, that's right, you can't talk, can you?"

Borchardt again screamed, his face turning beet red. For several seconds he screamed, though it was muted.

Dewey took another sip.

"You never know with those Chinese guys. I mean, they like some weird shit. Take for example sushi. I mean, raw fish? Who wants to eat a piece of raw fucking fish? Why the hell do they like sushi so much, Rolf? Actually, now that I think about it, that's Japan who likes sushi, isn't it?"

Dewey smiled, staring into Borchardt's eyes. He took a last sip from the coffee mug, then hurled it over Borchardt's shoulder. It struck the wall and shattered, dropping pieces of the mug all over Borchardt's head and shoulders.

"Sorry," said Dewey, watching as Borchardt tried to shake shards of the mug from his shoulder. "I was aiming for the dishwasher."

Dewey reached for his ankle, pulling out his knife. He took it and thrust it toward Borchardt, who screamed, flinched, and yanked at his cuffs, all to no avail.

"Relax."

He stuck the tip of the blade next to Borchardt's ear, under the tape edge, then ripped the blade up, cutting the tape. Dewey grabbed the tape and ripped it from Borchardt's face, which made a loud noise, though not as loud as Borchardt's scream.

Dewey sat back and let him finish his wailing.

"Don't say anything you're going to regret," said Dewey. "There's an entire roll of tape, and I'd be glad to put some more on."

"What the hell do you want?"

"You know what I want, asshole. I explained it to you. I want help getting these fuckheads back."

"Then you kill me?"

"Maybe. But unlike you, I'm a man of my word. If you help me, there's a chance I won't kill you. It's not a promise, because sometimes I'm just in the mood, know what I mean? Even though you attempted to fuck me back at your house, Rolf, I still really actually don't care if you live or die. You and I are professionals. We know the drill. We understand the risks. But Jessica was innocent."

"I'll help you. I give you my word."

"Spare me, will you? You don't have a 'word' to give. You're a fundamentally dishonest human being, which is how I knew you'd rat me out. Just shut the fuck up, answer my questions, and do as you're told."

Borchardt nodded. "Got it."

"Now, my first question."

"Go ahead."

"Something I've been meaning to ask you since I first met you."

"What?"

"What the fuck is the deal with your hair? You're a wealthy man. Buy yourself a toupée. Or better yet, do what real men do: go bald. Be a man about it. It looks like a dead rat."

Dewey leaned forward and grabbed the end of the long bunch of hair that dangled to the side of Borchardt's head. He took his knife and put it next to Borchardt's scalp and sliced the entire piece of hair off, then tossed it into Borchardt's lap.

"There we go," said Dewey, sitting back, nodding slowly, assessing his hairdressing skills. "Much better."

Borchardt looked sadly down at the clump of hair on his lap.

"Okay, next question," said Dewey. "Weapons."

"Enough for whatever you want to do. A full cache of military-grade combat equipment. You're welcome to inspect it. It's in the cargo hold."

"Explosives?"

"SEMTEX, PBXN, gelatin, C4. Enough explosives to blow up Buckingham Place, or . . . the Ministry of State Security?"

"Good one, Rolf. What about shoulder-fired missiles?"

"MANPADs, RPG-7s."

"What sort of MANPADs?"

"Javelins.

"Oldies but goodies."

"There are also half a dozen Alcotán-100s."

"What are those?"

"Portable antitank missiles. Very easy to use. No recoil. Very effective too. I sold a bunch to Syria last year. They couldn't afford all of them, so I kept a few."

Dewey nodded.

"Okay, next question," said Dewey. "Tell me about Fao Bhang."

"What do you want to know?"

"Do you have a relationship with him?"

"I've never met him. Few have."

"Where does he live?"

"I have no idea. Presumably Beijing. If he's like all of the rest of the State Council, he also has a house somewhere, Hong Kong, Macau, Shanghai. But I don't know."

"What do you know?" asked Dewey. "Because I can tell you right now, your life span is directly correlated to how much you can help me."

"He's a buyer of information. Loves information. What sort of weapons system so-and-so bought, what sort of satellite setup this or that government has. That sort of thing. Very price agnostic. Big spender."

"What else? What's his deal?"

"His deal?"

"Yes, his deal. What's his fucking deal?"

"Bhang is the brains behind whatever nasty thing China does. He's the strategist and the implementer. He was without question the one who sent the team in to kill you last night. He would've been the one to organize the wet work down in Argentina."

"What about his brother, Bo Minh?"

"I know Minh. I know him quite well, as a matter of fact."

"How?"

"He's on my payroll. Bo Minh is the top technologist at the ministry. He designs various cryptographics, eavesdropping, profiling algorithms, lie-detection devices. He's as ruthless as Bhang, but a recluse, an introvert; he doesn't have the political skills or ambition of Bhang. But he's brilliant."

"Why is he on your payroll?"

"He keeps me apprised of developments within ministry weapons programs. He helps ensure I continue to play an active role in their decision-making process."

"Bribery."

"Something like that."

"How much have you paid him over the years?"

"Tens of millions."

Dewey stared at Borchardt.

"You really are a scumbag, aren't you?"

Borchardt smiled.

"I'm a businessman."

"Are they close?"

"Who?"

"Bhang and his brother, shitbrain."

Borchardt's eyes grew sharp.

"I'm not sure."

"Rolf," Dewey said, shaking his head, scolding in his voice. "Remember our discussion a little while ago about answering my questions? There is one individual on the entire planet you need to keep happy. And right now, that individual is a little upset. He'd like nothing better than to fire one of these Alcotáns up your constipated German ass. Answer the fucking question."

"Yes, they're close," said Borchardt, sighing. "Very close."

"What's 'very'?"

"Very. Bhang protects him. Minh is smart but weak. Bhang is not weak. They say even Li has a healthy dose of wariness about Bhang. His people are everywhere. Bhang watches out for Bo Minh. Minh was once caught in a Ponzi scheme. This was in Shanghai, several years ago. There were two men. They were caught and convicted, sentenced to thirty or forty years in a labor camp. The day after arriving at the camp, both men were shot in the head."

Dewey nodded. He sat back, pausing, then smiled.

"Well, you better hope I succeed then."

"Why?"

"Because Bhang's going to be mighty pissed off at you after his brother dies."

52

Calibrisi, Katie, and Tacoma grabbed a few hours of sleep at the American embassy, then were driven to MI6 headquarters on the banks of the Thames. They were escorted to the top floor, to a glass-walled conference room whose windows were lined with copper mesh, designed to prevent eavesdropping.

It was 5:00 A.M. Chalmers was already seated when the three Americans walked in. With Chalmers was Veronica Smythson, who ran paramilitary operations for MI6.

"Did you go home?" asked Calibrisi, noticing that Chalmers had on the same clothing from the night before.

"No," said Chalmers. "It's been a long night."

Calibrisi sat down and poured himself a cup of coffee.

"What's going on?"

"China is demanding to know what happened to their ambassador."

"They should ask one of the goons they sent in," said Calibrisi.

"Met's dealing with it," said Chalmers, referring to Scotland Yard. "Nobody knows we were even there."

"Have you heard from Dewey?" asked Smythson.

"No," said Calibrisi. "Any signs of Borchardt?"

Chalmers shook his head.

"What about the plane?" asked Tacoma. "Did they file a flight plan?"

"Yes," said Smythson. "Moscow. They never landed."

"So what are you guys thinking?" asked Calibrisi.

"We don't know," said Smythson. "He's obviously improvising. My best guess is he's headed to another foreign capital. Perhaps he'll try to take out more ministry assets. He could also be heading to China."

"Hector, would Dewey actually even consider entering China?" asked Chalmers, incredulous.

"He's not crazy," said Calibrisi. "But he is unpredictable. He was a Delta. He was taught to improvise and to act alone. Whatever it is he's up to, I can guarantee you one thing: it will be bold."

"If he's headed for China, he's not getting in," said Smythson. "Certainly not a six-four American whose face, by now, is at every border crossing in PRC. Bhang, by now, knows damn well what happened to his agents. It wouldn't surprise me if the Chinese knew Borchardt's plane had gone missing."

"If that's true, they'll look for the flight plan too," said Katie. "They'll know the plane hasn't landed in Moscow."

"We took care of it," said Smythson. "We altered a tail number on a Moscow-bound BA flight out of Heathrow. If they're tracking Borchardt's plane, they'll believe it actually landed. It should hold."

"Why the hell is Dewey not coordinating with Langley?" asked Chalmers.

Calibrisi looked at Chalmers with an icy stare.

"Because we got his fiancée killed," said Calibrisi. "Why is that so hard for you to understand, Derek? It was our goddamn operation that led to Jessica's death. Dewey wants nothing to do with Langley, MI6, or anyone else. Can you blame him?"

Chalmers paused, considering his response.

"No, of course I can't blame him," said Chalmers, calmly. "I feel terrible. But I have a job to do. The removal of Fao Bhang has to be our top priority, now more so than ever."

"President Dellenbaugh authorized us to take action," said Calibrisi. "America is going to hit China back. But Dewey Andreas isn't the one who's going to do it. He's in no condition to execute a black-on-black right now. It will be a suicide mission, and it will fail."

"If we want Jessica's death to mean something, let's figure out how to help Dewey kill Fao Bhang," said Chalmers.

"I'm all for killing Bhang," yelled Calibrisi, slamming his fist on the conference table. "But we're not using Dewey. We're finding him, then I'm bringing him home. If I have to have President Dellenbaugh call the prime minister to tell you to back the fuck off, I will. I'm not going to kill Dewey too!"

There was a long, uncomfortable silence in the conference room. The anger and emotion between Calibrisi and Chalmers was palpable.

Chalmers had a blank look on his face. He scanned Calibrisi's eyes for several moments.

"How long have we known each other, Hector?"

"Too long."

"Twenty-five years this December. Cape Town. Remember?"

Calibrisi calmed down. A small grin even appeared on his face.

"Yeah, I remember. A couple of rubes, huh?"

"Speak for yourself," said Chalmers.

"Okay, one American rube and a Cambridge dilettante."

"That's more like it," said Chalmers. "You taught me something important in South Africa. Remember the girl, the Danish girl, at the consulate?"

"Annika."

"You said, 'Don't get emotional.' She ended up being KGB. My career at MI6 would have been over."

"I was young and naïve," said Calibrisi.

"Do you at least want to hear what we have in mind?"

Calibrisi took a sip from his cup and sat back.

"Why not."

Chalmers nodded to Smythson.

"We have the rough architecture of a structured assassination of Fao Bhang," said Smythson. "MI6 has an asset inside the ministry hierarchy; a high-level agent who was recruited six years ago. This agent has been an important source for the UK, and the West, for some time. MI6 is willing to sacrifice that asset in order to strike at Fao Bhang. The operation is code-named 'Eye for an Eye.'"

"Revenge," said Calibrisi.

"It's a double meaning," said Smythson. "The obvious one: revenge. But we will also attempt to deceive Fao Bhang, to make him believe that what he is seeing is something different than it actually is and not, in fact, a drama, a play, an orchestrated fiction whose final act is his very own death. We will be, in a sense, replacing Bhang's eyes with our own, at least for a few hours."

Calibrisi poured another cup of coffee, intrigued. He glanced at Katie, then Tacoma, both of whom were also rapt at attention, fascinated by Smythson's words.

"But," said Smythson.

"But what?"

"But we're missing a key element. And without that element, the operation simply will not work."

"What is it?" asked Calibrisi.

Smythson looked across the table at Chalmers. Chalmers turned to Calibrisi.

"We need Dewey."

53

Xu Qingchen, the top general in the People's Liberation Army and the second-highest-ranking official in the Chinese military, was seated on a wooden bench. He finished a sandwich, then tossed the last piece of crust to the lawn. A pigeon pounced.

The red wooden bench sat at the center of a private lawn atop the roof of the Ministry of Defense building. Except when he was traveling or during inclement weather, Qingchen ate lunch every day on the roof, usually alone. Today, he was not alone. Seated next to him was Fao Bhang.

Between the two men was a yellow pad. Except for the occasional innocuous chitchat, Qingchen and Bhang communicated by writing notes. Bhang knew what eavesdropping technology was capable of.

"X met with council this morning," wrote Qingchen.

"X" was shorthand for Premier Li.

"You were a subject," Qingchen continued, "of discussion."

"What about?" scribbled Bhang on the pad.

"The ministry budget. X proposes slashing it. This led to bigger discussion. It became agitated."

"Continue."

"Photos were produced."

Bhang looked up from the pad, nostrils flaring.

"Photos?" he said aloud, barely above a whisper, yet seething with anger.

"A corpse," said Qingchen. "An ax in the skull."

Bhang abandoned any concern he might have had about speaking aloud.

"Gruesome," said Qingchen, continuing.

"Mossad did it," said Bhang.

"Who was the dead man?"

"It doesn't matter. An asset."

"What happened in London?" asked Qingchen.

Bhang stood up.

"How do you know about London?"

Qingchen stared at Bhang, a calm anger in his eyes. He remained silent.

"An operation," said Bhang, defensively. "They don't always go well. You should know that. It's nothing, a trifle. A person we're trying to remove."

"Sit down," ordered Qingchen. "And calm down."

Bhang remained standing, taking a cigarette from his jacket.

"You know I dislike smoke, Fao."

"What was Li's objective in all this?" asked Bhang, ignoring him.

"He had no objective, other than cutting the budget, but that is a ruse," said Qingchen. "It seems clear to me, you've upset him. He has started to politicize his paranoia about you."

"I can handle him."

"Not if he moves to quell a perceived threat from you. If the premier senses a threat, a real threat, you are in danger. The council favors you, but more important to the council is rule of law. Political hierarchy. To the extent he politicizes his paranoia, you risk losing support within the council. It's only a matter of time. He's very good at politics."

"What should I do?" asked Bhang, taking a hard drag on his cigarette.

"You have two choices," replied Qingchen.

"What are they?"

232

"Appease him. Apologize. Do something to make him—how shall we say?—less concerned about your ambitions. Politicians also like flattery."

"What's the other choice?"

"Move on him."

"When?"

"Now."

"What is the condition of your support within PLA?"

"As always, it is nearly unanimous," said Qingchen. "Those generals loyal to Li are well known to me and would be easily removed. But . . ."

"But what?" asked Bhang.

"You must want to be premier," said Qingchen. "I'm too old. You know this. And there is nobody else capable."

Bhang sat back down. General Qingchen's words were surprising but not unexpected.

Bhang had pledged his loyalty to Qingchen many years ago. Both men, and a sizable piece of the upper ranks of the PLA, didn't trust Li. Like all leadership changes in China, the outside world would know little of the internal machinations that ended up paving the way for a new leader. The elevation of someone new, like Qingchen or Bhang, would be seen as yet another mysterious though placid transition by the West. But in China, power was taken. It had been that way since the beginning.

The general's words represented the culmination of a decade's worth of work.

Bhang had correctly guessed that Qingchen would not want to rule when the time came. Like many military leaders, politics was a business he wanted little to do with. It was enough for the old general to have his man at the helm, in this case, Bhang.

Bhang attempted to control his excitement. He knew he could never be the one to suggest it. It had to be Qingchen. Ironically, it was Li who'd pushed him to it. He would have to remember to thank Li someday.

"With your support, I would do it," said Bhang.

Qingchen stood.

"Clean up this London affair," said Qingchen. "You give him needless ammunition. Clean it up."

"It is a mosquito," said Bhang. "I swung and missed. Next time, I'll not miss."

54

IN THE AIR

Dewey wrapped tape around Borchardt's mouth again. He went to the back of the plane, opening doors until he found the entrance to a small circular stairwell that led belowdecks. There, he found another door. Inside was the weapons hold. The storage area seemed endless: like a low-ceilinged warehouse, the shelves of various firearms, explosives, and ammunition-lined walls that ran to the front of the plane

Over the next hour, Dewey wired up a large block of SEMTEX, which he knew was not only effective but idiotproof, hence the reason it was popular with terrorists. It was forgiving and resilient to the accidental bumping or grinding that might trigger an explosion in other materials.

There were several types of detonators, and he rigged one that would allow for remote detonation, testing it before inserting it, feeling the slightly painful tickle of the electric pulse between his fingers.

He carried the detonator, a pair of Glocks, and an Alcotán-100 back upstairs and sat down.

Borchardt had nodded off.

"Wake up, Mary Poppins," said Dewey. "Rise and shine."

Borchardt opened his eyes. He groaned from behind the tape. Dewey grabbed a piece, then ripped it off.

"Fuck!" yelled Borchardt.

"That never gets old," said Dewey.

"You really are a mean son of a bitch, aren't you? Can I please get something to drink?"

"Like what?"

"Like water. I've been sitting here for at least six hours."

"Clean or dirty?"

Borchardt chuckled.

Dewey stood up, went to the galley, and got a bottle of water, then returned and held the bottle up to Borchardt's lips. He chugged down the entire bottle.

"So, two things," said Dewey.

"What?"

"First, we need another plane."

"Another plane?"

"Yes. It needs to be in Beijing, near where we're landing this monstrosity."

"Monstrosity?"

"This flying homage to greed, barbarism, and ego. This gaudy symbol of what happens when you're willing to sell weapons to terrorists."

"Why do we need another plane?"

"The answer is, none of your fucking business. Number two. You need to call Bo Minh."

"Why Bo Minh?"

"Because you'd like to meet with him in," said Dewey, pausing, looking at his watch, "three hours. At the airport."

"Beijing Airport?"

"On the plane. I don't care what you have to offer him. What you have to give him, promise him, threaten him—whatever. But you need to think of something, and it better be good. He's going to visit you on this plane."

"They found the dead bodies by now," said Borchardt, pleading. "They'll know the team failed. They'll know Ambassador Mǎ is dead. They'll know, Dewey. They'll assume I'm with you."

"Well, now, that's the most insightful thing you've said all day. Which means you better be pretty fucking clever when you call the little retard."

Borchardt glanced at the shoulder-fired missile. Then his eyes moved to the remote detonator. His eyes grew wider.

"What's that?" asked Borchardt.

"It's a detonator. I thought you knew about weapons?"

"I know very well what it *is*. What's it *for*?"

"Oh, yeah, I did a little art project downstairs while you were napping."

Borchardt's face flushed red.

"I made a sculpture out of some orange plastic stuff. It was like Play-Doh. I felt like I was back in kindergarten. I forget what it's called."

"You!" screamed Borchardt. "You fucking idiot, Dewey!"

"SEMTEX. That's it. I hope I did it right. Anyway, according to the instructions, if I press this little button here, it'll make the orange stuff change colors and get all hot. Doesn't that sound friggin' awesome, man? Then again, the instructions were in German, so who knows? Only one way to find out."

Borchardt became frantic, his face turning red, sweat appearing on his forehead and upper lip.

"You're a fucking maniac!" he screamed. "What have you done?"

Borchardt kept yelling and pulling at his cuffs. Finally, Dewey took the roll of tape and wrapped another piece across his mouth to shut him up.

"Can I bounce a few ideas off you?" asked Dewey. "You don't need to talk, just grunt if you agree, okay? So here's what I'm thinking."

Dewey stood up and started pacing the aisle next to the frantic Borchardt.

"When we get to Beijing, me and those pilots of yours are getting off the plane. If it's okay with you, I'm going to keep this with me."

Dewey held up the remote detonator.

"You, on the other hand, should probably stay to meet your guest, don't you think? Catch up on old times. I think it would be bad etiquette to not be here when he arrives. By the way, is that what you're wearing? Do you have anything more colorful? Maybe a light blue or yellow, something that would complement that tape across your mouth?"

Borchardt yelled hysterically and yanked at his cuffs.

"Sorry, it was just a suggestion. Wear what you have on."

Dewey walked to the galley and opened the refrigerator. He took a bottle of beer and twisted off the cap, took a large gulp, then walked casually back to Borchardt.

"Can you behave?"

Borchardt nodded yes.

Dewey leaned over and ripped the tape off Borchardt's face.

"Ow! Fuck!"

"I know. Tape hurts, doesn't it? Not as much as being vaporized in SEMTEX, but still."

"You said I wouldn't die."

"I said you might not die. Get the dork on the plane and a plane for us to leave on, and you'll live. We won't take off without you."

"What if I can't get Bo Minh to meet me? What if he tells his brother and the plane is intercepted?"

Dewey stared at Borchardt, his blue eyes as cold and blank as a winter sea. He held up the remote detonator and placed his thumb on the button.

"Then it's hard-count time. We all die."

55

Lacey James leaned over his Big Bertha driver, staring at the golf ball that was perched on a tee.

"So what's the answer, Lacey?" said a tall dark-haired man standing behind him, his agent, Chris George. "I need to get back to them this afternoon."

"I told you," said James in a clipped, aristocratic British accent. "I want ten million and some points. You figure out the points."

"Iger is not going to give you any points," said his agent. "It's fucking *Star Wars*, for chrissakes."

"Then tell them to find someone else."

"They don't want anybody else."

"Which is why I want the points, especially if I have to deal with those miserable communists at Disney."

James's large, rotund belly dangled over his belt as he stood still, trying to concentrate.

"By the way," added George, eyeing his gut. "That P90X is really working wonders on you."

James's bushy beard itched and he wanted to scratch it. Instead, he raised his middle finger off the club.

"Some of us don't need to be good-looking in order to get laid," said James.

"It helps though."

Lacey James didn't look like an Eton-educated Oxford grad. He also didn't look like someone worth millions of dollars, but he was that too.

James was universally considered the foremost special-effects makeup man in the film industry, with more than two hundred film credits to his name. He could make a donkey look like a *Sports Illustrated* swimsuit model, and vice versa, as one actress had said before handing James his second Oscar.

"I'll tell you what," said James, getting ready to hit. "If I drive the green, I'll do it for twelve, no points."

James pulled his club back. As the head of the driver reached its apotheosis in the sky, George let out a loud, wet belch, booming from his throat for at least three seconds, right as James started his swing at the ball. His club came down awkwardly, he skulled the ball and sent it flying into the parking lot. A pregnant moment of silence was followed by the sound of a windshield shattering, then the siren from someone's car alarm.

James turned and stared at George.

"I'll try for the points," said his agent.

James felt a vibration in the pocket of his shorts. Technically, he wasn't supposed to have a cell phone at Lakeside. He looked at the number, glanced about nervously, then put the phone to his ear.

"Hello?"

"Lacey," came the voice, British, confident, unmistakable: James's uncle, Derek Chalmers. "It's Uncle Derek."

"Hi, Uncle Derek," said James. "Is this about my mother?"

"No," said Chalmers. "It's about you. We need your help."

"Who's we?"

"The agency. I'm texting you a photo. I need to know if you can make someone look like this man."

James examined the photo. It showed a Chinese man.

"The short answer is yes, of course. It's a fucking Chinese guy."

"It needs to hold up under scrutiny," said Chalmers.

"What do you mean by 'scrutiny'?"

"Close inspection," said Chalmers. "The consequences of it not working would be quite negative."

"Understood," said James. He turned from the tee box and started walking back toward the pro shop. George tried to get his attention, but James ignored him. "How much time do I have?"

"I don't know. At most, a few days."

James crossed the parking lot, walking by a good-looking silver-haired man and his friend, who were examining the broken windshield of a brand-new Porsche Panamera. James pointed back toward George, who was walking down the fairway, indicating to the owner of the car that George was the one who'd put the golf ball through the windshield.

James climbed into a red and white Bugatti Veyron.

"I'll do it, Uncle Derek," said James, turning on the car. "Send me more photos if you can."

"Will do," said Chalmers. "Thanks, kid. By the way, what will this cost us?"

"Nothing," said James, firing out of the Lakeside parking lot.

56

Bo Minh was already up when the phone rang. He looked at the caller ID. The number was blocked. He pressed a small device that looked like high-tech wire cutters to the phone line. He squeezed the teeth of the device lightly against the phone line. The identity of the dialer appeared.

BORCHARDT, R. H.

"Hello?"

"It's Borchardt."

"Mr. Borchardt. It's nice to talk to you. What can I do for you?"

"I'm upset with you, Bo. I pay you a lot of money."

"What exactly are you referring to, sir?"

"The documents that were sent last week."

"What is the matter with the documents?" asked Minh. "Those are highly classified. It's a system that the army plans to spend more than ten billion dollars on. I thought you would be pleased."

"You're telling me about a missile defense system more than a month after the decision has been made?" said Borchardt. "This is what I pay you for? What's the point?"

Minh looked out the window. Borchardt had always been kind to him. He felt himself becoming upset. He shut his eyes.

"I don't know what to say, Mr. Borchardt. I sent the documents immediately after I received them. I even helped to design the specifications."

Minh waited for Borchardt to respond, but he said nothing.

"I don't know what to say, sir," continued Minh.

"There still may be time, but I'll need your help," said Borchardt. "Can the specifications be amended during the bidding phase?"

"Yes, yes, absolutely. I can't promise—"

"I leave Shanghai in a few minutes. I could divert to Beijing if you could meet me."

Minh considered the two agents outside the door to his apartment, sent by Ming-huá. He couldn't bring them; Ming-huá couldn't know about his relationship to Borchardt. Of course, evading them would be simple enough. His deck attached to a neighbor's deck, who lived in a duplex. He would go next door, then take the elevator from the floor above.

"When would you like to meet?" asked Minh.

Borchardt looked at Dewey, who was leaning over, cheek to cheek with him, holding the SAT phone between them, eavesdropping.

Dewey held up a single finger.

"One hour," said Borchardt, into the phone. "The private terminal, near Terminal Three."

When Dewey heard Minh's phone click, he stood and hung up the phone.

"Not bad," he said to Borchardt. "You're an unusually good liar. Almost like you've done it before. By the way, you need a shower, dude."

"I thought that was you."

"It could be," said Dewey. "Who knows. Maybe we can take a shower together when we get back to London? My back could use a nice loofah."

Borchardt started giggling.

"You're not funny."

"Everyone always says that but then they laugh at my jokes."

243

The plane abruptly arced left and one of the copilots came on the intercom.

"Buckle up, we're on approach to Beijing. We land in about fifteen minutes."

Dewey used the restroom, then sat down across from Borchardt.

"You need to uncuff me," said Borchardt.

"Why?"

"How will I get off the plane?"

"That's not my problem, Rolf," said Dewey. "If I untied you you'd run screaming from the plane like a little girl."

"What the hell do you expect me to do?"

"Honestly? I expect you to blow up. Then again, I haven't used SEMTEX in a while. For all I know I made a chocolate soufflé down there."

Borchardt screamed.

"Help!"

Dewey took the tape and wrapped it across his mouth. Borchardt squirmed and fought against the cuffs, his screams muted by the tape.

Dewey sat and stared at Borchardt for a few minutes. Finally, he stood and walked to the galley. He searched through drawers until he found some tools. He removed wire cutters, then returned to the seat. He held up the tool.

"Wire cutters," he said, putting them down on Borchardt's lap. "They should be able to cut through the flex cuffs."

The plane's landing gear went down and the plane shook.

"As much as I'd like to continue this enlightening discussion," said Dewey, "this is my stop. Good luck."

57

Borchardt sat in the same seat he'd been seated in, with the exception of one bathroom break, for twelve hours straight.

He was alone. His hands and feet remained tethered to the seat. On his lap sat a pair of wire cutters, taunting him with their proximity and their stillness. He calculated that once his hands were free, it would take him less than ten seconds to clip the flex cuffs from his ankles, then run down the aisle to the open cabin door and down the stairs. The reality, he knew, was a little different. Right now, he was one itchy American finger away from being immolated in the white-hot hell of a SEMTEX explosion.

Out the window, to Borchardt's right, two hundred yards across the empty tarmac, was another plane, a white Gulfstream G250. Fortunately, Gulfstream had it in Hong Kong, a short flight away. The plane had already been sold to a Chinese coal tycoon named Junbei. It had cost Borchardt twenty-five million dollars over the asking price of the jet to convince the CEO of Gulfstream to break the contract with Junbei and force the thirty-six-year-old to wait two extra days for another G250.

Borchardt stared at his new plane, wondering if he would ever actually get to use it.

Over time, Borchardt knew, his weapons had been used to kill thousands, perhaps even tens of thousands of people, on every continent and in almost every country in the world.

But Borchardt had never actually killed someone.

Borchardt's eye was suddenly drawn to the door of the private terminal building, behind the Gulfstream. The door opened and a man emerged, alone. Borchardt recognized Minh immediately. He was short and thin, and he walked with a stoop. His hair was down to his shoulders.

Minh surveyed the tarmac suspiciously, then started walking toward Borchardt's plane.

In his hand he carried a large briefcase. He wore the typical uniform of seemingly half the men in China, a dark plain Windbreaker and dark plain pants.

Dewey leaned to the porthole window of the Gulfstream, as a small man—who he assumed was Bo Minh—stepped from a blue corrugated-steel building and started walking across the tarmac toward Borchardt's brightly lit plane.

As he walked across the blacktop, Minh glanced in Dewey's direction, in fact, for one brief second, into Dewey's eyes, at least that's what it felt like.

Dewey walked to the cockpit. Inside, the two Israeli pilots were both seated. Their hair looked matted and slightly greasy. They were clearly exhausted.

"Let's start getting ready to go," said Dewey. "And when I say 'go,' I mean we're going to need to get the fuck out of here lickety-split."

"Okay," said the pilot on his left.

"What about Borchardt?" asked the other.

"Jury's still out on that one," said Dewey.

Dewey went back to the leather sofa and sat down. He watched as Bo Minh stopped at the bottom of the mobile airstairs that led up into the Boeing.

———

The rattle of Minh's shoes on the steel stairs made Borchardt's heart race. He felt like his heart was about to explode. He counted the steps as Minh climbed. Finally, Minh's head popped into view. Long black hair with specks of gray; thick, square glasses. Minh had a fearful look on his face as he entered. Then, as he focused in on Borchardt, tethered to the seat, duct tape across his mouth, his head jerked forward in shock and his glasses tumbled to the ground.

Borchardt yelled. The tape muffled the sound.

Minh picked up his glasses, put them on, and gently placed the large briefcase on the floor. He walked quickly down the aisle to Borchardt.

"Hold on, Mr. Borchardt."

Borchardt nodded at the wire cutters, still yelling.

Minh grabbed the wire cutters and cut the flex cuff at Borchardt's left arm. Borchardt reached up and pulled the tape from his mouth, panting.

"Oh, thank God, you're here," Borchardt said, panting. "It was unbelievable."

Borchardt grabbed the wire cutters from Minh. He slashed them through the air, stabbing Minh in the neck, then again, two fierce blows that made blood abruptly flood from Minh's neck. Minh dropped to the ground, screaming.

Borchardt cut the cuff at his left wrist, then the cuffs at his feet.

He dropped the wire cutters and ran to the galley kitchen, but fell down, his knees and legs weak from inactivity. He got back up, looking back to see Minh crawling after him, his front covered in crimson. At the galley, Borchardt pulled a drawer out and found a small knife. He grabbed it with his left hand, then turned, but Minh was already on him.

The sharp points of the wire cutters struck Borchardt just behind the ear. Minh swung again, from Borchardt's right, ripping a gash into Borchardt's ear. Borchardt screamed as he fell to the aisle floor, covering his ear.

Minh was screaming in Mandarin, a rabid, bloodcurdling yell, as he stabbed again, viciously, hitting Borchardt above the right eye. Blood spurted forward. Minh swung again as, from the ground, Borchardt stabbed the knife into Minh's calf. Minh screamed but landed another blow to Borchardt's forehead. Borchardt crawled toward the front of the plane, trying to get away, as Minh pulled the knife from his calf.

Minh picked up the steel briefcase with both hands. He slammed it into Borchardt's head as the German attempted to crawl away. After the second blow, Borchardt went cold. Minh hit him one more time, cursing him in Mandarin as he did so.

Minh stared for several minutes at Borchardt, who was unconscious, bleeding badly on the ground. Minh tried to catch his breath. He reached his hand to his neck, then looked at it. The fingers were covered in wet blood.

Minh limped to the cabin door, clutching the briefcase.

The engines on the Gulfstream were fired up, and a smooth electric din permeated the cabin as the pilots prepared to take off.

Dewey stared at the entrance door to the Boeing, watching the light, waiting for signs of life. He gripped the detonator. The first minute turned into a second, then third. Then a shadow appeared in the Boeing door, at the top of the stairs.

But where Dewey expected to see Borchardt, Bo Minh suddenly appeared. His head darted wildly about. He stepped into the light atop the stairs, and Dewey could see blood covering one of his hands and his neck. He was limping. He started descending the stairs.

"Motherfucker," said Dewey.

Dewey held the remote detonator. He put his thumb to the red button. He was about to press it, then paused. He put it down on the seat.

He bolted to the cabin door and jumped from the top step to the tarmac ten feet below. He sprinted toward Borchardt's plane. As he ran, Dewey pulled a Glock from his shoulder holster. He closed in on Bo Minh, who was limping beneath the shadows of the Boeing.

Minh saw Dewey sprinting toward him. He dropped the briefcase as Dewey closed in. Minh did not even have time to move as Dewey fired a round from point-blank range into his chest.

Dewey caught Minh as he fell, throwing him over his shoulder, fireman style. He sprinted the last few yards to the Boeing, then climbed up, two steps at a time. At the top stair, he tossed Minh's body to the floor. He saw Borchardt. Dewey grabbed him and lifted him up onto his shoulder. He ran back to the cabin door, then descended the airstairs, still clutching the handgun. He ran the last hundred yards to the Gulfstream, then climbed aboard. He tossed Borchardt onto one of the leather sofas, then turned and hit the door lever. The stairs began to rise.

"Get this thing in the air," yelled Dewey into the cockpit. "And I mean right fuckin' now."

The Gulfstream's engines flared and grew louder. The plane bounced into motion, then moved toward the end of the runway.

"Hold on," barked one of the Israeli pilots. "We're goin' hot."

The engines roared. The jet accelerated down the runway, to the right of the Boeing.

Dewey went back to the sofa and picked up the detonator. As the front wheels lifted off the tarmac, he pressed the small red button.

There was a pause of no more than half a second, then a tremendous thunderclap slammed the sky as the Boeing exploded.

Dewey watched through the porthole window. White, red, orange, and black flames, along with billows of thick smoke, exploded up into the sky in a spectacular radius around the plane. Dewey had to turn his eyes away from the explosion.

More loud thunder echoed across the sky as heat and flames from the explosion spread havoc within the plane's explosive- and ammunition-laden cargo area.

The Gulfstream was punched sideways, shaking and tilting as it lifted off into the sky. Dewey almost fell to the floor, but he held on to the seat. He forced himself to look again. The tarmac was a smoldering inferno of steel, inside of which was the now very charred remains of Fao Bhang's beloved half brother, Bo Minh.

Dewey looked above the burning jet. The lights of Beijing were visible in the distance.

"You're next, motherfucker," Dewey whispered.

58

The black sedan reached the steel gates at the edge of the entrance to the private terminal. Dozens of flashing red and blue lights atop police cruisers made the scene look festive—until one moved past the gates and the line of soldiers and police officers standing guard. On the tarmac, the plane was still burning. It had been more than an hour since the blast. The object was was virtually unrecognizable, a destroyed carapace of charred steel, melted parts, atop a small crater torn into the tarmac.

The line of soldiers and officers were held back at least 150 yards by the intense heat still emanating from the wreckage.

Closer to the Boeing was a convoy of green and yellow fire trucks. Teams of firefighters in protective clothing sprayed water at the smoldering wreckage.

Bhang's sedan passed through the gates, then past soldiers and officers. It came to a stop between two of the fire trucks. The driver leapt from the front seat and opened the back door.

It was 9:00 P.M. in China's capital city.

Bhang stepped from the sedan. An unlit cigarette dangled from his lips. Despite the heat, which at this distance still hovered at approximately one hundred degrees, Bhang wore a black suit. Not realizing the irony of the act, he took a lighter from his pocket and lit the cigarette.

Bhang's driver climbed back inside the air-conditioned limousine.

Bhang stood alone smoking the cigarette, listening to the loud crackling of the plane burning, watching the torrents of water strike the flames, creating steam that made clouds climb into the sky along with the smoke.

The chief investigator for the Beijing Fire Authority approached. Bhang saw him coming, from the corner of his eye, and held up his hand toward him without looking, telling him in no uncertain terms to stay away.

He stared at the burning jet, trying to imagine where Bo Minh had been and what had happened. He already knew who did it.

Bhang realized, as he took a long drag on his cigarette, that he'd let his personal feelings affect his professional judgment. But he never could have foreseen this. In all his years of covert activities, of killing, assassinations, being the target of attempts on his life, this was the first time anyone had succeeded in hurting him.

He stood in the intense heat. Sweat dripped down his forehead. He didn't want his driver or anyone to see the tears that now flowed down his cheeks at the thought of his poor brother, his helpless brother, always the weakest one on the playground, always the one being picked on. The only person Bhang had ever truly loved. Now he was gone.

The one thing Bhang was there to do and was capable of doing— protecting Bo—he'd failed at. There was no other way to look at it. At that moment, Bhang knew that the dark knot in his stomach, the bitter woe and paralyzing guilt, was a feeling worse than dying.

He also knew what he had to do, the only thing he had to do, the only thing that mattered anymore.

Bhang flicked his cigarette butt down on the ground. He opened the door of the sedan and climbed into the cool air.

"Headquarters, Minister?"

"Yes. Hurry."

Ming-húa and a swarm of other senior-level ministry officers were already assembled in Bhang's large corner office at the ministry when he entered. He said nothing to the six men standing around the conference table as he walked to his desk. He placed his briefcase on the desk, picked up a silver lighter, and lit another cigarette.

"Minister Bhang," said Ming-húa, bowing. "We are all deeply, deeply sorry for what happened to your brother."

Bhang did not look up. Instead, he removed his suit coat and hung it on the back of the chair. He opened the top drawer of his desk. Reaching in, he removed a small, stainless-steel handgun, a Walther PPK/S 380CP. Next to it was a long suppressor. Methodically, Bhang screwed the suppressor into the muzzle. When he was done, he raised the weapon in his right hand and aimed it at Ming-húa. He fired one shot. The bullet struck Ming-húa between the eyes, dropping him to the ground, as the other five men stared in horror.

"Nobody leaves this building until Andreas is dead," said Bhang. "His elimination is now the top priority of the ministry. Drop what you are doing. Delegate any projects you are currently working on."

None of the five men still standing at the table said anything, but all nodded yes.

"We have learned something in the last few minutes, Minister," said Dheng. "We found several Hong Kong–based accounts we know to be Borchardt's at the Bank of China. This afternoon, Mr. Borchardt wired seventy million dollars to the Gulfstream Aerospace Corporation of Savannah, Georgia, presumably for an aircraft."

"It could have been someone working for Borchardt," said Bhang, "paying an old bill."

"Yes, but it was wired into a Gulfstream account at the Bank of Hong Kong," said Dheng. "The account is designed so that when Gulfstream sells something in China, it can keep the profits in China and not have to repatriate the money and thus pay American taxes on the transaction."

"In other words," said Bhang, "he bought a jet in China?"

"Today," added Dheng. "An hour and a half ago."

Bhang nodded. He lit another cigarette.

"Excellent work."

"My team is now attempting to locate the plane," said Dheng. "Gulfstream embeds standard tracking technology into all of its planes. But in order to do so, we must penetrate Gulfstream, and that's not easy.

The company is owned by General Dynamics. We need to access their internal servers to be able to access the GPS."

Bhang looked at a tall bearded man, Xiao.

"I want the roster of every ministry operative, regardless of rank and regardless of current mission," ordered Bhang. "I also want personal information on Andreas. Dig deeper. We know he was born in Castine, Maine. Does he have family?"

"Did we not already kill his fiancée?" asked another man at the table, who immediately regretted asking it.

Bhang glanced at him, nostrils flared.

"It's a fair question," said Bhang, hatred and fury inflecting in his normally calm voice. "What you all want to know is, when will it end? It ends when Andreas is dead. Until then, we take as many pieces off the chessboard as we can."

59

Chalmers stuck his head in the door of the conference room, interrupting Calibrisi, who was on a phone call. Katie and Tacoma were seated at the conference table, looking at their laptops.

"We have something," said Chalmers.

The group took an elevator to the second floor of MI6 headquarters. When the doors opened, they entered a cavernous, brightly lit room filled with dozens of men and women at workstations. This was MI6's operations room, Smythson's nerve center for the management of MI6 paramilitary teams.

"Close your eyes, guys," said Chalmers as they walked through.

Technically, Calibrisi, Katie, and Tacoma shouldn't have been allowed on the second floor of Vauxhall Cross. But while there existed plenty of information that the two agencies kept separate, including activities inside each respective country, the fact is that MI6 and the CIA were more like siblings than adversaries. The occasional courtesy, such as allowing Langley's well-liked director to pass through, was looked at by everyone on the floor with a mixture of amusement and pride.

In the middle of the floor stood a small frosted-glass conference room. In each corner, a large plasma screen was hanging. In the center of the room was a steel conference table. Smythson stood at the table, looking across it at two men who were seated behind computer screens.

Chalmers, Calibrisi, Katie, and Tacoma entered the room.

Smythson's brown hair was brushed back from her face, tousled after so many hours of stress and work. She looked up at Chalmers, a blank expression on her face.

"Punch it up on two," said Smythson.

One of the plasmas lit up, and the group watched as video started to play on the screen.

"We've been monitoring SIGINT coming out of PRC," said Smythson. "Video, audio, data. This came off a British Airways flight four hours ago. The jet was on approach to Beijing International Airport."

The screen was black. After several moments, the orange and yellow lights of Beijing twinkled across the screen as the plane descended.

"Watch for it," said Smythson.

Flashing green and yellow lights pulsated in a long line, which indicated the runway that the jet was headed for. To the right of the runway, an orange mushroom cloud of flames was visible. As the lights on the ground grew larger, the plume of bright orange spiraled spectacularly into the sky, the flames lashing orange and white into the black of the night.

"It's an explosion," said Smythson. "We'll get a closer shot, here."

The jet moved lower. As it closed in on the runway, the size of the inferno grew larger. An analyst paused it. The right side of the screen was now taken up by a still frame of the explosion. Within the flame stacks was the skeleton of a plane, now aflame.

"So there was a plane that caught fire at Beijing International," said Calibrisi.

Smythson smiled at Calibrisi.

"It's Borchardt's plane," said Smythson.

Calibrisi's eyes grew wide.

"Once we saw the burning plane," said an analyst, "I called MIS to see if we could look at all SIGINT for Beijing International starting six hours ago, the approximate earliest point in time I thought they could fly in from London to Beijing. I got a hit on a flight plan, an inbound private flight, Boeing 757, which landed three hours before the video was snapped. The plane crossmatched against a British customs filing that one of Borchardt's companies made almost a decade ago, an ownership certificate, necessary if your plane is British domiciled."

Calibrisi nodded. "Excellent work."

"What does it mean?" asked Katie. "Could they have attacked the plane? Perhaps on landing?"

"We're not there yet," said Smythson. "There are a number of different possible explanations."

"There aren't that many," said Katie, walking to the screen, pointing at the skeleton of the jet. "It landed, so it wasn't shot down, right? It's in Beijing, which could mean Dewey flew right into the waiting arms of Fao Bhang."

"Yes," said Chalmers. "Or there's simply a different explanation. In any event, we need some real-time intelligence on Dewey. Hector, this guy is your guy. Do you have any way of reaching him?"

Calibrisi shrugged his shoulders.

"What can I say?" asked Calibrisi. "The guy's AWOL."

"We need to find Dewey," said Smythson.

Calibrisi nodded, then pulled his phone out.

"Get me Bruckheimer over at NSA," he said into the phone, to an operator at CIA control. "Tell him it's important."

60

Dewey leaned into the cockpit.

"No radio," said Dewey, "unless you feel like having China shoot us out of the sky."

Dewey went back to the seat and opened his leather bag. He removed a half-empty pint bottle of Jack Daniel's. He sat down in the seat and kicked his feet up on the seat in front of him.

"Why did you save me?" asked Borchardt. They were his first words since taking off from Beijing several hours before.

Dewey held the bottle in his hand, reading the label on the side of the bottle. He took another sip but said nothing.

Borchardt sat up, a pained grimace crossing his face. He felt for his ear. It had turned into a large red scab. The gash had clotted up. Dewey had left it alone, even though it needed a bandage. Eventually, the blood had stopped trickling.

Borchardt touched the raw, fresh scab, then grimaced again. He glanced around the interior of the plane.

"This must be the new plane," he said, admiring it. "They're too expensive, of course, but Gulfstream makes the best planes. Look at it."

Dewey stared at the seat in front of him, his mind a thousand miles away.

Killing Bhang's brother had done little to make the pain go away.

His mind kept replaying the sight of Jessica, her eyes looking help-lessly up at him from the ground.

"Nothing," Dewey whispered to himself. "You did nothing wrong."

"Dewey," said Borchardt. "Why did you save me?"

Dewey glanced at Borchardt, a look of contempt and sadness on his face.

"You wouldn't understand."

"Try me."

"Because I gave you my word," said Dewey, looking away, shutting his eyes for a moment, trying to shut out the sight of Borchardt, of the plane—trying to shut out the world.

Borchardt sat back.

"Well, thank you," said Borchardt. "Whatever you did it for."

Dewey opened his eyes. He stared impassively at Borchardt. Borchardt was a mess. On one side, his shirt was covered in blood. He had a raw, fresh contusion on his forehead. His ear looked as if a bear had clawed part of it off.

Dewey had inflicted the counterblow he wanted to. He'd struck hard at Bhang, in a way that had undoubtedly hurt him. But Bhang wasn't expecting it. He would be anticipating Dewey's next move.

Dewey knew Bhang would bring the weight of the ministry to bear now. He would scour the earth looking for him, much as Aswan Fortuna had done. Yet, unlike Fortuna, Bhang had an army of committed, disciplined warriors, not just a cell of half-crazed jihadists.

And the first place they'd be looking is somewhere in the vicinity of the disheveled, blood-crusted, ashen-pale little German billionaire with the odd haircut seated across from him.

Dewey glanced at his watch. They'd left Beijing nine hours before. They would be over Europe soon.

Dewey knew that now was the time to move beyond improvisation. Bhang would come looking for him, and when he did, he had to be ready. He would have, at most, one chance at Bhang.

Dewey knew he couldn't do it alone. He needed Hector.

But would Hector ever forgive him?

Dewey shut his eyes, feeling shame, as his mind replayed the look in Hector's eyes as Dewey held him by the neck, against the concrete wall.

"So what now?" asked Borchardt.

"What do you mean?"

"What are you going to do now?" asked Borchardt.

Dewey took a sip.

"You killed his brother," continued Borchardt, "but he's still alive. What's next? I could help you."

"Gee, thanks, Rolf," whispered Dewey, contemptuously. "Let's do it together. Me and you. The Lone Ranger and Tonto."

Borchardt nodded.

"I guess I don't blame you. I wouldn't trust me either. Then again, who else do you have?"

Dewey leaned over and looked out the window. They were passing over water. Suddenly, Dewey pictured his brother, Hobey, standing on the town dock in Castine, shirtless, eating a popsicle, staring up at the Maine Maritime Academy ship, mesmerized by its size, towering over the dock and the two boys. Something about the memory made him feel anxious, even upset. He stood up and walked to the cockpit.

"Where are we?"

"We'll be over Italy soon," said the copilot.

"Let me see a map."

The copilot handed Dewey a navigational chart, which he studied for several minutes. He'd been to most of the larger cities on the map. He wanted someplace familiar, where he could hide out for a few days and figure out his next steps. A place where he could reach out to Hector and apologize.

"Drop me in Lisbon," said Dewey. "Then you guys can go back to London and get some sleep."

Dewey went back to the seat across from Borchardt.

"Dewey," said Borchardt, "I would like to know where we stand. I know my apologies mean nothing to you, but I am sorry."

"You certainly deserve to die," said Dewey, "but I'm better off with you alive. Properly managed, you have a certain utility. There aren't many people who could've done what you just did. Besides, Fao Bhang will probably get you after he figures out what happened to his brother."

A look of anxiety hit Borchardt.

"You better hope I kill him," said Dewey. "Because if I die, my guess is, you'll be next. Then again, maybe a sincere apology from you would suffice for Bhang. Throw in a box of chocolates. He seems like the sentimental type."

Dewey pulled his handgun from his shoulder holster.

"No," said Borchardt, holding his hands up, pleading.

"I'm not going to kill you," said Dewey.

He clutched the barrel of the weapon, then swung the butt at a precise spot on the side of Borchardt's head. Borchardt tumbled to the floor, unconscious.

"But I am going to knock you out for a while."

61

BEIJING

Dheng's desk was a large X made of glass and stainless steel. It sat in the middle of a gargantuan floor of stone-faced computer geeks, hundreds in all, seated in row after monotonous row of computer terminals, each of them staring into computer screens.

Dheng sat at the intersection of the X. Dheng was a computer engineer by training, with two Ph.D.s in computer science, including one from Caltech. Within the ministry, Dheng was considered, at least to those who knew him, the most intelligent person in China.

Sixteen flat-screen plasma TVs lined the axis of the large X, two on each axis, facing outward, enabling Dheng to monitor activities; he had access to the activities of every hacker inside the ministry and could drop in on any individual screen at any time in order to ask the hacker a question, make a recommendation, or take over the screen.

It was Dheng who had written the cryptographic algorithm that enabled the ministry to hack into the Pentagon four years before. Although access inside had lasted only eleven minutes, Dheng stole a variety of informative documents.

Dheng was a short man with unusual curly black hair and glasses. He moved along each axis, looking quickly at each screen for no more than a minute before stepping to the next screen. Occasionally, he would stop and type something quickly into a keyboard, usually a suggestion or actual code, before moving on.

All sixteen screens mirrored the screens of Dheng's most notorious and capable hackers, scattered about the large floor. All sixteen hackers were working on the same thing: trying to break into Gulfstream's computer network.

As Dheng long ago learned, the U.S. private sector had much more robust antihacking protection than the U.S. government had. Everyone knew where the talent went after getting their degrees from MIT, Carnegie Mellon, or Caltech.

Dheng's small brigade of hackers had been at it now for more than five hours.

Dheng was suddenly interrupted by a loud commotion half a room away, almost out of eyesight. A group of employees was yelling. Dheng looked up.

A young, overweight man came running from the commotion, down the aisle between rows and rows of workers. By the time he reached Dheng, his face was beet red and sweat darkened the armpits of his blue plaid shirt.

"One sixty four," he wheezed, "sir. I have gotten inside, sir."

Dheng smiled. He stood upright and started clapping.

"Fine work. What is your name?"

"Hu."

A brief round of applause filled the room.

Then Dheng moved to a screen and started furiously typing.

He took over Hu's computer screen. As the young, obese hacker had said, he was indeed inside Gulfstream.

Analyzing the access route, Dheng saw that Hu had used a cat-and-mouse strategy, luring a high-level General Dynamics employee in their computer security area to chase after Hu in what was a persistent but illusory attempt at getting in through an employee e-mail server. While fleeing, Hu had painted a simple brushstroke of nearly invisible metadata into the General Dynamics employee's own seemingly successful lockdown code. Once the employee booked it into a separate data cache, the metadata had communicated back to Hu through the employee's own CPU. It was a clever strategy that depended on persistence and upon the mistake of an unwitting person on the receiving end.

"Excellent work, Mr. Hu," said Dheng, who started typing. "Are you married?"

"No, sir."

A crowd started to gather behind Dheng. His fingers moved across the keyboard.

"Parents?"

"Yes, sir."

"Well, they will be very proud," said Dheng as he typed. "Tonight you may tell them you received a raise and a promotion."

"Thank you, sir."

Within forty-five seconds, Dheng was inside Gulfstream's servers. Three minutes after that, he'd penetrated the massive GPS feed, which collected second-by-second location information about every Gulfstream jet ever made, whether it was parked or flying. Exactly eighteen seconds later, he knew where Borchardt's new plane, the plane with Dewey Andreas aboard, was located.

Dheng pressed the earbud in his right ear, turning on the wireless phone.

"Get me Minister Bhang," he said.

Fao Bhang marched into the conference room down the hallway from his office. Inside the room were the seven men who had, until a few hours before, reported to Ming-húa. These were the top agents within the clandestine paramilitary bureau.

Bhang had ordered them to convene ten minutes before, after Dheng had let Bhang know that the American who'd murdered his brother and who was responsible for the death of Mikal Dillman, was headed into southern Europe.

Dheng entered the conference room, a cigarette in his mouth, walking quickly and reading a laptop as he moved toward the table.

"The plane is descending," said Dheng, staring at his laptop as he spoke. "He's going to land in one of the following airports: Madrid, Sevilla, Porto, Lisbon, Rabat, Casablanca, Marrakech. We will know more as he gets closer."

"I want every ministry agent in those cities positioned at the airports," said Bhang, calmly. He lit a cigarette. "Get them all on live COMM."

"Yes, sir."

"All contractors in Spain, Portugal, Morocco—same thing," said Bhang. "Get an alert out. We need to stop him right now, at the airport. He's running. We need to find him before he gets far, and we need to take him down."

Bhang looked at Dheng.

"As soon as you know," Bhang said to him.

"As soon as I have his end location, Minister, you and everyone here will know," said Dheng. "It shouldn't be that long. In fact, based on the plane's altitude, we can now rule out Madrid."

"Tell them all, to the man or woman who kills Andreas, the Order of the Lotus," said Bhang, "awarded by me personally."

Every man at the conference table paused. A few exchanged glances. They each understood the significance of what Bhang had just said. The Order of the Lotus was the ministry's highest honor, a medal that had not been awarded to anyone in more than five years.

"Good luck, gentlemen. I know we will be successful."

62

Near a private exit off the Baltimore–Washington Parkway that read NSA EMPLOYEES ONLY stood a black glass rectangular office building, one of two newer buildings in a cluster of four—the Big Four, as they were referred to—headquarters of the world's foremost cryptologists, eavesdroppers, and hackers: the National Security Agency.

On the third floor of the building, in a windowless conference room, Jim Bruckheimer, director of SID, was seated with two of his most trusted SID analysts, Serena Pacheco and Jesus June.

SID had primary responsibility within the United States for the acquisition of all foreign signals intelligence; SID was the behemoth that went out and eavesdropped, stole, code-broke, and did all manner of legal and illegal information gathering, in every region and country of the world, on behalf of the U.S. government, then processed signals with NSA's massive computers for use by the president and other military and intelligence officials.

Bruckheimer, Pacheco, and June were seated around a triangular phone console. On the line with them was General Piper Redgrave, NSA's chief, along with Hector Calibrisi.

Calibrisi had just finished briefing the group on the explosion in Beijing.

"Is there a finding on this?" asked Redgrave.

"Yes," said Calibrisi. "President Dellenbaugh signed it two days ago."

"Care to share some of the details?" asked Redgrave.

"No," said Calibrisi. "I don't. What I need is a very immediate off-event scan in regard to this explosion, focused within PRC. We are flying in the dark here, and we can't be."

"Can you point us toward something?" asked Bruckheimer. "Words, names—whatever will help us cut to the quick."

"Andreas, Bhang, Borchardt, Ming-húa. That's all I can think of."

Pacheco and June started typing.

"That's a good start," said Bruckheimer.

"What's the end goal here?" asked Redgrave.

"Finding Dewey Andreas," said Calibrisi.

"Do we have a precise timeline on the explosion?" asked Bruckheimer.

"We have an approximate time," said Calibrisi. "We stumbled onto the burning wreckage after the explosion, so we don't know how long it had been on fire. However, eight minutes before the explosion, another plane landed and there was no fire, so we've got it narrowed. It was between 8:12 and 8:18 Beijing time."

Bruckheimer nodded at Pacheco.

"You take the explosion," he said.

Bruckheimer looked at June.

"Let's look at ThinThread real quick," Bruckheimer said, off-line. "Get it sniffing for Andreas."

"I thought ThinThread got shut down?" said Calibrisi on speaker.

"You weren't supposed to hear that," said Bruckheimer.

"Call me when you have something."

The NSA's ThinThread program was created in the late 1990s and designed to gather, synthesize, and contextualize vast amounts of data in real time in order to then cherry-pick relevant communications targeted around specific dates, times, locations, or people. ThinThread was able to gather and subsequently marry seemingly unrelated data from such real-time, innocuous trigger events such as credit-card purchases, e-mails, financial transactions, travel records, use of GPS equipment, Internet activity, and any other electronic imprint that an NSA analyst might find helpful in locating virtually any individual anywhere in the world.

Though ThinThread had been shut down, much of its internal engines still hummed along under various names. Bruckheimer was old-school, however, and had been part of the team that designed and named the system. He refused to call it by anything else.

Unfortunately for Bruckheimer and June, Dewey was precisely the sort of individual who could elude ThinThread based not on intent but solely on the way he lived his life. Dewey rarely used credit cards and didn't like the Internet. He didn't have a Facebook account and was serially plagued with the same problem, trying to remember his password for his e-mail account. He found it easier to simply not communicate.

For the first hour after the conference call with Calibrisi, June found little to nothing on Dewey. His e-mail hadn't been opened in more than two weeks. He didn't own a cell phone. The most recent travel records, Dewey's flight to London, they already knew about. After that, Dewey's life was a blank slate, at least as far as ThinThread was concerned.

Serena Pacheco, on the other hand, quickly found a veritable treasure trove of information coming off the explosion at Beijing International Airport.

First were various radio transmissions coming from firemen and policemen who were on the scene. While interesting, they were useless. Then Pacheco hit paydirt. When she entered the name Andreas into an e-mail system based in Morocco and owned by a private Russian company, it was like striking oil. Attached to five different e-mails of individuals using the Russian e-mail server, a document was attached. On the document was a large photograph of Dewey. The document had five separate encryptions off a base Chinese text; Pacheco fed this document into a NSA code breaker algorithm that was designed to run text and figures through a massive store of mathematical and language possibilities. It took the program less than ten minutes to decrypt the document with Dewey's photo on it. Once it was decoded, the document had five separate versions: Chinese, Spanish,

Russian, French, and English. Pacheco hit print on the English version, then grabbed the document from the printer.

Across the top of the document, above Dewey's photo, were the initials in bold black letters on a red stripe: **TEP.** It looked like an FBI most-wanted poster at the local post office.

Pacheco ran out of the SID conference room to Bruckheimer's office down the hall.

"Jim," she said. "I got something."

Bruckheimer took the sheet from her. He looked at the photo of Dewey, then called Calibrisi and put it on speaker.

"We're e-mailing this to you now," said Bruckheimer. "It'll be on MI6 1422 in a few seconds."

"Great work, guys," said Calibrisi, from London.

"By the way, what does TEP stand for?" asked Bruckheimer.

"Is that what it says?"

"Yeah."

"Termination with extreme prejudice," said Calibrisi.

Calibrisi hung up the phone, then turned to Smythson as Chalmers came back into the glass conference room.

A few moments later, one of the corner plasma screens lit up with the document.

→ TEP
ANDREAS, DEWEY   AGE: 39
CURRENT LOCATION: 11798700ADE
NATIONALITY: U.S.A.
BIOGRAPH: FORMER U.S. SPECIAL FORCES (DELTA)
WANTED: MURDER OF TOP-RANKING MINISTRY OFFICIAL
COMMENTS: TARGET IS ARMED AND EXTREMELY DANGEROUS

"That might explain the explosion," said Chalmers.

"Do we have a time stamp on this?" asked Calibrisi.

"It was sent out more than two hours ago," said the analyst.

"What's the location?" asked Chalmers, pointing at the long coded number.

"The SID code breaker couldn't figure it out."

"They know where he is," said Katie, urgency in her voice. "They have a location on him."

Calibrisi opened his phone.

"Get me Jim Bruckheimer again," he told the CIA operator.

A few moments later, Bruckheimer came on the line.

"How can I miss you if you won't leave?" asked Bruckheimer.

Calibrisi didn't laugh.

"I need you to find out where that location is. This termination order went out more than two hours ago. We're behind here. Dewey is a sitting duck."

"If it didn't decrypt, it means it won't, Hector," said Bruckheimer. "That thing went through the mainframe. They formatted the document into five different versions. Each version was the same except for the code. It's different on each version. We also opened the document that was attached to other e-mail accounts. Again, all the codes were different. I can't explain it other than to say, we can't decrypt the locale."

"That doesn't do much for me," said Calibrisi. "What about Thin-Thread?"

"We need an electronic event. You know that. He needs to buy something. But he hasn't done that. Until he does, we got nothing."

"What about Borchardt?"

"Same. Try and be patient."

"I can't," said Calibrisi. "Let's keep a line open here. I'll have control set up the bridge."

Calibrisi pointed at the phone console in the center of the table. Smythson hit the conference button, and the CIA operator created a secure bridge between MI6 and Fort Meade.

Calibrisi then had the CIA operator connect him with Bill Polk in Virginia.

"Hi, Bill," said Calibrisi, stepping into the corner of the conference room, away from the larger group.

"What've you got?"

"Where are you?"

"Langley."

"We've got a situation," said Calibrisi.

"Dewey?"

"Yeah."

"I talked to Katie a couple hours ago."

"China has a termination order out on him," said Calibrisi. "They have a hard location."

"Where?"

"We have no idea."

"What can I do? I've got a tac team waiting here. As soon as we get a location, we'll redeploy whatever assets we have in the theater. I've got every operative I have on standby. If you want, I can call JSOC and see about getting some Deltas and SEALs good to go."

"Do it."

"Hector, one more thing. If they do succeed in killing Dewey, I'd like permission to change the rules of engagement, at least for a day or two. Let my guys clear some of these Chinese motherfuckers off the face of the earth."

"They won't succeed," said Calibrisi.

"But if they do."

"They won't."

63

A quarter mile off the coast of Lisbon, Huong lay winded atop his surfboard, an Al Merrick 6´2´ Tangent, his most prized possession, floating in the cold ocean, catching his breath. His arms and legs, after a morning of surfing, were sore and aching.

Huong was surfing his favorite spot, Guincho, an exposed, west-facing beach that picked up some of the first and thus biggest of the fast-moving swells coming off the Atlantic Ocean. Guincho was not for the faint of heart nor the technically challenged. Add the occasional shark to the mix, and it was not a mystery as to why most of the people on this warm autumn day were watching from the beach or from the crumbling rock jetty next to it, rather than trying to tame one of the double-overhead sets that came like rolling thunder from the open ocean.

Huong was paddling just a few feet behind the notorious, intimidating Guincho break when he felt a sharp vibration at his wrist. It was coming from his ministry-issued wristwatch. He pulled his wet-suit sleeve up. The face of the watch displayed a red light that flickered on and off. It meant one thing and one thing only: get in.

Something was going down inside his station, meaning Lisbon proper. He nearly screamed with excitement. But he didn't. In fact, Huong didn't show any emotion.

Huong saw an oncoming wave and paddled hard to get into position. He dropped onto what turned into a vicious, eighteen-foot-high wall of deep blue, which he caught a tad late. But once he was atop it, he knew what to do, shaping the front of his board into the wave's sharp upper edge. Huong and board were thrown forward and down. He slashed like a dagger across a hard wall of blue water, just inches from the foaming white barrel that wanted to rip into him from behind and pummel him into the oblivion. He crouched, skimming his fingers along the wall of blue, as, in the distance, he could hear excited screams from onlookers atop the jetty, cheering him on. He emerged from the chute as the wave collapsed like a falling building, and he popped out the side, unscathed. He let the massive wave's remnants fire him gently onto the sandy beach.

At the beach, Huong dried off, took off his wet suit, then sprinted up the hill to his car, carrying his board. He strapped his board to the roof of his car, then climbed in the front seat. He ripped the bright blue Porsche 911 out of the parking area, nearly hitting a woman, as he fumbled for his phone.

"Where have you been?" It was Huong's team leader, somewhere in Beijing.

"Surfing."

"Get to the airport, now."

"What terminal?"

"The private terminal. You'll get further instructions when you get there."

64

It was late morning as the Gulfstream made its approach into Lisbon.

Borchardt was still out. He'd be unconscious for a few more hours at least. Borchardt was going to no doubt require a few days in the hospital. Then a month or two of psychotherapy.

Out the window, Dewey saw the curvilinear slope of the Portuguese coast, Lisbon like a white-and-red patch at the northern apex. Lisbon was one of the most beautiful cities in the world, and from the sky, the dark, muted ocean behind the green curvature of the land was like a painting.

"Buckle up," said one of the pilots from the cockpit.

Dewey ignored the suggestion.

As the plane arced down toward the tarmac and the city of Lisbon drew closer, its rich panoply of low red-roofed buildings, Dewey pondered his next steps.

The Chinese would be looking for him, but they would have no idea where he was, unless they had somehow tracked the plane. Dewey knew that was possible, though highly doubtful.

Lisbon was a random decision, just as he'd been trained to make. He thought back to his training:

Move quickly. Never stay in the same place for long. Stay in crowded areas. Seek crowds. Blend in. Don't hide. Avoid locations where you've been in the past or where they assume you will go. Move with speed. Know when you are found. Always know what your weapon is, and have it within reach at all times.

The smartest thing for Dewey to do would be to simply take a taxi-cab to the American embassy. There, he would be beyond the reach of Bhang. He could do what he should have done already: call Hector. Go back and figure out a way to get at Bhang.

The jet's wheels kissed the tarmac. The plane sped down the landing strip, then slowed.

Dewey checked the calf sheath on his left leg, making sure his knife was there. He stood up. He checked the magazines on the two Glocks he'd taken from the weapons cache in the other plane. He tucked one of the guns into his belt, in front. He took the other Glock and holstered it beneath his left armpit.

Dewey leaned into the cockpit.

"Move it around so the stairs face away from the building," he said, pointing at the modern glass building that served as the entrance area for the private terminal.

Dewey hit the door lever. The stair hydraulic vibrated as the stairs lowered. He stepped down the stairs. His eyes darted from side to side as he scanned the tarmac. He peered beneath the fuselage. In the distance stood the private aviation building. Dewey started walking in the opposite direction, toward the main terminal. There was a long strip of hardtop he would have to cross. He started a fast walk across it. After a hundred yards, he was near a line of commercial jets. He fell in with a line of passengers disembarking down a set of stairs. He walked into the terminal building, his eyes scanning, the hard steel of the Glocks pressing, in an uncomfortable but familiar way, into his torso and side.

The private aviation lounge was a small modern glass building with a comfortable seating area. It was reserved for passengers on private planes. In the far corner of the lounge area sat Huong. He was in the back, in a black leather chair, sipping a coffee. He looked at his iPhone. The words were in Mandarin.

"Wheels down."

Despite the heat, Huong had on a black Windbreaker. Across his chest, inside the Windbreaker, a 5.7x28mm FN P90 close-quarters combat submachine gun was strapped, its unusual bullpup shape easy to hide, the top-mounted magazine loaded, the safety off, the fire selector set to full auto.

Huong first eyed the Gulfstream when its silver nose reflected a sun flash in the low western sky, coming toward the runway. The jet barreled down the runway, then moved toward the terminal. It was unmistakable; it had to be the jet.

Huong hit a few strokes on the iPhone.

"Target in sight. Do I have backup?"

Huong waited for the response, his heart beating wildly.

"Yes. Lei and Shin are outside the main terminal."

Huong knew both men. Lei was young, early twenties. Shin was in his forties, tough as nails, the second-ranking agent in Portugal.

Huong looked one last time at Andreas's photo, then pocketed his phone.

In addition to a compact, extremely lethal FN P90 submachine gun, Huong had a suppressed, Spanish-made Star Megastar .45 ACP tucked in a specially designed pocket of the Windbreaker. He knew it would be better to use the suppressed Megastar. Inside the terminal, he would have to go quiet. But he'd never killed someone with the P90, and he longed to do it.

He looked around and counted only two other people in the spacious, brightly lit lounge area, a woman behind the reception desk and a businessman seated in the center of the reception area, reading.

The plane came to a stop directly in front of the building, a few hundred feet away. The right side of the jet faced the building. Huong walked to the window. He searched the tarmac near the jet, looking for people, security guards, maintenance crew. But it was empty.

He felt the rectangular block of steel against his torso. He could do it outside, as he crossed the tarmac. The sound would be barely intelligible above the loud noise and confusion of the airport.

Then Huong remembered his training. To show off was frowned upon.

The sound of a gun is the sound of the soldier; silence, the signature of the professional.

He moved to a seat against the far wall, a seat removed from the line of sight of the entrance door. He put his hand in his pocket and gripped the butt of the Megastar, waiting, heart racing, the warmth of adrenaline coursing through him, warmth ten times that of the feeling off Guincho, when the front of his Tangent board slashed horizontally across the front wall of the wave.

Inside the main terminal, Dewey went into the first store he could find. He bought a baseball hat with a Benfica football logo on it, along with a pair of dark sunglasses and an international phone card.

In the distance, he saw a sign for the taxi stand. Against the wall, he noticed a line of public phones. He went to one of the glass semiprivate booths, put his bag down, keyed in the calling-card number, then dialed. Though he'd picked up the receiver with the intent of calling Hector, when he started to dial, his fingers struck different digits, another number he knew by heart. After nearly half a minute, the phone started to ring. It rang four times, then picked up.

"Hi, this is Jess," said the voice. Dewey shut his eyes, picturing her face.

"I can't come to the phone right now; please leave me a message."

He forgot how warm her voice was, how soft and shy, and he remembered that it would have been his voice to listen to, to laugh with, for the rest of his life.

He fought to push the thoughts away. He hung up, then leaned his head against the wall.

Leave it behind, Dewey. Walk away. Get it through your head and walk away. Leave her behind. Yesterday's gone. She's gone.

Fight. It's all you can do. It's all you could ever do.

Against his better judgment, he dialed again. He listened until he felt someone's eyes on him. He looked up. An old woman was staring at him, politely waiting for the phone. He hung up the phone and walked away from the phone booth.

Dewey walked quickly through the terminal, keeping his head down. He rode an escalator to the baggage-claim area. Near the glass doors to the outside, he saw a sign for the taxi stand.

The area outside the terminal was crowded with cars, buses, rental-car shuttles, taxis, and people. There were three separate lanes. The first was reserved for taxis. A center lane was reserved for public transportation and shuttles; a procession of buses, hotel and rental-car shuttles lined the concrete sidewalk. The far traffic lane was for everyday cars and was crowded with double-parked cars, as passengers hustled to climb in.

Dewey saw the taxi line to the left. He fell in line behind a young black couple. They were holding hands and laughing. From their accents, they sounded French. The man was tall; Dewey moved into line as close to the couple as possible, using them to provide a visual shield as he scanned the sidewalk for anyone even remotely Asian.

The airport was chaotic and crowded. This, Dewey knew, was exactly what he wanted.

Seek crowds. Blend in. Know where your weapon is.

Dewey began to relax slightly as the French couple came to the front of the taxi line. Still, he felt perspiration beneath his armpits.

"Are you here on holiday?" asked the woman behind Dewey. He turned. She looked Middle Eastern; her accent was British. She smiled at him.

"No," said Dewey.

The line moved again. A small green taxi pulled in front of the French couple. As they climbed in back, the woman giggled watching the man attempt to squeeze into the tiny vehicle. The driver climbed out and opened the trunk of the taxi, then grabbed the couple's bags and tossed them into the trunk. A few seconds later, the taxi sped away.

Dewey was at the front of the line now. He was exposed to anyone driving in any of the three pickup lanes. He stooped a bit, pulling the hat as low as he could without looking suspicious. He registered a long succession of buses and rental-car shuttles in the next lane. In the far lane, cars were backed up, double parked, horns honking intermittently.

Dewey glanced left, toward the airport entrance. There wasn't a taxi in sight.

"Fuck," he whispered.

Dewey turned.

"How about you?" he asked politely, looking at the woman. He surveyed over her shoulders, to both sides, scanning the terminal entrance for spotters.

"Yes, I'm on holiday. I'm meeting my sister."

Dewey turned from the woman, looking again for a taxi. There wasn't one in sight.

"Would you like to share a taxi into town?" asked the woman. "It's so frightfully expensive."

Dewey looked into the woman's eyes for a brief moment, saying nothing. Then, out of the corner of his eye, he caught sight of a bright red sedan with black checkers on its doors and a flashing yellow sign on its roof. The taxi barreled into the airport and, moments later, sped down the taxi lane.

"Thank God," he muttered.

The red taxi moved quickly down the lane and stopped in front of Dewey.

"I'm afraid I can't," said Dewey to the woman.

Dewey reached for the taxi door and noticed, for the first time, a white van parked two lanes over, its windows tinted jet-black.

A chill spiked in the back of Dewey's neck as the van's lights suddenly flickered. Someone inside the van had turned the key.

"Where to?" asked the cab driver.

Dewey leaned down, into the passenger window, making eye contact with the driver.

"I have luggage," said Dewey.

"I'm sorry," said the driver, putting it in neutral and climbing out. "Let me help you."

"Thanks," said Dewey, remaining with his head down, next to the passenger window as the driver moved to the rear of the taxi.

Through the canopy of the taxi, he scanned the van. It was shiny and new. It sat still, its running lights now on. The black of the windshield and passenger window prevented Dewey from seeing anyone.

Am I being paranoid, Dewey asked himself?

Fight. It's all you can do. It's all you could ever do.

The taxi driver stepped to the back of the taxi and opened the trunk.

"Where is your bag, sir?" he called in a thick accent from behind the taxi.

Dewey glanced at the driver. He was now shielded by the trunk.

Dewey ripped open the front passenger-side door. He climbed in the taxi, then moved across the passenger seat to the driver's seat, keeping his eyes glued to the van.

Suddenly, the black passenger-side window of the van cracked, then lowered.

Dewey thrust the taxi into reverse just as the muzzle of a rifle emerged from the window. Dewey ducked and slammed the accelerator to the floor, tearing backward, just as the first slugs pelted the window, shattering it.

Unmuted automatic-weapon fire exploded out above the general din of the airport. It was followed by screams, then all-out pandemonium as anyone within earshot dived to the ground or ran for their lives.

The taxi driver screamed as Dewey burst backward, leaping out of the way as the taxi accelerated up the lane, in reverse, the back bumper barely missing him.

Dewey kept the gas pedal slammed against the floor. Tires screeched and thick black smoke clouded the air as Dewey let the tires rip across the hot tar. The taxi hurled backward, trunk open, back up the taxi lane, wrong direction, smoke from burning rubber darkening the air around the cab.

Slugs pelted the side of the taxi as the gunman in the van fired at Dewey.

Screams blended with the sound of gunfire and screeching tires.

Dewey ripped the vehicle backward, speeding in reverse for a hundred feet, then slammed the brakes. He was now behind the van.

Dewey jammed the car into gear and slammed the gas pedal to the floor as hard as he could. The tires screeched even louder this time, creating more black smoke. The rear of the taxi fishtailed slightly. Dewey jacked the steering wheel left as the taxi fired dead ahead, toward the van, accelerating. With his right hand, Dewey pulled the G19 from under his armpit. People scrambled, screaming, dropping bags, trying to get out of the way of the speeding taxi, which Dewey targeted toward the white van, two lanes away.

Dewey hit the low concrete curb at fifty miles an hour, then barreled over it.

A line of people waiting for a bus was directly in front of him. He slammed the horn but didn't slow down a bit, keeping the gas floored as he flipped the safety off the 9mm. People scattered, screaming, as Dewey accelerated through the line, leaving hysterical people on both sides of the taxi, now blazing at seventy-five miles an hour and climbing.

Ahead, now only one lane away, Dewey could see the unmistakable face of a Chinese gunman on the passenger side of the van, as he triggered an assault rifle at the taxi.

Several people were struck by errant bullets. They tumbled to the concrete sidewalk, blood spraying the ground. Hysterical bystanders dived to the ground, fortunate enough to be spared from the fusillade.

Dewey kept low, tucked against the door, his foot hard on the gas pedal, his right hand clutching the G19.

Suddenly, the rear double doors of the van flew open. The Chinese agent appeared. He went into a crouch, military style, on one knee. He clutched a short, stubby black assault rifle, which Dewey recognized: FN F2000, a bullpup assault rifle that was easy to handle and blisteringly lethal. A moment later, the muzzle erupted as the gunman triggered the 5.56x.45mm assault rifle at Dewey, who was now moving at almost ninety miles an hour straight at him.

The first slugs pelted the steel hood of the taxi. The line of big holes moved in a jagged line up the hood, toward Dewey, hitting what was left of the shattered window.

Dewey reached left and opened his door. He ducked lower, away from the spray of lead. He tucked against the front of the door, near the hinges, next to the steering wheel, shielded by the dashboard, as slugs tore the seat next to him.

The engine revved furiously as he charged ever closer to the van. Dewey braced himself as yards turned to feet turned to inches. The sound of the F2000, firing full auto, combined with a hurricane of slugs. The air between the two vehicles was drowned in chaos.

Dewey heard the gunman shout, a panicked scream in Mandarin. Then, a moment later, the taxi slammed into the back of the van. Metal crushed against metal as the gunman was launched into the air. He tumbled out the back of the van, thrown to the taxi hood, where he landed just in front of Dewey. Dewey moved the Glock, then fired a slug into the man's skull, just as—ahead of Dewey—the van peeled out, the driver now desperate to get away.

Dewey hit the gas again and burst right, accelerating to the side of the now-screeching van, which was running for the airport exit. Both vehicles were accelerating down the lane, Dewey trying to catch up in the badly hobbled taxi. Smoke billowed from the taxi's engine, rising up through the pockmarked hood.

Dewey had the accelerator hard against the floor. He looked down and saw the speedometer hit sixty. Screams mixed with the sound of screeching tires and revving engines. For the first time, Dewey heard a siren in the distance.

Dewey pushed the taxi until it finally reached the back bumper of the van. He was gaining on the slower vehicle as, up ahead, cars swerved out of the way. Inch by inch, the taxi came abreast of the van. When he was finally parallel to the front tire of the van, Dewey jacked the wheel left, aiming at the van. A second later, the taxi slammed into the passenger door. The van jerked abruptly to its left, careering toward a thick steel pole. The van slammed dead center into the pole, crushing into the engine, in the same moment the taxi smashed into the door. Both vehicles came to a grinding halt, the dead gunman tumbling off the hood.

Dewey punched up at the shattered windshield, then climbed up onto the hood, clutching the Glock. He raised the gun as he leapt toward the van. He started firing. Unmuted gunfire sounded above more screams and an approaching chorus of sirens. He fired into the black glass of the passenger-door window, shattering it. Another agent sat in the driver's seat. The man's head was forward, against the steering wheel, though he was still alive. He turned his head to look at Dewey. Blood covered his forehead.

Dewey fired. A bullet tore into the man's forehead, spraying the far glass with blood and skull.

Dewey leapt from the hood of the cab and sprinted toward the parking garage, as, behind him, sirens wailed in the distance and screams continued to echo through the warm air.

Inside the parking garage, he sprinted down an aisle of cars, Glock clutched in his right hand, searching for an escape vehicle. Dewey came upon a large man climbing into a white Mercedes E63 AMG.

"Keys," said Dewey.

The man turned, shocked, saw Dewey's sidearm, then tossed Dewey the keys.

He climbed inside the sedan, jammed the key in the ignition, started the car, then peeled out of the parking space. He turned the wheel and headed toward the garage entrance, quickly removing his sunglasses and hat. Dewey fell into the airport exit line, driving cautiously, scanning for more agents.

At least half a dozen police cars descended upon the terminal, their blue and red lights flashing, their sirens blasting the air, as they barreled past buses, taxis, and cars, all of whom pulled over to let them pass by, including Dewey.

He drove through the airport exit. He kept a calm eye on the rearview mirror, looking for trailers. He saw nothing. Dewey moved onto the freeway, heading for downtown. He glanced up at a large green sign:

BEM-VINDO A PORTUGAL.

65

NATIONAL SECURITY AGENCY
FORT MEADE, MARYLAND

Jesus June sat in front of two large computer screens, angled in front of him, watching, waiting. Thirty-one separate applications were running on the SID mainframe, all of them visible and accessible on his two screens, icons layered like tiles on a checkerboard.

ThinThread had still not produced anything on Dewey. June had strategized with one of the other analysts inside SID about other programs that might possibly be able to trace Dewey's whereabouts. June's main hope, at the moment, rested on a facial-recognition program that allowed Dewey's photo to be analyzed by ThinThread and compared to the database's massive electronic warehouse. If a security camera anywhere in the world was tied into any sort of network that NSA had access to—legally or not—and Dewey stepped in front of the camera, ThinThread would call it out, and they would have their location.

So far, however, only four sightings had occurred, and none were Dewey. Two of them had been photos of the same man, someone in Kiev, videotaped twice at a train station in Kiev.

Like all successful NSA hackers, June was patient. Patience was perhaps the most important quality in an NSA employee. That, curiosity, and persistence. June, like Pacheco and Bruckheimer himself, had all three qualities, along with a big brain.

On the right-hand plasma screen, a small red-and-gold triangle abruptly lit up on the screen, signifying activity of some sort, then made a short burst of chiming noises. The program wasn't related to ThinThread. In fact, it was an old program called FireBite, developed in the 1970s, which allowed NSA programmers to wiretap within the United States but not listen to the calls. In other words, if NSA was monitoring a phone number, and that number received a call, the number of the caller was immediately cataloged. Beyond that, the program was "dumb"; FireBite couldn't eavesdrop.

He double-clicked the triangle, and the FireBite user interface appeared on the screen. June had set the program up to monitor a handful of phone numbers he thought Dewey might call. The home, cell, and work numbers of Calibrisi, Katie, Tacoma; his parents' home in Castine; his brother's home in Blue Hill.

On the screen, one of the numbers was boldened and had two messages. The calls had just occurred. June clicked the number. Then he did a double take. It was a number he'd stuck into FireBite as an afterthought; after all, Jessica Tanzer was dead.

His eyes bulged as he looked at the numbers, then hit the trace feature. A few moments later, the location of the calls appeared.

"I found him!" screamed June. "I got Dewey!"

At MI6, June's yelling boomed over the speakerphone.

"Where is he?" asked Calibrisi.

"Lisbon. Hard location four minutes ago. He made two calls from a public pay phone at Lisbon Portela Airport."

Smythson snapped her fingers, ordering one of her staffers to run down the hall and retrieve Chalmers.

"How do we know it was Dewey?" asked Calibrisi.

"We don't," said June. "But who else would call Jessica Tanzer twice in a row from halfway around the world?"

"Nice work," said Calibrisi. "Langley, patch in Polk."

Chalmers entered the glass conference room.

"What do we got?"

"Lisbon," said Smythson.

Polk, the head of Special Operations Group, came on speaker.

"Hi, guys," he said. "Whaddya got?"

"Lisbon," said Calibrisi.

"Let me see what I have in theater. Hold on."

Smythson pointed at one of her staffers, seated at the table in front of his laptop.

"Hurry, James," she said. "Tell me what sort of manpower we have down there."

"I'm already on it, Ronny," he said, staring into his screen.

He banged the enter button, then pointed at the large plasma in the corner of the room, which lit up with what looked like a lineup from the roster of a football team. There were four photographs in a grid and names, ranks, current operations beneath each photo.

Chalmers and Smythson stepped to the screen.

Polk returned on speaker.

"I got one paramilitary in Lisbon," said Polk. "I have a full black squad in Madrid, but I assume we don't have the time to haul them down there."

"No. What about Delta or SEAL?"

"Hold on."

Polk went off the line again.

"Gatewood, O'Toole, Farber, Mueller," said Smythson, turning, barking over her shoulder. "Get them over to the airport right now. Brief them en route, get them Andreas's photo, and tell them to watch the hell out for counterfire. They'll be swarming."

Polk came back on speaker.

"I got a couple Deltas," said Polk. "Where do you want 'em?"

"Airport," said Calibrisi. "CIA, patch those Deltas into the MI6 feed; same with Special Ops; we'll brief all of them at the same time. Billy, get them moving, safeties off. We're goin' in hot."

"On it, chief."

"I have a ton of police activity coming out of the airport," said Serena Pacheco from Fort Meade, on speaker. "Gunfire."

Calibrisi took his blazer from the back of a chair. He looked at Katie and Tacoma.

"I'm getting on a plane," said Calibrisi.

"Let's go," said Tacoma.

"Hector," came Pacheco again, "ThinThread is hitting hard. There were at least two killings, both Asian males, just happened. It's a mess. They're shutting down the airport."

Calibrisi looked at Smythson, then Chalmers.

"He won't be at the airport," said Smythson.

"You guys and Billy figure out where to send the Deltas. We're heading for the plane. You got a chopper we can borrow, Derek?"

"Absolutely. I'll walk you there."

Chalmers opened the door and exited, followed by Katie, Tacoma, then Calibrisi, who stopped just before leaving and turned back to the room.

"Thank you, MI6, for your work," Calibrisi said, smiling at Smythson and her staffers, before turning and hustling to catch up with the others, who were running toward the elevator.

66

Bhang's office phone buzzed. He put a cigarette in his mouth, lit it, then hit the button on the console.

"What?"

"First sighting, Minister."

"I'll be right there."

Bhang hustled across his empty office, then through a door that connected to a conference room.

At least a dozen people were in the room, either looking at laptops around the conference table or staring at one of the two massive wall-sized plasma screens.

The left screen displayed a detailed live satellite shot of Lisbon, taken from a low-orbit Chinese military satellite in outer space. It was tied into the ministry network; flashing red lights indicated the precise location of every agent in the city. Already, eleven separate members of ministry paramilitary were in the area, along with four contractors.

On the second wall-sized screen, a grid displayed fifteen individual squares; inside of each one was live video, coming off each agent or contractor in Lisbon, video that was being shot at various source points, including gun-mounted microcameras, on the weapons of the agents, or from cameras clipped to clothing, belts, backpacks. Several of the feeds were black, meaning the weapons were holstered or the cameras hadn't been turned on yet.

The room became hushed as Bhang entered.

"We have a live report from an agent at the airport," said Cho, one of Bhang's deputies. "Andreas killed two men, outside the main terminal. They positioned the van across from the taxi stand. He saw them, killed them, ran."

Bhang took a long drag on his cigarette.

"Okay," he said, surprisingly calm. "Do we have video?"

Cho nodded at one of his men, seated at the table, who punched some keys on his laptop. One of the fifteen squares on the right plasma screen enlarged; they were now looking at a live video feed from Huong's camera. A late-model white van was sideways, its front smashed into a steel pole. A red taxi was perpendicular to the van and had collided into the front passenger side. Flashing police and ambulance lights were everywhere, along with various uniformed officers, security, EMTs. The shot was choppy, as Huong was jostled by others trying to get a better view. The scene was pandemonium.

"I have the others fanning out from the airport."

Bhang stepped to the left screen. He studied the map.

"Get men to the American embassy and the train station."

"Yes, Minister."

Bhang stepped to the video, standing before it, studying it. He pointed with his lit cigarette at the upper left corner of the screen. A small cluster of people was standing away from the chaos of the van.

The video was silent; there was no audio.

"What is this?" asked Bhang.

"I don't know, sir."

"Get Huong over there. Tell him to turn on his COMM."

After a few moments, the picture focused in on the cluster of people.

As Huong approached, four people were standing in a group, three policemen and a large Portuguese man in a red shirt. Huong moved closer. One of the officers was explaining something to the Portuguese man as Huong approached.

288

"My guess is, he drove it somewhere and abandoned it, sir," the officer said, as Huong approached from behind. "I wouldn't be surprised if you have your car back by the end of the day."

"Very well," the man said. "Can someone give me a ride?"

The policeman nodded at the accident scene.

"You'd be better off getting a taxi, sir. We have your information. We'll be in touch."

The man started to walk away, across the street, toward the central terminal.

"Excuse me," said Huong, approaching him. "Did something happen to your vehicle?"

"Yes," said the big man, looking at Huong. "Someone stole it, at gunpoint."

"Is this the man?"

Huong held up his iPhone with the photo of Dewey on the screen.

"Yes, that was him!" yelled the Portuguese man angrily, pointing at the phone. "How did you know? Show that to the policemen!"

"What kind of car was it?"

"A white Mercedes AMG."

Huong turned away from the man, running toward the satellite lot where his 911 was parked.

Back in the ministry conference room, Cho leaned into the speaker.

"Why didn't you shoot him when he stepped off the plane?" barked Cho at Huong.

"He went the other way. I never saw him."

"Enough," yelled Bhang, waving his arm in the air to shut Cho up. "It doesn't matter what happened. Focus. Where is Andreas going? Why is he going there? What does he need? If we can figure that out, we will know where he's going before even he does. And find that white Mercedes."

Dewey moved the Mercedes at more than a hundred miles an hour along the A2 toward downtown Lisbon.

In America, his speed would have stood out. In Portugal, where there were no speed limits, he was just one of several other cars moving at more than a hundred. In fact, he was in the middle lane and was passed every half minute or so by a car moving much faster than he was.

He tried to think, to put the pieces together. He needed a plan. He needed it right now.

China had had a kill squad at the airport by the time they'd touched down. It was impressive and disconcerting. Dewey knew if they were able to find him in Lisbon, if they were able to figure out where he was going, they were doing things that even he couldn't anticipate.

They might already have the make of car he was in. Maybe there were more men on the kill team than just the two he'd already gunned down.

Dewey kept an eye on the rearview mirror. He didn't see anything suspicious. Twice, he exited the freeway then made abrupt cross-lane U-turns, swerving, then got back on the road; standard countersurveillance. He saw nothing suspicious.

Still, act as if they know. Doing just that had saved his life back at the airport.

The American embassy was the most logical destination. Next in line, train stations, then bus stations.

He felt in his pocket for the phone card. He needed an exfiltration. He could evade Bhang for only so long. With the technology they were using, the sort of tracing and hacking Dewey only vaguely understood, he knew it was only a matter of time before they found him.

He needed to get ahold of Hector.

Johnny Dowling had on a black motorcycle helmet with a black glass visor. It wasn't a normal helmet that you could buy from a motorcycle shop, however. It had been modified by someone at the Pentagon, DARPA to be exact.

In addition to being wired for audio and phone, the upper right corner of the helmet's interior glass could, with a few clicks on a small ceramic ring around his thumb, ignite a graphical user interface that enabled Dowling to connect to a remote-network feed, including the Internet.

Dowling had the black BMW S1000RR ripping down the A8 at more than 120 miles per hour.

To Dowling's right, a few yards behind him, was Dino Athanasia, his teammate from 1st Special Forces Operational Detachment—Delta. Athanasia straddled a bright red-and-white MV Agusta F4 RR.

They hadn't taken either bike full-out yet, but Dowling suspected that Athanasia would beat him in a race; Athanasia was slightly nuts. Most Deltas were nuts, but Athanasia was one click more so. Something suddenly caught Dowling's attention. He looked back: Athanasia was doing a wheelie, cruising down the A8 on only the back wheel of the bike. Dowling glanced down. His speedometer read 134 miles per hour. Case in point.

In his right ear, Dowling heard the beeping of a phone call.

"Dowling."

"Go COMM, soldier."

Dowling clicked the ceramic ring, then saw the upper right screen of his visor light up. On it was a photograph of a man with brown hair, American, handsome, tough-looking.

"This is Colonel Black at the Pentagon," came a voice in their helmets. "Dowling, Athanasia: you're on a live briefing with Langley and MI6. This is a Tac One, Code Red project. You are reassigned effective immediately. Johnny, Dino: it could get messy. Watch yourselves, and good luck."

Dowling knew Athanasia was examining the photo as well. He glanced left; Athanasia's front tire was still in the air.

"Comm check," came a woman's voice, in a stern British accent.

"MI6 O'Toole."

"MI6 Gatewood."

"MI6 Farber."

"MI6 Mueller."

"CIA Lamontagne."

"Dowling," said Dowling. "Delta."

"Athanasia, Delta."

"Gentlemen, this is MI6 Smythson," came the female British voice again, "along with Langley Polk. You are joining a live MI6, CIA, Pentagon operation with no in-theater command control. The situation you're entering is extremely fluid and highly lethal. You're on your own, and you need to be really careful, guys. Rules of engagement no longer apply."

Dowling nodded at Athanasia, trying to get his attention to slow down and exit the highway. Athanasia looked back, but instead of slowing, he have him a thumbs-up and accelerated.

"The photograph you're looking at is American Dewey Andreas," continued Smythson. "He is a former member of U.S. Special Forces."

"What branch?" asked Athanasia.

"Delta," said Smythson. "Andreas landed in Lisbon less than thirty minutes ago. He is being targeted for assassination by agents from Chinese intelligence. This a Code Red exfiltration. Andreas is a high-value asset."

"Any idea where he is?" asked Farber, one of the MI6 agents.

"He was at the airport when we flagged him. He killed two ministry agents at the airport before fleeing."

"Where's he going?"

"We don't know."

"Would he head for the embassy?"

"He might," said Smythson. "But we don't know. We're not going to speculate."

"Guys, Polk here in Virginia," came the gravelly voice of Bill Polk, who Dowling knew was the top dog at CIA Special Operations Group. "Andreas ain't necessarily gonna want to be exfiltrated. He's a rather independent-minded fellow. I strongly suggest that if you can, you work in pairs. You might need to help convince Andreas of the need for your assistance."

Dowling and every other person on the call knew what Polk meant: Andreas wasn't going to come easy.

"Why is China trying to capture him?" asked Dowling.

"They're not trying to capture him," answered Smythson. "It's a kill squad."

Dowling saw an exit sign ahead. He revved the bike, pushed it to 150 miles an hour, and cut across the road in front of Athanasia. Athanasia had to slow down or else crash into him. Dowling swerved down the exit ramp, forcing Athanasia to his right, down the ramp with him.

"Where do you want him if we get him?" asked O'Toole, another one of the MI6 agents.

"Nearest embassy," said Polk. "U.S., Britain, Israel, Canada, in that order. Avoid PSP. China has too many people there, and neither he, nor you, will be safe."

"Is anyone near the airport right now?" asked Smythson.

"Yeah," said Dowling. "Delta One and Two."

"Are you mobile?"

"Yes," said Dowling. "Very."

"I want a screen of the highways leading into the city," said Smythson. "Run hard. Stay together. Do it quickly. Special Ops, get to the train station. I want Gatewood and Mueller over at the U.S. Embassy. Watch for snipers. O'Toole, get to a central spot downtown and work circuits, bus stations, and hotels. Farber, where are you?"

"A Five."

"Head east, toward the airport."

"Roger."

"Everyone stay live on COMM. We're looking hard for more intel, and we'll pass it on as soon as we get it."

"How many on the kill team?" asked one of the MI6 agents.

"Assume it's at scale," said Smythson. "Ten to fifteen guys."

"What this means, gentlemen," added Polk, "is that you need to be really fucking aware of your fields of fire. There's a shit-ton of Chinese guys running around Lisbon right now, and, as you know, they're not very nice. They have a head start on you. If you suspect someone is Chinese intelligence, take him down."

"And watch yourselves," said Smythson. "They'll assume we're there. I don't have to tell you what that means. Good luck."

67

In Beijing, a voice abruptly interrupted the low din of conversation. It came from the speakerphone.

"This is Chiu," said the Chinese agent, his voice faint and scratchy. "I see him. I have him in my sights."

Bhang walked to the speaker.

"What do you have, agent?" asked Bhang.

"I have the white Mercedes, moving along the A Two," said the agent. "I assume it's him."

"How fast is he moving?" asked Bhang.

"Very fast."

Bhang stepped in front of the left plasma screen, quickly assessing the live map of Lisbon proper. He found the agent's flashing red GPS moving along the A2. Bhang studied the map, taking a drag on his cigarette. He pointed to the A2, tracing the path forward, where they were headed. A few miles ahead, he saw another flashing light, along another freeway, the A5.

"Huong," barked Bhang.

"Yes, Minister," said Huong.

"They're coming at you. Get ready."

"Yes, Minister."

"Agent two, you have Huong in approximately five miles," said

Bhang. "I want a pinch and cut: push the Mercedes toward Huong. Don't let him get off the road if you can help it."

"He marked me," said Chiu.

"That doesn't matter. When you see Huong, attack the Mercedes. Watch your fields of fire, both of you. In the meantime, I want everyone else on the A2 heading north; provide backup. They will be in the opposite lane. No mistakes. Let's finish the job."

Dewey noticed a plain-looking silver sedan in the passenger-side mirror.

He was getting close to downtown Lisbon. The highway was congested, though still moving at more than fifty miles per hour. Something about the car made him look twice. It seemed to hover back there, clinging to him but not taking him on.

Dewey switched lanes once, then another time; after half a dozen quick lurches, he slowed up, then went faster. The sedan stayed in approximately the same position, five or six car lengths back, center lane. It was a silver Ford Taurus.

Their tactics were good. That was obvious. The surveillance was textbook. Dewey knew they had found him and were now calling in the cavalry.

He didn't think about how they'd figured it out. It didn't matter now.

He floored the AMG, hopping into the right lane, and was soon at 110 miles an hour, swerving in and out of car traffic, horns blaring at him.

In the rearview, the silver sedan kept pace, hovering five car lengths back.

Huong was moving east on the A5, his left hand on the Porsche's steering wheel, right hand reaching behind him and pulling out his QBZ-95G Arsenal 5.8×42mm/DBP87 assault rifle.

Huong glanced down at the speedometer. He was cruising at a

relatively moderate seventy-five miles an hour; he knew precisely how far he was from the A2, and he wanted to get on the road just behind Chiu and the American.

Huong wasn't going to miss his chance to kill him this time.

"I'll be at the A Two in three minutes," said Huong. "Chiu, stay behind him. I'll pass him and then we'll converge and attack."

"Understood."

A minute later, Huong saw the first sign for the A2, two miles ahead.

"I'm two miles out," said Huong. "Where are you?"

"About to pass the exit," said Chiu.

At the entrance ramp to the A2, Huong barely slowed, banking around the sharp curve of the on-ramp. He swerved into the breakdown lane and passed two cars on the ramp, then surged into the heavy traffic of the A2. He slammed the pedal down, shifted with paddles on the back of the steering wheel, and ripped across three lanes into the left-hand lane, hitting ninety miles an hour in a handful of seconds.

"Be right there," said Huong.

"He's in the middle lane."

"I'll approach from the driver's side. When you see me pass you, fall in line and join me from the back. Fire on my go."

Dewey kept the Mercedes throttled hard, hitting upward of one hundred miles an hour but needing to slow down quickly and often to avoid hitting other cars.

The AMG was fast and extremely responsive. The car's brakes were unbelievable.

Yet no matter what he did, the silver Taurus stayed with him.

Horns blared as he swerved in and out of the freeway's crowded lanes.

The bright blue Porsche appeared out of nowhere. Dewey saw it immediately. It was a shiny blue apparition in the rearview mirror, with a surfboard attached to the roof. Dewey knew it was coming for him.

The car was tearing up the left-hand lane. When it reached a car in front of it, the Porsche simply swerved into the breakdown lane on the left, barely avoiding the concrete divider, and kept going.

Dewey was going as fast as he could without losing control. The Porsche would be with him in no time.

Dewey pulled the Glock from his holster. He put his left knee under the steering wheel and steered with his left thigh as he jammed a fresh mag into the sidearm.

He saw a long straightaway without a car on it, and he slammed the pedal down hard. The AMG burst like a cannonball and was soon at 140 miles an hour.

The 911 moved into line behind Dewey, gaining on him despite the accelcration.

"Fuckin' A," Dewey said, watching as the Porsche moved to within a car's length.

The Porsche's windshield was tinted black.

In Delta, there were two core tenets to evasion when being chased in a car. The first was speed. The second, the element of surprise. Unfortunately, neither tactic was going to work: the 911 was faster than his AMG, and surprising what were clearly highly trained agents would be next to impossible. He was moving much too quickly to attempt a braked 180; and if he slowed down, the two cars would pounce and start firing at point-blank range.

In fact, that was about to happen anyway.

Dewey swerved right, onto a short, empty stretch of road along the right side of the highway. Out of the corner of his eye, he saw the bright blue of the 911, scorching into the fast lane. A red BMW was now between Dewey and the blue Porsche.

Dewey lowered his window, then lifted the Glock in his right hand.

Shots suddenly echoed across the highway, above the traffic and horns. Then came the sound of glass shattering, and a faint, awful scream. The BMW popped abruptly left, spinning, glass and metal shattering as the car was riddled with slugs from the Porsche. The BMW flipped over and came to a spinning rest on its roof.

The Porsche moved toward Dewey now, as, behind him, he caught sight of the silver Ford Taurus closing in.

Dewey glanced left and saw the muzzle of an assault rifle in the window of the Porsche, then a long-haired Chinese man with sunglasses on.

Dewey triggered the Glock, firing as fast as his finger would move. Bullets struck the side of the Porsche, then the back window. The driver swerved, braked, then accelerated, trying to throw Dewey off.

In the rearview mirror, a gun emerged from the window of the Taurus. The low, dull boom of a large-caliber carbine arose above the chaos, just as the first big cartridge ripped steel at the back of the AMG. The next slug hit the back window, shattering it.

Dewey saw a large truck in front of the Porsche, a quarter mile ahead. He memorized his position, then ducked, flooring it toward the right breakdown lane, as slugs pelted the Mercedes from the Porsche to his left and the Taurus from behind.

The Porsche had to slow at the back of the truck, then was temporarily boxed in to the right. Dewey pressed the pedal to the ground and eyed the speedometer as the Mercedes climbed to 165 miles per hour. He put the Glock down, reached to his left, and put his seat belt on.

In the distance, sirens grew louder and seemed to come from all directions.

"This is Pacheco," came a voice over Dowling's COMM. "I have PSP reporting a high-speed chase on the A Two, near downtown. There were multiple gunshots."

"Delta One, Two are on the A Two," said Dowling. "Which direction, NSA?"

"Southbound."

"I need a map, MI6," said Dowling.

"You got it."

A graphic shot up in the right corner of Dowling's helmet, showing a map of the A2, with his position on the highway a blinking yellow light; a green circle showed where the gunfire had come from.

"Delta One and Two have it," said Dowling. "Where are they in relation to the A Five?"

Dowling glanced to the lane next to him, at Athanasia. Dowling nodded, then cranked the throttle. The motorcycle rocketed forward, hitting 130 miles per hour in seconds. Athanasia moved in line behind him.

"PSP south of the A Five, toward April Two-five Bridge."

Dowling knew exactly where they were. He and Athanasia were at least two miles behind them.

"How many cars?"

"They've APB'd a blue 911 and a white Mercedes AMG."

"Okay, Langley, I need a street-level view of the bridge."

"Here we go."

A street-level terrain view replaced the map in the upper right corner of Dowling's helmet, showing Lisbon's 25th of April Bridge. As Dowling moved at more than 140 miles an hour, he studied the terrain he was about to engage the enemy on.

"Okay, shut it off, MI6."

Ahead, traffic had come to a dead stop. In the distance, smoke was billowing into the air.

Athanasia swerved into the breakdown lane, with Dowling just behind him. They kept moving at more than 130 miles per hour up the breakdown lane.

Two police officers were standing in the lane, holding traffic, which was at a complete stop.

Ahead, in the middle of the road, was a red BMW, flipped over on its roof. The car was crushed, flames were darting out from the engine, smoke poured into the sky. Glass littered the highway. The wrecked car was flanked by the first responders—a pair of police cruisers. Two police officers were on their hands and knees, trying to pull the unconscious driver from the BMW.

Athanasia and Dowling charged toward the police line. One of the police officers saw them coming, then raised his weapon. Dowling and Athanasia accelerated, firing past the officer.

Past the accident scene, the highway was deserted. Dowling ripped the throttle again, moving alongside Athanasia, who also accelerated. Dowling glanced at his speedometer: 184.

The occasional random car was stopped in the middle of the road out of fear. Dowling and Athanasia had the bikes tearing along at full speed now. Dowling could feel the force of the air trying to push him back, off the bike, as he clutched the handlebars, leaning down, flying along the hot blacktop at almost two hundred miles per hour.

Ahead, far in the distance, Dowling caught the bright blue of a Porsche, then, to the right, a white Mercedes. Behind them was a sedan. All three cars were going blisteringly fast and swerving wildly. The Porsche and Mercedes were trading gunfire. As he gained on them, the air had a smell of gunpowder and burnt rubber. Dowling saw a man leaning from the window of the sedan, behind the Mercedes, firing a rifle toward the Mercedes.

"We're at surface zero," yelled Dowling into his COMM. "We're gonna need backup."

"On it, Delta," came a British accent. "MI6 Farber northbound."

"Andreas is the white Mercedes," yelled Dowling. "I see a bright blue Porsche and a second car, a silver sedan, behind him. Watch your field of fire, MI6. We're right behind where you'll be shooting."

"Roger that, Delta One and Two. Be there in approximately ninety seconds."

The Mercedes's engine was smoking now. The hood and left front of the vehicle looked like a piece of Swiss cheese, riddled with bullets. Still, it moved, and moved fast. It was responding to every demand Dewey made of it.

In addition to managing the gunman in the Porsche to his left, Dewey had to deal with the sedan behind him. He fluttered between the AMG's gas and brakes, quickly and unpredictably changing speeds to throw off the Porsche. For the sedan, Dewey zigzagged, trying to lead the sedan into other slower-moving vehicles. The Taurus was having a hard time keeping up with the two lead cars. Yet the unmistakable boom of the trailing car's rifle sent a shiver through Dewey every time he heard it.

Dewey stayed calm, his eyes darting between the rearview mirror and the terrain ahead, looking, searching, praying for an exit. He saw the arches of a bridge in the distance.

He aimed the Glock across his body, without looking, and fired at the Porsche.

Huong had the Porsche at more than 150 miles an hour. He had his left hand on the steering wheel while he held a carbine in his right and aimed out the shattered window, trying to hit the American. Each time he had a clear shot, the American sensed it, then slammed his brakes or gunned it; it was hard to predict.

Huong sensed something in front of him, glanced ahead, and saw a stopped minivan in the middle of the lane. He swerved just feet from the vehicle, barely avoiding a crash. He looked back for the Mercedes. Just as he did so, he saw him, one lane over, then heard the boom of the American's sidearm. The slug smashed into the windshield, barely missing Huong's head, shattering the glass. Huong slammed the brakes to avoid the next shot he knew would be coming.

Huong wanted his machine gun, but it was in the backseat. Reaching for it would force him to drop the rifle for a few precious seconds. But he needed the field of fire the weapon offered; the carbine was just not giving him—in the conditions—the targeting power he needed.

He dropped the assault rifle then reached in back for his FN P90.

Dewey watched as his slug hit the Porsche's windshield, shattering it. The Chinese agent swerved, then recovered. He'd almost taken him down.

The AMG's engine made a sputtering noise. Dewey heard a high-pitched revving coming from it, though he felt no drop-off in performance. Smoke from the hood was growing thicker, coming up from holes in the hood and in through the dashboard.

He glanced left. The Chinese agent clutched a different weapon in his right hand. A shiver of fear shot involuntarily up Dewey's spine. It was a firearm he himself had used, a nasty little submachine gun called a P90. Short, lethal, with a closed-bolt system for better aim than a typical submachine gun, the P90 was capable of emptying one of its fifty-round mags of slugs in less than four seconds.

Dewey watched as the Chinese agent lifted the submachine gun and trained it out the window. For a brief moment, Dewey stared right down the muzzle of the weapon. He floored the AMG, ducking just as the submachine gun—less than a lane away—erupted in full auto hail.

Huong waited until he had the Porsche at the same speed as the Mercedes, then ripped the trigger back. The P90 exploded, spraying slugs at the white sedan. He felt the blowback from the submachine gun, kicking against his hard biceps, but he held it stable and kept firing. He swung the weapon toward the midsection of the sedan, then washed the muzzle forward, spraying slugs as the two cars raced at nearly 175 miles an hour. The line of slugs tore up the body of the car, toward Andreas. Slugs pelted metal, then shattered the glass just behind the American. It was about to happen. The line of bullets would soon be at Andreas.

Suddenly, the American accelerated, bursting ahead, hitting a speed Huong didn't think the German car possessed. Huong's aim was thrown off, but he managed to rip the last of the magazine's slugs into the American's back tire.

Dewey listened as slugs pocked the side of the car, moving in a line deliberately from the middle of the Mercedes toward him. He heard bullets striking the door, coming at him, getting closer with each shot. He sensed the forward momentum of the muzzle as the agent swung the submachine gun up the car.

Still, Dewey waited, letting the line of slugs get closer, knowing it might be his last opportunity to escape.

He listened as slugs ripped into the window just behind him, shattering the glass of the back window. Dewey glanced left again, and again saw the muzzle, sparking red and silver, the sound of auto hail mixing with the staccato echo of bullets shredding the car behind him.

He slammed the pedal to the floor, pushing the badly smoking AMG for whatever it had left.

For a brief, precious second, he listened as the line of bullets was interrupted. The agent kept firing, but his aim had been thrown off, and the slugs flew wide, behind the AMG. Dewey swerved right, trying to get distance. Then Dewey heard a bullet hit the back of the car, then the back tire. A low explosion ripped the air. Dewey quickly lost control of the vehicle.

The back of the AMG bounced left, heaving violently, pulling against his weight as if the car had been grabbed by a gust of hurricane wind. Dewey heard the tires screeching wildly beneath him, then watched as the highway in front of him was torn abruptly sideways, into a breathtaking blur, and he knew he was flipping over at more than 150 miles an hour. He tried to brace himself, but even that was impossible, so fierce was the tornado that now controlled the car.

Dewey looked left just as the car was thrown sideways and over. The black of the road shot at him, and he knew he would hit. He pulled his left arm inside the car just as the side of the Mercedes smashed brutally into the tar, his arm barely avoiding being crushed by the full weight of the now-tumbling sedan. His face went flying uncontrollably forward, into the steering wheel, his nose smashing hard against the wheel, and blood spurting out from both nostrils. And still he knew it was only just beginning.

The momentum of the rolling car was ferocious, aided by the tremendous speed he'd had the AMG racing at. It took all of Dewey's strength to reach forward, against the fierce torque, trying to grab something to brace himself, anything—the steering wheel, the nylon of the seat belt—while at the same time he shut his eyes and heard screaming, which after a moment he realized was his own.

The car kept tumbling forward, in a blurring eddy of steel and pavement. The car bounced from its side to the roof, crushing it down toward Dewey's head, then kept rolling, flipping completely upright, then rolling more, pushed by a violent momentum, until finally the destroyed car landed upside down for a second time, crushing the roof, pushing against Dewey's head.

As the destroyed car came to rest, upside down, it went into a slow spin. Dewey finally opened his eyes. He was strung upside down, tethered by the seat belt, dangling. He could see nothing but the spinning

303

of the highway outside the ruined car, a dizzying scene cloaked in red, as blood gushed from his nose down into his eyes. He was close to passing out, and he fought to stay conscious. He felt for the seat-belt release, but couldn't reach it, as the sound of gunfire abruptly rang out anew, somewhere nearby.

Huong watched as the back tire of the Mercedes exploded. The back of the Mercedes lurched left. Its tires made a terrible squealing. The sedan was thrown out of control. It flipped over onto its side, rolling over, then landed on its roof, then seemed to almost bounce up, carried by the momentum of the car's original speed. It landed on its wheels and kept rolling, bouncing yet again, up into the air. It landed upside down again, on its roof, coming to a loud, jarring crash on the freeway.

Huong slammed on the brakes. The Porsche shuddered wildly, tires screaming a high-pitched cry as the 911 spun out. When he finally stopped, Huong grabbed a fresh mag from the passenger seat. He grabbed the door handle and leapt from the car. Weapon in hand, he began a furious sprint toward the flipped-over Mercedes, which was still spinning in place, smoke chimneying up into the warm sky.

He ripped the spent mag from the P90 and hurled it to the tar as, on the run, he slammed the new mag into the submachine gun. Huong was downrange of the wrecked Mercedes, forty feet away, running as fast as his feet would take him.

Huong heard gunfire. To the left, he saw another man—it was Chiu—clutching an M4 and moving at the overturned Mercedes from behind. The wrecked sedan was still spinning slowly counterclockwise as the two agents converged from both directions. As he came up to the Mercedes, Huong felt almost high; adrenaline flamed in his veins, and his heart felt like it was in his throat.

All of a sudden, he became aware of the loud roar of a motorcycle, then the telltale staccato of a submachine gun—someone else's submachine gun—firing on full auto.

Dowling was less than a hundred feet behind the silver Taurus when the white Mercedes suddenly bounced into the air and spiraled into a violent, unsightly crash. The Taurus skidded to a halt behind the overturned wreck. Smoke shot from the Mercedes's engine as the door to the silver sedan opened and a man emerged, running.

Dowling kept the bike tearing down the highway at full speed, barely slowing, then reached behind him and pulled out his MP5 without taking his eyes off the chaotic scene ahead. He was upon the silver sedan now, just yards away, as a tall Chinese agent looked toward him, then swept a carbine through the air at him, firing.

Dowling pulled the brake, then yanked back, sending the bike sliding down the tar, as he'd been taught, as he'd practiced so many times, in so many conditions, falling back onto his feet as the seventeen-thousand-dollar BMW went sliding on its side down the highway.

Athanasia was still on his bike, still moving recklessly fast down the highway toward the chaos. He was the first to fire, triggering his MP5 from the moving bike, ripping slugs up the highway at the Chinese agent who'd just leapt out of the silver sedan and was shooting at Dowling. A hail of Athanasia's bullets struck the agent in the head, destroying his skull, pummeling him forward to the ground in an awkward heap.

Dowling sprinted up the highway toward the overturned Mercedes.

Beyond the wreck, through clouds of thick smoke, he saw another man, a long-haired agent, running toward them, submachine gun in his right hand. The gunman caught sight of Dowling and Athanasia, then raised the weapon and fired just as Dowling dived to the blacktop.

Athanasia, still on his bike, was abruptly struck, chest high, by the shooter. He was pummeled sideways, blood arcing across the road, knocked backward by the slug. Athanasia fell from the motorcycle in the same instant it cartwheeled sideways, crashing to the tar.

Athanasia landed on the back of his head, then came to a limp, contorted stop.

Dowling knew from the point of entry—from the way the slug ripped chest high, dead center—that Athanasia was dead. He stared, mesmerized and in horror, as his bunkmate, teammate, as his best friend took his last breath.

But he knew he couldn't stand still.

Dowling jumped back up, running at the Mercedes, triggering the MP5 at the long-haired killer on the other side of the smoking, destroyed AMG.

Huong registered the sight, the sound, the feeling of the bullet strike, dead center, his bullet hitting the biker, knocking him backward. Huong knew he'd killed him.

Time seemed to stand still. He felt nothing, not fatigue or fear or exultation. He was moments away, feet away, from his purpose, from the man who an entire ministry of agents was now hunting. Huong would be the one to kill him.

Huong saw the other man, right of the fallen biker, coming toward him, weapon trained on him. Huong lurched right at the same time the man fired. Huong swept the P90, firing on auto hail, toward him.

Dowling fired at the oncoming agent but missed, then was kicked in the left arm by a slug, which ripped into his biceps. Dowling was thrown backward and he fell to the ground. He groaned in pain as he tumbled to the blacktop. The MP5 fell from his hands.

Dowling looked up from the ground. He was partially shielded by the Mercedes's frame. He reached for the MP5 with his right hand, trying to reach it before the Chinese agent had a clear line of fire on him.

He heard multiple sirens in the distance, along with screams and gunfire.

Dowling grabbed the submachine gun as the killer approached the Mercedes. From the ground, Dowling triggered the SMG; he weaved a disjointed line of slugs across the sky, his aim unsteady, as debilitating pain, then a sense of numbness, abruptly burst in his arm, chest, and body. He struggled to avoid the blackout he knew was upon him, still firing. His line of automatic weapon fire found the agent as he came point-blank to the side of the Mercedes. Dowling watched as a slug ripped the man's forehead, splattering crimson, kicking him backward, just a foot or two before the assassin would have enjoyed a clean shot at Andreas.

Dowling got to his knees and unzipped his orange jacket, then ripped his shirt aside. It was then that he realized he'd been hit twice, the second slug striking his chest, and he tasted blood in his mouth, bubbling up from somewhere inside him.

He stood, picked up his MP5, and moved clumsily toward Andreas. He knew there would be more men coming to kill the American. But his feet wouldn't hold, and he tumbled to the ground. With the last of his strength, he took up position next to the overturned wreck of the Mercedes.

Sirens now wailed through the Lisbon air from all directions. Traffic was at a standstill. Whatever cars were on the freeway, in either direction, had stopped. Except for one.

A blue Audi S8 moved toward the wreck from the opposite direction, its engine revving above the din, tires screeching, as it hopscotched between car after stopped car, moving at more than a hundred miles per hour toward the pandemonium.

Innocent bystanders, closest to the scene, climbed frantically from their cars. A long-haired woman climbed from a station wagon, clutching a baby and screaming, running away from the carnage.

Farber, from MI6, didn't see the woman until the very last second; he swerved the Audi, coming within a foot of hitting the hysterical woman.

Farber slammed the brakes on the Audi as he arrived at smoke-clogged ground zero.

He grabbed the car door, opened it, then leapt from the Audi in a hard sprint down the highway. He hurdled the concrete divider as the first flames danced from the AMG's engine.

Farber registered two motorcycles behind the wrecked Mercedes, both on the ground, one of them in two pieces. He counted four men on the ground in the vicinity of the Mercedes, lying in various stages of contortion, amid growing pools of blood.

One of the men—an American in a bright orange motorcycle

jacket—was still alive. Their eyes met. Blood coursed from the American's mouth down onto the ground.

Dowling was close to darkness now. He saw the MI6 agent as the man jumped the concrete divider, running toward him.

Dowling's eyes caught a white van in the background, speeding down the road, weaving through abandoned cars. Dowling lifted his left hand, pointing, trying to warn the British agent.

The agent turned. He saw the approaching van. In one smooth motion, he swept his M4 to the van, firing, ripping slugs through the windshield. A cartridge tore into the driver's head. His head bounced sharply forward against the steering wheel. The van fishtailed and crashed into the concrete highway divider one lane away from the smoking, wrecked Mercedes.

The British agent charged at the van, firing as he ran, pelting the vehicle with slugs.

The back of the van opened, and two more men, both Chinese, jumped out, firing assault rifles from behind the van.

Dowling watched helplessly as the MI6 agent caught a slug in the head, dropping him lifeless to the highway.

With what life remained in him, Dowling moved his right index finger to the trigger of his MP5. His arm was shaking badly.

Dowling saw the first Chinese agent hurdle the divider and dash toward the Mercedes. Dowling triggered the MP5. The submachine gun made a dull clicking noise. The magazine was empty.

Dowling watched, helplessly, as the two gunmen came closer, leaping over the dead British agent.

Dowling couldn't feel his body anymore. He was going into shock.

Dowling's eyes drifted to the Mercedes. His eyes found the American, Andreas, who was hanging from the ceiling, helpless, upside down, his face drenched in blood.

Dowling watched as the American turned and looked in his direction, blood pouring from his ears, nose, mouth, their eyes making contact over the smoke-choked air.

Dewey tried to mouth words, but he couldn't.

Run, he tried to shout. Run.

But he couldn't.

The world was spinning badly around him as he tried to focus on the young American now lying next to him, the American he knew had come to save him.

Dewey felt the cold, wet dripping of blood, coming from his mouth, his nose, running up his cheeks and into his eyes, as he hung upside down.

He struggled to remain conscious as, outside the car, he heard the high, incomprehensible words, yelling in Mandarin. Sirens and gunfire. Hell.

Through the groggy haze of semiconsciousness, Dewey looked down at the ceiling of the wrecked Mercedes. Lying on the roof, above his head, was one of the handguns. He reached up slowly for the weapon as the sound of automatic weapon fire drew closer, as yelling from the killers became louder, more frantic.

He heard the low, dull thuds of slugs striking the seat next to him, piercing leather. His right hand could almost touch the handgun. *One more inch*, he thought, as salt from the blood stung his eyes. He touched the steel, but instead of pulling it closer, he accidentally pushed it farther away. He stared for what seemed like forever at his badly shaking right hand, so close to the Glock yet so far away.

Dewey saw the shadow first, running on the road. Then he saw legs, running quickly. Through the destroyed windshield, he watched as a Chinese gunman ran toward the American in the orange jacket, trying to get a clear line of fire.

Fight. It's what you were meant to do.

Dewey stabbed his arm up at the butt of the Glock, reaching it this time, clutching it. He wheeled his arm around just as the gunman started firing. Dewey fired through the open slat of the windshield. The bullet tore into the agent's cheek, kicking out the back of his head, dropping him to the tar.

Dewey swung the Glock around to the other side of the car, marking the other Chinese agent as he approached. All he could see was the man's legs. They were blurry, tinted red by the blood in Dewey's eyes, moving quickly. All Dewey could hear was the sound of bullets ripping into the Mercedes as the gunman came closer, firing.

Dewey pumped the trigger. The slug struck the gunman in the ankle. He dropped to the road, screaming, his carbine dropping to the road. The gunman looked up at Dewey, a pained expression on his face, then to his rifle. He was young, no more than twenty-five. He lurched for the rifle. Dewey fired. The bullet hit him in the chest, dead center, his white T-shirt erupting in crimson as he was kicked back to the tar.

Dewey turned to look at the American, lying on the road, just outside his window. His brown eyes stared blankly back at him. Then he blinked. He was still alive.

"Dowling," the man whispered. "I'm Delta."

"Hold on, Dowling," said Dewey, mustering every ounce of strength he had left. "Hold on. Don't fucking give up on me, man."

"I won't," Dowling said quietly through the smoke, looking at Dewey.

68

Huong?" barked Xiao. "Chiu? Answer!"

On the opposite side of the glass conference table stood Bhang. His arms were crossed. An unlit cigarette dangled from his lips. As he listened to Xiao attempt to raise the agents on COMM, Bhang was studying the large electronic map of Lisbon, now imposed on the glass of the table.

There were ten flashing red lights in all. Two at the airport and four on the highway, near the 25th of April Bridge, represented the agents who weren't responding. Bhang already knew the two at the airport were dead, based on police reports coming out of Lisbon. Now it was clear the four men sent to take out Andreas on the A2 were also gone.

Xiao completed the COMM check and looked to Bhang for guidance.

"Should we send in the others?"

"No," said Bhang, shaking his head.

Bhang pointed to one of the flashing lights, which was close to the bridge, on a side street beneath the highway, moving toward the scene.

"Who's this?"

"Lo," said Xiao.

"Lo," said Bhang into the COMM mic on the desk. "Can you see the scene?"

"Almost, Minister."

Bhang lit the cigarette. He glanced at Xiao. "Does he have a rifle?"

Xiao nodded yes.

"I can see it now," said Lo, over the COMM. "It's a . . . well, it's hard to describe, sir. It's a mess. Let me put it up on video."

One of the plasmas suddenly lit up. The view was blurry. The screen bounced around as Lo focused and framed the shot. After a few seconds, the scene sharpened. A side shot, from beneath the highway, showed the pandemonium on the roadway above. Smoke clouded the sky. Cars were strewn about haphazardly, along with several overturned motorcycles. Bodies of injured or dead people were strewn about on the ground.

All of it was clustered around an overturned sedan, which Bhang recognized as the Mercedes.

Multiple sirens could be heard. Lo panned right to show police cruisers and ambulances hurrying from up the highway.

Bhang, Xiao, and the other men in the situation room back in Beijing watched, transfixed, as a pair of green-and-white ambulances zigzagged toward the wreck, then stopped.

"Focus on the wreck!" yelled Bhang, pointing at the Mercedes. "Get us in tighter!"

The view sharpened and moved in on the overturned sedan, just as two uniformed medics sprinted to the side of the car.

The sound of a helicopter, off camera, became louder. Lo suddenly shot the camera right and up. A black military chopper rushed overhead, descending toward the chaos. Lo followed the chopper as it hovered above the roadway, then descended in a slow loop to the highway, just a few feet from the overturned Mercedes.

As the chopper touched down, the blood-covered head of Andreas emerged from through the crushed side of the car. The medics struggled to pull the driver from the wreck. A third man ran to the far side of the car. Finally, they pulled him completely out. Bhang stared expectantly, hopefully, as the American's torso, waist, then legs were pulled through by the medics. Was he dead?

"Don't move the camera," ordered Bhang.

Two medics lifted Andreas up to a gurney as a third medic stuck an oxygen mask on his face then stuck an IV into his left arm. The two medics, trailed by the third, ran the gurney to the chopper. All three men climbed aboard. The chopper lifted into the smoke, then crossed the blue sky and shot away.

"See if you can track the chopper," said Xiao.

"Don't bother," said Bhang.

Bhang reached forward and shut off the COMM speaker.

"Minister?"

"Andreas is gone. He's alive, and he's gone."

"Are you saying the operation is over, Minister?"

"No, of course not," snapped Bhang. "It's simply moved to a more-complicated part of the playing field."

Bhang turned and walked to the door. He paused there. He turned, smiling, and pointed at Xiao.

"Kill his family," said Bhang.

69

US Airways flight 132 from Quebec City landed at Bangor International Airport at 8:50 A.M. There were four passengers aboard the fifty-seat Embraer jet. One of them, a Chinese woman, thanked the flight attendant, then stepped quickly down the airstairs and onto the tarmac.

Her name was Dao. She was twenty-three, had short black hair, and was a level-two operative in the paramilitary branch of the Ministry of State Security, assigned to territory U-8, eastern Canada and northern New England. U-8 included Maine, Vermont, and New Hampshire.

Dao headed for the main terminal, a few hundred feet away. Inside, she found the Hertz counter.

"Good morning," said a pretty blonde behind the counter. "How can I help you today?"

"I'd like to rent a car." She handed the woman a credit card along with a forged Maine driver's license.

"My pleasure," she said, picking up her license, "Miss Dao. Let me see what we have."

The woman typed a few keystrokes into the computer.

"Here we go. How about a Camaro? That's a nice car, if you ask me. I also have a Dodge Challenger. That one's fast as heck. My boyfriend has one. Sometimes he—"

"Camaro," Dao said, interrupting her.

The Hertz woman typed away as Dao studied the map on the wall.

"And what brings you to Bangor?" the Hertz woman asked absent-mindedly, making conversation as she typed.

"I'm visiting some friends," answered Dao, studying the map, a cold look on her face, "in Castine."

70

DEYROLLE
RUE DU BAC
PARIS, FRANCE

Xiua Koo stood beneath the mounted head of a rhinoceros, admiring it. The leather skin looked like armor, hardened by a lifetime's worth of fighting. Koo was always amazed at how marred, ripped, and pockmarked the rhino was upon close inspection, but it was also why he liked the beast so much. He imagined what the animal had faced in its abbreviated life, what elephants, other rhinos, cheetahs, and other predators had attempted to kill him, before the hunter had finally succeeded in shooting him.

A small white price tag was affixed to the wall next to the head.

1914
British East Africa
€75,000

A short bald man with round gold-rimmed glasses stepped to Koo's right, also admiring the head.

"The hunting was good that year," said the man.

"It's not for sale," replied Koo. He turned, without looking at the man, and left the taxidermy shop.

Koo walked slowly, on thin cobblestone sidewalks, toward the Seine, stopping to look in the windows of different art galleries, chocolate shops, and patisseries. He didn't look behind him.

Koo knew he was possibly being watched, and the next few minutes were important. The chances they were following him were slim but real. After all, Koo himself had spent his first years at the ministry doing nothing except surveillance of other ministry agents. It had always struck him as being inefficient and uneconomical. And yet he'd discovered two different traitors during his time in the surveillance unit, both ministry agents who'd gone to work for Russia.

If they were following him, looking back could be construed as paranoia, a cue; it had the potential to cause more men to be called in. And so he walked casually, pretending to enjoy the warm fall afternoon despite the speed with which his heart now beat.

He replayed the exchange at Deyrolle:

The hunting was good that year: We must meet immediately.

It's not for sale: Shakespeare and Company.

At the Seine, he turned right and walked in front of the small booksellers and antiquarians who lined the banks of the river. He aimed for Notre Dame and its ornate spires.

Inside the main door to the cathedral, he stepped quickly to his left, then sprinted down a set of stairs to the basement. He ran down a dimly lit hallway, past a man in vestry garments, who did not even look up. At the end of the hallway, he went through a small wooden door to another stairwell, this one darkened. He went down to the next level, using his phone light to guide him. At the next landing was another door. He opened it and stepped into an alley, a recessed flood channel at the back of the cathedral, two stories below ground level. Koo climbed an iron ladder attached to the masonry and was soon back at street level, near the verdant lawns that flanked the cathedral. Koo walked quickly to the street. Across the busy traffic, he saw the sign: SHAKESPEARE AND COMPANY.

Inside the crowded bookstore, Koo climbed thin stairs to the second floor, then passed customers browsing old, used books. Near the back, he stopped at a shelf of dust-covered volumes, next to a door that said EMPLOYEES ONLY. He pretended to browse, glancing around him until, finally, there was no one else in sight. Koo removed a key from his pocket, placed it in the door lock, and turned.

Koo stepped into the small office, shutting the door quickly behind him.

Against the wall sat an old wooden desk, piled high with documents, bills, and paper, much of it yellowed and frayed. Two chairs were next to the desk, along with an old, torn leather club chair, which served as the desk chair. A beautiful glass lamp on the desk provided the only light in the windowless room.

Two people were seated in the chairs, waiting for Koo. In the left chair was a woman in a stylish black trench coat, with brown hair that was combed neatly back and a serious look on her pale, unattractive face. Koo had never met her before but knew exactly who she was: Veronica Smythson, head of MI6 paramilitary operations.

In the other chair was someone Koo did know, the man who'd recruited him to be a double agent for MI6 six years before: Derek Chalmers, the head of the agency, his blond hair longer and more unruly than Koo remembered.

"Hello, Koo," said Chalmers. "Please sit down."

Koo sat down in the leather chair, saying nothing.

"It's time to make preparations," said Chalmers. "We're bringing you in."

Koo stared at Chalmers impassively, without emotion.

"Why?"

"You're going to be exposed," said Chalmers.

"When?"

"Tomorrow."

Koo stared at Chalmers. He knew the day might come. Indeed, sometimes he dreamed of it, of the day, the time, the place he would go, the day everything would be wiped clean and he would be brought in.

"Where will I be sent?"

"You know we can't tell you that."

"Do I have a choice about where I am to go?"

"No," said Chalmers. "I'm sorry."

Koo reached to his pocket and removed a pack of cigarettes.

"Do you mind?" he asked, looking at Smythson.

"Not at all," she said.

Koo lit a cigarette, then took a long puff.

"So tell me about the operation," said Koo, exhaling.

"It has to do with the ministry," said Smythson. "More than that, I cannot tell you. Excepting, of course, your role."

Koo nodded, and suddenly it made sense now.

"The American," said Koo.

"Andreas," said Smythson. "What is your knowledge of him?"

"It is the highest priority of the ministry," said Koo. "Every agent in the clandestine bureau has been repurposed until he's found and terminated. I would imagine there are other efforts going on as well."

"Tomorrow, the American will be in Paris," said Smythson.

Koo's eyes became more alert.

"Do you have informants at any of the hotels?" asked Smythson. "A parking valet? A concierge? Front-desk person?"

"Yes. I have people at many of the hotels."

"The Bristol?"

"Yes."

"Does he work afternoons?"

"Yes, his name is Vonnes."

"Good," said Smythson. "This afternoon, you will show him a photo of Andreas. You will ask him to call you if he happens to see him; offer him money. Make the rounds. Make the same offer to all of your informants. It's important that you show them the photo."

Koo nodded.

Smythson reached to her right. She lifted a paper bag with the Shakespeare and Company logo on the side. She handed it to Koo.

He reached into the bag and pulled out an old hardcover edition of *Anna Karenina*. Koo lifted the cover. There were no pages. The book was a storage box, designed to look like a book. He pulled out a handgun. It was the same sidearm Koo already had, a slightly weathered 9x19mm QSZ-92 with an undermounted laser pointer. He popped the magazine. The gun was loaded.

319

"Tomorrow afternoon, just before four P.M., your man at the Bristol will call you," said Smythson. "You will be somewhere close by. What's the first thing you should do?"

"Call it in."

"Precisely," said Smythson. "You call it in. What next?"

"Go immediately to the Bristol," said Koo.

"Are there rules of engagement?" Smythson asked.

"It's a TEP," said Koo. "It means we are to take any risk necessary on behalf of the state."

"I'm talking about procedural rules," she said. "Do you have to wait for backup? Kill or capture? Day or night?"

"None of that. The only one is that we must have our microcamera mounted and running."

"Can I see it?"

Koo reached inside his coat. He removed his handgun, a QSZ-92, the twin of the 9mm Smythson had just given him. He handed it to her.

Smythson examined it. At the end of the muzzle, a small silver bead, like the round head of a pin, was affixed.

"How is it engaged?"

Koo held up his watch. "A code typed into either our watch or phone."

"Can Beijing turn it on remotely?"

"No."

Smythson disassembled Koo's weapon, taking everything but the barrel and handing it to Koo. She then took apart the other sidearm. She switched barrels, so that the handgun she'd given Koo now had the camera on it.

"It's important that the camera be running when you enter the hotel," said Smythson.

Koo nodded.

"Where will he be?" asked Koo.

"In the lounge. When you see him, you pull your weapon from your coat. You will shoot Andreas at close range, here, once."

Smythson gestured to her chest, pointing at her heart.

"One kill shot."

Koo listened but said nothing.

"But, as you might expect, there are other American agents in the lounge," said Smythson.

She pulled two photographs from her trench coat pocket. One showed Katie, the other, Tacoma. She handed them to Koo.

"Your shots alert them," continued Smythson. "They are part of the operation."

"Who are they?"

"It doesn't matter," she said.

She pointed at the fake book. Koo reached inside. He pulled out a neatly folded white T-shirt. It was unusually heavy.

"You'll have that on," she continued.

"What is it?"

"The shirt is embedded with a chemical. The man in the photo will be at a table in the lounge. When he sees you move at Andreas, he'll stand up and shoot you."

Koo said nothing.

"His gun will have blanks in it, Koo."

A small grin flashed on Koo's face.

"The first bullet misses, and you return fire. Then you step forward and shoot Andreas three more times, proving without question to your handlers that he's dead. But you fail to kill the other man. He shoots from the ground and hits you in the shoulder. You fall to the ground. When you do, the chemicals in the shirt will combine and your shoulder will be covered in what appears to be blood. Wear something light above it, so that the blood is visible."

Koo stared at Smythson, then his eyes drifted to Chalmers, who stared back.

"After falling, get up and run for your life," said Smythson. "Hail a taxicab and run."

"Where will I be taken?"

"You call it in. Remember, you'll be on a live feed to Beijing. You're in pain. By the way, how do you say 'pain' in Mandarin?"

"*Téngtòng*," said Koo.

"*Téngtòng*," repeated Smythson.

"Yes."

"Repeat it over and over as you ride in the cab. Our guess is, you'll be directed to a safe house or back to your apartment. They'll want to get you out of the country. Once we know where they're going to exfiltrate you from, you hang up, and you're done."

"Done?"

"For good. We might need you to wait it out, but by suppertime you'll be in the UK."

Koo studied the photos of Katie and Tacoma. He held up the picture of Katie.

"Pretty," he said.

"Yes."

"What is her role?"

"She's going to kill the other ministry agents who will be coming after you call it in," said Smythson. "Don't get in the way of her bullets, Koo; they're real."

Koo lit another cigarette, reclining in the leather chair, contemplating everything.

"What about Tammy?" asked Koo, looking at Chalmers.

Chalmers stared back.

"Xiua," said Chalmers, "you know the drill. If she knows, if she does anything, it won't work."

Koo took a puff, nodding.

"If we're successful, you have my word that we'll make arrangements at the first opportunity," added Chalmers. "But there are no promises."

"By the way, no keepsakes," said Smythson. "No photos, mementos—nothing. It all stays behind. A normal day at the office, so to speak."

"I understand," said Koo. "However, I must also ask: Is there no other alternative?"

Chalmers shook his head.

"This is important," said Chalmers calmly. "Important enough to kill off one of MI6's most valuable assets. By my estimates, you should have at least five million euros tucked away somewhere. It's been my experience that others, after a similar transition, learn to be very happy. We will be there to support you at every turn. But you must also understand something."

"Yes?"

"We've invested a lot in you," said Chalmers, leaning toward Koo, his voice barely above a whisper, a polite but unmistakable hint of threat in his voice. "As you might have anticipated, you and Tammy will be under surveillance for the duration of the operation. I don't need to explain to you what that means."

71

Ji-tao Zhu, governor of the People's Bank of China, sipped from a martini glass as he sat alone, looking out at the Bund, Shanghai's famous waterfront, the Huangpu River, and its most famous building, the Pearl Tower, a concrete needle that stuck up into the sky, with two large round balls, like pearls, strung at either end of the needle, one near the top, the other closer to the ground.

Like most top government officials, Zhu had a weekend apartment away from Beijing. His was in Shanghai.

On this night, Zhu did what he liked to do every Friday night he was in town. He sat in a seat at Sir Elly's alone, having a cocktail, before heading into the restaurant for a private dinner with his mistress. That was another accoutrement enjoyed by Beijing's governmental elite. Zhu, a short, stooped, pasty man of fifty, was no exception. If anything was a testament to the homely Zhu's power, it was the stunning beauty of his mistress, a twenty-six-year-old Shanghai native named Tai-lin.

He sipped his cocktail, looking out on the neon-lit cruise ships and myriad party boats that moved around the harbor.

Zhu was used to getting a seat at the rooftop lounge. It didn't matter what time Zhu showed up. Beyond being a regular customer, and a generally nice person, Zhu also happened to run the largest financial institution in China. It made sense to keep a seat warm for him.

Most Friday nights, the rooftop lounge was crowded with people, and his reserved chair at the rooftop bar was the only one available. For some reason, on this night, Zhu was the only person at the bar. He took a few more sips, relaxing, staring out at the Bund. At some point, he noticed another man seated at the far end of the bar. His back was turned.

Had he been there before? Zhu didn't think so. Something about the man was familiar. Zhu finished his cocktail. He left money on the bar, climbed down from his chair, and walked toward Sir Elly's, where he knew Tai-lin would be waiting.

"Tai-lin is not there," said the man.

Zhu hesitated.

It wasn't a loud voice, and the man's back was still turned. Had he been speaking to someone else? Or, perhaps Zhu had misheard him?

Zhu shook his head and continued walking. As he got to the door, he turned to get one last look at the man. As he did, the man, as if sensing Zhu's eyes, turned. It was Fao Bhang. An unnatural shudder vibrated down Zhu's spine as he stared at the spymaster.

"Fao, how are you?" asked Zhu, waving awkwardly.

Bhang continued to stare at Zhu.

"I must go," said Zhu. "I . . . I have a dinner appointment."

Zhu turned to leave and found himself standing face-to-face with two large men in suits, guarding the entrance.

Zhu turned and walked back to Bhang, who was smoking and looking out at the Bund. He had a small pair of binoculars pressed to his eyes.

"The Bund is so beautiful at night, don't you think?" asked Bhang, looking through the binoculars. "I particularly love the Pearl Tower. So ugly during the day, but so pretty at night."

"I did what you asked," said Zhu quietly.

"No, you did not," said Bhang, turning.

"We cleaned up the situation with the White House for you," said Zhu. "We expended considerable political capital to do so, I might add."

"That was only part of it," said Bhang, icily.

"It is not my position to demand that the United States turn over a citizen for extradition," said Zhu.

"I can certainly understand your hesitancy, Governor."

"I am the top official of the largest financial institution in the world," said Zhu, stammering. "The public face of China's fiscal policy. This man, Andreas, I don't even know who he is. You must seek the legal avenues. There is a process for this, I'm sure of it. I am not a prosecutor, a judge, or a special agent, Fao. I'm an accountant."

"Ah, so I'm told," said Bhang, smiling. "So perhaps you can help me with a math problem?"

Zhu's face turned red. He stared at Bhang.

"What is it? Is it some kind of joke?"

"No," said Bhang, "a simple mathematics problem."

"Fine, ask your question, then I must go. I am late."

"Thank you for indulging me, Ji-tao. Here is my question: If one were to drop something from the top of the Pearl Tower, which is a thousand feet high, and it landed on top of the lower floor, which is two hundred feet, how far would the object drop?"

Zhu's eyes shot across the water to the Pearl Tower, lit up in the distance. He grabbed Bhang's binoculars. He searched the Pearl Tower until he found the round upper pearl. There, he saw the silhouette of a woman whom he knew immediately was Tai-lin. She was hanging by one foot, upside down.

"Keep watching," said Bhang.

"No!"

Suddenly the woman fell from the sky, dropping quickly and silently to the lower pearl, which she slammed into with an awful force, bouncing visibly. Her limp corpse then slid down the curvature of the ball and fell to the ground below.

Zhu's mouth went agape. He couldn't say anything. He had a hard time even breathing. A pained, terrible expression wrinkled his face as tears came to his eyes.

"There is a plane waiting for you at the airport," said Bhang, standing up and flicking his cigarette to the ground. "It will take you to Washington, D.C. I have gone ahead and taken the liberty of having the chef at Sir Elly's prepare your favorite meal, diver scallops, which was sent ahead to the plane, along with a bottle of wine, which I asked the sommelier himself to select on your behalf."

Bhang stared at Zhu as he cried. He leaned closer to Zhu, a look of pity on his face.

"Do you need help remembering his name, Ji-tao?"

"Andreas," whispered Zhu. "Dewey Andreas."

72

MILL CREEK ROD & GUN
ORRINGTON, MAINE

Dao took a right off Route 15 and parked in front of a sign that read MILL CREEK ROD & GUN. The shop looked like an old house whose bottom floor had been converted into a gun shop a long time ago.

Inside, the shop was empty except for an older gray-haired man who wore a flannel shirt, clip-on suspenders, and Carhartts. He had a long thick beard and mustache. He was smoking a pipe. He looked at her as she stepped into the shop, scanning Dao from head to toe.

"What can I do you for?" he asked in a hard Down East accent.

Dao quickly scanned the small shop. Gun racks lined the walls and were filled with dozens of shotguns and rifles, new and used. The wall behind the counter was a checkerboard of handguns of all types and calibers, also new and used. The glass counter case had a variety of new handguns.

"I'm in the market for a rifle," Dao said. "I'd like to do some target practice. Long-range."

"New or used?"

"I don't care."

"You are aware of Maine gun laws, young lady?" the shopkeeper asked.

"That there aren't any?" she replied.

The man grinned.

"Well, you need a permit to carry a handgun, although you can still buy one, of course. Not sure I understand the distinction on that one, but that's politicians for ya. Other than that, there's just the instant background check."

Dao stared at him.

"I'm not buying a handgun," she said. "I want a rifle."

"All right. I hear ya."

The man nodded at the wall behind her. A gun rack held a line of rifles, locked behind a steel bar.

He walked out from behind the counter and unlocked the bar. He swept his arm across the air, pointing at the line of firearms.

"Other than the Browning there on the right, which ain't for sale, those'll all do fine."

He lifted a rifle up, then handed it to her.

"Kimber Classic," he said. "Used by a fella up in Winterport."

Dao picked up the rifle. It was light, about five pounds, with a handsome walnut stock. She swung it up, aiming at the corner of the ceiling.

"What else do you have?" she asked.

"We have the SuperAmerica, also by Kimber," he said, pointing. "Brand-new. Beautiful rifle. To be perfectly honest, it's pretty much the same rifle as that other one. The America's more of a collector's item. We also got a few Remingtons, the Woodmaster, which I think is a decent gun, especially for the price."

"What's that one?" asked Dao, pointing toward a rifle that was hanging on the wall alone, above the others, although she already knew the answer. It looked heavily used, even beat-up, with a patina of scratched metal and wear. A worn sling dangled beneath it.

He glanced up at the rifle.

"That there's a Panther," he said, reaching up and lifting it from the wall. "That was my nephew's. That's a military rifle right there. Great rifle. I'd have to sell you the ten-round mag. Lawman won't let me sell the nineteen, which is what it was designed for."

He handed the rifle to Dao. It was heavy, but Dao already knew that. The DPMS Panther LR-308 was the rifle she'd been trained on. It was an easy-to-use, incredibly reliable sniper rifle, ideal for medium-range precision shooting that required speedy setup and pickup.

Dao took it to the counter. She made sure it wasn't loaded, then quickly fieldstripped the weapon; shutting the bolt assembly, pressing the rear takedown pin and pulling it out the other side, pivoting the upper receiver and barrel assembly away from each other, pressing the front pin, pulling it out the other side, separating the upper and lower receivers, pulling the charging handle back, removing the bolt assembly, then removing the charging handle until it fell free. She laid the parts neatly on the counter.

Dao did the fieldstrip in exactly five seconds, her long fingers dancing over the steel of the firearm with dizzying speed. The shopkeeper watched her do it, his eyes bulging in awe. She inspected the weapon, then reassembled it. When she was finished, she handed it back to him.

"I'll take it," she said.

73

NORTHERN SPAIN

The steady rhythm of the train was familiar and comforting. Clickity-clack, clickity-clack. Feeling the slow swaying of the car beneath him was the first sensation Dewey had, and it calmed him. He tried to open his eyes but couldn't; he was still deeply groggy, drugged. He tried to move his hand, but it was fastened down. Then he slipped back into unconsciousness.

A distant train horn is what awakened him the next time. How much later was it, where he was, he didn't know. The rhythm of the train soothed him, the steady bouncing of the wheels, steel turning atop steel. This time he opened his eyes.

It was, at first, blurry and dark. It was nighttime. His eyes were trained at the window, which was black. He was lying down. His throat hurt, and he tried to move his arm up to feel it but could not. His right arm was shackled to something; looking down, he saw the black synthetic band of the flex cuffs, tight around his wrist. He tried the same with his left hand, but it too was shackled down. He tested his legs. They were shackled tight. He couldn't move.

The light in the compartment was out, and it was pitch-black. He tried to keep his eyes open, tried to achieve a level of lucidity, but without the light, it was hard to stay awake. He willed himself to.

The horn sounded again as the TGV approached a town somewhere, not slowing one iota. The lights from the station cast soft yellow patches into the compartment. In the wan light, Dewey looked around. That was when he saw a figure—seated across from him, dark slacks, a striped shirt, suit coat. Dewey's eyes drifted up to his face. Where he expected to find the closed lids of a man sleeping, he found himself staring into eyes as dark, as blank, as angry as he'd ever seen, staring back at him. Their eyes met and locked for several still, quiet moments, the man communicating in those moments his anger.

"Hi, Hector," Dewey said.

Calibrisi didn't move. He didn't respond.

"Why am I cuffed?"

"So you don't run away."

"Where am I?" Dewey asked.

"Spain."

Dewey tried to turn his head, wincing in pain.

"What happened to the Delta?" Dewey asked. "Dowling?"

"He's going to live. The bullet missed his heart by a quarter of an inch."

Dewey pulled at the restraints.

"Is this really necessary?"

Calibrisi ignored him, not taking his dark eyes away, staring at him with cold fury.

"Well, if you're not going to talk to me, could you at least get me a beer?" asked Dewey.

Calibrisi lurched forward and slammed the back of his right hand at Dewey's face, hitting him hard enough to hurt, to jerk his head sideways. Dewey absorbed the punch, then looked back at Calibrisi.

"One Delta and one British intelligence officer died saving your motherfucking ass today," said Calibrisi. "Athanasia. You know where he's from? Well, I do. I spoke with his dad tonight. Montana. The British kid, Farber? From a little town outside London called St. Alban's. They had nothing to do with this. You're a selfish son of a fucking bitch."

Dewey let Calibrisi burn through his point, his anger, listening.

"I didn't ask for your help," said Dewey. "I didn't want it. I didn't ask for it. You sent those men in, not me."

Calibrisi's nostrils flared, then he lurched out again, hitting him in the same exact spot, harder this time. Dewey absorbed it again.

"It was your fault, and you know it, Hector."

"You would've died."

"So what. That's not your choice."

"You think you're so fucking tough, don't you? 'I don't care if I live or die. I'm Dewey Andreas.' The world is always out to get poor little Dewey Andreas."

"Pretty easy to say that when you have me tied down, ain't it, chief? Untie me and say it again."

Calibrisi shook his head, more furious now than ever. He reached into his pocket and pulled out a folding combat knife. He stood, flipped it open, stepped to the other side of the compartment, leaned down, then cut the cuffs from Dewey's hands and legs. Then he sat back down.

"Well, tough guy?" Calibrisi said.

Dewey slowly sat up.

"Cool down," said Dewey.

"Don't tell me to cool down."

"Fine. Don't cool down. I'm sorry they died. Obviously, I'm sorry they died. Is that what you want to hear? You're the one—"

"Don't say it."

Dewey leaned back, wincing from pain in his neck.

The train horn made a distant blow. Dewey and Calibrisi sat in silence for more than an hour as the train pushed through the Spanish countryside.

"Where are we going?" asked Dewey.

"Paris."

"Why Paris?"

"You'll see."

"What does that mean?"

"You have a job to do."

"A job? I didn't realize I work for you."

"You don't. But if you don't do it, the SAS team down the hallway is dropping you off at the Chinese embassy when we get to Paris."

Dewey looked out the window.

"You want Fao Bhang dead?" continued Calibrisi. "Well, you're going to get your chance."

Dewey tried to read Calibrisi's stony, emotionless eyes.

"What's the catch?"

"The catch? The catch is, the odds of it working are about one in a million. Oh, and after it's done, whether it works or not, you're either gonna spend the rest of your life in a Chinese prison or, more likely, you're gonna get a nice slug right between those blue eyes of yours."

Dewey nodded. "Sounds like fun," said Dewey. "And please remind me, why would I do this?"

"Because you don't have a choice."

74

Eleven-year-old Reagan Andreas clutched the roof of the golf cart as it barreled toward a large grass-covered knoll at the side of the fairway. Reagan wore cutoff khaki shorts, a white polo shirt, and was barefoot. Her knees were green and brown with dirt and grass stains. Reagan was seated in the passenger seat.

"Not again, Sam," she implored. "Your ball isn't anywhere near here!"

The golf cart was speeding along as fast as it could go. Its driver, thirteen-year-old Sam Andreas, had a devilish smile on his face as he ignored his younger sister for the umpteenth time that day. Sam's only thought was that he hated the fact that the cart couldn't go faster.

Sam had on his favorite shirt, a blue Lacoste polo shirt with a large rip across the back, a hand-me-down from his Uncle Dewey. He wore bright red madras shorts and flip-flops. Sam had curly blond hair, which he hadn't brushed or washed since the beginning of summer, letting the salt water of the ocean do the job for him. He wore sunglasses, was tan, and was as thin as a beanstalk, despite the fact that he ate at least five meals a day and snacked incessantly.

Reagan clutched tighter as the cart crested the hill, then launched out into the air, becoming airborne for the briefest of moments. The cart came to an awkward, bouncing landing, the clubs jangling in back, as everyone within earshot turned their heads, including a small crowd of onlookers on the terrace of the green-and-white clubhouse in the distance, including their father, Hobey Andreas.

"Did you see that?" Sam screamed.

He straightened the cart out, then weaved in an absurdly sharp left turn toward the clubhouse.

"Let me out," said Reagan. "Honestly, you are the most immature human being I have ever met. I can't believe I'm related to you."

"You're not," said Sam. "You were adopted. Mom and Dad didn't tell you?"

She rolled her eyes.

"I wish I was adopted. It would mean I wasn't related to you."

Sam drove the old cart back to the clubhouse. Standing on the porch, arms crossed, a pissed-off look on his face, was their father, Hobey.

"Sucks being you," Reagan sang as she climbed out of the cart.

Hobey Andreas crossed the gravel parking area. Like his father and his brother, Hobey was tall and good-looking, with a mop of unruly brown hair. He came up to Reagan and gave her a little pat on the shoulder.

"How'd you shoot 'em, muffin?" he asked her.

"Okay. I almost got a hole in one on four."

"You did not," said Sam.

"Did I ask you?" said Hobey sharply, without looking at his son. "I don't want to hear a peep out of you. Is that understood?"

"Dad, technically, if I say 'I understand,' that would be making a peep," said Sam.

Hobey Andreas smiled at his daughter, trying to control his temper. "Mom's inside, sweetie. Why don't you go grab some lunch."

"Okeydokey," Reagan said. She looked at Sam and smiled. "Bye, Sam." She turned and walked toward the clubhouse.

Her father waited for her to go through the screen door, then leaned into the cart.

"Five complaints," seethed Hobey, holding up his hand to show all five fingers of an open fist. "That's a new record."

"Five? What are you talking about?"

"The hill jump," said his dad, holding his thumb up to count. "Hitting the Anderson's roof." He held up another finger.

"It was an accident."

"Leaving Reagan on the tee box at one," he continued, holding up a third finger.

"How'd you know about that?"

"Playing chicken with Mac."

Hobey held four fingers up.

"What's the fifth?" asked Sam.

"Mrs. Penske said you made a lewd comment while cleaning your golf ball on the third tee?"

"Oh, yeah."

"What the hell is wrong with you?"

Sam was silent. He remained seated in the cart.

"Sorry," he said, sheepishly.

Hobey shook his head back and forth.

"It's a nice Saturday. You have to go and act like a knucklehead."

"Does this mean I can't play the back nine?"

Hobey pulled his cell from his pocket and hit a button. He let it ring.

"Hi, Pop," Hobey said, staring daggers at his son. "What are you up to?"

Sam started shaking his head back and forth, mouthing the word "no" to his father, who stared at him with a small grin on his face.

"So, I have someone here who'd like to come up and do some work," said Hobey. "And I mean work. Anything. Shoveling cowshit. Cleaning the stables. Getting rid of the wasp nests. Nothing fun or even remotely pleasant. Don't let him sweet-talk you or Mom. No lemonade, iced tea, soda—nothing. If he gets thirsty, let him drink from the hose."

Hobey paused, listening to his father, smiling at Sam.

"Oh, I'm sure Sammy would love to give Homer a bath," said Hobey, his grin becoming wider.

Sam looked as if he might cry. Homer was the Andreas' ill-tempered, three-hundred-pound three-legged pig, known for the time he bit the UPS man.

"Thanks, Dad," said Hobey. "No, he can walk. We'll pick him up around dinner, if we remember."

75

The train pulled into Gare Saint-Lazare at 11:00 A.M.

Dewey was led from the train directly into a waiting sedan, one of three onyx Mercedes S550s, windows tinted black, waiting at the station. Dewey had a dark hood over his head and his arms shackled behind his back. No one—no security personnel, no camera, not even his own mother—could have recognized him.

The three-car convoy took Calibrisi, Dewey, and a half dozen other CIA staffers and security personnel away from the station, north. Calibrisi went in a separate car from Dewey. There wasn't room in Dewey's sedan, not with the driver and two operatives from CIA Special Operations Group, weapons loaded and trained on Dewey at all times. Not that Dewey necessarily wanted to run, but Calibrisi wasn't taking any chances.

The small convoy drove through Paris to Neuilly-sur-Seine, a wealthy, quiet neighborhood just outside the city. There was a large black iron gate at the end of the driveway. The sedans rolled through the gates and sped down the long gravel driveway, lined on each side by massive, ancient elm trees.

At the end of the driveway sat a beautiful rambling limestone mansion, with large black wooden shutters. The front of the house was half covered in ivy, which had grown and spread in pretty bunches up toward the copper gutters and slate roof. The lawn was neatly manicured. The gardens were ornate, more than two acres of carefully trimmed alders, dogwoods, cherry trees, and rare pines, intercut with ordered rows of boxwoods.

They parked near the front door of the house, three abreast, in front of a round fountain, which had long ago been shut off and filled with boxwoods. To the right of the house, an old swimming pool stood out in the middle of the acreage, brick-tiled gunite, with water a tempting light blue. A helipad sat just beyond it, with a black chopper at rest, just before deep woods that bordered the land.

The Neuilly safe house was the epicenter of what would be an MI6-designed operation to assassinate Fao Bhang.

When the three cars emptied, Calibrisi made a quick hand signal to one of the agents, instructing him to remove Dewey's hood and cuffs. When the hood was removed, Dewey's hair was messed up, his face sweating and red, his expression emotionless and blank.

As Dewey followed Calibrisi toward the front door, it didn't take much to guess the general mood in regard to him. He already knew Calibrisi's state of mind; his slightly sore cheek was testament to his anger. Dewey already understood CIA paramilitary from experience; they were mostly ex-Delta or ex-SEAL, so it wouldn't have surprised Dewey if they knew the American who died on the highway back in Lisbon.

As for the British, Dewey could immediately see anger in the eyes of the two plainclothed agents, suppressed carbines strapped around their necks, standing at the large green door. They eyed Dewey like the soldiers at Buckingham Palace might. Dewey looked back without reacting, ignoring them, and entered the house.

Through an entrance foyer filled with antiques, Dewey and Calibrisi walked into a spacious, high-ceilinged living room, with bookshelves, dark blue walls, and a back wall that was filled with French windows, giving a sweeping view down into the gardens. The doors were open, and the sound of birds was the only noise that could be heard. More agents with machine guns stood outside the doors in back of the house; Dewey quickly counted three gunmen.

In the center of the large room, a glass chandelier was hung. Four long sofas in dark maroon velvet were squared around a modern wooden coffee table. Seated on the sofas already was a group of five people.

On the right, next to each other on one side of the seating area, were Katie and Tacoma. On the sofa opposite them sat a middle-aged woman with brown hair and a dignified but stern, even harsh, demeanor. Next to her sat a bald man with round gold-rimmed glasses, young, perhaps only thirty years old, with a laptop open on his lap.

The last man faced the gardens, his back to Dewey and Calibrisi as they entered the room. The man saw the heads of the four others look up when they walked in. He stood up and looked at them. He had slightly messed-up, slightly long blond-and-gray hair, an angular nose, and was the only person, other than Calibrisi, wearing a tie.

He eyed Dewey without saying anything, scanning him head to toe then back up.

"Hi, Hector," he said. "This must be Dewey."

"Dewey, this is Derek Chalmers," said Calibrisi, introducing him. "He runs British intelligence."

Chalmers extended his hand, but Dewey ignored it. He looked at Chalmers icily, then glanced at Katie and Tacoma. Katie revealed nothing, said nothing, and didn't move. Tacoma had a poker face as well.

"Sit down," said Chalmers, looking at Dewey, nodding at the far sofa.

Calibrisi took a seat next to Chalmers. Dewey walked to the far sofa and sat down.

"What do you want?" asked Dewey calmly, looking at Chalmers, then Calibrisi.

Chalmers spoke first.

"The first thing I'd like to do is apologize," said Chalmers. "It was my idea, not Hector's, not anybody else's, that resulted in the death of Jessica Tanzer. There is an unwritten code in this line of work: people who are innocent bystanders should be left alone. Fao Bhang crossed that line. That said, it was my operation that brought him there. And all I can say to you is that I am sorry."

Chalmers looked at Dewey for several tense moments.

"I'm not looking for an apology," said Dewey. "What do you want?"

"It's not what we want," said Chalmers. "It's what you want. You want Fao Bhang dead, am I correct?"

Dewey didn't answer.

"Is this going to be a one-way conversation?" asked Chalmers.

"I didn't ask for this meeting. Tell me what you want me to do, and I'll tell you if I'm willing to do it."

Dewey looked around the room.

"Yeah, sure, I want Bhang dead, but I don't need your help."

"That's where I beg to differ, Dewey," said Chalmers. "I can tell you, there is no man who can single-handedly take down Fao Bhang. It can't be done. I know what you are, Dewey. I know what you're made of. You're programmed to act alone, to improvise. Theoretically, you're the best. But there are some mountains that are, quite simply, too high to climb, even for you."

"You're entitled to your opinion," said Dewey, "but I don't really give a fuck what you think, Derek. I was minding my own business. You're the ones who dragged me up here."

"Minding your own business?" asked Calibrisi. "You were dangling upside down in a fucking car. You'd be dead—"

"That's my choice," said Dewey, calmly.

"Yes, it is," said Chalmers, agreeing. "And you're right, you didn't ask for our help. The truth is, we want Fao Bhang dead too."

"So kill him."

"You're the one he's developed the obsession with," said Chalmers patiently. "That obsession is the only reason he's vulnerable right now. Inserting ourselves into that obsession is the only way anyone is going to get within a hundred miles of Fao Bhang. So you're right, you can try to do it on your own. You killed his brother on your own. I would imagine Bhang might be slightly more difficult, but, yes, you might be able to pull it off. Let me say this: I'd give you better chances than anyone else I know."

Chalmers paused, then smiled at Dewey.

"But in the end, we both know, if you step foot out of this house, you're a dead man," said Chalmers. "I'd give it a day, maybe two. You know it, and I know it. What occurred in Lisbon is simply a taste of what awaits you. And not just here—everywhere."

"That's my choice. Let them try. And if they succeed, then I'll wait for that motherfucker in hell."

Chalmers shook his head.

341

"Okay, for the sake of argument, let's say you do manage to not get killed. Bhang hasn't left China in ten years. How would you infiltrate China? Then, once you were there, how is it you'd get close to him?"

Dewey stared icily at Chalmers.

"Why don't you worry about protecting Queen Elizabeth, and I'll worry about killing Fao Bhang," said Dewey.

Chalmers shook his head in disbelief.

"Oh, that's brilliant," Chalmers said. "Do you want to fail? To die trying? Do you think there's some sort of nobility in that? And is that what Jessica deserves? Doesn't she deserve more?"

"She deserves to be alive, which she isn't."

The room went silent.

"I need a break," said Chalmers, struggling to maintain his composure. He stood up and walked behind the sofas to the French doors. He walked onto the terrace and stood looking out at the gardens.

Calibrisi stood up and walked out of the room. He was followed by Katie, then by the two Brits on the couch. Only Tacoma remained in the room. He was seated on the sofa. He had removed one of his shoes and was scratching between his toes.

"Dewey?" asked Tacoma after a while, quietly clearing his throat. "You know I'm not good at saying stuff. So I'm just gonna say it. I'm sorry for what happened. It sucks, man."

Dewey stared at the coffee table for several moments. Finally, he looked at Tacoma. Tacoma's long hair was a disheveled mess. He looked more like a hippie than a highly decorated former Navy SEAL. He had on a flannel shirt with paint stains on it, and a prominent rip on the right shoulder. His face was covered in stubble. Their eyes met.

"But are you so fucking selfish you'd rather die than forgive the people in this room?" continued Tacoma. "Are you so fucking selfish you'd rather die than kill that son of a bitch, the one who actually did kill her?"

Dewey didn't quite know why—he'd served alongside many men—but for some reason he couldn't explain, Tacoma was like the little brother he never had. He had an older brother, but not a younger one, and it was different. He stared at Tacoma and he felt embarrassed, even ashamed. And in that moment, Dewey found something he needed badly, something that no amount of revenge or killing or alcohol or running could ever give him: in that brotherhood, he found a reason for living.

Dewey smiled. "Well, since you put it so politely, Rob."

76

MARGARET HILL
CASTINE

Sam walked up the long gravel driveway toward his grandparents'
farm.

Before he left the club, he'd grabbed the nine iron from his golf bag.
As he ambled slowly toward the farm, he was swinging it at the yellow
dandelion heads that sprouted in the grass strip that ran up the middle
of the driveway, and at anything even remotely hittable in the low
bushes alongside the driveway—flowers, pinecones, even the occasional
rock.

Truth be told, he didn't like golf very much, so he actually didn't
care about not playing the back nine, which was, at nine-hole Castine
Golf Club, simply the front nine all over again. But the thought of
scrubbing down the cantankerous old pig Homer made Sam walk as
slowly as humanly possible without drawing the suspicion of his grandmother, who was apt to go looking for him if he took too long walking
up the meandering drive to the farm.

Sam came to a small green apple that had fallen in the middle of
the road. He considered eating it, but then changed his mind. He got
into a golf stance, then swung, firing the apple in a hail of scattering
parts into the bushes.

After admiring his shot for much longer than it actually deserved,
he started walking again, practically smelling Homer as he drew

closer. His momentum was suddenly interrupted by the dull red speckles of a raspberry bush.

They wouldn't want you to starve, he said to himself as he dropped the club and leaned over to pick a few raspberries and waste more time.

John Andreas stepped to the side of a large fenced-in pigpen. Three pigs were inside the pen, but there was little question as to whose pigpen it was. Homer lay on his side, covered in dried mud, sunbathing in the morning sunshine. He occupied the entire center of the pen, next to the feeding trough, guarding access to it and snoring.

"Hey, Homer," called Andreas. "Sam's giving you a bath. Don't bite him, or I'll cut another one of those legs off."

If the pig understood anything that his sixty-six-year-old owner had just said, he didn't act like it. Indeed, the sound of the big pig's snoring hummed on through Andreas's words, uninterrupted.

Andreas, trailed by an old sheepdog named Ginny, walked back across the lawn toward the farmhouse.

Inside the kitchen, he sat down at the table where his wife, Margaret, was already seated. Three plates with sandwiches on them, along with three glasses of lemonade, were on the table.

"Well, that was nice of you, Marge," he said. "Who's the third one for?"

"Sammy."

"Hobey's trying to teach him a lesson, hon."

"Well, as far as I'm concerned, there's nothing wrong with that kid. He's a spitting image of his uncle. How did *he* turn out?"

"That's not the point, Marge. It's not our place to get in the middle of that."

"We'll tell him to keep it hush," she said, patting his hand. "And before you have him clean that damn pig, I need his help in the garden. My arthritis is acting up. He can weed for a spell."

Less than a half mile away, just past Hatch Cove, Dao took a right turn on Wadsworth Cove Road. She drove a few hundred feet, slowly, looking ahead and behind, making sure no one was around to see her. She turned into a grassy cutout lot to the left. She aimed the car across the thick field grass and parked between a pair of pine trees, out of sight of anyone driving or walking on Wadsworth Cove Road.

Outside the car, she took off her leather boots, then removed her white blouse and jeans, tossing them in the back of the Camaro. She pulled on tight green camouflage running pants, a matching running shirt, then a camo ski mask, which she pulled down over her head. She slammed a magazine in the Panther LR-308, then strapped the rifle across her back.

Dao began a fast run into the woods, due south, guided by the small compass on her watch. She'd never been to Castine before, but she knew precisely where she was going.

The stand of trees soon dissolved into thickets of overgrown shrubs, but it didn't slow her down. She came to a thin stream, jumped across it, then kept moving south. Soon, she was cloaked in the shadows of the forest, the North Woods, as it was called in Castine.

When she hit the first of the tall trees, Dao turned, stopped, and faced due east. She walked off exactly four hundred paces. She then turned to face south and walked slowly straight ahead, being careful not to make any noise. After half a minute, the red of a barn suddenly appeared through the trees. Dao was at the farm.

She walked a slow, stalking, meticulously quiet path along the edge of the trees that encircled the large farm. When she finally stopped, she was south of the farm, looking up at a pretty, rambling white farmhouse.

In the yard, she saw a fluffy dog walking alongside a tall, silver-haired man and a much-shorter woman.

Chang continued to stalk around the perimeter of the farm, shielded by the shadows of the trees, looking up at the couple as they walked across the front lawn of the farm to a garden. The couple—John and Margaret Andreas—went inside the garden. Dao stared as they each pulled on yellow gardening gloves and went to work.

Dao glanced quickly around her, scanning for a place to set up. She quickly found it. An old stone wall was just a few feet away. She walked to it and found a place to set up the Panther for a nice, clean shot. When she found a stable, flat boulder, Dao removed the rifle from her back, set up the bipod on the rock, then lay down behind the stone wall.

Thirty feet up in the air, Sam sat on the branch of a massive maple tree. He stared down at the camouflaged figure on the ground.

Sam's heart was beating so loudly, he feared the person might hear him.

He looked in front of him. Carved into the bark of the old maple tree were brown letters, carved many years ago, long before he was born:

Hobey

Then, just below it:

Dewey

Sam tried to focus on the letters, looking at them as if they might give him some sort of guidance.

When Sam had first heard the sound of someone walking on dried leaves below, he'd been halfway through the letter "A" of his own name, a few inches below Dewey's. Sam was about to yell at the person— "Hey, who is that?"—when his eye caught the sight of the long black rifle strapped across the person's back, and he caught his words.

Now Sam tried to keep from fainting, from screaming, from moving, as he watched the camouflaged figure set up the rifle on a rock below him.

Straight ahead, through the trees, Sam watched as his grandparents walked across the green front lawn. Ginny was between them.

"Oh, God," Sam whispered, shutting his eyes as tears welled up and he fought against them. "Please help me."

He finally opened his eyes as the figure set the weapon down on the stone wall and lay down on the ground behind it. It was aimed at his grandparents up in the garden.

He looked back at the tree.

Dewey

Sam took a deep breath, then put his left foot gently down on a branch below where he sat. His tears abruptly stopped, and he felt a warmth that he'd never experienced before, invading his body. Silently, he stepped down onto the branch as, with his other foot, he searched for another branch even lower, a branch he knew by heart, a branch one step closer to the mysterious figure.

77

In a small apartment near Luxembourg Gardens, Koo finished toweling off, then went to the bedroom. His clothing was laid out on the bed. Next to his clothing, a nurse's outfit was laid out.

Koo didn't get dressed. Instead, he walked downstairs. Tammy was in the kitchen, reading the newspaper.

"Good morning," he said.

Tammy smiled. "Why are you not dressed?"

"I don't have to work until this afternoon," he said.

She smiled and slowly put the paper down, then followed him back upstairs to the bedroom. There, they climbed into bed and made love.

Afterward, she watched from beneath the covers as he got dressed.

"I was thinking of inviting Sam and Kelly for dinner tonight," she said. "I could make chicken and forty cloves, your favorite."

Koo pulled the heavy white T-shirt over his head.

"That would be wonderful," he said, without looking at her. "I'll pick up a bottle of wine."

"My shift ends at eight. I'll invite them for eight thirty, all right?"

"Sounds perfect."

By the time Koo finished getting dressed, Tammy had fallen asleep. He reached into the drawer and took the QSZ-92 from beneath a pair of pants, sticking it into his shoulder holster.

Koo walked to the side of the bed, then leaned down and kissed his wife on the forehead.

"I love you," he said, then, in Mandarin, he whispered a Chinese proverb: "How lucky I am to have known someone who was so hard to say goodbye to."

As he lifted his head, his wife's eyes opened. She stared at him without moving.

"Must it be?" she whispered.

Koo stared at her for several moments. He said nothing. Finally, he averted his eyes from her, turned, and left.

In Beijing, General Qingchen was dressed in his green khaki uniform, a gold rope sash from right shoulder across his waist; a block of colors was over his left breast, gold stars atop both shoulders, and a beautiful red-and-gold neck ribbon, reserved for the highest-ranking military leader in the People's Liberation Army. At seventy-four, General Qingchen was not the oldest man in the room, but he was the only one not dressed in a black or dark blue suit.

He was seated on a gold-colored damask couch, in a room called the Gold Sun Room on the grounds of Zhongnanhai, the palace that was the home of China's paramount leader, Qishan Li, as well as headquarters for China's Communist Party and its governing State Council, both of which Qingchen was a member.

Qingchen was one of twelve members of the State Council invited to the meeting, which had been called by Premier Li, who was seated on the sofa across from Qingchen. The others, Qingchen had realized as soon as he sat down, were Li's closest allies.

For the preceding hour, Qingchen and the others had been listening to a detailed briefing by China's foreign minister regarding Portugal and a series of violent killings in Lisbon that had occurred the day before, involving men that the president of Portugal believed were Chinese agents, four of whose corpses were being held in a Lisbon mortuary.

"This is the second incident in a week involving the Ministry of State Security," said Li, looking around the room, making eye contact with every man in the room, Qingchen noted, but him. "First America's national security advisor dies in some sort of botched operation, and now this thing in Lisbon. Bhang's missteps are becoming a deep embarrassment to us all. I didn't want to have to do this, but I must insist we consider Bhang's removal. We all know he's a capable and talented man, but he's beginning to harm China's reputation abroad."

"What would you like from us?" asked one of the members of the council.

"You are my most trusted circle," said Li, again glancing around the room, and again, either consciously or unconsciously, avoiding Qingchen. "I know already that I have your loyalty. I would like your support with the broader membership. It is time for action. Bhang must be removed."

Li flashed Qingchen a look.

"He is a powerful self-advocate," said another council member. "He has many allies."

"He is not the paramount leader," snapped Li. "He would be afforded the honors and awards becoming of a high-ranking official who has decided to retire. A stipend, a seat in the congress, medals, et cetera, and other such things."

Qingchen felt a chill as Li looked his way.

"As for his allies," said Li, "we will continue to expect and appreciate their service to the republic. Indeed, I like to consider myself one of Bhang's strongest allies. This need not be contentious. But it must be."

At noon, a silver GV touched down at Orly Airport on the outskirts of Paris.

But for the man aboard the jet, Lacey James, it was 3:00 A.M.

With James was his girlfriend, a svelte, beautiful twenty-eight-year-old Swarthmore grad named Didi, with ghost white skin, and a face that garnered ten thousand dollars an hour modeling, when she felt like it, which wasn't often. She had on a pair of glasses and was reading a book, her third on the flight.

James was dressed in bright yellow leather pants, cowboy boots, a

J.Crew flannel shirt, and a cowboy hat. As the plane taxied toward the black Mercedes sedan parked on the tarmac, outside the private terminal, he opened a can of Red Bull and guzzled it.

The jet came to a stop a few feet from the Mercedes. James looked out the window. An MI6 agent climbed from the car's driver's seat. He was tall, dressed in jeans and a long-sleeved green Under Armour T-shirt.

"See you in a few hours," he said.

Didi looked up.

"Are we here already?"

"Yes. They're going to fly you to London. I'll get there tonight."

"Cool. See you then, L.J."

James smiled at her nickname for him.

As far as Didi was concerned, he was getting off in Paris to meet with a French film director named Bruggé, who was interested in hiring him for an upcoming film about the French Revolution. She'd agreed to come when promised a long weekend in London, her favorite city, mainly because she loved its bookstores.

One of the pilots opened the cabin door and lowered the stairs. James lifted a large stainless-steel trunk from a back seat and walked toward the door.

"You need a hand, sir?"

"I got it."

"London, then back to get you, correct, sir?"

"That's right. See you later."

The sound of footsteps on the stairs made him turn just as the agent from the tarmac stuck his head in the cabin. He scanned James from head to toe.

"You got any other clothing?" he asked.

"Yes, why? You don't like what I'm wearing?"

"The pants are hideous, but that has nothing to do with it, sir," said the agent. "We're going to be passing through a residential neighborhood. You can't stand out. Lose the pleather."

James went to the back of the plane.

"They're leather," he muttered to himself under his breath, as he changed in back. "Versace. Twenty thousand dollars."

The agent had already put the steel box in the trunk. James went to open the passenger-seat door, but the black window suddenly lowered. Another agent was already seated. Across his lap was a submachine gun. The agent looked up.

"Why don't you sit in back, Mr. James."

"If you insist," said James.

Dewey took a shower and put on clean clothing. When he returned to the library, someone had placed a mug of fresh coffee in front of his seat. He looked around, trying to figure out who had done it, but no one said anything, which was, he realized, the point.

He took a sip, ran his hand through his still-wet hair, and looked across the room at Chalmers, then Calibrisi.

"I'm in," Dewey said. "Tell me how we're going to kill this motherfucker."

Chalmers smiled then looked at the woman on the sofa.

"I'm Veronica Smythson," she said to Dewey. "I run paramilitary operations at MI6."

"Nice to meet you."

"First, some context. Two weeks ago, you succeeded in finding the name of an elusive double agent working inside Mossad. The discovery of that mole, Dillman, began a chain of very brutal, very lethal reprisals and counterreprisals. For a variety of reasons, what began as a fairly traditional East–West intelligence battle has become personal between its two protagonists. Bhang's behavior, we believe, holds the key to the operation. In his increasing obsession with killing you lies the architecture of his own demise."

"Speakay Anglay," said Dewey, sipping from his coffee cup, "*s'il vous plaît.*"

Smythson grinned.

"As reckless as killing Bo Minh was, it served a vital purpose," said Smythson. "You personalized it."

"Bhang issued a worldwide kill order on you," said Chalmers.

"In Bhang's eighteen years running the ministry, he's issued six," said Smythson. "Killing you is now the highest priority of Chinese intelligence. Every move you've taken—killing his brother, killing the squad over at Borchardt's house, escaping from Lisbon—has only added to the anger that now drives Bhang. It's his obsession with you, ultimately, that's going to be his undoing. Or yours. The operation we've designed takes that anger and directs it back at Bhang himself. The code name is 'Eye for an Eye.' It means revenge. But it also means deception; we are going to manipulate what Bhang sees for a brief period of time. Unknowingly, he will see something different than what is actually occurring. A series of lies. We will be substituting an eye for an eye."

Smythson nodded at the bald man next to her on the couch, who began typing on his laptop. Suddenly, the curtains slid shut over the windows, and the lights in the room dimmed. A large screen lowered from the ceiling behind Smythson. The screen lit up. It displayed a picture of the exterior facade of a hotel.

"This afternoon, at approximately three fifty-five P.M., you'll check into the Bristol Hotel," said Smythson. "You'll pay with a credit card that we'll provide you. The name on the card will comport with a passport we'll also provide."

A photo of a passport appeared showing Dewey's face. The name "Walker, Dane M." appeared next to it, along with "Kansas City, Missouri." Next to the photo of the fake passport was a black American Express card, the name "Dane Walker" in the lower corner.

Something about the name triggered a memory in Dewey.

"Does that name sound familiar?" asked Smythson.

"Yes," said Dewey. "I don't know why, though."

"Delta," said Smythson. "That was your alias when you went to Munich and exfiltrated the Russian, Vargarin."

Dewey nodded.

"When that credit card is swiped," continued Smythson, "it will trigger the alias. It's one of the aliases we assume the ministry will be in possession of. When that credit card is swiped, they'll know within approximately ten seconds you've checked into the Bristol."

Smythson nodded at her aide, and the screen changed. A photo appeared of a man in a baseball hat. He was middle-aged, with a mustache and dark complexion.

"We also have a backup, for redundancy. This man, Louis Vonnes, is a parking valet at the hotel. He's also a Chinese informant. Yesterday afternoon, he was shown your photograph and promised a bunch of money if he sees you and phones you in. We would like you to smoke a cigarette outside the hotel before you check in."

"Does Dewey need to worry about this guy doing more than phoning it in?" asked Tacoma.

"There's always unpredictability," said Smythson. "That said, we checked him out. He doesn't own a gun or have any sort of criminal background."

A photo of the hotel's front desk appeared.

"After checking in, you will place your bags in room one-oh-one-one," said Smythson. "You'll put on this shirt."

She stood up and walked to a credenza on the side of the room. From a leather weekend bag, she lifted a blue button-down shirt and held it up. It appeared normal from the outside, but on the inside of the shirt was a thin sheet of mesh that resembled Bubble Wrap. Four fist-sized bladders of transparent liquid were attached to the mesh. It looked like water.

She carried it to Dewey. "Put this on; let's make sure it fits."

Dewey stood up and pulled his T-shirt over his head. He tried the shirt on. It was snug but would work.

"Look in the pocket," said Smythson.

Dewey looked in the chest pocket and removed a ceramic ring. A small button stuck out of one side of the ring.

"Don't press it," said Smythson.

"Why not?"

"I'll get to that. Now take the shirt off."

She folded it up and walked it back to the leather bag.

"Sometime after four, you will return to the lobby of the hotel, wearing the shirt. The ring will be on your finger. Head for the Bristol lounge."

A floor plan appeared, showing the elevator marked with a big X. To the elevator's right was a large red star. An arrow showed the route.

The floor plan disappeared and was replaced by a photo of the Bristol lounge. The room was fancy, like a tearoom at a palace, with cavernous ceilings, chandeliers, large double-decker windows, booths, and tables filled with people.

"Unfortunately for the Bristol, I'm afraid we're going to be making quite a mess of it this afternoon," Smythson went on.

"It's critical you understand the next sequence," said Chalmers. "If any aspect of the operation from this point forward goes south, you're a dead man."

Three photographs popped onto the screen. On the left was a head shot of Katie. To the right, Tacoma. In the center of the screen was a photo of a Chinese man.

"These are the three role players in our drama," said Smythson. "Katie, Rob, and a third individual."

Dewey stood and walked in front of the screen, studying Koo's face.

"Who is he?" asked Dewey.

"His name is Xiua Koo. He is a high-rank ministry agent. For six years, Koo has also worked for England. Koo is being sacrificed by MI6 for the greater objective of this operation. He's playing a key role in our deception, and then he will be brought in from the cold."

Dewey studied Koo's face.

"As of three thirty this afternoon, Katie and Rob will be in the lounge," Smythson went on. "They will not be together and will not do anything to acknowledge each other. Rob will brush his hair and put on some decent trousers so that the Bristol allows him inside."

Tacoma smiled and ran his hand through his hair.

"That could be the most challenging part of the whole operation," said Katie.

"When you emerge from the elevator, Dewey, you'll go to the lounge. You'll be provided a table near the front. You'll take the seat facing the entrance. By my estimates, time will be approximately five after four."

The screen flashed to a handgun.

"QSZ-92," said Dewey, standing in front of the screen, looking at the photo. "Nine by one-nine. Undermount red-dot laser."

"Correct," said Smythson.

356

The screen zeroed in on the muzzle. At the end of the barrel, where the site was located, was a small silver object. Dewey thought it was a smudge on the photo or a nick on the site. When the shot came into sharp relief, it looked like a tiny ball bearing.

"Dewey, this is the most important part of the briefing."

"What is it?"

"A camera," said Smythson. "From the moment Koo walks into the hotel, everything will be watched live back in Beijing. Everything. Assume Fao Bhang will be watching."

"No flipping him off," said Calibrisi.

"That little camera is what this entire operation is about. That is our eye. Do you understand?"

"Yeah, I get it."

"Xiua Koo will enter the hotel at approximately four ten," said Smythson. "He'll be wearing a tan trench coat. You'll be in the lounge, sitting, perhaps having a spot of tea. When he sees you, he'll pull the QSZ from the coat. Koo will then fire at you from close range, like this."

Smythson pretended to pull a sidearm from her coat, then stepped toward Dewey, aiming the invisible weapon at Dewey's chest.

"Bang, bang," she said. "That's when you press that little button on the ring, twice. You need to time it so that the second time you press it is right when he fires. It would also be helpful if you fell backward and pretended to be dead."

"So obviously the QSZ will be loaded with blanks," said Dewey. "Unless, of course, he has a change of heart. Or Bhang gets to him. Then what happens?"

"Then you won't need to press the button," said Tacoma.

Dewey smiled and shook his head.

"Koo is trustworthy," said Chalmers.

"That's easy for you to say."

"If it was just about him, I would understand," said Chalmers. "It's not. If you die, some people Koo cares about will also die."

"What if those people have already been exfiltrated by China?" asked Dewey. "Or shot?"

Chalmers looked at Smythson.

"There's no way around that one, Dewey," said Smythson. "But, if it's any consolation, that's one of the smaller risks you're signing up for."

Dewey said nothing.

"92's a decent gun," said Tacoma. "You won't feel a thing."

"Will you shut the fuck up?" said Dewey.

"Okay, let's get back to it then," said Smythson. "At this point, two different sequences begin, and you two"—Smythson pointed to Katie and Tacoma—"come into the picture."

Smythson turned and nodded at her staffer. A generic photo of a man appeared on the screen.

"Rob," said Smythson, "you're there to keep an eye on Dewey. When you see Koo pull his weapon, you stand, pull yours, and fire, aiming here."

She pointed to her left shoulder, then to the screen. A red star appeared where she wanted him to aim, atop his shoulder.

"Of course, you'll be firing blanks, Rob," she said. "Your first will miss. Koo will shoot at you, and you'll take the fall, like Dewey. Koo puts a few more rounds in Dewey, giving the folks back in Beijing a nice view of a very bloody and very dead Dewey Andreas. From the ground, you fire again, Rob. That one hits. Koo will fall to the ground. He'll run for the door, bleeding badly. Exit Koo. Katie, at the same time this is happening, you are watching the door to the hotel and the lobby. At some point, sooner rather than later, we have to anticipate the arrival of more ministry agents. Your firearm will be hot; you need to take them down. Otherwise, this will all be for naught. If any tertiary assets get into a firing zone, Dewey will die."

"What will I be carrying?"

"Anything you want."

"MP7A1," said Katie. "A Glock 30, also."

"Done," said Smythson. "Now, this is important. There will be witnesses. Also, you should assume one or more of the Chinese agents have cameras. People in the lounge might have cameras, even the hotel. We should expect that all of it will be examined by MSS. What this means—Dewey, Rob, Katie—is that you need to play your parts, even after Koo is gone, and even after Katie has taken down whatever comes her way. Katie, you should tend to Dewey."

"Then what?"

"At this point, I would expect full-out pandemonium," said Smythson. "Police, ambulances—you name it. Dewey and Rob, you'll be taken away in ambulances that we happen to own. Katie, guard Dewey the entire way to the ambulance in case there are any more agents. You'll have identification that, if necessary, will let you pass any French police. Get in the ambulance with Dewey."

Smythson looked at Tacoma, then Katie, and finally Dewey.

"Everyone got it?"

"I think I can handle that," said Dewey. "Am I done at that point?"

Smythson looked at Dewey, then to Chalmers, in silence.

"Not quite," said Chalmers. "Why don't we take a five-minute break."

Bhang stood on the deck outside his brother's empty apartment.

The sun was setting in the distance, and he understood then why Bo had chosen to live where he lived, far away from the ministry's offices, from the city, in a place where, beneath the burnt orange sky, acres upon acres of trees, fields of wildflowers, and the serene, dark blue water of the lake spoke a different language than anything available from human beings.

He smoked his third cigarette in a row, standing in silence on the small terrace.

Back inside the apartment, Bhang walked one last time through the rooms. He'd already had all of Bhang's computers and technical equipment shipped back to the ministry. Furniture, such that it was, would be picked up in a few days and donated to a local orphanage. As for Bhang's personal effects, such as clothing and dishes, Bhang had it thrown away. He'd boxed up the photos, and they now sat in a cardboard container near the door.

Bhang walked one last time through the apartment. He looked in the closet, off the bedroom, finding it empty. Then he stared at the bed for a few moments. He crouched and peered beneath it. There, he saw a small object tucked away, near the wall. He crawled on his stomach and grabbed its edges. He pulled it out, then set it on the bed. It was a homemade radio, the radio Bo had made, with help from their father, when he was all of seven years old. He touched the wires to the old battery, and the radio made a faint static noise. He moved a small wooden dial until he could hear the sound of a man, coming through the small speaker. He was giving a weather report. After a few seconds, the battery died out.

Bhang stared for several moments at the radio, feeling an emotion he hadn't felt in so long that at first he couldn't recognize it: sorrow. He felt his eyes become wet, and then he began to cry, a high-pitched, childlike cry, his head bobbing up and down as tears fell to the floor.

As he was driven back to the ministry, his composure reestablished, Bhang listened to his voice mail, a number that only three people possessed, two of whom—Bo and Ming-huá—were now dead. He dialed the third.

"General Qingchen," said Bhang, after he'd answered.

"We must talk," said Qingchen. "Time is moving faster than I anticipated. Events are occurring."

"I'll be right there."

Dewey saw Calibrisi standing alone on the terrace. He went outside.

Calibrisi turned. He put his hand on Dewey's shoulder.

"I'm sorry for slugging you earlier."

"It's all right. Sorry for choking you. Now, what are you not telling me?"

Calibrisi paused.

"Let's go back inside," said Calibrisi.

The rest of the group had reconvened in the library.

Dewey sat down.

"We need to hurry," said Chalmers, looking at his watch. "We're going to start running into time issues."

"Next steps," said Smythson. "You're shot. You're down on the ground. You'll be taken from the Bristol in an ambulance. The ambulance is going to take you to a garage near Luxembourg Gardens. It's near where Koo lives and where we believe he'll be exfiltrated from."

Dewey listened without reacting.

"I'll meet you there," continued Smythson. "Your hair will be dyed and cut. Then a cast of Xiua Koo will be attached to your face."

Smythson nodded at the screen. The photo of Xiua Koo appeared.

"I'm six-four."

"Koo is six-three," said Smythson. "As for the cast, you won't be able to tell the difference."

"I don't speak Mandarin," said Dewey, his doubt starting to show.

"You only need to know one word," said Smythson. "*Téngtòng.* It means, 'pain.' Remember, you just got shot. Everyone will understand if you don't say anything for a while."

"They'll examine my shoulder," said Dewey.

Smythson looked at Dewey, then to Calibrisi and Chalmers. Dewey's eyes followed hers.

"That part will be real."

Dewey sat back, saying nothing.

"You'll take the place of Xiua Koo," said Smythson. "You'll be exfiltrated today and flown to China. That's the part of the operation you'll have to architect, Dewey. It is our belief that soon after your arrival, either at the airport or when you get to the hospital, Bhang will visit you. Of course, he'll think he's visiting Koo, the ministry hero who killed his nemesis. What you do at that point, what tools or weapons you may or may not improvise, that will be solely up to you to innovate. Perhaps break his neck or strangle him."

"What if he doesn't visit?" asked Dewey.

"He will," said Chalmers. "The agent who succeeds in assassinating you receives the highest award the ministry has. Bhang is awarding it in person. This is all going to go down quickly—right when you arrive or soon thereafter. But if you miss the opportunity, they're going to find out sooner rather than later. Then you're dead, and Bhang lives on."

Dewey leaned back.

"Sounds like I'm dead no matter what."

"You wanted your shot at Fao Bhang," said Calibrisi. "Now you've got it."

"You can still back out," said Katie. "You don't have to do it."

"She's right," said Chalmers. "We're going to do everything we can to figure out how to get you out of China. But there are no guarantees, and I would be lying if I said the odds of rescuing you are good."

Dewey thought of Jessica. She wouldn't want him to do it, of course. Were she alive, the operation would've been killed in its infancy. But she wasn't alive, and Hector was right: he did want a shot at Bhang. He wouldn't be able to live with himself if he didn't take it, even if the odds were low and the aftermath fatal.

Deep down, it wasn't about Jessica anymore, it was about him. It was about being a man. Dewey knew he'd rather die than spend the rest of his life knowing what it felt like to be a coward.

Dewey stood up. "Let's go."

Chalmers and Smythson led Dewey into the kitchen. Lacey James was standing next to the island, sleeves rolled up.

"Take a seat."

James's steel trunk lay open on the ground. Inside, it was lined with bottles and canisters of various sizes, shapes, and colors.

"What are you doing?" asked Dewey.

"We need to make a mold of your face," said James.

James reached into the trunk and pulled out a see-through polycarbonate case. Inside was a mask of a Chinese man. Other than the fact that it had no eyes, hair, ears, or teeth, it looked exactly like Koo.

"We need something to adhere the life cast of the Chinese agent to," said James, holding up the mask of Koo. "Otherwise, it will fall off. The cast of your face lets me build a positive of your features. Then I attach the mask to it. It's the same thing as wearing a mask on Halloween, only this time the mask looks and feels like it's real. We glue it to your face and, *voilà*, you'll be Chinese, at least for a few days."

"What's it made of?"

"Silicone," said James. "We use medical adhesive. It's safe, and perhaps more important, has the same texture as skin. Now sit down."

James pulled out two gallon-sized canisters, both labeled BODY DOU-BLE. He unscrewed the lids. Inside the first canister was a thick, gooey pink liquid; the other held a similar-looking liquid, only it was blue. He poured equal amounts into a bowl and mixed them. The liquid turned purple.

Next, James immersed a small stack of damp plaster strips in the purple liquid. He waited a few seconds, then lifted a strip into the air.

"This is going to feel somewhat disgusting," said James. "I apologize in advance."

He leaned over and wrapped the wet strip across Dewey's forehead. Working quickly, he covered Dewey's entire face with wet purple plaster strips.

James then removed a pair of specially designed blow dryers, plugged them in, and blow-dried Dewey's face until the color was gone, indicating the strips were dry, replaced by a dull, translucent hue. He took a small plastic tool that looked like a spatula and inserted it between the dried cast and Dewey's chin. He gently worked the end of the tool around the edge of the cast. When he finished a full circle, he popped the cast from Dewey's face.

Smythson nodded to Dewey.

"Let's go. We don't have a lot of time."

78

The limousine carrying Ji-tao Zhu sped quickly along Rock Creek Parkway. It exited at Connecticut Avenue, then moved up Connecticut until it was in front of a large art deco apartment complex called the Kennedy-Warren. Zhu's driver pulled into an underground parking garage. Zhu climbed out the back of the limousine alone and took the elevator to the top floor. He walked to the door marked 1809.

Zhu rang the doorbell. When no one answered, he rang it a second time. Finally, he heard footsteps. The door opened. Standing in the doorway, dressed in a blue bathrobe, wearing a pair of worn-out Timberland construction boots, his curly blond hair in a wildish Afro, was Wood Uhlrich.

"You're two hours early," said Uhlrich.

"The plane was faster than I anticipated, Mr. Secretary," said Zhu. "May I come in?"

Uhlrich opened the door.

"Why not."

Zhu followed Uhlrich into a spacious, light-filled apartment, its windows overlooking the treetops of Rock Creek Park.

"I'll be right back," said Uhlrich. "Do you want coffee?"

"No, thank you. I won't be here long enough to enjoy it."

Uhlrich disappeared into the kitchen, where he poured himself a cup of coffee. He returned to the living room.

Zhu scanned Uhlrich's outfit as Uhlrich stood staring at the much-shorter Zhu, who was neatly attired in a plain-looking black business suit and tie.

"You gonna say something?" asked Uhlrich.

"Thank you for seeing me on such short notice," said Zhu.

Uhlrich took a sip of coffee but didn't say anything.

"This concerns our last conversation," said Zhu.

"Yeah, I figured that. The one where you told me, and the United States, to go to hell."

"That's not exactly what I said, Wood. I said that China will not lend you any more money."

"It's the same thing," said Uhlrich, "and you know it."

Zhu smiled, then looked at the window.

"Such a nice view, Wood. I am very jealous. It must be such a joy to wake up every day and see the trees."

"Cut the bullshit."

"I said we'd be in touch. The conditions for China's continued lending to the United States. Remember?"

Uhlrich sipped, staring at Zhu with a blank stare.

"What do you want?" asked Uhlrich.

"There's an American citizen," said Zhu. "He is wanted by my country. He has committed certain crimes against my country."

"What the fuck does this have to do with the United States Treasury or the People's Bank?" asked Uhlrich, turning red.

"Nothing, except that unless he's handed over, we will not lend America any more money. So I suppose it has very much to do with you and me, yes, Wood?"

Uhlrich stared into Zhu's eyes for several pregnant moments.

"He's a criminal," added Zhu, smiling. "A common criminal. A thug. You will be happy, I'm quite sure, to be rid of him."

"What's his name?" asked Uhlrich.

"Andreas. Dewey Andreas. Have you heard of him, Mr. Secretary?"

A smile crossed Uhlrich's lips as he nodded to Zhu.

"I've heard of him."

"Perhaps that will make it easier to find him."

Uhlrich said nothing as he watched Zhu smile, then squirm uncomfortably. Finally, after taking another sip from his coffee cup, Uhlrich pointed to the door.

"Get the hell out," said Uhlrich, calmly. "American heroes aren't for sale."

79

Sam descended the tree in silence, each step a delicate, slow-motion progression toward the forest floor. He needed to act before it was too late. In his hand, he held his red Swiss Army knife, blade out.

Could he stab someone? He couldn't imagine actually doing it, and yet it was the only option he had.

The knife abruptly fell from Sam's hand. He watched it as it plunged toward the ground. But it didn't make a sound. The knife handle jutted up in the air. The blade had stabbed straight into an exposed root of the big tree. His temporary relief was ruined, however, by the realization that he didn't have a weapon. He kept going.

When he reached the bottom branch of the tree, Sam was at the point of no return. His next step would be on the ground, atop dried leaves. Noise was inevitable.

Sam arched his head around the trunk, spying. The gunman was no more than ten or twelve feet away, motionless, clothing blending perfectly into the green and brown forest floor. The gunman was tight against the sniper rifle, eye to the scope, right hand gripping the trigger.

There was only one option left. He had to jump and run, then try to tackle the gunman before he turned and shot him.

You'll never make it.

"Should you call Hobey?" asked Margaret Andreas.

Sam's grandmother was kneeling on the ground next to a tomato plant, kneepads strapped on, clutching a pair of hand trimmers.

She looked at her husband. He was at the corner of the garden and had his right boot on top of a shovel, about to push down and lift another pile of dirt out of the ground. Perspiration covered his face.

"Stop worrying, Marge. He'll be along."

Dao breathed slowly in and out, staring at John Andreas through the scope. His chest was dead center in the crosshairs of the scope. She preferred a head shot, but his digging, which caused him to move up and down, made this more difficult. A chest-tap would have to do.

The sequence was obvious. Shoot John Andreas, swivel the weapon slightly right, then take out the woman. Drive to the brother's house and kill him too. Get out of Castine—out of Maine—out of the United States—as quickly as possible.

Without moving her eye from the scope, Dao moved the safety off. She put her right index finger on the trigger. She pulled it back.

Sam sat on the lowest branch of the maple tree, just a few feet above the ground. Suddenly, like a gymnast, he fell backward, letting his arms, head, and torso fall down toward the ground, so that he was upside down, his legs still over the branch, keeping him from tumbling to the ground below. Sam's head was inches from the ground. He stretched out his right arm. He grabbed his golf club, which was resting on the leaves. He lifted it gently up, then pulled himself back up to the branch.

Sam stood on the branch and leaned around the trunk of the tree, studying the gunman. The ground surrounding the gunman was a carpet of dried leaves, which he knew would make noise no matter how delicately he tried to tiptoe across them.

He looked up and studied a large branch at least fifteen or twenty feet in the air, which extended out directly over the gunman. Sam climbed to the branch as quietly as he could, as he felt the adrenaline charging through every part of his body.

He put the golf club between his teeth, biting down. He reached up and grabbed the big branch with his right hand, then his left. Slowly, quietly, Sam moved down the branch, hand over hand, out into the air above the gunman.

When he was directly over the gunman, he could feel his arms burning in pain. It was a pain unlike anything he'd ever felt before, a pain he would remember for the rest of his life. It was the pain of the fight, the pain that came when you risked everything, when you challenged death itself.

Sam let go with his left hand, holding himself aloft with his stronger right arm. He dangled silently in the air. He took the golf club into his left hand.

Sam began a slow, deliberate swinging motion, his feet and legs moving back and forth in the air above the killer. As his momentum picked up, he suddenly kicked his feet. Both flip-flops went sailing through the air, over the gunman, landing atop dead leaves just in front of the muzzle of the rifle.

Clutching the branch in his right hand and the golf club in his left, Sam watched from above as the gunman raised up from the weapon, frantically searching for whatever had caused the noise. Sam let go of the branch, falling through the air, swinging his right hand to the club, where it joined the left. By the time his bare feet landed on the ground, he was already swinging the nine iron through the air with every ounce of strength he had in his thirteen-year-old body. He clubbed the gunman—who was searching in the opposite direction—in the back of the head. A loud scream came from the ski mask as the gunman fell to the ground. It was a woman. She hit the ground, rolled over, then tried to stand up. Sam swung again, whiffing completely as she ripped off the ski mask, revealing short black hair and the eyes of a Chinese woman.

The killer touched the back of her skull, then looked at her fingers. They were drenched in blood. She said something in a language Sam couldn't understand, then ran at him.

He swung again just as she leapt. The club landed with a brutal thud on the side of her head. Blood shot from her face as she fell to the ground, screaming. Sam stepped closer and raised the club again. He brought it down in a fierce axing motion. The club struck the woman's forehead. Her eyes shut as she went limp, blood suddenly gushing from a small crack in her skull.

Sam stood, drenched in sweat, staring at the woman. He raised the club again but didn't swing. He stared at her limp body for almost a minute, club raised over his head in case he needed to use it again.

"Sam?"

Sam's eyes glanced right. Standing at the edge of the woods was his grandfather.

"We heard screaming. What the hell is going on?"

His grandfather ran toward him. His eyes bulged as he saw the blood-covered skull of the Chinese woman lying on the ground. Then he registered the rifle on the rock, aimed up at the farmhouse, and did a double take. He followed the trajectory of the muzzle and realized it had been aimed at the garden.

He turned to look at Sam. They were both quiet for a few seconds, then the older man spoke.

"That was very brave of you, Sam."

80

HÔTEL LE BRISTOL
RUE DU FAUBOURG SAINT-HONORÉ
PARIS

Dewey climbed out of the taxi in front of the hotel. He walked a few feet from the door and pulled a pack of cigarettes from his coat.

In the distance, he could see soldiers guarding the Élysée Palace, home of France's president.

A parking valet was milling about the entrance to the hotel. It wasn't Vonnes, the informant.

"*Un feu?*" he asked.

The man pulled a lighter from his pocket and lit Dewey's cigarette.

It looked like it was going to rain, with dark, gray clouds creating a foreboding roof over the Paris afternoon.

Dewey glanced about, looking for the man. Finally, he finished the cigarette, just as a white Maybach pulled up to the hotel's entrance. A man in a black uniform climbed from the front seat; another parking valet, bringing someone's car around. Dewey recognized him. He made eye contact, then looked away, watching from the corner of his eye as the man pulled a cell phone from his pocket and started typing.

———

"May I use your restroom?" Koo asked the woman.

She looked at him with a snobby sneer. All of the people at Hermès were like that.

"The restrooms are reserved for customers," she replied.

Koo held up a small orange bag, inside of which was a tie Koo had just purchased for two hundred euros. The last thing he would ever buy in Paris, he realized.

In the restroom, Koo locked the door. He pulled out his QSZ-92, a suppressor jutting from the muzzle, inspecting it. He looked at the small camera near the site.

He felt his iPhone vibrating. He pulled it from his pocket.

"*Il est ici.*" He's here.

Koo put the QSZ back in his trench coat. He checked his watch, unlocked the door, then walked unhurriedly out from the back of the store and up rue du Faubourg Saint-Honoré.

Dewey stepped through the glass entrance door of the Bristol Hotel. He glanced at his watch: 3:58 P.M.

"*Bonjour, monsieur,*" a concierge said as he stepped inside the lobby. "Welcome to the Bristol."

Dewey scanned the lobby, then stepped to the front desk.

"Checking in?" asked a young woman, smiling at Dewey.

"Yes," said Dewey. He pulled a wallet out and took a black American Express card and handed it to the woman.

"Welcome to the Bristol Hotel, Mr. Walker. I have you here for six nights, correct?"

"That's right."

"City view suite."

The woman reached into a file and pulled out a piece of paper. She placed it down in front of Dewey, handing him a pen to sign.

"Does this look correct, sir?" she asked.

Dewey flashed his eyes to the paper without reading it, then took the pen and signed.

"Looks good."

Over the woman's shoulder, to her right, ran a sweeping set of marble stairs. A little past the stairs was the lounge. It was filled with people, seated at luxurious sofas and chairs—couples, a few business-men, a family; drinking espresso, tea, or coffee as the afternoon sun splayed cuts of soft yellow through a massive window.

Back against the far wall, sitting down, Dewey saw a woman with short blond hair wearing a bright orange blouse, her arms bare; turn-ing quickly, teacup in hand, their eyes met: Katie.

The woman swiped Dewey's Amex, then handed it back to him.

"There you are."

"Thank you."

"How many keys would you like, Mr. Walker?"

"One."

"Premier Li was using me as a messenger," said Qingchen, looking at the ground but speaking to Bhang. They were seated in their usual place, atop the roof of the Ministry of Defense. "He is savvy enough to know I am an ally of yours. He is also savvy enough to understand I will deliver a message, which I'm doing."

"That I am to be pushed into retirement?" asked Bhang, calmly enraged.

"He was extending an olive branch. The next time it won't be an olive branch."

"So what are you saying, General?" asked Bhang. "Is this what you think I should do? I would never resign. Li and his minions will have to kill me first."

"You misunderstand me," said Qingchen. "You're still too impa-tient. No, I see today's meeting as a grave error on the part of our leader. Today he revealed his weakness. He let us know that he has become aware of the impending transition away from him to you. He is less worthy an adversary than I had expected. He abandoned politics today, his field of expertise, and now would like to engage us on the battlefield of deception and power. In my opinion, power is now ours; all that's left is for you to take it."

"How long will it require?" asked Bhang.

"Hours."

"I'm ready when the PLA is ready."

"Good," said Qingchen. "I would ask one favor of you as I move ahead with the preparations. Please, whatever happened in Portugal, as with London, the sloppiness of your activities only makes it harder. Understand, Fao, you are but a vehicle for a change which must take place no matter what. I would like it to be you, but it doesn't have to be."

"I understand, General," said Bhang.

Just then a steady beeping noise came from Bhang's phone. Emergency. Bhang pulled the phone from his jacket, then read the coded text:

16/339-2
G1-y

Andreas had been found; he'd triggered an alias, using a credit card in Paris, and every ministry asset in the city had been notified, nine in all.

Bhang put the phone away.

"That little problem is about to go away," said Bhang, trying to contain his excitement. "I can promise you there will be no further interruptions. Now, if you'll forgive me, General, I must go."

Dewey opened the door to room 1011. He went inside, bolted the door, then threw the leather bag to the bed. He pulled off his sweater and T-shirt. He put on the blue from the bag. He took the small ceramic ring and put it on his left thumb.

Dewey went to a large mirror. He stared for a moment at his week of stubble, coating his cheeks and chin. His heart was starting to beat faster, he could feel that now for the first time. He stared into the mirror, into his blue eyes. The man who looked back at him looked tired, sad, but mostly just blank and emotionless. Inside, Dewey felt a combination of emotions—anger, grief, nervousness, fear, excitement—which he allowed to build, pool up, to grow into a single feeling: desire. Desire for vengeance.

He shut his eyes, took a deep breath, then moved to the door.

Katie held a newspaper, a copy of *Le Figaro*, as she scanned the lounge with trained calm. Her legs were crossed in front of her.

On the blue-green chintz sofa cushion next to her, her slightly worn toffee-colored Hermès Birkin bag sat on its side. For all pretenses and purposes, she looked like any other young, stunning, wealthy French woman, out for an afternoon espresso.

Inside the bag was an MP7A1. It had been sanitized by MI6, in case the operation went south. A snub-nosed suppressor jutted from the muzzle. The MP7 was a terrific close-quarters combat firearm, with lethal kill power, accuracy, and reliability. She also had a Glock 30, in case she burned through the MP7's magazine.

Katie checked her watch. In the reflection off the face of the watch, she saw Tacoma's unmanageable hair. He was seated a few tables away, sipping water.

Lijun—along with eight other ministry agents assigned to Paris—received the text as he was in the middle of a bite of a ham sandwich at a café on Montparnasse.

8U 8U Di7

Lijun jumped up so fast that he knocked over the table, sending dishes, glasses, and silverware crashing to the sidewalk.

Two minutes later he was in the back of a Citroën taxicab as it moved across the Pont Neuf, the black water of the Seine underneath. A few minutes later, the Louvre's signature glass and steel pyramid appeared to the right. To his left spread the ordered birches, gardens, and walking paths of the Tuileries Gardens. But he wasn't admiring the scenery.

Lijun made sure the driver wasn't looking, then popped open his briefcase. Inside was Lijun's Steyr TMP, a select-fire 9x19mm machine pistol, in essence a handheld, extremely compact submachine gun. He attached a custom snub-nosed suppressor, upon which was attached a small camera, then inserted a thirty-round magazine.

He checked his watch. Finally, he removed his cell phone. He typed in:

R5 999

That told Beijing he was approximately four minutes from the target. It also engaged the small camera at the end of his weapon. He tucked the Steyr TMP against his chest, then zipped up his Windbreaker.

Dewey took the elevator to the lobby, where it opened to the left of the lounge. He walked across the marble floor and stepped to the entrance of the lounge. A tuxedoed waiter approached him, held his arm out, and pointed to a table in the middle of the crowded lounge.

To the right, against a far wall, Dewey saw Katie.

Next to Dewey's table, where the waiter now held out a seat, was Tacoma, drinking water, reading the *International Herald Tribune*. Their eyes met briefly; Tacoma looked calm.

"May I get you an aperitif?" asked the waiter. "Perhaps a coffee or glass of wine?"

"Coffee," said Dewey.

Koo received the text from the ministry as he crossed rue de Miromesnil. He waited for a large group of schoolchildren to pass by before replying. In the distance, he could see the entrance to the Bristol Hotel, the flag of France, of the EU, and of several other countries, all billowing in the wind above the entrance.

He removed the Hermès tie from its bag, folded it, and stuffed it in his pants pocket. He threw the bag in a trash can. Then Koo typed into his iPhone:

P+ KK1 8U

The code activated the camera on the end of his QSZ, which he felt sticking into his side. His words also communicated something to Beijing: "I am within one minute of target."

Koo put the iPhone back in his coat pocket, crossed Miromesnil, and walked toward the Bristol.

As the cab moved up Avenue Matignon, Lijun was sweating, his body a live wire, filled with tension and nervous energy. In the distance, he saw soldiers standing at the gates of the Élysée Palace.

The taxi turned onto Faubourg Saint-Honoré. To the left, a short line of cabs sat waiting in front of the Bristol. Multicolored flags, tossed by a breeze, waved above the majestic entrance canopy. Then Lijun saw someone he recognized: Cao Chong, another agent, running down the sidewalk from the opposite direction toward the hotel door. In Chong's hand, swinging in the air, was a black steel handgun, a suppressor sticking from the end.

Lijun did not wait for the taxi to get to the hotel, instead he ripped the door open and leapt from the back, leaving the briefcase behind, going into a hard sprint toward the hotel entrance.

The waiter walked toward Dewey with a tray in his hand. As he was about to arrive at the table, Dewey's eyes were drawn across the lobby to the glass doors at the hotel's entrance.

Through them walked a man with dark hair in a tan trench coat. He was tall. His eyes scanned the lobby. There was no question: it was Koo.

"Monsieur—"

"I changed my mind," said Dewey, raising his hand to stop the waiter. "A glass of wine."

From the corner of his eye, Dewey watched as Koo crossed the lobby quickly, moving like an athlete. As he descended the marble steps near the lounge, his arm reached inside his trench coat. He ripped a sidearm from inside the coat, walking with it at his side as he approached.

Dewey felt the small button on the thumb ring.

"Very good, monsieur," said the waiter. "What kind of wine would you like?"

"Anything," said Dewey, impatiently. "Red."

Koo came to the lounge entrance. His dark eyes scanned the room. In his right hand he clutched a suppressed QSZ-92.

"Bordeaux, monsieur? Beaujolais?"

"Anything," said Dewey. "I trust you."

"Very good."

As the waiter moved from in front of Dewey, Koo's eyes scanned a moment longer, then found him, then locked. Koo's arm flew up, the black suppressor swung in line, and found Dewey.

Bhang stood before the plasma screen, which was divided into three separate views: the live shots from the cameras on the weapons of Koo, Chong, and Lijun.

Bhang's suit jacket was removed, as was his tie. His sleeves were rolled up to the elbows. He was smoking a cigarette. The room was filled with at least a dozen other men, all transfixed on the plasma.

On another screen was a map of Paris with live GPS locations on all nine ministry agents in the city, indicated by flashing green lights. Bhang studied the map quickly. The three green lights—Koo, Chong, Lijun—were clustered in and around the Bristol.

"Tell the others to hold back," said Bhang calmly. "Three agents should be enough."

Bhang, recalling his meeting with Qingchen, didn't want to create any more violence than necessary.

"Don't enter the hotel unless we tell them to."

Bhang went back to the screen showing the live video feeds. Koo was on the left. He was now inside the hotel, walking across the lobby. The view was grainy but clear. He came to a stop at the front of a lounge full of people, seated at tables.

In the middle screen, Chong was entering quickly through the door. To the right, Lijun's view was dark; he still had his weapon concealed, but he'd activated it. Suddenly, his section of the plasma lit up. The back of Chong, running across the hotel lobby, was plainly visible.

Dewey lurched forward, tossing the table over, lunging in the direction of Koo, as a woman to Dewey's left suddenly started screaming. Dewey leapt at Koo, his arms outstretched. But before he could reach him, Koo fired.

The mechanical staccato of the suppressed weapon played low, beneath the screams, in the same moment Dewey pressed the button on the thumb ring twice. Dewey's shirt exploded in a riot of dark red above his heart. His forward motion was halted. He tumbled sideways, down to the ground, onto his back, chest sopped in crimson.

Tacoma leapt up from his chair, pulling his P226 from his shoulder holster. In one fluid motion, he swung it toward Koo and fired, missing, the sound of Tacoma's unsuppressed sidearm only adding to the screams, the sense of chaos, that now filled the lounge.

Koo swung the QSZ to the right and fired at Tacoma. Tacoma was struck in the center of his chest as he grunted loudly and was kicked backward, tumbling to the ground, his T-shirt abruptly ruined in dark red.

Screams filled the Bristol lounge; patrons ran toward the back of the lounge and dived under tables for cover.

From the lobby, a commotion ensued, voices raised, then suddenly there was more gunfire, this time from near the entrance to the hotel.

Koo stepped above Dewey, weapon trained at his chest. Dewey looked up at the agent. His mouth moved, but no sounds came out. Koo fired once, twice, three more times as, behind him, through the lobby, another man stormed toward the lounge, running with a weapon outstretched in his hand, a long black suppressor sticking out from the muzzle.

The loud, unmuted sound of Tacoma's gun exploded as Tacoma got off a round from the ground. Koo lurched backward, clutching his left shoulder, falling to the ground, screaming in pain.

Katie saw the second gunman as he came into view, near the front of the lounge. He was running fast, weapon out. Katie stood up. She ripped the MP7 from her bag just as the gunman rounded the entrance, saw Dewey on the ground, and swung his weapon.

Katie triggered the submachine gun, full auto. A hail of slugs tore into Chong, arresting his forward motion and kicking the back of his skull out in a spray of blood. He fell in a contorted heap to the marble floor, dead.

For the first time, sirens pealed in the distance from somewhere outside the hotel.

Katie moved to Dewey, crouching at his side. Suddenly, her eye was drawn to the lobby. Another man was charging. In his left hand, he clutched a squat black CQB machine gun, which she recognized: Steyr TMP.

From the ground next to Dewey, Katie swept the MP7, trigger flexed, and sprayed slugs across the agent's torso, ripping holes through him before he could even fire, felling him a few feet behind the other gunman, the wall behind him abruptly splattered in red.

Koo ran through the lobby, toward the entrance, clutching his weapon. He pushed through the now-abandoned doors.

Sirens moved closer now, becoming louder.

Outside, Koo ran to the first taxi he could find. He climbed in back, clutching his shoulder.

"Drive."

The driver eyed Koo in the rearview mirror, holding his shoulder, a pancake of red now covering the shoulder of the trench coat.

"*L'hôpital, monsieur?*"

"*Non.* Jardin du Luxembourg."

Koo removed his iPhone from his pocket and typed.

009 YT-6

The code told Beijing a number of things: Andreas was dead, he needed an exfilt, and he was injured.

It also turned off the camera.

———

Bhang stood in front of the plasma screen as Koo's video feed went black. The other feeds—from Chong and Lijun—had already gone black.

"Rewind it to the point of conflict," said Bhang. "Then put it full screen."

A few moments later, the video from Koo's camera started playing.

A man holding a small tray stood at the center of the picture, his back to the camera. As he moved out of the way, Andreas appeared, seated, behind where the waiter had been standing. Koo raised his weapon. Andreas lurched toward the camera. The frame then bounced as Koo fired, but the sight of blood erupting as the bullet hit his chest was plainly visible. Andreas fell to the ground. The lounge devolved in chaos. Another man stood and fired at Koo; Koo swung his gun and shot him in the chest, knocking him to the ground. Then the view moved back to Andreas. Koo moved above him. The shot was grainy. He aimed the weapon at close range and fired three more times; each time the view became interrupted as the QSZ kicked back on Koo. To the right, in the corner of the screen, the other American could be seen on the ground. Then the feed went abruptly haywire as Koo was shot.

"Stand down the other men," said Bhang, standing before the plasma screen. "Get them away from the hotel and out of Paris, immediately."

"Yes, Minister."

"I have a message from Koo," said another agent. "He's injured and is requesting exfilt."

"Get a logistics team moving," said Bhang. "Make sure they have medical equipment aboard the plane."

The first French police arrived a minute later amid a growing chorus of screams, ambulance sirens, and shouting. It was a two-man detail, carbines out and aimed forward as they stormed into the Bristol.

The first ambulance arrived just behind them. Two EMTs sprinted through the open doors, pushing a gurney across the lobby toward the blood-soaked lounge.

Blood was splattered all over the place. A woman was dead at the foot of the marble stairs; she'd been gunned down by Chong as he ran through the lobby.

Chong lay in a growing miasma of blood outside the lounge entrance, his head destroyed. Lijun, the third man on the scene, was just behind him, contorted on the ground, lying in a growing pool of blood, eyes staring up at nothing.

Inside the lounge, Dewey lay on his back, eyes closed. Tacoma lay just feet away, motionless, drenched in red.

At least a dozen more French police entered the lobby of the Bristol, followed by soldiers.

Another pair of EMTs charged through the doors, running a gurney across the lobby.

The first pair of EMTs went to Dewey. One of them put a stethoscope to his chest, felt his neck, then shook his head as he looked at the other EMT, who quickly turned and performed the same ritual with Tacoma.

They hoisted Dewey to the gurney, wheeling him out of the lounge, back across the lobby. Katie trailed them, holding her MP7 in her right hand, lest any more agents arrive at the scene. In her left hand, in case she was stopped, she had an ID, issued by French intelligence, but amid the chaos, no one stopped her or even noticed the weapon at her side.

Outside, Faubourg Saint-Honoré was shut off, taken over by police, SWAT teams, soldiers, and ambulances.

The EMTs with Dewey pushed to the open doors at the back of the ambulance, collapsed the gurney, then lifted him in. Katie climbed in the back along with one of the EMTs. The other shut the door, then ran to the front, climbed in, and hit the siren.

The ambulance shot away from the hotel, siren blaring.

In the backseat of the taxi, Koo looked out the window as they moved across Paris, trying to memorize the views of the city he loved and would likely never see again.

On boulevard Montparnasse, his iPhone vibrated.

Exfiltration in forty minutes, your apartment. Congratulations.

Koo removed the magazine from his QSZ, opened the window, and tossed it out. From the pocket of the trench coat he removed another magazine and jammed it in.

Koo took a separate phone from his pocket. He typed in a text.

"Exfilt forty minutes rue Madame."

The taxi pulled onto rue Guynemer, a block from his apartment.

"*Ici*," said Koo.

He climbed out at the curb, removed the trench coat, folded it so that the red area wasn't visible, then laid it atop his shoulder to conceal the red.

Koo walked around the block, past his apartment building. He glanced around, making sure he wasn't being followed. On rue de Fleurus, a large green garage door went ajar as he approached. He slipped inside.

Koo's eyes registered the brightly lit work area and a variety of people milling around. A woman walked across the large bay toward him.

"Hello, Koo," said Smythson, extending her hand.

Outside the Bristol, the doors to the ambulance shut. Dewey sat up and ripped his shirt open, sending buttons flying.

"That was fun," Katie said.

"Speak for yourself."

The shirt was a storm of red, as was everything beneath. He stripped off all his clothing. Katie looked away. He handed the clothing to the EMT, who stuffed it into a black plastic bag. The EMT handed Dewey a warm, wet towel and he quickly wiped off every part of his body. Dewey wrapped a green hospital gown around his waist.

The ambulance siren turned off as it pushed through the city's streets. At the back of the Musée d'Orsay, the ambulance pulled into an underground unloading dock and stopped beside a white van, which was idling. Dewey and Katie followed the EMT to the van then got inside. The van sped back up the ramp and out of the loading dock.

A few minutes later, they pulled onto rue de Fleurus. The van stopped in front of a set of green garage doors.

Bhang watched the video sequence six more times, not saying a word. Then he performed the same exercise with the other feeds, watching as his two agents, Chong and Lijun, were killed, both by the same woman, obviously, along with the long-haired man that Koo shot, CIA or some other agency, there with Andreas. That fact alone told Bhang that the killing of Bo Minh had probably been executed by the intelligence agency. It also told him that they would need to expect reprisals; France, though amoral, was a U.S. ally. They would quickly ID Chong and Lijun.

"Shall I attempt to do anything regarding the dead agents?" asked Dheng. "We could, perhaps, alter certain aspects of their back-grounds—"

"No," said Bhang. "Don't bother. We should expect a healthy coun-terstrike from Langley."

"I'll send out a warning."

"Yes," said Bhang. "Standard rules of engagement. I want to cool things off. The mission has been completed. Make arrangements as per usual protocol regarding pension for the two dead agents. See that their records reflect their part in this mission."

Bhang picked up his coat from the back of a chair.

"One more thing," said Bhang. "Please call the Bureau of Central Supplies. We will need to cast a new medal; the Order of the Lotus is to be awarded. Tell them it is their top priority."

Bhang walked toward the door, then turned.

"Thank you, everyone," he added, his words barely above a whis-per. "I appreciate your work today."

Smythson met Dewey at the door.

"Follow me," she said.

They moved across the garage bay, which looked like an operating room.

Dewey climbed onto an elevated stainless-steel platform as two nurses pulled the hospital gown from him. He stood naked atop the table. Dewey wasn't shy; everyone there knew it was business.

The two nurses, looking at photos of Koo on a large plasma to the right of Dewey, shaved his chest and legs. One of the nurses took out a small glass dish, which she placed on the stainless steel table next to Dewey. She took a paintbrush and painted Dewey's pubic hair, staining it black. After she finished, the other nurse handed him a towel to wrap around his waist.

"Here, Mr. Andreas," said a man in a white surgeon's uniform. He pointed at a large chair in the center of the room, similar to a dentist chair. "Sit."

The man jabbed a needle into Dewey's shoulder, as another man started cutting Dewey's hair to resemble Koo's.

"This will numb it up," he said. "It's still going to hurt."

They dyed his hair black, then dried it.

"We're twenty minutes out," said Smythson, her voice stern and loud. "We need to get moving."

Lacey James, the makeup artist, approached.

Dewey looked left. Xiua Koo was standing next to Smythson, watching with a blank look on his face.

"Lean, back. Contacts first."

James put brown-tinted contacts in each of Dewey's eyes.

"Okay, now I need you to shut your eyes," said James. "Hold your breath for the first minute or so, or you're going to get really stoned."

Dewey shut his eyes and took a deep breath. He felt a warm, rubbery substance moosh into his eyes, like clay but with a synthetic feel. Dewey felt pressure against his right eyelid for more than a minute, then the same pressure on the other eyelid. Then he heard what sounded like a blow-dryer, and felt heat on his forehead, cheeks, and around his eyes.

"We have to hurry up," said Smythson.

"Eyebrows," he heard, then moments later, felt a hand rubbing across his eyelids.

"Okay, I need you to hold really still," said James. "And I mean *really* bloody still. Whatever you do, don't open your eyes."

He felt coldness, like ice, then hard pressure against his nose, cheeks, and forehead.

"Eyes closed now, until I say open."

Dewey felt pressure against his right eye, followed by the same sensation above the left eye. He heard a suction device, then felt suction at each eye. Finally, warm liquid was poured over his eyes, which was then vacuumed out.

"Okay, open up," said James. "It'll sting, but that should be gone soon."

Dewey opened his eyes. It was a strange sensation, as if he were numb around his eyes, nose, and forehead. But he could see perfectly.

"Can you see?"

"Yeah."

"Blink. Fast."

Dewey blinked.

"Well, I won't win another Oscar for it, but it should do. By the way, it'll last a week. Then it'll harden and start to flake off."

Dewey felt another needle jam into his shoulder, to the left of his neck.

"A little more anesthetic," said the doctor.

"Let's go," said Smythson. "We're down to minutes here."

"Stand up," said the nurse. "Put this clothing on."

Dewey dressed quickly: white underwear, black slacks, socks, black shoes, belt, white sleeveless undershirt, shirt. Someone handed him a tan Burberry trench coat.

Behind him, he heard wheels squeaking. He turned to see a large portable wall being moved into the lights. The wall looked like some sort of thick corkboard.

"Dewey," said the surgeon, "the pain shots will help, but you're going to feel this. I injected a six-hour anesthetic. Anything more powerful and it will leave a trace when they read your blood. In about five hours or so, it's going to start hurting. In six, you're going to be in real pain."

Dewey said nothing.

"Stand in front of the wall," said Smythson.

Dewey moved to the corkboard wall.

Smythson stepped in front of Dewey, a suppressed SIG P226 in her hand. She stepped to a piece of blue tape that had been put on the floor, replicating the distance from which Tacoma had fired at Koo in the lounge. She raised the weapon and fired.

A slug tore into Dewey's shoulder. He was kicked back, into the wall, and he grimaced as a ripping burn kicked out from his shoulder, like fire. His hand shot to the bullet wound. He held his hand up. His fingers were coated in blood.

The surgeon pulled the trench coat aside and examined the wound.

"Clean exit," he said. "Couldn't be any less harmful, even though I'm sure it kills."

"What was in that needle, doc?" Dewey asked, looking down at his shoulder and grimacing. "That fucking hurt."

"I might've injected you with estrogen," said the surgeon, smiling.

Dewey grinned, through the pain.

"Why are you smiling?" asked Dewey, looking at Smythson. "You enjoyed that a little too much."

One of the nurses handed Dewey a mirror. He looked into it. For a moment, he thought it was Koo. He held it closer to see the artificial skin around his eye sockets.

"We need to move," Smythson said. "We need to beat the recon team."

Smythson showed Dewey a map, telling him where the apartment was. She gave him a key.

Dewey was having a hard time concentrating as his shoulder wracked him in waves of sharp pain.

"Third floor, unit twelve. Remember: *téngtòng*."

Dewey slipped out of the garage.

His shoulder hurt badly. He remembered the feeling in Cali, when he'd been struck by the cartridge from the Kalashnikov. That slug had remained inside him. He was grateful for that experience now; the 9x19mm from the SIG SAUER was smaller. It was embedded in the cork back at the garage, not inside him. Still, the pain was excruciating, making him breathe hard and fast. The trench coat was covered in blood.

Dewey stepped into the apartment building, climbed the stairs, then entered the apartment.

He felt thirsty. He went to the kitchen and drank a large glass of water. The screech of brakes came from the street below.

Dewey went into the bathroom and glanced at himself in the mirror. A sheen of perspiration had now formed on his forehead. The patch of fresh blood had grown larger, down to his shoulder blade and across his chest. He peeled back the trench coat, which caused unbelievable pain, and he moaned but looked at the wound. Blood was everywhere. The hole pumped a small amount out every few seconds. He felt nauseated as chills ran through him. Most of all, he felt pain.

In one sense, however, it wasn't a bad thing: he hurt too much to be nervous.

He stumbled back into the living room, feeling dizzy. He sat down in a leather armchair. He shut his eyes just as the recon team put the pick gun in Koo's lock and opened the door.

81

Dellenbaugh was seated at his desk. In front of him stood Wood Uhlrich, the treasury secretary, and Adrian King, his chief of staff.

Uhlrich had just finished briefing Dellenbaugh and King on the visit by Ji-tao Zhu, the head of the People's Bank of China, and Zhu's ultimatum: hand over Dewey Andreas or China stops lending the United States money.

Dellenbaugh and King were incredulous.

"What did you say?" asked Dellenbaugh.

"I used some words which may not have been in the spirit of China-U.S. relations," said Uhlrich.

"What'd you say, Wood?"

"I told him to go to hell," said Uhlrich.

"You reacted emotionally," said Dellenbaugh.

"Yes, Mr. President. I wasn't thinking about the financial implications."

Dellenbaugh sat back. He looked up at Uhlrich, a blank expression on his face.

"Good," said the president, finally. "I would've punched the son of a bitch in the nose."

"If we can't borrow the money, sir, we will be in a very precarious spot," said King.

"What are you suggesting?" asked Dellenbaugh. "You wouldn't actually consider handing over Dewey, would you?"

"No, sir," said King. "But it's time to elevate this. If Premier Li is aware of what occurred today, we need to know that. If he isn't aware, it means something entirely different. It's time to pick up the phone, Mr. President."

82

Two men entered the apartment. They shut the door and moved silently to Dewey.

One of the men gently slapped Dewey's cheek, but Dewey didn't open his eyes. He heard a zipper, then his nostrils were abruptly stung by smelling salts.

He opened his eyes and looked at the two men. Both were Chinese, one in a suit, the other in jeans and a dark Windbreaker.

One of them said something to Dewey in Mandarin, but Dewey didn't respond. The two men looked at each other, then whispered back and forth, speaking rapidly.

"*Téngtòng*," whispered Dewey.

The man in the suit pulled the trench coat aside and stared at the wound. He leaned down and patted Dewey's head, then said something in Mandarin; but Dewey knew it was something along the lines of "It'll be okay," or "Good job."

Dewey shut his eyes.

They lifted him up and wrapped his arms around their shoulders. Dewey acted as if he could barely move, though the truth was, it wasn't much of an act; the wound was increasingly degenerating his ability to function and think properly. He groaned, and it was a real groan. He was losing a lot of blood.

They moved through the door, then, step-by-step, as fast as possible, down the three flights of stairs. Both men were smaller than Dewey, but they were strong and athletic.

In the lobby stood a third man. He was also Chinese, with dyed blond hair. He was smoking a cigarette. He wore a dark green trench coat. Inside, Dewey could see, he clutched some sort of weapon, ready to be drawn.

The gunman glanced through the lace curtain that hung over the front door. He turned, nodded, said something, then opened the door.

They carried Dewey down the front steps of the apartment building. A blue minivan idled, and the side door opened as they came closer. They lifted Dewey up into the minivan and laid him down on the first bench seat. The team climbed in, gunman in the front passenger seat, the other two behind Dewey.

Dewey shut his eyes. He felt weak. The pain was abating. He knew the signs. He was going into shock.

Again, one of the men attempted to speak to him. But Dewey didn't say anything. This time, he didn't even open his eyes.

"*Téngtòng*," he whispered.

The driver moved out into traffic.

They carried Dewey into a large unmarked private jet, an Embraer Lineage 1000. Dewey was laid out on a long leather sofa near the front of the cabin. Within minutes, the jet taxied down the runway, then took off.

Dewey willed himself to hold off going into shock, at least for a little while. He'd walked through, in his mind, how the operation would unfold, but what he hadn't anticipated was the deleterious effects of the gunshot. He knew how to handle pain. It was one of his greatest strengths, an asset that enabled him to reach a little deeper than most men, to fight through situations. But it wasn't the pain that worried him now. It was the shock that was coming. Unconsciousness. With it could come anything. One of the operatives could somehow cut into the skin around his eyes. They could take his fingerprints, which would reveal immediately who he was.

Dewey realized that his desire for vengeance had caused him to jump on board what was a suicide mission. Had Calibrisi really wanted to just get rid of him? Had he caused too many problems for him, for Langley, and for the United States?

Stop feeling sorry for yourself. You're not dead yet.

A gauzy, numb feeling made the ceiling spin and blur. Then Dewey drifted into unconsciousness.

One of the men removed Dewey's trench coat, unbuttoned his shirt and pulled it off. Another man brought a stack of towels from the bathroom, along with a first-aid kit. The agent cleaned the wound with alcohol, then applied pressure to it. He sat next to Dewey's head, pressing the towel into his shoulder.

The other agent prepared a needle with painkiller and injected it near the wound. He also injected Dewey with an antibiotic to prevent infection.

After pushing against the wound for more than an hour, the bleeding had abated somewhat. The man placed a large bandage on the wound, then wrapped gauze and tape over the bandage and around Dewey's armpit.

"Hold on," said the man, speaking in Mandarin to the unconscious Dewey.

83

BEIJING

At midnight, Bhang was still at his desk. Although he didn't normally drink, he had a glass of vodka in his hand. He'd been sitting and staring out his large window at the Beijing evening, thinking not of Andreas but of his father, his mother, but mostly of Bo. It had been a long if memorable day. He'd expected to feel more elation when they finally succeeded in killing Andreas. Instead, he felt something altogether different and better, a happiness that was deeper than mere excitement. The guilt from Bo's death was gone, replaced by a sense of personal satisfaction and closure.

Suddenly there was a knock on his door, and Xiao stepped into Bhang's office.

"I thought you would be interested," said Xiao. "Koo lands in the morning. He is to be taken to Beijing Hospital."

"How is he?"

"In a great deal of pain. He's not saying much."

"He should receive a hero's welcome," said Bhang. "The best room at the hospital, that sort of thing."

"When would you like to present him the award, sir? Of course, if you'd like, we can handle it for you, if you're too busy."

"I will present it personally to him tomorrow. What time does he land?"

"Early," said Xiao. "Around six."

"Good." Bhang smiled. "The Order of the Lotus, Xiao. It has been far too long."

After Xiao left, Bhang had one more task to do before leaving for the night. He picked up his phone and dialed.

"Yes," said Qingchen.

"Good evening, General Qingchen."

"Hello, Fao. It's midnight."

"I'm sorry. I had to inform you: the matter is cleaned up. The interruption is now behind us all. I'm ready to lead, though I would reiterate my sincere belief that you would be a better leader than me."

"Your flattery is as unnecessary as it is fictitious," said Qingchen.

"I am as sincere as it is possible for me to be, sir."

"Then thank you," said Qingchen, "but now it's time to put away the mutual admiration society and discuss next steps. The military is now solidly behind you and is prepared to act. In addition, we have made all necessary preparations as it relates to getting support from a quorum of party leadership and the State Council. Tomorrow morning at eight o'clock, the premier has called another meeting of his inner circle. I've once again been invited. We will detain them all until a peaceful transition has occurred."

"Good," said Bhang. On his desk, he saw the mahogany box, inside of which was the Order of the Lotus. Bhang smiled. "I have something that I must attend to first. It will be completed by eight, general."

"Excellent. We can ride over to to Zhongnanhai together. Come by my office, Premier Bhang. It has a nice ring to it, don't you think?"

84

Several hours after take off, Dewey awoke. His shoulder throbbed.

He looked up to see the blond agent, seated across from him. Dewey looked around nervously; part of him expected to see a gun, aimed at him. But the agent simply smiled. When he saw Dewey wake up and stir, he said something, in Mandarin.

"*Téngtòng*," said Dewey.

The man reached to his left and opened the first-aid kit, removing a needle.

Dewey held up his hand, shaking his head no. As much as he wanted more pain medication, he needed to wake up, to become sharp again. Now more than ever, he had to endure the pain.

You wanted your shot at Fao Bhang.

He would have, at most, one chance to take that shot.

He stood and went to the restroom. He examined first his face. It was remarkable, even scary, to see how much like Koo he looked. He pulled aside his blood-soaked shirt. Just doing that caused him to moan loudly. He examined the wound. It had sealed up, but he needed stitches. A large-diameter radius encircled the wound, its color black-and-blue, bruising from the trauma of the bullet.

Dewey went to the bathroom, then returned to the seat. As he sat down, the three agents all looked at him. Then the two copilots came out of the cockpit. One of the pilots said something that Dewey again couldn't understand. Then all five men began to clap loudly and bow repeatedly as they acknowledged the apparently now well-known actions of their illustrious passenger, Xiua Koo.

Dewey sat down, barely nodding, and shut his eyes.

The Embraer landed six hours later, coming into Beijing Capital International Airport at dawn.

By the time the plane landed, Dewey felt stronger, though the shoulder still ached.

An ambulance, two police cars, and two black sedans with agents were waiting on the tarmac at the airport when the jet touched down. A steady rain fell from gray clouds overhead. At least a dozen people were standing on the tarmac. As Dewey descended the stairs, the group started clapping and cheering.

A wheelchair was waiting for him at the bottom of the jet's stairs, but Dewey chose instead to walk slowly to a waiting ambulance. Inside, he lay down on a gurney as a female EMT strapped an oxygen mask to his face. When she went to insert an IV into his forearm to deliver fluid and antibiotics and, Dewey feared, painkillers, he pushed her away and shook his head.

They drove to Beijing Hospital, through the crowded city, escorted by two police cruisers. Dewey remained silent as the EMT spoke in rapid Mandarin to him.

The hospital was a massive complex of white concrete that spread for several city blocks. They pulled in front of the main entrance, beneath a large glass-and-steel canopy adorned with the flag of the People's Republic of China.

Through the ambulance window, beneath the canopy, a large group of people awaited his arrival.

It was happening quickly. Too quickly. The pain in his shoulder seemed to go away as adrenaline abruptly warmed him.

The back doors of the ambulance swung open, and he was face-to-face with a crowd of at least fifty people; doctors, nurses, police officers, and others, who clapped wildly as the doors opened.

Bhang climbed into the back of a long black limousine. It was the vehicle reserved for special occasions. Today there would be two.

The window behind the driver lowered.

"The ministry, sir?"

"No," said Bhang. "Beijing Hospital."

"Very good, sir."

The window lifted back up.

As Bhang sat alone in the back of the large limousine, driving through Beijing, he considered what was now upon him.

He'd avenged the death of his brother, a death, he now realized, that had been caused inadvertently by his own vanity and paranoia. As much as he didn't like Premier Li, the fact is, as paramount leader, a different set of responsibilities existed. Li was well within his rights to be upset at the appearance of the dead double agent, Dillman. Li was also justified, Bhang now realized, in his horror at the violence in Lisbon and England.

The leader of a country was supposed to set a moral example; could he himself set a moral example?

Bhang shut his eyes as he thought of Zhu. His expression had been so pathetic and sad as he watched his mistress fall to her death. He was embarrassed by what he'd done to Zhu, the cruelty he'd exhibited. Could he put aside that quality and lead a country? Could he react in a different, more-measured way when faced with the sort of challenges that would undoubtedly face him as China's next leader?

Bhang smoked a cigarette as he stared out at the Beijing morning. He realized how absurd his self-doubt was.

It was, after all, his viciousness, his savageness, that had given him power in the first place. His willingness to kill Xiangou, so many years ago, was what had not only given him the ministry, but also saved his own life. Saved it from Xiangou, another man just as vicious as he. Even Li himself had paved his way to power with the corpses of those who would have prevented it.

Yes, Bhang realized, as the limousine pulled into Beijing Hospital, the very qualities that worried him most—his viciousness, duplicity, and cunning—were the only reason he now stood at the precipice of leading the world's largest country.

Any self-doubt washed away as he saw his security detail waiting at the hospital door. In a way, the ceremony this morning was the very culmination of his time at the ministry; he would present China's highest intelligence award to a man who had avenged the cruelest of deaths. It would be, he now realized as a smile crossed his lips, his final act as minister.

85

The lobby of Beijing Hospital was a cavernous, light-filled atrium, its walls adorned with colorful murals.

A large crowd had gathered, hundreds of people—nurses, doctors, hospital administrators, even some patients. When Dewey appeared at the door, the crowd started clapping enthusiastically, and many started shouting.

The entire left side of Dewey's shirt was stained with blood. He walked slowly into the atrium as the crowd cheered.

A photographer approached. He took several photos of Dewey as he walked to a podium that had been set up. Did they want him to say something?

He walked closer, nodding politely to the crowd, who cheered his every step. A man in a suit approached him and bowed before him, then shook his hand. Dewey guessed he ran the place.

There was a sudden commotion as, at the far side of the lobby, the doors opened and in stepped four men in paramilitary attire, walking two by two, shoulder holsters visible. One of the men held a carbine, which Dewey recognized: Beretta CX4 Storm, with Picatinny rails, forward grip, red-dot sight, and tactical light. The man had the deadly-looking firearm trained at the ground.

Dewey's eyes shot left, then right, looking for an escape route. The four members of the security detail parted, and a short man in a black suit emerged from behind them.

The man was clapping as he entered the lobby and walked toward Dewey. He was shorter than Dewey expected, thinner, older, more frail-looking. But his eyes told a different story. He stared at Dewey as he drew closer; in their blackness, their focus, their cold assessment of Dewey, he saw the man who'd murdered Jessica.

Dewey's heart raced. He scanned the lobby as, around him, the crowd began to applaud even louder, watching as Bhang approached. He was looking straight at Dewey as he walked across the shiny white floor. A wide smile was plastered across his lips. Under his arm was a beautiful mahogany box.

Bhang bowed as he stopped before him and looked up into his eyes.

Dewey eyed the gunmen with the carbine. The gunman was studying Dewey as hard as Dewey was studying him; Dewey registered the man's finger was on the trigger of the Beretta.

Fight, Dewey. It's all you can do. It's all you could ever do.

You died doing something you believed in. You died for Jessica.

He didn't want to die, but he knew he would never be able to live knowing he'd let the evil creature in front of him get away with it.

Bhang stepped in front of Dewey. The applause grew louder. Bhang opened the wooden box to the cacophonous cheering of the crowd. Inside the box was a large gold medallion attached to a beautiful red ribbon.

Dewey's hair was soaking wet; his face was covered in perspiration. He stepped toward Bhang as Bhang held out the medal to wrap around his neck.

Dewey looked down at the medal, admiring it as Bhang smiled and started clapping. Slowly, Dewey leaned forward, bowing before Bhang. Pain shot from his shoulder. Time stood still.

Dewey remained bowed and reached to his ankle as the crowd continued to clap and cheer. He ripped his knife from the ankle holster, then stood up.

Bhang's smile disappeared. A confused look shot across his face as he alone could see the black steel of the Gerber combat blade in

Dewey's hand. Bhang scanned Dewey's eyes, his clothing, his shirt. Then Bhang's black eyes flashed anger.

Bhang pointed at Dewey and started yelling in Mandarin.

Dewey lifted his arm above his head. He lurched for Bhang as Bhang turned to run, ripping the knife down, swinging with all his strength, slashing into the center of Bhang's chest. Dewey felt the blade puncture Bhang's tissue just as he was tackled from behind. They were too late. The strike ripped deep into Bhang's chest as the two men went down, Dewey on top of him, beneath a horde of people, which pushed the Gerber straight through Bhang's chest. Dewey felt the tip of the blade hit the hard marble of the hospital floor beneath Bhang.

Dewey's face was above Bhang's. Their eyes were just inches apart. Dewey watched as Bhang's eyes fluttered. Their anger seemed to dissipate, replaced by calm, even resignation. Blood started pouring in thick, dark bursts from his nostrils, ears, and mouth. They stared at each other, eyes locked, as chaos gripped the hospital lobby and screams filled the air.

Bhang's lips moved, but no sound came out, just blood, which poured from his lips in dark crimson. He coughed, struggling to get out his final words:

"Well done, Mr. Andreas," he whispered, in English. Then his eyes shut.

86

BEIJING HOSPITAL
BEIJING

The hard staccato of automatic-weapon fire cracked the air. People dispersed, running in terror. More screams echoed through the atrium.

Dewey turned his head in time to see the gunman sprinting toward him, the muzzle of the Beretta CX4 trained at his head, the red laser beam from the red-dot sight flashing across his eyes. Terror enveloped the room. The man fired.

Dewey ducked as slugs tore out of the carbine, but he felt nothing except sharp pain in his shoulder. He looked behind him; one of the other guards was pummeled backward by the slugs.

A third gunman, to the right, charged at Dewey, pulling a sidearm from his shoulder holster. The gunman with the Beretta swiveled and pumped more slugs, which struck the other gunman in the forehead and kicked him backward in the air.

"If you want to live," the gunman shouted at Dewey, "get the fuck up."

Dewey followed the gunman, sprinting, through the lobby. Outside, a white Toyota Land Cruiser idled. The gunman sprinted to the back passenger door and opened it for Dewey.

"Hurry up," shouted the gunman.

Dewey climbed in back as the gunman covered the SUV. He slammed the door and climbed into the front passenger seat. They sped away.

Seated in the front seat was another man, young and tall, dressed in paramilitary gear. In the backseat, next to Dewey, was a man in a suit. He had slightly longish black hair and was smoking a cigarette.

"Who are you?" asked Dewey.

The man stared forward, not responding, then took another drag from the cigarette.

"Where am I going?" asked Dewey. "Where are you taking me?"

Dewey reached up and touched his shoulder. His fingers came back red.

The Chinese man in the suit slapped the back of the passenger seat. He said something in Mandarin. The gunman reached into the center console and found a small box of tissue, which he handed to Dewey.

Dewey sat back, for the first time noticing a dark sedan just in front of them. He turned and saw another just behind them.

They moved through the crowded city center of Beijing, then climbed onto the highway. They moved fast, at least a hundred miles per hour, in the left lane.

They drove for an hour in total silence. Throughout the trip, none of the men so much as glanced at Dewey.

Somewhere in the country, where the highway cut through endless hills of green trees with seemingly no inhabitants, they exited the highway. They drove for several more miles. At some point, Dewey's eyes caught the sight of tall, foreboding metal fencing with large cables of razor wire unfurled across the top. They drove alongside the fencing for what felt like an eternity. Finally they came to gates and passed through. Two soldiers saluted as they swept inside. Past the gates was an enormous military base that looked as if it ran to the horizon, crowded with soldiers, camouflaged troop carriers, and barracks.

On a tarmac deep inside the base, the Land Cruiser stopped beneath the wing of an old medium-sized tan-and-blue four-prop transport plane, which Dewey knew was a Shaanxi Y-8. The plane's engines were already running.

A soldier opened Dewey's door. He followed him to the plane and climbed aboard the plane. Before he even had time to sit down, the Shaanxi was moving down the runway. They were airborne a few moments later. Other than the two pilots, Dewey was alone.

Dewey found a restroom. For more than an hour, he peeled silicone and glue from his eyes, nose, and forehead. He scrubbed his face, then sat down in one of the plane's canvas seats.

It wasn't until then that he let himself try to figure out what had happened. It had to have been Calibrisi or Chalmers; and yet, he was brought to a military base. It didn't add up.

It doesn't matter. You did what you came to do. It's over. Walk away.

Dewey didn't feel happy or satisfied. He'd killed Bhang, and yet he would have traded a million Bhangs for Jessica. It was an unfair trade. But it was all he could do. It was all he could ever do.

Four hours later, the Shaanxi began its descent. He looked out the window. The hills were pitched in lush, bright green jungle. In the distance was the low, sprawling chaos of a city. Behind it were dark blue pockets of water, which he guessed were lakes.

Dewey stepped into the cockpit as the plane arced lower.

"Where are we?" he asked.

"Hanoi," said one of the pilots.

It was humid and hot as Dewey climbed down from the plane onto the tarmac. Standing at the base of the stairs were Calibrisi, Katie, and Tacoma.

"Hi, Dewey," said Calibrisi.

Dewey stepped toward Calibrisi and wrapped his arms around him. "Thanks."

"Don't thank me," said Calibrisi. "Thank the captain of your hockey team."

87

More than a thousand people were gathered at the cemetery on what was a beautiful autumn day. The cemetery's entrance had been secured. Armed FBI and Secret Service agents stood just inside the gates, checking names against a master list. Past the gates, the road ran through row after row of headstones. Near the center of the cemetery was a large meadow. Two metal detectors stood on the lawn just outside the rope cordon.

The memorial service was supposed to begin at eleven, but one of the guests, a guest deemed important enough to wait for, was running late.

At 11:15, a black limousine, with flags flying at each of the four corners of the vehicle, pulled through the entrance gates. The vehicle rolled slowly through the cemetery to a reserved parking area. The limousine's red flags, with gold stars arrayed in one corner, ruffled lightly in the wind.

Three armed Secret Service agents, carbines out, stood guard along the perimeter of the marked-off parking area.

Waiting there, dressed in a navy blue suit, was President J. P. Dellenbaugh. With him was his wife, Amy, who wore a black dress with thin white stripes.

The limousine stopped a few feet from Dellenbaugh. The back door opened, and Qishan Li, the premier of China, climbed out.

"Mr. Premier," said Dellenbaugh, reaching out and shaking Li's hand, "we're happy you're here."

"Mr. President," said Li, a somber but kind smile on his face, "as I told you, I wouldn't have missed it."

As they crossed the grass, Dellenbaugh glanced at Li.

When Li had called him three days earlier, Dellenbaugh didn't know quite what to expect.

"Mr. President," the soft-voiced Chinese leader had said after listing out a series of transgressions committed by the Chinese government against the United States. "I am calling for a very simple reason. I am calling to apologize for the murder of Jessica Tanzer by employees of the Chinese government; for the attempted murder of an American citizen, Mr. Dewey Andreas, as well as his parents and brother; and for the unauthorized, illegal use of the People's Bank of China in an attempt to extort your country. I did not sanction any of these actions, and I am deeply embarrassed that it required so long for me to reach out to you. The Chinese government accepts full responsibility. While we both know actions do occur in the world of covert operations that sometimes lead to death, on both sides, I am personally, ethically, and morally opposed to the taking of innocent life as part of that effort. I am also opposed to the use of our financial resources in a way that can only be called extortion."

Dellenbaugh, in his typical blue-collar manner, hadn't beaten around the bush.

"What does 'accepts responsibility' mean, Mr. Premier?"

"Whatever you want it to mean."

Dellenbaugh's next call, to someone who was quickly becoming his closest advisor in government, began what was to be Dellenbaugh's first real exposure to a world he only vaguely knew about.

"I need to talk to you, Hector."

"Mr. President, I'm in the middle of a shitstorm. Dewey is two hours from landing in Beijing, and there's a decent chance he's dead once he steps off the plane. I have no assets on the ground there, and I'm down to begging the Taiwanese government to lend a hand, which they will only do if I promise them the first two dozen F-35s to roll off the line at Lockheed. I'm sorry, sir, but I can't talk."

"The person I just spoke to might be able to help."

"Unless it was the Chinese premier, I highly doubt it."

The president and Amy Dellenbaugh walked with Li to the seating area, which was quiet except for a lone violin player, who played a concerto by Bach.

They moved down the hushed aisle, past dignitaries, business leaders, ambassadors; past congressmen and senators, governors and cabinet members, members of the Supreme Court, foreign leaders, journalists— there as attendees, not to cover the story—and family members; all of them there to celebrate the life of Jessica Tanzer.

As they reached the front row, Dellenbaugh stepped to the couple seated in the first two seats.

"Don't get up," said Dellenbaugh. "Mr. and Mrs. Tanzer, I would like to introduce you to Premier Li of the People's Republic of China."

Li reached his hand out.

"I am deeply sorry for what happened," said Li. "The death of your daughter was the fault of people within my own government. Even though I abhor what these criminals did to Jessica, I cannot change what happened. What I can do is accept responsibility for it and apologize to you sincerely from the deepest springs of humility and sadness that, today and always, shall flow from my heart."

Three rows back, Katie sat next to Tacoma. He was dressed in a gray Brooks Brothers suit, and was wearing a blue tie. It was the first time she'd ever seen the former UVA middie and Navy SEAL ever wear one. He pulled at his collar, which was too tight. Katie was dressed in a simple black sleeveless dress, her tan arms clutching a small bag of tissues, her blond hair parted neatly in the middle.

They were, like everyone else in the large crowd, silent, reverent, listening to the soft strains from the violin.

Down the row from Katie and Tacoma sat Calibrisi. His eyes were red and sad. Next to him was an older couple who'd traveled from Castine for the funeral of the woman who would have been their daughter-in-law. John Andreas looked distinguished, dressed in a new gray suit. Margaret was in a simple, pretty green dress. Beside her sat Reagan Andreas, then, to her right, her mother, Hobey's wife, Barrett. Three seats sat empty at the end of the row.

At half past eleven, the minister gave an almost imperceptible nod to the woman playing the violin. He stepped slowly to the dais.

"Welcome to Princeton, and to a celebration of the remarkable life of a unique and special American, a daughter of Princeton, and someone I had the pleasure, some thirty-eight years ago, of baptizing. Today we cry, we mourn, and we rejoice the life of Jessica Cavendish Tanzer."

Hobey and Sam stood just inside the gates to the cemetery. Despite the fact that the memorial service had begun, they remained at the gates, waiting for Dewey.

"Maybe it was just too hard," said Hobey. "I don't blame him."

"He's coming," said Sam.

A few minutes later, Sam saw him first, walking down the road toward the gates. Dewey's head was shaved. As he approached the gates, he pulled out his wallet to show ID.

"Please put it away," said the agent. "I'm sorry for your loss, sir."

Dewey walked through the gates. He looked at Hobey, who stepped to Dewey and hugged him. Then Dewey looked at Sam, who could only stare up at Dewey. Dewey's eyes were bloodshot, red with tears. He eyed his nephew's mop of curly blond hair and grinned through his grief.

"What, they don't have barbers in Castine anymore?" said Dewey. He stepped toward Sam and hugged him.

"I know," said Sam. "It's a little long."

"I heard what you did, Sammy," Dewey whispered into Sam's ear. "Pretty fuckin' ballsy, if you ask me."

"Thanks, Uncle Dewey."

They walked down the cemetery road together, Sam in the middle. They passed a long line of limousines, SUVs, and government vehicles.

Dewey was dressed in a navy blue suit, a blue button-down shirt, a gray-and-white houndstooth tie. It was a tie that Jessica had given him; a tie she had picked out for him to wear to their wedding.

"You go ahead," said Dewey, looking at his brother, then at Sam.

"You okay?" asked his brother.

"No," said Dewey. "But seeing you two guys sure helps."

Dewey went left, off the road, into the field of gravestones. He walked down a long line of headstones toward the funeral. He walked until he was just a few feet from a woman who was seated in the chair at the end of the last row. She glanced at Dewey; he didn't recognize her. She looked at him for several moments, then turned back to the front.

Jessica's sister, Percy, had asked Dewey to speak, but he said no.

Dewey shut his eyes, listening to Calibrisi's normally loud, authoritative voice, softened by emotion, as he talked about Jessica.

There were times, minutes, moments that etched themselves into your memory, Dewey thought, like letters carved into an old maple tree. They were carved there, and there they would remain. Sometimes, those memories could be obscure and trivial. For whatever reason, at that moment, he thought of the color of a girl's socks, a girl whose name he couldn't even remember, on the first day of elementary school back in Castine, so many years ago. And yet that memory was a permanent marker that would never disappear. Other memories were like letters written into sand, there for only brief, fleeting moments, then gone, washed away forever by the water and the wind.

As Dewey listened, with eyes shut, to Hector speak, as he felt the warm breeze across his face, as he smelled the fresh-cut grass beneath his feet, as he fought back tears, anger, and frustration, he finally understood that his entire life had amounted to nothing; Jessica was but a set of letters, a word, now gone. And that as much as he fought to carve his life into the thickest of maples, he was little more than a boat, helpless on the incoming tide, watching the water wash away his dreams; an eyewitness to the tragedy that was the life of a warrior.

EPILOGUE

Dewey parked his pickup truck in front of a large, rambling, white-brick, three-story 1885 colonial, the home of Hector and Vivian Calibrisi.

Dewey's hair had grown out a bit, perhaps a quarter inch, and he'd let his beard and mustache grow out. He looked like a spot-on twin for the young man who, more than a decade before, had been the first-ever Ranger to make it through Gauntlet; big, tough, and plain-out mean. That wasn't his intent when he got up, but it's the way it was.

He knocked on the front door, and a young woman with long brown hair, dressed in plaid pajama bottoms and a Northwestern sweatshirt, appeared, then opened the door. She had a cup of coffee in her hand. She looked like a young Sophia Loren. She scanned Dewey from head to toe.

"You must be Dewey."

"Yeah."

"I'm Daisy."

"Hi."

"Come in."

Dewey followed her inside. He smelled wood burning in a fire-place somewhere off inside the big house.

"Your dad talks about you a lot."

"He does, huh?" she said. "My background is supposed to be kept classified."

"Seriously?" Dewey asked, believing her.

She glanced around.

"I'm a secret agent," she whispered. "Russian. Deep cover. My real name is Svetlana."

Daisy looked up at Dewey and smiled; he couldn't help smiling back.

"I know," said Dewey, whispering back. "That's why I'm here. Moscow sent me. They have a job they want you to do."

Daisy giggled.

"Really?" she asked conspiratorially. "What is it?"

"It has to do with the truck out front," said Dewey, glancing around suspiciously.

"The truck?" she asked, leaning closer to Dewey. He could smell her shampoo. She put her hand on his forearm and stood up on her tiptoes to be closer to his ear, then whispered, "Do they want me to blow it up?"

"No," he whispered back. "They want you to clean it, then wax it."

Daisy started laughing, and soon Dewey joined her.

"What's so funny?" asked Vivian Calibrisi, who heard the commotion and walked out from the kitchen.

"Dewey," said Daisy, smiling at him, then turning and walking toward the stairs. "This is going to be a fun Thanksgiving!"

"Come on in, Dewey," Vivian said, walking to him.

Dewey hugged Vivian, then followed her into the kitchen.

"It's great to see you."

"You too. Thanks a lot for having me. I hope I'm not intruding or anything."

"Are you kidding? We're going to have a blast. Hector said he wants you to carve the turkey. He said he thinks you'll do a good job."

Dewey smiled. He looked around the big kitchen. A racing green AGA stove was covered in various shiny pots and dishes. A fire roared in the fireplace. In the middle of the kitchen, a long harvest table had flowers on it. A beautiful chandelier dangled overhead.

"Where is the old geezer?" Dewey asked.

"He's in back. Just look for the forest fire."

Dewey walked across the back lawn, toward a pond that sat in the middle of a field, beyond which were trees. Next to the trees, a chimney of smoke swirled into the late-autumn air. He came to the source of the smoke: a brick fire pit at the edge of the forest. Standing there was Calibrisi. His back was turned, oblivious to the outside world. He was singing a song to himself, "Feed the World," in a jarringly off-key tone. He had on boots, a flannel shirt, and jeans and was stirring a large pool of brown liquid which was in a steel pan simmering on the fire.

"First of all," said Dewey, "you are the worst goddam singer I have ever heard."

Calibrisi turned, stopped singing, and smiled.

"Second, what the fuck are you doing?"

"You guys never made maple syrup?" asked Calibrisi. "I thought you were raised in Maine."

"We just bought it from the idiots who spent all day making it," said Dewey.

Calibrisi laughed, then reached down with a spoon and took a small amount of the piping hot liquid, blew on it then slurped it up.

"Getting there," he said. "You wanna try?"

"Tempting, but no thanks."

Calibrisi put the large wooden spoon down and gave Dewey a hug.

"How you doing?" asked Calibrisi.

"Good," said Dewey. "Good to see you. Your daughter is hilarious."

"We're all glad you're here," said Calibrisi.

"I am too," said Dewey, reaching for the wooden spoon. "Let me stir a while. You rest that pretty head of yours."

Dewey took the wooden spoon and stirred as they both stood next to the fire.

"So you going to stay the night? Vivian made up a bed for you."

"Sure," said Dewey. "If it's not too much trouble."

"So have you thought about things?" asked Calibrisi.

"No."

"You want to know what your options are?" asked Calibrisi.

"Do I have a choice?"

"No," said Calibrisi. "I spoke to Giles Smith down at Fort Bragg. You'd be welcomed back with open arms. You could be part of the training team, new Deltas. He said they could really use you."

Dewey nodded.

"Don't get too excited," said Calibrisi.

"I'm honored."

"Then there's Katie and Rob. They'd make you a partner. If you ask me, that would be a lot of fun. You'd make a shitload of money, travel all over the place."

Dewey nodded.

"Okay," continued Calibrisi, shaking his head. "Jesus Christ, you're a hard man to please. Third, finally, there's Langley. You can come and work for me. We could send you into the field, you can train guys at the farm, whatever you want. The money isn't great, but I think you'd enjoy it."

Dewey said nothing.

"To be honest," continued Calibrisi, "that's what I think you should do. I think you should work in an environment where the guy you're reporting to understands what you've been through."

Calibrisi paused.

"Dewey, I think you need to talk to someone. I'm talking about lying down on a couch somewhere and reflecting, rebuilding a little. I've done it. You'd be an incredibly valuable CIA asset, but on a personal level, I'm worried about you. I think you need to talk to someone. No one person can go through what you just went through and be fine. I hope you don't take that the wrong way."

Dewey smiled.

"Not at all."

Just then, Daisy approached from across the field. She was carrying two beers, which she handed to Dewey and her father.

"Mom made me bring these out to you," she said, smiling at Dewey, then her dad.

"Thanks, kiddo," said Calibrisi.

"Yeah, thanks, kiddo," said Dewey.

Daisy had showered and was now dressed in a tight brown sweater and white jeans which may have been a size too small but were unlikely to garner any criticism, except perhaps from her parents.

"You look nice," said Calibrisi, looking at his daughter, then at Dewey, who was trying not to look. "What's the big occasion?"

"It's Thanksgiving, Dad," she said, smiling at Dewey. "Can't I put on something nice?"

Daisy stuck out her tongue at her father, then turned.

"By the way, Mom wants to know what time you two idiots are coming inside."

"Soon," said Calibrisi. "Give us a few more minutes."

"Okay," she said. She glanced at Dewey, then turned and headed back inside.

Dewey watched her walk away, then looked at Calibrisi.

"She's too young for you," said Calibrisi.

"Please," said Dewey, "give me a little credit, will you? The last thing I'm looking for is a twenty-one-year-old girlfriend."

"She's twenty-three," said Calibrisi.

"She is?"

Calibrisi smiled.

"Anyway, back to reality. Those are your choices, at least the ones I can help you out with. But I want you to know I'll do anything for you. At the end of the day, you deserve to be happy."

Dewey said nothing. He picked a log and tossed it on the fire.

"So what are you thinking?"

"I'm not thinking anything."

"Nothing? Trust me, I've heard some weird shit over the years."

"Okay, you want to know what I'm thinking?" asked Dewey.

Dewey leaned down, grabbed another large piece of wood, and threw it into the fire. He crouched down and held his hands up toward the warmth of the burning wood.

"I think I only have two choices, Hector," said Dewey. "And to be honest, I'm not sure which one I should go with."

"Well, talk to me," said Calibrisi.

"I'm just not sure you're the right one to talk to."

"Dewey, trust me. You can tell me anything. You're not going to upset me."

415

"I know I'm not. I just think it's a very personal decision."

"Let me guess. Langley or Katie and Rob? Let's go though the pros and cons."

"That's not the choice, Hector," said Dewey.

"Bragg or Langley? Bragg or Katie and Rob?"

"No. I hate to break it to you, but I'm not thinking about any of those things you talked about."

Calibrisi said nothing. For a brief moment, he appeared crestfallen. He stirred the syrup. Finally, he cleared his throat and spoke.

"Okay," said Calibrisi. "What's the choice?"

"I think the choice is, white or dark meat," said Dewey. "Which one should I eat first? I like 'em both. What are you going to go with?"

Dewey glanced at Calibrisi, a shit-eating grin on his face.

"Asshole," said Calibrisi.

BEIJING

General Qingchen sat in his normal position, on the wooden bench, alone, atop the Ministry of Defense building. It was a rare day in Beijing, clear, without smog or clouds. Qingchen could see the roof of the Forbidden Palace in the distance. He made eye contact with the white pigeon who sat on the far arm of the bench, staring politely at Qingchen's sandwich, waiting for his usual reward. After an hour, Qingchen still had not taken a bite. Finally, he took the sandwich and ripped it into small pieces, then placed the plate on the ground. The pigeon hopped down, picked up a small piece of bread, and began eating what would undoubtedly be the biggest feast of his life.

He looked around the rooftop. The grass had been his late wife's idea. Qingchen had been to many places in his life, all over the world, but this was his favorite.

It had been a long month, a month whose repercussions inside Beijing, and in particular the Ministry of Defense, were still being felt. Li had begun his purges within a day of Fao Bhang's death, and the upper ranks of the military, Chinese intelligence, the Communist Party, and the State Council, were but shadows of their former selves. Dozens of officers had been rounded up and now awaited military tribunal. It had all come crashing down, as violently, as suddenly, as the dagger that tore through Bhang himself, though far more blood would be spilled in the days and weeks to come than anything Bhang left on the white marble floor at Beijing Hospital.

Qingchen had yet to be touched. Part of him believed it was because they hadn't gotten to him yet. But he knew that wasn't the case. The truth is, as much as Li might have suspected him, he didn't have proof. How, after all, can you prove a man guilty when the only witnesses—Bhang, and Kai-wen, Qingchen's deputy—were both dead; Bhang by the American, and Kai-wen by Qingchen himself, with poison, less than fifteen minutes after Bhang was killed and the wily general figured out that unless he killed his loyal deputy, he himself would swing from the gallows.

The pigeon chomped away at the sandwich, and then heard a noise. The bird abruptly flew off into the clear sky as, at the far side of the rooftop, the door opened.

One man stepped onto the rooftop and started to walk toward Qingchen. He kept walking until he came face-to-face with Qingchen.

"Good afternoon, General."

"Premier Li. To what do I owe the pleasure of your visit? I would have been more than happy to make the trip to Zhongnanhai."

"On such a beautiful day, I thought it would be nice to visit you here. I would like to speak candidly with you, General. May I do that?"

"Yes, of course."

Li and Qingchen began a stroll across the lawn, toward the edge of the roof, where boxes of white lilacs were growing.

"I believe it's time to announce your retirement, General Qingchen," said Li, as they arrived at roof's edge. Ten stories below, the city traffic teemed.

"My retirement?" asked Qingchen. "I had assumed that was a decision that would be made by the State Council. Please don't take that the wrong way. But that is not only customary, it is in fact the law."

"Yes," said Li, "I assumed you would take that approach. There have been rumors, General."

"Rumors?"

"Of your involvement. You know what I refer to."

"Ah, yes, the purported elevation of Bhang," said Qingchen.

Li put his shoe up on the knee-high brick balustrade that ran along the edge of the roof. He looked out at Beijing.

"Were you involved?" asked Li.

Qingchen paused, then, after a moment, nodded.

"Yes, Mr. Premier."

"Thank you for your candor," said Li, "but now I am left with the challenge of having to conduct an investigation, charge you, that sort of thing. The alternative would seem much more appealing to everyone concerned."

Qingchen stared for several moments at the shorter Li. Just then, the door opened and a soldier stepped onto the roof. It was one of the members of the general's personal security detail. Qingchen nodded to him, then subtly waved him over. Li glanced at the soldier as he approached. He held a carbine, which he had strapped across his chest, aimed at the ground.

"Mr. Premier, I have a riddle for you," said Qingchen as the soldier approached. The soldier stopped a few feet away from them, then trained the muzzle of the rifle at Li.

Li was silent.

"What is more powerful," asked Qingchen, a smile appearing on his face, "information or strength?"

"I don't know," said Li.

Qingchen's face adopted a sinister stare.

"If you can't answer my riddles, Mr. Premier, what good are you to me?" asked Qingchen, nodding at the soldier.

"Wait," said Li, eyeing the muzzle of the soldier's rifle. "The answer is neither."

"What do you mean, neither?" asked Qingchen.

"Neither information nor strength, General, is as powerful as luck."

"This meeting only becomes more amusing," said Qingchen, laughing. "Your weakness and stupidity confirm whatever plans I had to remove you from power, Qishan. The answer is strength. After all, you

418

have enough information to hang me, and yet, it is my strength that will now determine not only my fate, but yours as well."

"It's luck," said Li. "If you don't believe me, ask the soldier."

Li pointed at the young soldier, then reached out and politely moved the muzzle of his weapon so that it was aimed at Qingchen.

"How else could you possibly explain how my nephew came to serve on your personal security staff?" asked Li, smiling. "Is it not luck, General? In fact, I feel so lucky I think I'll go to Macau this weekend and play some blackjack."

Li walked away as the sound of a gunshot echoed across the rooftop.

MCLEAN, VIRGINIA

Dewey was brushing his teeth when the door to the bathroom opened ever so slightly. He pulled it open as he brushed, looking around. He saw nothing. He looked down. Sitting there was the Calibrisis' German shepherd, Lizzie. She looked up at him with a kindly look, her tongue out, a dog's version of a smile.

He finished brushing, then walked down the hall to the guest bedroom. When he went to shut the door, Lizzie was standing there. Dewey leaned down and scratched her gently. She was an old dog, and some of the hair around her eyes and mouth was gray.

"Good dog."

The old German shepherd put her nose in the crack of the door when he went to shut it. Dewey smiled and let her in. He climbed into the king-size bed. When he went to turn out the lamp on the bedside table, Lizzie was lying on the floor, next to the bed, curled up.

Dewey was tired. He'd eaten three helpings of turkey, two pieces of pecan pie, and drank down a respectable amount of beer along with a glass or three of whiskey. He'd watched football, gotten mauled several times by Daisy in Scrabble, and taken his revenge on the basement Ping-Pong table.

He put his hand behind his neck, smiling, staring at the moonlight-crossed ceiling.

Suddenly, he heard Lizzie rustling beside the bed. He turned on the bedside light. The dog was sitting obediently next to the bed, looking at him. She took her paw and reached up to the bed.

Dewey smiled. He pulled the covers aside and climbed out of bed. He lifted Lizzie onto the bed, then climbed back under the covers and turned out the light. He again lay down, his arm behind his head. Lizzie inspected the bed for a minute or two, then found a spot next to Dewey. She curled up against him.

"So what do you think I should do?" Dewey asked the old dog.

He put his arm under the dog's head, patting her chest. He looked up at the white and black pattern made by the moonlight across the ceiling. Soon, he heard the soft wheezing of the old German shepherd as she drifted off to sleep.

"I couldn't agree more," said Dewey.

ACKNOWLEDGMENTS

Writing the acknowledgments is one of the best parts of writing a book. It means you're done. All that's left now is to sit back and wait for the book to hit the bookstores, then cross your fingers and hope everyone likes reading it as much as you enjoyed writing it. So let me start by thanking some people without whom I couldn't, and wouldn't, be writing.

First, there's you, my readers. As I write this, I'm on a plane, heading out west for a few weeks with my family. Out the window, I can see the green and blue land of America, spreading so perfectly to a black line at the horizon. I know many of you are down there. Knowing that makes the land, seen from up here, five miles up in the sky, feel like I'm looking across the town square in my hometown. Thank you for doing that, wherever you happen to be. Let me tell you, it's an amazing feeling for me to look down and know I'm among friends.

Next, I want to thank America's veterans. A gentleman wrote to me a few months ago and asked if I'd send a signed copy of one of my books to his son, who is at a veterans' hospital; he lost his right arm in Afghanistan. His father was worried about him, and thought I might be able to cheer him up. He said I was his son's favorite author. Though that should've made me happy, I found myself picturing a young soldier, a kid really, lying in a bed somewhere, his arm gone, his spirits, too, and it took every ounce of strength I had not to lose it. I'm not sure you could ever adequately thank our veterans, but for what it's worth, I write these books for you guys.

Writing a book is truly a team effort, and I'd like to thank the big team who helped me with *Eye for an Eye*.

Aaron, Nicole, Lisa, Lucy, Frances, Arleen, Melissa, and John, my "kill team" at the Aaron Priest Agency: you guys are the best. A special thank-you to Nicole Kenealy James; you somehow find a way to be amazingly gentle and brutally tough; you're my fiercest advocate and I'm grateful to have you on my side.

To Sally Richardson, Matthew Shear, Keith Kahla, Matthew Baldacci, Paul Hochman, Nancy Trypuc, Jeanne-Marie Hudson, Anne Marie Tallberg, George Witte, Jeff Dodes, John Murphy, Hannah Braaten, Stephanie Davis, Loren Jaggers, Phil Mazzone, Rafal Gibek, Malati Chavali, and everyone else at St. Martin's Press: thanks for your patience, guidance, and confidence. A special thanks to Keith, my editor: your patience is surpassed only by the diplomatic skills with which you deliver your "suggested" changes.

Thanks to: everyone at Macmillan Audio, including Mary-Beth Roche, Robert Allen, Brant Janeway, Samantha Edelson, and Esther Bochner; Chris George, my man in Hollywood; Caspian at Abner Stein and Trisha at Pan Macmillan in London; Lizzie, Lora, Alyssa, and Andrea at Scratch.

As with every book, I needed the help of experts to nail some of the subject matter in *Eye*. Thanks to: Michael Murray, James Lacey, Rod Gregg, and Charlie Speight.

The kitchen cabinet: Shortsleeve, Miguel, Michelle G., Rorke, Alex, Sam A., Tad, Ed Stackler, Ranger, Mabel, Ray L.

Last but not least, thanks to my family. This time, I decided to let my four kids each write their own acknowledgment. I cannot in good conscience vouch for the accuracy of the following, but it did come from their mouths:

To Esmé, you are a great sharer to your friends and a great example to your mean brothers and a great hockey player on your team. Oscar, you're an amazing hockey player who is also skilled with guns and knives. Teddy, you are a great cook, a football genius, and you like a nice pair of slacks. Charlie, you're a nice guy who should be allowed to do whatever you want.

To Shannon, thanks for your tremendous support, excellent advice, true friendship, and undying love (I wrote that—and it is 100 percent accurate).